s ᴏne of Hungary's best-known living
᷐e ₁9ᴏ̃7 he has published eleven novels and many other
ᴏꜰ prose, earning critical acclaim in Hungary as well as in
the German-speaking countries and France (his novels *Követés* –
based in large part on the author's own experiences during the Nazi
occupation of Budapest – and *Drága Liv* have appeared in translation). Sándor has been awarded Hungary's highest literary
honours, including the Sándor Márai Prize (2000) and the Kossuth
Prize (2005). Earlier in his career he was a prominent theatre critic
and playwright. He lives in Budapest.

Tɪᴍ Wɪʟᴋɪɴsᴏɴ (born 1947) grew up in Sheffield but has lived much
of his adult life in London as well as spending several years in Buda-
pest. He is the principal English translator of Imre Kertész (including
Fatelessness, Fiasco, Kaddish for an Unborn Child, Liquidation and
Dossier K) and more recently Miklós Szentkuthy (*Marginalia on
Casanova, Towards the One and Only Metaphor*), among others, as
well as shorter works by a wide range of other contemporary
Hungarian-language authors.

IVÁN SÁNDOR

LEGACY

Translated by Tim Wilkinson

PETER OWEN
London and Chicago

PETER OWEN PUBLISHERS
81 Ridge Road, London N8 9NP

Peter Owen books are distributed in the USA and Canada by
Independent Publishers Group/Trafalgar Square
814 North Franklin Street, Chicago, IL 60610, USA

Translated from the Hungarian *Követés: Egy nyomozás krónikája*
First published by Kalligram Kiadó, Bratislava/Pozsony, 2006

First English language edition published in Great Britain 2014
by Peter Owen Publishers

PAPERBACK ISBN 978-0-7206-1571-5
EPUB ISBN 978-0-7206-1572-2
MOBIPOCKET ISBN 978-0-7206-1573-9
PDF ISBN 978-0-7206-1574-6

A catalogue record for this book is available from the British Library

Typeset by Octavo Smith Publishing Services

Printed and bound in the UK by
CPI Group (UK) Ltd, Croydon, CR0 4YY

Sponsored by the Hungarian Academy of Sciences
Füst Milán Foundation for Translators

This book has been selected to receive financial assistance from English PEN's
"PEN Translates!" programme, supported by Arts Council England. English PEN
exists to promote literature and our understanding of it, to uphold writers'
freedoms around the world, to campaign against the persecution and
imprisonment of writers for stating their views, and to promote the friendly
co-operation of writers and the free exchange of ideas. www.englishpen.org

Supported using public funding by
ARTS COUNCIL
ENGLAND

I

By the time the cyclist had whisked around the corner of Bem Quay and Halász Street we had recognized our shared failure in each other's looks. Seeing the handlebars of his bike brought to mind another cyclist's bull-like figure, pumping the pedals as he was draped over the drop handlebars, in the very same place fifty-eight years before, although then it had been called Margit Quay. None the less, it was as though my viewpoint were not my own but that of a fourteen-year-old boy marching in a column who was trying to catch the eye of the cyclist beside him.

All he saw, however, was the slits of his eyes.

A flash of the tightly clenched line between a swollen eyelid and a puffy cheek.

The looks of the armed escort gave nothing more away.

Once again new orders were being shouted out. Once again he had to run between the lines of men with submachine guns.

What was I doing anyway on the Buda bank at the corner of Bem Quay and Halász Street?

Fifty metres further along, on the right, is Pala Street as it drops to meet the Danube. At the top of a flight of steps stands the ancient house where P., one of the designers working on my most recent books, resides. I had been searching for days to find an appropriate image for the jacket to take to him for the book we were working on now. I had settled on a Hieronymus Bosch painting. Maybe that was why in my dream I encountered the figure of a midget monstrosity: the legs of an insect, wings of a locust, human face. Bespectacled. He nodded, and we started. Just before there had still been two of us, but as it was I was already pushing ahead on my own. The midget figure had been me.

*

What I had chosen for the jacket was a detail from Bosch's triptych *The Haywain*, which shows people trapped between the massive wheels of the wagon, two of them already crushed, several driven over on top of one another, yet others reaching out with arms raised in the air, although there is no way of telling whether they are praying for their lives or trying, while they are at each other's throats, to lay hands on some food from the cart's payload. Dotted around are several monsters with the bodies of animals but human legs. Four figures are on top of the hay cart. Two have musical instruments; a third – a young woman in a white headdress – is holding a sheet of paper covered in writing on her lap that the lad with her is perusing. This detail from the scene seems to express the idea of a text that denies the distance between writer, reader and subject.

In another picture by Bosch, St John the Evangelist, book in hand, is listening to the words of an angel on the island of Patmos.

When I looked more closely at this picture, I noticed a tiny monster in the seemingly peaceful surroundings. Insect legs, a devilish body, locust wings, a human face; on its head is a basket of live coals, and perched on its nose are a pair of pince-nez, giving the air of an intellectual.

In other words, Bosch sought to have a narrator for the spectacle.

It's rather as if he painted in the right-hand corner someone who would be able to open the story: I was there.

In my dream it was on the insect legs of this little monster that I set off to go to Pala Street.

The column leaves the Erzsébet Bridge.

Where are we going? I ask Mother. This is Döbrentei Square, she says. Fine, but where are we going? She glances at my father. I am walking between them. Father's look indicates no. We reach Margit Quay. Mother is slipping behind. We are proceeding in lines of four: the fourth is an elderly man. I don't know who he is.

At one side of the column is a conductor from Budapest Municipal Transport, the BuMuT, with an armband with the pale-blue stripes of the House of Árpád used by the Nyilaskeresztes Párt – Hungarista Mozgalom, the fascist Arrow Cross Party; in front of him is a member of the Home Guard with an armband. On the other side a policeman with submachine gun. Bringing up the rear of the procession are men in black uniforms and green shirts; at the head is a Home Guard lieutenant and a MP NCO.

What are you staring at? the BuMuT conductor roars. Don't look to the right, says Father. We are passing in front of the site of a blown-up statue of former Prime Minister Gömbös (Gömbös had died in office in 1936). Toppled from its plinth, the figure has already been taken away.

On the left a cyclist sweeps alongside us. A racing bike. He is leaning on the drop bars, counting us. He says something to the BuMuT conductor. He pushes on ahead, then wheels around and turns back.

It is sleeting. For the first time I see the arches that have been blown up between the exit from Margit Bridge on to Margit Island and the Pest side of the bridge.

Could I have seen blown-up stretches of Margit Bridge on 15 November 1944?

Dusty old newspapers. Rustling in the library's hush. Margit Bridge was blown up on 4 November.

In turning the pages one of the thin sheets is torn.

> All means necessary will be employed to compel every fighting-fit and work-fit person unfailingly to complete whichever task is allotted to them and which is considered necessary to attain our goal, because we dare to proclaim, and we shall enforce, our principle that we consider life to be too good for those who withdraw themselves from the demands of the life-and-death struggle of our nation or who even attempt to do so. Anyone not with us, with our Nation, is against us. Any such person must perish. That is the call of the Arrow Cross Party Hungarist Movement to the Hungarian Nation.

On 16 October President Miklós Horthy, following due constitutional ceremonies, charged Ferenc Szálasi with forming a government.

Jews were required to remain in houses designated with a yellow Star of David.

On 26 October an amendment was made to the preceding order whereby one family member, wearing a yellow star, would be permitted to shop between the hours of 10 a.m. and midday.

On 27 October a speech by Ferenc Rajniss: anyone wishing to be called civilized must now fight. The sole refuge from fighting is to die . . .

On 4 November it is decreed that all Jewish property has devolved to the state.

On 10 November it is decreed that any activity by Jews on the street is forbidden on the 10th, 11th and 12th.

On the day on which our column reaches Margit Quay in the early afternoon hours US forces breaks through the German line of defence at Metz.

The Battle of Jászberény in east-central Hungary commences.

On Szálasi's orders a unit of anti-tank volunteers of between eighteen and twenty-two years of age is deployed.

The Hungarian branch of the Swedish Red Cross officially declares that for the time being it will discontinue the issuing of safe-conduct letters.

I am not the only one who is trying to catch the voice of a boy panting from the quick pace of marching, because it is as though he is himself trying to get me to hear what he is saying, but, although I hear it, I hear it only as though it is being filtered to my ear from the depths of a sea that has turned to glass.

I had read those few words two years ago. My own name appeared under the lines.

There was a sense of satisfaction at having fashioned time into language. Before long I would have to deny the fact that, although my name appeared beneath the lines, I was not the author of those words.

It was a palimpsest: the motto of a novella by Sándor Balázs that he had dedicated to me. He said it in one our conversations, which used to stretch out into the early hours of the morning, not long before he died. I can hear his voice as if it really was being filtered in time from a distance that had turned into glass. We had been talking about it on that particular morning.

I helped him across his apartment into the room overlooking Mexikói Road. After midnight we made an infusion of the special herbs that he always had about him in little tins, and, glancing at the distance in the steam floating up from the cup, I said that if he were to look out of the window then he would just be able to make out where, fifty-six years earlier (relative to the time of the conversation), I had set off in the procession from the sports ground on the next block, at the corner of Queen Erzsébet Avenue in the XIVth District.

I couldn't bear the look he gave me.

He stepped over to the window. He pulled back the curtain, which had been set swaying by the touch of his hand. The windowpane misted over from his breathing. He then turned back with the air not so much of someone who had spent such a long time looking and had got tired as of someone who had seen something.

As if my finger, which just before had been pointing downwards, had been directed at his approaching fate, about which he no longer had any doubts, because he had insisted that his doctors speak frankly with him.

As I said, I found it hard to bear the look he gave me, yet when, on reading the poems he had written about his imminent death, I glanced up from the text, we were able to look at one another at length, as if it were the poem that carried the weight of our gaze.

He turned back towards the window. I moved beside him. We looked at the emptiness of the barely illuminated Mexikói Road, at the skeletal arabesques of the trees at the side of the railway embankment, marvelling as he looked down like someone who could see to the very end of the fate which was unfolding before his eyes – further than any point I had ever reached.

But was that point before me or behind me?

And that sense of indefinability helped me to recapture the look with which I made my way down here at the age of fourteen.

Notwithstanding, my two looks cannot have met, since as I was making my way in that column I could not have lifted my eyes to the window of the house from where everything was now presented to my sight, because then I was looking at the backs of the necks, knapsacks and boots of those stumbling along in front of me. But only by following his look did I feel I had a chance of approaching the crime scene, as I called it, and, if I managed that, of preserving

9

what had happened there, provided I was able to arrange a meeting between what I saw then and what I see now.

The point at which the investigation is directed is also a landscape, only an internal one, deeper than I have ever reached before – the point where, while I step into a space created by memory, everything is presented in the incorruptible continuity of how it had once happened.

The line of his mouth, mute, supercilious, is as if it were asking, Have you any idea where you are treading? What is this empty street down below that we are looking at together? What city are you living in? But he didn't ask, so who knows what he was thinking then, whereas it is easier for me to ascribe to him questions which, it seems, I did not dare, either then or since, to ask as my own, although all my life I had been waiting to ask them.

At all events, I had taken the first step in the interests of the investigation. I figured that in order for it to work I had to learn how to see and hear as my fourteen-year-old self at the same time as myself now.

I stepped over to the stereo.

I put on a record of old waltzes that he owned.

It is a waltz that I hear when the column – which is proceeding along Mexikói Road with the Home Guard lieutenant and a gendarme NCO at its head and the submachine-gun-toting Arrow Cross duty functionary as rearguard – reaches Thököly Road.

Two hundred metres from the outdoor Erzsébet Ice Rink, on the corner with Kolumbusz Street, the loudspeakers crackle. There was always a crackling, even back then, every time I leaned forward as I skated to trace a large circle in the ice.

Red scarves; short fur coats; crocheted caps with tassels; the surface of the rink cut up by the blades of ice-hockey players; the burning-hot iron stove at which they warmed themselves.

Father took over my backpack first on Hungária Outer Circle, the third and outermost of the concentric roads around the Pest side of the city.

The cobblestones on Thököly Road are the same today. They are changed every twenty to twenty-five years with another surface of the cobblestones' six sides being turned uppermost each time the street undergoes a routine repair.

Shortly before the waltz is heard I can also hear the crack of the shot.

I also hear the ring of the alarm bell before the crack of the shot.

It's six o'clock. Father is seated on the edge of his bed; Mother watches with her head tucked under her pillow; Grandmother doesn't open her eyes.

We are living in the home of the Róbert family. Sixteen square metres. Four sleeping places, a wardrobe, two seats, a small table.

Father gets dressed on hearing the bell.

I can hear Misi's voice out in the hallway; I bring the keys. He's eighteen, deserted from his forced-labour brigade a month ago. He's lying low. At night he would hide at his parents' place.

Six armed men burst in. The commanding officer is in an officer's green raincoat, holster open; the others have submachine guns. All of them are wearing Arrow Cross armbands. We are given half an hour. The old woman can stay, the officer says, pointing to Grandma. She will die later in the ghetto. Grandma is now sitting on the side of the bed, searching for her slippers with her feet.

We stuff things into the long-prepared knapsacks. Yet one more pair of warm socks, another can of food. I can't make up my mind whether to put on my winter coat or the windcheater I was given for school trips. The windcheater, says Father, with two pullovers under it. Mother pauses her packing. We wind scarves around our necks, pull our caps down to our eyes.

Misi, having called out through the door that he's fetching the keys and putting a coat on top of his pyjamas, slips out of the back door of the kitchen, clothes over one arm. The caretaker's apartment opens on to the yard at the back. Ten minutes later Misi returns with documents belonging to the caretaker's son's, who is away. Misi raises one hand to the peak of his cap in salute before showing the papers, looking at his parents, his younger sister and his grandparents.

One of the men with an Arrow Cross armband is already wrapping up the cut-glass vases. Misi rebukes him. Watch it, says the man in the raincoat, your own head is far from securely attached to your neck.

I am not able to witness that, Misi's younger sister Mádi tells me

11

fifty-eight years later. She was paying a visit to Budapest from Paris. We drink cups of coffee in my home. How long I have known these cool, not indifferent faces that speak meaningfully of a world which, strictly speaking, is now inaccessible.

The KISOK football ground of the middle-schools' sports club, the gate in its wooden fencing wide open. Several thousand of us gather in the slush. Groups escorted by Home Guards with armbands of the Arrow Cross, BuMuT conductors and black-uniformed soldiers arrive from Queen Erzsébet Avenue, from the direction of Kolumbusz Street, Amerikai Road and Rákosrendező Railway Station.

Many are poor. Worn-out shoes, threadbare trousers, ragged shawls.

I stand near one of the goals. I used to play on that pitch. An inter-schools championship. White football jersey, black satin shorts. It's hard to move inside the ring of armed men.

The first shot cracks out.

A number 67 tram turns in from Mexikói Road, wheels squeaking. Passengers stare at us from the tram windows. I am sitting on the other side; they must be able to see the sign of the well-known Woman of Trieste tavern and eating-house in Zugló.

It is sleeting as we set off. The older people stumble. I get sleet splashed on to my britches.

Between Hungária Outer Circle and Hermina Road, at the place where yesterday I bought a pair of black socks from a street vendor, several dozen bystanders watch the procession. A young lad wearing a cap of Hungary's quasi-military Levente youth movement jumps in among us. He is two or three years older than me. He runs forward, beckoning to his friends. He points me out. He has a scar on his chin. Lives in the neighbourhood. We have met more than a few times at the ice rink. He is pointing in the same way as I do in front of the monkey cages to my classmates on school trips to the zoo.

We have seen each other plenty of times on the streets of Zugló, the XIVth District, in the yard of the film factory on Gyarmat Street. Maybe that was his workplace. He always steers away from me; I never thought to ask about it . . .

What would I ask?

The subconscious is a huge storehouse; forgetting is instantaneous. Yet just a sound, a look, can conjure up what has been forgotten.

I buy bread from the baker's on the corner of Hermina Road. Housewives queue up silently with their shopping-bags. The counters are located on the spot where the comfortable armchairs once stood in front of the mirrors in Mr Zsilka's hairdressing salon on lino that every ten minutes was swept clear and wiped over with a damp rag.

Mr Zsilka, on his kiddies' swivel chair that could be raised or lowered with a twirl, is my hairdresser. He drapes a pink cloth with a floral pattern around my neck. Mother waits in an armchair by the cash desk. She tells Mr Zsilka what kind of haircut we want. I know, I know – *küss-die-Hand* – the same as last time. In the mirror I can see the assistants soaping the cheeks of the clients with shaving brushes. Mr Zsilka has a rubicund face; his breath smells of lavender water; he has a grizzled crew cut; his potbelly is pressed to my back as he leans over me.

He is standing in the open doorway, watching the procession.

I can see inside the shop as far as the mirrors.

A gust of wind snatches at his white cap. He starts to raise his hand; as though seeking to assist him, Father gives a nod. We'll work later, he is saying as he does this. We'll work later in Germany.

Groups like ours are marching along other streets.

Budapest is a city of yellow-starred children, women and the elderly stumbling along with escorts of armed men.

At the Outer Circle, on the corner with Népszínház Street, a boy somewhat like me is able to look at the crowd gathering on the pavement, the same way as I am taking a look at Thököly Road.

He can see on the pavement, just like I see, the chin-scarred, jumping lad, a tall, slim, fair-haired young fellow who after fifty-eight years is now speaking. I remember, I was standing there as a nineteen-year-old in the open street and I was amazed that a column with hands behind their necks was passing. There must have been two or three hundred of them, with yellow stars on their chests. At the head, on the left and right and bringing up the rear, were young men with Arrow Cross armbands and submachine guns, four of them in all, between them two or three hundred people, women, children and the elderly, and since they were going along the middle of the road even the trams had to halt, sneakily bided their time – just take your time, please, take all the time in the world, we're in no hurry – and there were three or four thousand there, watching from the pavement. I was also standing there, D., a big actor, recollects in a newspaper article. I watched it as a spectacle. If those three or four thousand had done nothing else but set off towards the column, blocked the way, then those people would have remained alive, but nobody set off, and what remains of such experiences is the deep, gnawing shame of knowing one was there but did nothing.

The elderly man, the fourth in our row, is wheezing as he breathes and stumbles. Father would have taken over his knapsack if he were not already carrying mine as well.

I can no longer hear the waltz from the loudspeaker at the rink.

A few days before the cyclist peeled off at the corner of Bem Quay and Halász Road the Hungarian edition of the 1995 book *Carl Lutz und die Juden von Budapest* appeared – about the man who was Switzerland's Vice-Consul in Budapest from 1942 until the end of the Second World War – written by Swiss church historian Dr Theo Tschuy.

We reach the Outer Circle.

From the left, coming out of Népszínház Street, another column attaches itself to ours.

At around this time Carl Lutz enters the office of Hungary's Foreign Minister. His way is barred by a hulking, brutish ministerial aide whose diplomatic experience consisted of having been a body-guard and gang leader in the royal household of the Emperor of Abyssinia. Three days before that, when the concentration (as the official regulations term it) of Budapest's Jews in the Óbuda Brick-works had already begun, Lutz had written a five-point letter of protest. The government is working out the details of the concentration, and plans for deportation by forced march from the Óbuda Brickworks to Germany are being worked out under the direction of Gábor Vajna, Minister of the Interior. Friedrich Born, the authorized representative of the International Committee of the Red Cross (ICRC) in Budapest, demands to be allowed to inspect the site, writes in his report that crammed together there are people of all ages, from teenagers to those in their eighties; Arrow Cross Party men choose who is able to march, but they declare as unfit only the disabled and the terminally weak, and nobody is allowed a blanket or any food.

At the Hungarian Ministry of Foreign Affairs Lutz is urged to check seemingly forged Swiss protective passports, *Schutzbriefe*, that participants in rescue operations had produced – with his approval and in more than a few cases his cooperation – and he is also urged personally to separate 'genuine' and 'forged' safe-conduct papers at the Óbuda Brickworks, failure to acknowledge any document, he writes, being tantamount to a death sentence to the holder of the paper.

> At one time my wife and I stood four hours in snow and ice inside the ill-famed Óbuda brickyards performing this sad business of sorting out *Schutzbriefe*. We witnessed soul-searching scenes. Five thousand unhappy human beings stood in one row, freezing, trembling, hungry, carrying small bundles with their belongings, and showed me their papers. I shall never forget their terrified faces. Again and again the police had to intervene because the people almost tore off my clothes as they pleaded with me. This was the last upsurge of a will to live before resignation set in, which usually ended in death. For us it was mental torture to have to sort out these documents. On these occasions we saw human beings hit with dog whips. They fell to the ground with bleeding faces, and we were ourselves openly threatened with weapons if we tried to intervene . . . I drove towards the brickworks past a procession in order to show the people that not all hope was yet lost.

There are two people sitting on the back seat behind the driver, the man on the side nearer the kerb. He has a longish face, thin-rimmed spectacles, thin, tightly clamped lips, hair sleeked and with a parting, chiselled chin – I see that on a photograph fifty-eight years later.

There are also lots of people on the pavement in Bécsi Road. Yesterday it was repeated on the wireless that on 30 January 1942 Hitler announced to the world at large what, at the Wannsee Conference ten days before, had still been kept secret, namely, that the war was going to come to a successful conclusion with the annihilation of Europe's Jews.

A black Packard is now driving in front of us. We are not to know that it will shortly reach its destination, turn off under a massive wooden gate, pull up in the mud in front of the dead bodies lying on the ground, and the long-faced man and a fur-coated woman get out.

We are still proceeding along Bécsi Road.

The boy should not look over there. Father does not say to me, Don't look over there, but instead speaks to Mother, as if it were her responsibility that I should not look over there – but where? I am walking between them. I can see them exchange looks; this is an unspoken agreement between them. It is Father's task to recognize that the time has come for something unavoidable for all of us, and after that come Mother's tiny tasks, but in this case she can do nothing as she is walking on my left and can do nothing to stop me looking over to the right.

There is a dead body lying in the gateway.

Pulled out of the column and just now being covered with newspapers.

The two booted feet and right hand are poking from underneath. The fingers stretched out. The palm of the hand rigid in shellfish-like fashion. The hand looks as if it were charred.

Heart attack, says someone in front.

Can a heart attack be like an electric shock? Flashing through one and charring the flesh?

We have to pick up our step.

Those who lag behind get beaten with rifle-butts.

It is possible that what I thought was charring was a threadbare black glove. Some of us gave a fleeting glance at the dead body.

A young man steps out of another gateway and turns up the collar of his winter overcoat, pulls the visor of his cap down over his eyes. He steps off the pavement when the BuMuT conductor with the Arrow Cross armband and the submachine-gun-toting Home Guard move away from each other. He slips an envelope into the hand of one of the men who is marching just ahead of us, says something to him, turns around and vanishes into another gateway.

So, at six in the morning Misi sees an armed detachment through the spyhole in their front door at 78 Amerikai Road, asks for time to get the keys, but he doesn't bring them; instead he hurries out of the back door into the caretaker's apartment and ten minutes later reappears with a few papers that belong to the caretaker's absent son, watches his family's Swiss *Schutzbriefe* being ripped up, hurries off to the Glass House at 29 Vadász Street (an annexe of the Swiss Legation and home to the local office of the Jewish Agency and where *Schutzbriefe* were produced) in Pest's inner-city Vth District. He pushes his way through the crowd of several hundred who are pleading for such documents, acquires authenticated copies, heads across the city in search of our column, reaches it, hurries ahead, waits under a gateway on Bécsi Road, steps out at an appropriate moment, slips the documents into the hand of the man on the outside of the row, who immediately passes them on. Misi vanishes, and all that is what his sister tells me fifty-eight years later while we drink coffee. I, though, do not recall this, whereas she does not recall a dead body covered with newspaper.

Misi is average-sized. Wears spectacles. Not the sporting type. He goes to the opera, sings Verdi arias. His voice is none too good. The column leaves the dead body behind. Him, too.

On the stretch of the Millennium Underground, which runs from the city centre to Zugló, in one of the showcases recently installed at the Opera House station is a group photograph of the pupils at the Israelite Gymnasium who took their school-leaving examinations in 1944. Dark suits, white shirts, ties, regulation six-point stars on the breast pockets of the jackets. Misi is on the second row, fourth from the left.

Hung. Royal Government on the matter of decree 1240/1944 concerning the distinguishing marks for Jews. Outside the home, from the time the current decree comes into force onwards, all Jews regardless of gender who have completed their sixth year of life are obliged to wear on the left breast of the outer garment a readily visible canary-yellow star of 10 x 10 cm in diameter and made of silk or satin cloth.

M. is blinking in the photograph. He looks young for his age. Seven months later he would be breaking through detachments in the city. He does not his clean his steamed-up spectacles. He knows which gateway to wait in, when he should step out, how he should approach the column and in what direction he should disappear.

I would like to get there. I would like to put the knapsack down, change socks, dry my clothes.

Far in the distance, at the end of Bécsi Road, in the last few minutes before darkness falls, the chimney of a brick kiln pokes up into the sky.

On the left is the entrance to the St Margit's Hospital, a sure point from which to get one's bearings in the gloom.

By now the sheds full of drying bricks are visible in the arch of the hillside.

The space behind the enormous, wide-open gate swallows up the columns ahead of us.

The sound of gunfire in the distance. I am able to tell from the gunfire the difference between rifle shots and submachine-gun bursts. These are dull-sounding cracks from a north-easterly direction.

A bend in the road. The front of our column flashes in the light of pocket torches. Bayonets are fitted on to rifles; submachine-gun barrels are directed at us. The lieutenant, as if this were a dress parade, is marching four paces ahead of the first row with two deputies falling in behind him – one the gendarme NCO, the other a Party functionary. We march in step on command – women, old people and children younger than me as well – as if we were marching in the schoolyard past the dais at some festivity. Or rather, no, as if I were sleepwalking. Not that the column is a dream, but everything that has happened, both before and after. The truth is my path to the gateway. I am a fourteen-year-old boy, and I see the face of an elderly man as he watches me, trying to write down what he see as he bends over a sheet of paper.

The light of pocket torches on dead bodies lying in the mud. On both sides are lines of submachine guns. The lieutenant salutes. Identifies himself. The front of the procession has now passed beyond the gate. Our row is next.

II

We pass through the wide-open wooden gate of the brickworks.

One of the escorts with an Arrow Cross armband, his sub-machine gun pointing up in the air, fires a short burst.

The piles of drying bricks are orange-coloured cubes.

The chimney for the kilns is a black point.

St Margit's Hospital is a green brick shape.

The first map to show the hospital was issued by the Hungarian Geological Institute Ltd (Budapest V, Rudolf Square) in 1905. The second is from the Hungarian Royal Home Guard Cartographic Institute (Budapest II, 7–9 Olaszfasor) in 1943. The third is from 2002.

A century ago brick kilns stood on both sides of Bécsi Road, from the start of Szépvölgyi Road, level with the middle of Margit Island, to Vörösvár Road near the far end. Sixty years ago they started only from Elek Fényes Road, the two central points being the Újlaki Brickworks on the right and the Bohn Brickworks on the left of Bécsi Road. The 2002 map shows Remete Hill with a new housing estate that has been built in their place.

The site where the chimney for the brick kilns stood is now at the entrance to a Praktiker DIY Store.

Where the gateway once stood, through which Carl Lutz's automobile passed not long before us, is a stone block: 'In winter 1944 many tens of thousands of our persecuted Jewish Hungarian fellow citizens were dispatched from this site, the area of the former Óbuda Brickworks, en route to Nazi concentration camps. Their memory shall be preserved.'

Students exit just fifty metres from the stone block through the gates of the Zsuzsa Kossuth Gymnasium.

I am unable to set my knapsack down, unable to change my sopping-wet socks; I have to hang on tightly, with Mother on my left holding on to my hands, Father holding on to my right arm, so as not to be carried off by the people who are pushing from behind.

A schoolmistress also comes out through the gymnasium gates and speaks to two schoolgirls.

Mother's grip is torn from mine in the mêlée; Father pushes his way between us and clasps both of us by the arm, dragging us along. The crowd is squeezed into one of the brickyard drying sheds. We tread on bodies. Father's name is being shouted. Lajos's family, Mother says. The light of a pocket torch flashes. The Róbert family. They are sitting on their rucksacks. I, too, have only as much space as my knapsack takes up.

The schoolmistress says goodbye to two of the female students. She heads for the Praktiker Store. It starts to rain. My feet are freezing in my thin-soled shoes.

Mother wraps a blanket round me; Father folded it before we set off, strapping the U-shaped sausage to his own, military-style, although he was never a soldier.

We open some tinned meat and tear off crusts of bread. Father and Uncle Lajos go off for water; there's a tap outside. When they get back Mother goes off with Aunt Bőzsi. Mother is forty-one, Aunt Bőzsi forty-four. When they return they say the ladies is in the same place as the gents. I set off in the dark. The sky is starry. Armed men surround the standing and squatting people. Beyond the brick-drying sheds is a semicircle carved out of the hillside. As I squat the kiln chimney looks even taller.

The first night passes; 16 November.

A second night passes.

On 17 November Friedrich Born, the ICRC's authorized representative in Budapest, will not budge until he is allowed into the Óbuda Brickworks, writes Theo Tschuy. When he gets back he says that 'he had seen a mass of men and women of all ages crowded together, including teenagers and people in their eighties. Marching columns were formed in one to three days to set off westwards.'

Carl Lutz's Packard drives in through the gateway another time. We must leave the brick-drying sheds.

We are lounging about in the mud. We see the automobile.

Young children are playing in the puddles.

At around this time Edmund Veesenmayer, the Reich's plenipotentiary representative, sends a fresh telegram to Berlin. 'Despite technical difficulties, Szálasi is disposed to continue energetically with removal of the Jews of Budapest.' At much the same time Carl Lutz and Raoul Wallenberg request the papal nuncio, Angelo Rotta, to pass on to Szálasi a memorandum of protest from the accredited representatives to Budapest of the neutral powers:

> On the day after 15 October the new government and His Excellency Ferenc Szálasi decided, and announced officially, that the annihilation of the Jews was not going to be continued. Notwithstanding this, representatives of the neutral powers have learned from absolutely reliable sources that a renewed decision had been made to deport all Jews, and this is being implemented with such merciless cruelty that the entire world is witness to the inhumanities that attend its implementation (small children forcibly separated from their mothers; all, including the old and sick, having to lie under the inadequate cover of a brickworks; men and women being left for days on end without any nourishment; the perpetration of rape on women; the shooting to death for trivial offences).
>
> Meanwhile it is asserted that it is not a question of deportation, merely of labour service abroad. The representatives of the neutral powers, however, are well aware of the dreadful truth that this term conceals for the majority of the unfortunates. The atrocities with which the transportations have been carried out make it predictable what the final outcome of these tragic events will be.

Mother apportions the food. We ate twice yesterday; today once.

The valley is sheer, in places twenty metres high. On top, submachine-gun-toting Arrow Crossers are posted every ten to fifteen metres. I venture close to the gate, peer beyond the barbed-wire fencing. People are chatting and pointing at us.

Two men get out of the Packard. Twenty or thirty people race towards them. An Arrow Crosser fires a shot in the air. My name is called from the far side of the barbed-wire fence. A pair of big, brown eyes; headscarf pulled down over the brow; well-worn winter coat. Jolán Bors is standing there, one of the three, at times five, employees in Father's paper-processing workshop. She's in her thirties, a former nun. She pasted paper bags; she had to lay out the precision-cut sheets of paper on a big trestle table; glue was applied with a brush, after which the paper could be folded. I have no idea she had been standing by the barbed wire. She had brought a few kilograms of apples. She had implored the commanding officer of the sentries to be permitted to hand in the bag – she had been allowed. Eat while you can, says a bespectacled old man. These people are going to kill everyone.

In the autumn of 1944 the wife of Dr Kővári, who was a next-door neighbour, made a trip home to Novi Sad (by that time known as Újvidék once more) to see her younger sister. They were both killed by Hungarian soldiers and their bodies tumbled into the Danube. Dr Kővári had been discharged as a first lieutenant at the end of the First World War. When he learned what had happened he put on his officer's uniform, pinned on his medals and, after donning an officer's kepi with its lacquered visor, went off to make the rounds of his patients. The block's air-raid warden admonishes him that his dress contravenes the law and if he does not take it off he will be reported. Standing next to him as he says that was his wife, wearing a fur coat that her younger brother, an army sergeant, had brought back from a village in Ukraine.

I lose the gaze of the fourteen-year-old boy; I can see only his back in the crowd. I try to keep track of him.

He tightens the belt on his windcheater.

At the gate is a renewed crackle of gunfire. Soldiers are again ripping protective passports in two. Dead people are lugged behind the brick-drying sheds. Father and Uncle Lajos come to an agreement that they will not show their Swiss *Schutzbriefe* even if challenged to do so – it's not worth taking the risk that they will be ripped up. A trench-coated diplomat whose identity is unknown to me, and all I see is that he is gesturing as if he were observing us; as if he were grateful that we are not flocking to him, not pleading for anything. It takes fifty-eight years until the two gazes find each other, and even then only I am able to see him while writing this.

What remains of our bread is dry. Mother gives me a square of chocolate.

The third morning. Father's face is grey. He has a leather peaked cap with a cloth lining that he can pull down over the ears; this was what he wore when he was a passenger in a car. Comes in handy right now, says Mother. Father finished six years of elementary-school education in the small town of Kiskunhalas; he was the seventh of eight siblings. He was able to invent stories as he sat at my bedside of an evening. One of the stories was about Jericho and a tall, spry black lad's adventures in the African jungle, while another was about Little Red Riding Hood and her being able to fly with outstretched arms and travel on clouds.

The first time Father went out on the streets wearing a yellow star was on 5 April 1944 to go to his workshop at 41 Francia Road. He leaves the barrier on Thököly Road, turns left, goes past József Rübner's timber shop. Single-storey working-class housing; dwellings consisting of just a single room and kitchen, communal latrines at the end of the corridor. Number 41 is the sole two-storey building with a garden. The balconied apartment on the mezzanine over the workshop is the home for the lawyer Dr Ernő Fogas and his family. That morning he sets off in a lieutenant's uniform. Father would like to turn back so that they could avoid each other, but now there is no chance. Twenty metres, ten . . . He saluted from a long way off, he tells Mother that evening. He halted. Saluted in anticipation. Set off again, saluted again.

I can't see a German soldier anywhere. Nor at the KISOK station.

Another column is sent off. They vanish at the bend in Vörösvár Road. Kafka's genius, Walter Benjamin wrote to Gershom Scholem, lies in the fact that he sacrificed truth for the sake of clinging to the Haggadic element of transmissibility; Scholem replied that in other words it was about a crisis in transmissibility of truth. Six years after that exchange of letters we, too, are falling in. The marching columns line up. Again Home Guards with Arrow Cross armbands, submachine gunners in black. Again an officer at the head of each column. Again gendarmes bringing up the rear.

I strap up my knapsack, wind my scarf round my neck. Shouted commands. The left-hand column sets off. It wheels off and vanishes in the fog. The right-hand column sets off.

I am approaching the intersection of Bécsi Road and Vörösvár Road on a number 1 tram.

On the right are two single-storey buildings with peeling

plasterwork. I can recall their like. They must have been built in the first couple of decades of the last century. Dwellings of a single room and kitchen with no mod cons. In the row of shops facing the street a depot for Suzuki scooters, a launderette, a discount paint shop. At the corner a Piazza Italia restaurant. On the valley slope stands a string of villas on Remete Hill. Big picture windows, balconies, underground garages.

I set off to the left along Bécsi Road. A SEAT automobile showroom, INTERSPAR, Eurocenter. They operate with huge bulldozers. Stone mounds. An asphalt road on top of the clay hillside leads to the string of villas. A parking lot in front of the Praktiker Store.

On 17 November, the day before we were lined up, Ferenc Szálasi issues a memorandum on the definitive settlement of the Jewish question.

> (2) The Jews loaned on behalf of the German government, whom the German government is prepared to employ as able-bodied in the interest of a shared conduct of the war. These Jews are obliged to work for the benefit of the Hungarian nation. Their fate will be determined by the Hungarian state consonant with European considerations in the course of a general resolution of Europe's Jewish question.

Those European considerations had been decided years before then, at the Wannsee Conference.

> (3) Jews remaining for the time being in Hungary are to be concentrated in ghettos. Each ghetto will have four gates located at the four main points of the compass. Jews may only leave the ghetto in the event that they are transported out as Jews on loan for forced labour.

On the afternoon of 18 November Carl Lutz, accompanied by Raoul Wallenberg, comes across several hundred people in possession of Swiss and Swedish passports heading for Gönyű on the highway to Vienna.

That same day the commanding general at the Wehrmacht HQ in Budapest reports to the SS Reichsführer in Berlin that the Swiss

Embassy is disrupting the Jewish action by distributing *Schutzbriefe* much as before. Guidance is requested as to what action should be taken.

Eichmann, the director of a special *Judenkommando*, added the following comment to the sentence in Szálasi's memorandum, according to which a boarded-up ghetto will have four gates under the supervision of the police and Arrow Cross functionaries: 'Jews must be escorted through these gates, but in principle no one may leave.'

In Ferenciek Square lie two Home Guards who have been hacked down. Around their necks are cards saying 'Army deserters'.

On the instructions of Joachim von Ribbentrop, the Reich Minister for Foreign Affairs, Edmund Veesenmayer, the German Ambassador to Budapest, lodges a protest note about how 'the Swiss are sabotaging joint German–Hungarian war efforts'. The Hungarian Ministry for Foreign Affairs takes immediate action, and additional Arrow Cross detachments arrive at the Óbuda Brickworks.

I am standing between Mother and Father in the marching column. They are holding my hands and are not wearing gloves. The trench-coated diplomat also has no gloves on. The man beside him is wearing a Red Cross armband. They are having a discussion with a lieutenant colonel. The latter orders the captain standing at the head of our column to come over to him. The captain then bawls out that those over sixty and children under sixteen may fall out.

There is no scrum, no rush. Everyone looks around. An elderly woman moves off. Someone asks what will happen to those who stay in line.

Father adjusts my cap; Mother rewinds the scarf round my neck. Put your gloves on, she says. She reels off a list of the rations I shall find in my knapsack; Father lists the documents that I have on me and slips some banknotes into my windcheater pocket.

The Róberts are also taking leave of Mádi.

A gendarme NCO lines us up.

Father is able only to call out names and ranks.

Mother would like her smile to be my memory of these moments.

We hold hands and wave with our free hands.

Mádi pulls out two tins of food from her knapsack. She darts over and gives them to her parents.

I don't remember that, however. It's something she tells me fifty-eight years later over a cup of coffee. Our parents had no doubt that we ought to stay behind, she says.

The column reaches the gate. It wheels to the left then disappears.

We are also lined up. In front of me is a short, slight old lady. She has applied lipstick; her face is sallow, but I can see traces of lipstick on either side. She whispers something.

She is someone I know, though.

The gendarme NCO leads the column. Beside him is the man with the Red Cross armband. I carry Vera's small case. Mádi has a knapsack. Vera's twelfth birthday had been in August. She's wearing a dark-blue overcoat and dark-blue beret. Her mother, in the same column as our parents, may by now be on the highway threading through the Pilis Hills. Her father has been away for two years on forced-labour service. There has been no news of him. Our first kiss was in the summer, in the back yard of the yellow-star house.

The yard was in part a garden, in part a storage dump for building materials: sacks of lime, piles of cement, ladders. We were sitting on a stack of bricks. We had seen in films how one was supposed to kiss, but I wasn't holding her hand, did not embrace her, did not bring my lips close to hers. She did not pull away, but I have the impression that I heard a frightened cry when we parted. The kiss must have hurt her; my groin is aching.

We reach another brick-drying shed. Here, too, a person has only as much room as one's body can squeeze out in the crush of people. Vera calls out to Mádi. They whisper. Mádi has already had her first period and passes on advice. After a while Vera feels bold enough to hold hands with me, squeezing when she feel a spasm.

The 1943 map marks the Bohn Brickworks on the left-hand side of Bécsi Road; on the right are the drying sheds of the Újlaki Brickworks. Zápor Street is to the east, Vályog and Föld Streets to the south.

These three streets are also marked on the map from 2002. Built-up housing blocks. Many old houses and a few recently built business establishments.

On the 1943 map, on the left of Vörösvár Road, are Óbuda's old cemetery and Testvér Hill; to the right are the Óbuda limeworks and new cemetery. Bécsi Road swings north-westwards toward Solymár

Valley; to the right are Arany Hill and Üröm Hill. That is the direction in which the columns disappeared.

We sometimes get to our feet then sit back down – that's how much room we have to move. In the evening we are herded down a set of wooden steps without banisters into a yard. Many stumble and fall so that those coming after trample over them.

We line up anew.

An officer once again heads the column. This time there are two men with Red Cross armbands accompanying us. We head towards town along Bécsi Road, at times under orders to proceed at a fast march. The streets are deserted. No light filters out from behind the blackout papers pasted on windows. The armed men are also silent.

We are nearing the Danube.

Those in front slow down; those behind run into us, and we pile up.

On to Margit Bridge.

But there's no bridge.

The armed men again bawl out the order to move ahead: By twos! By twos!

I can't see the Danube.

Now I see it.

The reason I could not see it was because I have never before seen it at the same level as my feet . . . The waves are slopping over the planks.

Two of us can fit on the planks alongside each other. I hold Vera by the hand. It is not possible to hang on to a swaying cable fastened to buoys bobbing on the water. The crossing was constructed by men on assault craft. An old woman slips, and we tread on her. One of the submachine gunners pushes her into the river with his foot. Armed men are also stumbling along among us. One right behind me is roaring 'Left, right! Left, right! His expression astounds me. Never before have I seen a look of naked terror on the face of an Arrow Crosser. The NCO yells out, Don't all step at the same time, you bloody fools! Stop swinging!

The moon is not shining. The stars cannot be seen. The wind is stiff. The column is swaying. It is not impossible we'll have to swim. Anything is possible. I step deliberately, not so much on the wooden planking, the end of which is separated from the wrecked stump of the bridge by a gap of half a metre. Some manage to jump across. The elderly and small children are helped across by elderly people and children. The old girl with the lipstick again ends up beside me. She has on a thin black coat. Dangling ridiculously from one arm is a leather handbag.

You, Luca, were not there, in the brickworks, I say thirty-two years later. We are sitting in her apartment at 30 Mexikói Road.

That morning when the Arrow Crossers came, by pure chance I happened to have gone down to the shed for fuel under the outside staircase, says Luca Wallesz; that's where I hid, but they took Mother and the others off to the brickworks. I don't remember anything of that. But she was, says Luca, you yourself told her that the over-sixties could quit the marching column. I don't remember that, I reiterate that time thirty-two years later, and now, a further twenty-six later, all I can remember is Gitta Gyenes's lips daubed with lipstick.

I don't even remember that when I was talking with Luca in 1976 there was also a young girl sitting in the room, which is why I don't recognize her, twenty-six years on, as she comes out of the gates of Zsuzsa Kossuth Gymnasium, exchanges words with her students and sets off towards the Praktiker DIY Store, and when she passes she looks at me as if she had recognized me.

At the Pest end of the bridge are three ack-ack guns. The barrel of one of them is slowly lowered and trained on us; the barrels of the other two are also not pointing up at the sky but towards the city.

The streets evaporate into the blank of my memory; the stumbling people into unrecollectability.

Why were the guns pointing towards the city and not at the sky? The gunners in charge were Hungarian artillerymen. It was as if they found that reassuring then; as if the two flanks of the valley that embraced the brick-drying sheds we had already left behind an hour before had moved stealthily to encompass the dark city.

The block of the Great Synagogue on Dohány Street.

The column is not herded towards the main entrance.

We go round the building and reach a smaller doorway. That, too, can only be entered two by two. Again we are crushed against one another. I hold Vera by the hand, pulling her after me. Stairs. A corridor. More stairs. A large hall.

A big purge is likewise commencing in the Chamber of Actors. In the course of his presidency Ferenc Kiss did all within his power to make sure that roses of Hebron, along with Jewish actors, should vanish both from before the film cameras and from stages, but despite all his efforts numerous Jews still remained members of the Chamber. To mention just a few: Gyula Bartos, Lajos Básti, Oszkár Beregi, Dezső Ernster, Ella Gömbaszögi, Gyula Gózon, Vilmos Komor, Andor Lendvai, Erzsi Pártos, Blanka Pécy, Gabriella Relle, Jenő Törzs. It is now at last curtains for them, together with many other Israelite contemporaries of theirs.

That, in the hush of the library, is from the edition of the daily newspaper *Magyarország* for 1 April 1944.

The main reading room, the devastated Goldmark Room.

Shattered chair fragments by the walls and the half-light merge with the old newspaper; the touch of the pen, refilled while writing this, merges with the voices of Dezső Ernster and Andor Lendvai heard in the winter of 1943 sitting in the eighth row of the theatre. Vilmos Komor is conducting the chamber orchestra.

By the time Jewish actors are banned from taking to the stage the Hungarian Israelite National Cultural Association has installed a theatre hall on the first floor of a building that adjoins the Dohány Street Synagogue.

I have a precise recollection of that eighth row. Dark-brown long trousers, herringbone jacket. An ageing gentleman singing on the small stage. That ageing gentleman was then all of forty-two years old.

According to the 1994 edition of the *Actors' Encyclopaedia*, Andor Lendvai was born in the town of Vác in 1901; he studied in Vienna, Milan and Munich. Between 1934 and 1961 he was a bass soloist at the Hungarian State Opera House and appeared with great success in guest roles at Vienna, Lucerne, Rome and Moscow; one of his main roles was as Mephisto in Gounod's *Faust*. What the *Encyclopaedia* does not underline is that when he sang Mephisto was exactly when he was *not* a member of Hungarian State Opera.

His voice strikes me as hard and rasping; so does Dezső Ernster's. He was forty-five. He set off on his globetrotting career from Germany in 1923. Until Hitler's accession to power he sang in Berlin, then after that, until the Anschluss, in Graz, then 'for a few years he lived in Budapest', it says in the *Encyclopaedia*, whereas from 1945 he was on the staff of the New York Metropolitan Opera.

We stumble between stacks of chairs piled on top of one another. The stage curtain is ripped.

Time relays the voices; it contracts, expands, has dimensions, raises barriers, constructs channels, prepares an open road to Lendvai's rasping baritone, to Ernster's soft-grained bass and to stage and screen actor Oszkár Beregi's 'to be or not to be', so let us leave time-related questions, they make no sense, because time is always present tense; in the past present of the past tense many past presents are superimposed on top of one another, and in the present of writing down I hear these voices together with the sound that, holding Vera's hand, I hear as I push ahead in the dark. I shall have something to say later to Vera and Mádi about these singing voices, *sensed* as being pursued, among the broken fragments of chairs that are piled up in the corner, but for the time being I try to get my bearings in the enormous space of the Great Synagogue. Everything is dark except for a few candles flickering by the Ark of the Covenant.

There are several hundred of us: men doing forced-labour service, immobilized older people, children of five or six. Everyone is searching for someone; everyone is calling out names. Those doing forced labour will be sent on further tomorrow morning – perhaps to western Hungary, perhaps Germany. Doctors are allowed to pull on Red Cross armbands. The dying are laid beside the walls. The candles in front of the Ark of the Covenant burn down. I enquire from some of the men on forced-labour service about my older brother and uncle, occasionally shouting out their post-box number. Everyone has heard something. My uncle's unit had boarded railway freight cars at Rákosrendező Railway Station, which used to exist in the XIVth District, but it was possible that this train could not be sent off because Russian troops had closed the lines. My brother's unit had set off on foot three weeks before from Bustyaháza, heading for Germany, and some of them managed to escape at Kassa. Vera would like to sleep. A man over by the Ark of the Covenant asks for quiet. Next to him is a military officer who fires a pistol shot in the air. The man distributes unfilled *Schutzbriefe* among the forced-labour servicemen.

Someone says it is Carl Lutz.

A rabbi joins them, the shadow of his figure in his vestments falling on the Ark of the Covenant.

I can see that shadow now better than the fourteen-year-old boy could in the dark. I close my eyes in order to seek him out, although, of course, it is not possible to write with eyes closed. It eases his position that he is able to vanish in a crowd; his movements are not weighed down by my acquaintances. He cannot know that around that time, maybe even on that very night in early November 1944, the last group of Jews was gassed at Auschwitz-Birkenau. The Germans began systematic elimination of all traces. The last 204 men of the Jewish *Sonderkommando*, or Special Detachment, who had been working in the gas chambers and crematoria were shot so that no witnesses would be left.

It could not have been Carl Lutz who stood in front of the Ark of the Covenant that evening.

It is as if someone were watching.

As if it were not just me making this journey of discovery but also someone else.

As if while I were searching for the tracks of the fourteen-year-old boy someone was accompanying my steps.

That there were three of us.

It gives a new dimension, let me put it that way, to this chronicle of the investigation.

I walked from the Praktiker DIY Store to Vörösvár Road. I wait at the terminal for the number 1 tram. Someone has been following me since I set off from the store.

Although the reason for my making the journey is because I am supposed to be the tracker.

I have encircled in my imagination the places where fifty-eight years ago, if memory serves me right, I once lined up, stood about or sat down on my knapsack; in my imagination I could chalk around the places where I had been present, in the same way as detectives mark the position of a corpse on the asphalt or the cobbles of a car park. I might as well mark the whole city and not just the traces of the steps with which, by now there is no doubt about it, someone is following me. I check behind but can see nobody. There may be more than one of us sleuthing, and someone is more cautious than me and I cannot identify them. If I were writing a story I might make so bold as to venture that the fourteen-year-old boy is watching, whose presence I have just recorded at various crime scenes in my imagination. There is room in a story for that, too. We create each other, the describer and the described, it's just a matter of which one is which. In a story they may even be interchangeable, but now it is not about an event, at best the story of a reconnaissance, and even if the fourteen–year-old boy and the person making their way to the terminus of the number 1 tram do correspond with each other, the event and its reconnaissance are nevertheless not the same.

More puzzling than that, someone really is following me.

Why did I have the feeling that it was the schoolmistress, even though presumably she took her customary route home from the school?

Still, it is worth noting that in that case she, too, must have tramped from Praktiker to Vörösvár Road on foot. I had paced what amounted to the distance between two tram stops because I wanted to note a few bits of information about the houses and shops on either side of Bécsi Road, but why did she not, lugging a full bag with one arm as she was, take a number 17 tram to get to Vörösvár Road?

We get on the number 1 together. I find a free seat near the rear platform. She is further off in front of me. She does not look behind her.

At Thököly Road I get down at the back; she at the front. She stops. Waits.

It is as if both of us had been charged with following the other. Might we truly be simultaneously observers and observed?

She is around forty. White blouse, close-fitting jeans. With her free hand she sweeps her shoulder-length auburn hair aside from her brow. It could be that behind me her husband is approaching. This is where they meet for him to take the full shopping-bag from her. Or maybe she spotted an acquaintance, and that's why she's waiting. Maybe her lover – this is a spot where they can rendezvous for a few minutes. I don't look behind me. I stand beside her. She does not look behind me; she looks at me.

You don't remember me, do you?

I am at a loss for words.

She tells me her Christian name; says that she is only telling me that because that was how she introduced herself the last time we met.

The single-storey house in which I met Luca twenty-six years ago had been in ruins. Four cats. As if nobody had cleaned the room for years. As if Luca had smeared powder and lipstick on the make-up she had worn as a girl. As if she were wearing her mother's moth-eaten cardigan.

She introduces her daughter as her girlfriend: Luca was sixty-five; the girl eighteen. A freshly ironed white blouse, a pleated skirt with a floral pattern. She was seated on the divan like someone who was afraid to get up because she would be unable to locate her place again on the same hollow between the protruding springs when she wanted to sit back down. I had been talking with Luca for a hour, and no longer about the time she made the acquaintance of the poet Attila József, where the three of them had strolled with his mother, a painter, whom I supposedly told in the Óbuda Brickworks, so Luca said, which row to she should move to. The eighteen-year-old girl in the white blouse finally gets up, with the springs in the divan twanging, and she goes out, presumably to the toilet.

As if she had been waiting for this, Luca quickly tells me that the girl's grandmother was her friend, she was a doctor in the ENT Dept at the Charity Hospital on Amerikai Road; she knows it is now Neurosurgery, says Luca. Yes, I know, I say. Oh, of course you still live there, opposite the hospital, says Luca. In 1976, when I am sitting with Luca, I still lived there, at the time it had been for thirty-five years and after that for another twenty-five. The reason I know Luca is that from 1936 until 1945 she, too, lived there at 74 Amerikai Road with her mother, the painter, and her father, a magazine editor who died during the war. My friend worked there in ENT, says Luca, while the girl with the white blouse was outside in the loo; they, too, lived on Amerikai Road; they, too, had amused themselves with her daughter on the KISOK ground; just a minute, her daughter then, in 1944, must have been seventeen, I know that because Attila was still visiting us and still writing poems for me at the time when my friend's daughter was born, so it was around 1927; anyway, they, too, were taken to the brickworks, my friend was no more than forty and her daughter was at least sixteen, which is why they both ended up in Ravensbrück. It was just pure chance that the over-sixties and under-sixteens were able to leave the marching column that day, I say. I know says Luca, in the same way as it was pure chance that I just happened to be in the wood cellar when the Arrow Cross came at 6 a.m., and I didn't dare come out, and they forgot to take a look there, so they did not take me away, but they took Mother. Of course, it was equally pure chance, I say, that both I and Auntie Gitta were allowed to leave the column, and I said that to Luca in 1976, when I still knew nothing about Carl Lutz, as the schoolmistress and I are crossing Hungária Outer Circle, so she must be Györgyi, and the fact that I meet her is just as much a matter of chance. Yes, I distinctly remember that, while she was out having a pee, Luca says that the girl's grandmother, her friend, was taken to the gas chamber, the girl, Györgyi's mother Klári, saw how her mother was taken away, and Klári's friend was also taken away, but she got back home to Hungary, she married the fiancé of that friend, gave birth to Györgyi and divorced. She had never told Györgyi what had happened to her and her mother, and she was telling me so that the child would not learn, she was unable to tell her, but she had to tell someone so she was telling me, I was her mother's best friend, and she had forbidden her to say anything to Györgyi, but it slipped out of my mouth when Györgyi paid a visit last week that you were going to come over to talk about Attila. It slipped out that you were also there in the brickworks, that's why you had come. Now, it is just possible she will try to ask you about things, but don't tell her anything, I swore to her mother, what could I say, I didn't know them then.

The girl comes back into the room.

We leave Hungária Outer Circle. She says nothing, just walks beside me.

You probably also don't remember, she says at the corner of Mexikói Road, that we came away together from Luca's, and I asked if you minded me tagging along at least until we were at the hospital where Granny worked.

In Ear, Nose and Throat . . .

With Pogány as the consultant in charge.

I don't remember us going together as far as the hospital, but Dr Pogány was the consultant who took my tonsils out in 1941 or '42, I say.

I need a rest.

I change fountain pens.

I put the Montblanc pen in its place and carry on writing with my Reform.

I write down that I am twelve. I am wheeled into the operating theatre. Blue lamps. I am strapped down. Faces lean over me: an oval bespectacled man's face; a longish woman's face. A gauze wax as a gag in my mouth. A narcotic anaesthetic is sprayed on it. The woman asks me to count to ten. A scalpel flashes. I make it as far as six. It is as if bells were ringing like in the ten-minute morning break at school. Where did my voice go while I was counting? I see blue lamps. The woman with the attentive face was that young woman's grandmother, I think to myself on the corner of Mexikói Road with Thököly Road. That night I dream of the two of us standing on that corner; I also see the face of the lady doctor leaning over me. Cats slink about in Luca's room. In my dream the girl with the white blouse is not eighteen but around forty, and she puts her full bag down beside Luca's divan, unbuttons her blouse, unbuttons some more, steps out of her skirt, the hair falling over her eyes as she tilts her head slightly back, she sets it back behind one ear with the fingers of her right hand, the gesture being repeated several times, rather as if it were recorded on film, but in my dream it is repeated by one of the members of a gathering seated around a large oval table. I am sitting directly opposite; the faces of the others are shaded, the face of the person who repeats the gesture as well; I can see the fingers and the strands of hair very clearly, also a white blouse, only not who these belong to, who is repeating the gesture of smoothing the hair back. In one corner of the room a stove of heat-resistant glass is glowing ruddily. This is another room, not the one where they are seated around the oval table. Homespun tapestries on the walls; a set of folk-art furniture; Luca in seated in one of the armchairs; high up there is a blue lamp giving a light like that of the lamp illuminating the operating theatre – I can even sense a smell of ether, but I can see nothing except a leisurely gesture of the hand sweeping the long strands of hair behind one ear.

I even remember, says Györgyi, that when we came away together from Luca's I asked you what you knew about my mother and grand-mother, and you answered that you knew nothing.

I wasn't acquainted with them, I say, there was nothing I could say. I understand, she says, but I didn't understand back then. What? Why I could learn nothing about them. Or maybe I did understand, even back then, but I was still not able to resign myself to it.

What couldn't you resign yourself to? She does not reply. I ask if it was just chance that she had been coming after me? Not at all, she says. I wanted to look for you on several occasions, ever since getting over the feeling that I couldn't let it go I desisted, but when I saw you in front of the school I was reminded again . . .

Her look is bright and warm. Once again she throws her head back and tidies the hair from her brow.

Are you still living in this neighbourhood? I enquire. She did not remember seeing me, but I remembered that she had lived in this neighbourhood? After a pause I say that even I could not explain why, but it simply was the case that I distinctly remembered she used to live in the neighbourhood.

She lives in Abonyi Street. Am I familiar with the area, she asks. I don't know what to say, and I say as much. She says she, for her part, does not understand. I offer to carry her bag, but she declines.

It could not have been Carl Lutz in the Great Synagogue that night. Someone else was distributing *Schutzbriefe*.

That evening of 10 November 1944 Carl Lutz was reading a report from Red Cross delegate Friedrich Born:

> Old people, men and women, young men and girls, but also children staggered slowly on the old road to Vienna, starved, in their columns of thousands. Arrow Cross guards were driving the children along the side of the road. Already early on in this journey of more than 200 kilometres even the lightest baggage was dropped by the wayside . . . Sometimes shots were heard when overtired marchers were unable to continue. The Vienna Road became a road of dread, and it will probably remain engraved in human memory as the road of hatred. Forty columns of a thousand each were driven towards Germany to their deaths.

A colleague at the consulate adds: 'Fear that they, too, will end up in a gas chamber pushes the persecuted into a state in which they can now scarcely be called human. They are completely at the mercy of the brutal guards.'

He read, as I read, a report from Police Captain Batizfalvy:

Those arriving at the border crossing of Hegyeshalom are handed over to SS Hauptsturmführer Dieter Wisliceny. The Hungarian committee handover is led by László Bartha. By their number, not their names: 10,000 human beings had already lost their lives before reaching the border, mostly shot dead, beaten or starved to death. At Gönyű several hundred people are lying on barges waiting for death as a result of many days of walking, starvation and torture. On the way back there were hundreds of dead bodies lying by the roadside, nobody having given any thought to burying them.

At the same time that Lutz was reading those reports an Arrow Cross squad burst into the Great Synagogue and picked out ten men who are hauled out into the yard outside.

I hear the burst of gunfire.

It is ten days since the Swiss Minister Maximilian Jaeger had left to travel back to Berne, and in their final talk had left it up to him whether he stayed in Budapest or went home, too. Every day Carl Lutz and his wife posed themselves the same question: should they go or should they stay. They had arranged weeks before for their furniture to be removed. He would have been delighted, I read, if his own name had been included in the telegraphed instruction that the head of the Swiss mission in Budapest had been sent by the Ministry of Foreign Affairs in Berne in response to the question as to whether he was willing to accept the invitation made by the government of the Hungarian Prime Minister Szálasi and relocate the Swiss representative mission to Sopron, the city in western Hungary to which the government offices were being withdrawn. 'We see little possibility of the Swiss Legation being able to follow the Szálasi government. We ask you to entrust Kilchmann and staff with the protection of the Swiss colony in Budapest and to report with Major Fontana to Berne.'

Frau Lutz asks her husband what will become of them. Neither our name nor what will happen to the department are mentioned in the telegram, says Lutz after he has discussed this with the minister. So what did Jaeger say? He said I was to do as my conscience dictates.

The following day he receives a request from the Hungarian Ministry of Foreign Affairs to relocate his Representative Department for Foreign Interests to Sopron or face the loss of all diplomatic rights should this not be done. An hour later the news came through that the German Embassy was on the brink of removing to Sopron. The person who transmitted this added enigmatically that as long as Lutz was in Budapest the Arrow Cross should not attack Jewish yellow-star houses under the protection of foreign embassies.

Who is sending you cryptic messages from the German Legation, Frau Lutz asks?

Lutz paces in front of the colonial writing desk. Dr Gerhart Feine, he says. Who's Dr Feine, if I may ask? His wife lights up a fresh cigarette and pours a brandy for herself; she does not pour one for her husband. The first secretary at the embassy, says Lutz. He's the one who, four years ago, when we were representing German interests in British-mandated Palestine always thanked me for my efforts. The parties, oh my God! says his wife, tossing back the drink; the parties were most agreeable; it was just the climate that was so unbearable!

He had likewise poured a drink for himself, and likewise thrown it back twelve days later, when Moshe Krausz, head of the Jewish Agency for Palestine in Budapest, placed on the Vice-Consul's desk a copy of the minutes of a meeting that he had attended on Lutz's behalf to represent the Swiss Legation.

Gertrud Lutz is in a négligé with a deep décolletage, from which the lace of her blue silk nightdress is visible. It is a quarter past midnight. The chandelier is shaking from nearby bomb strikes.

Lutz reads the minutes, which record what police captain Batiz-falvy had experienced on a more recent visit to Hegyeshalom. He supposed, he read, that he had seen them set off from the Óbuda Brickworks mentioned in the reports. In Batizfalvy's view, says Moshe Krausz, many members of the escorting guard could not bear the sight of people being tortured, some even saying they would prefer to be sent to the front rather than continue to take part in the horrors. Batizfalvy had acquired an open order, and if we were to set off in a registered legation car he undertook to accompany us to Hegyeshalom, says Moshe Krausz; if we were to take blank *Schutzbriefe* along we could fill those out at the border for the people who were in the worst shape. That is why the officers are here.

There are two officers: a slim, fair-haired first lieutenant in the artillery and a squat infantry second lieutenant. Both are members of a resistance group among army officers. Alongside the first lieutenant is a tall, blonde, attractive woman in her forties; she has one arm around him. Lutz's wife looks at her with interest, asking her what hair dye she uses, poppet; what is your natural hair colour? Brunette, says the woman, dark brown. Frau Lutz pours a drink for her and the two officers; she polishes it off in such a way that she does not wriggle out of the first lieutenant's embrace to do so.

Lutz seemed at a loss to start with, but then he swiftly made arrangements, the blonde woman told my mother later. Gizi could not tell her coherently what had happened, Mother later told me. Both of them left it up to me to try to assemble the words, like fragments of sentences on slips of paper floating in time, to restore order to the unrestorable – the fact was that Gizi had not paid much attention to the faces, and although she distinctly remembered Frau Lutz asking about her hair colour and that it was Hennessy cognac that they drank, still her clearest memory was that Károly had been woken up one hour earlier by his batman to be told that an order had come in that he should set off for the Swiss Consulate.

But that can wait five minutes, Gizi says in the bed. They had made love for five minutes; Gizi had related that, too, Mother later told me; Gizi even said that they had not had enough time to wash because Károly's fellow officer, the infantry second lieutenant, was waiting at the gate in a car.

Gizi was Mother's aunt, although no more than two years older – in 1944 she was forty-three years old.

On other occasions Károly was a stickler for formalities, but that time he permitted me to put an arm round him even at the Lutzes'. The woman was uninhibited: it was evident that she would happily go to bed with Károly and that she had made the drink for me in order to obtain my approval.

Lutz's hands were trembling, but he went ahead straight away with making arrangements. We knew he already had a long experience of consular duties, having worked in America and in

Palestine for the British; he issued the orders like clockwork . . . we, too, did everything . . . like clockwork . . . If we had not operated that way we would not have dared go out on the streets. Nor should I forget that Lutz kept his eye on me for a long time. How had I ended up there? Perhaps he thought I was a grass.

Lutz gives an order that the legation's other car should be brought out. The infantry second lieutenant declares that his own car is also available. The first lieutenant says that the two of them, along with the woman who was with them (only now did Lutz notice her Red Cross armband), were also ready to go. He says that they are in contact with the He-Halutz, the Zionist socialist pioneer youth movement, which has been organizing the rescue of Budapest's Jews, and they have at their disposal some cars camouflaged as Red Cross ambulances. Frau Lutz turns to Gizi. Won't this be too risky, poppet? Gizi says she has already made the trip once; she is looking for her younger sister, who was in one of the marching columns that had set off from the brickworks.

Moshe Krausz whispers something to Lutz. Lutz makes a telephone call. He demands that the under-sixteens among those collected in the Dohány Street Synagogue should be taken over by the ICRC.

At daybreak two cars set off from Vadász Street. Gizi is sitting on the back seat in the second of these, between the two officers.

Lutz is unaware that at dawn the daily log for the Budapest ambulance service records its inspection of the site after a fusillade had been unleashed on the first group to be dragged to the bank of the River Danube. He is unaware that at midday, in a speech he makes to Parliament, MP Károly Maróthy will point out that something must also be done about the dying scattered along the highway towards Vienna so that they could not be heard groaning all day long in the ditches; it would be better to dispatch the Jews; any dormant pity for them should not be allowed to be awakened.

An old man is sitting on a step leading to the Ark of the Covenant, his head covered by a tallit, a prayer shawl. He reminds me of how my grandfather used to sit at the head of the table in his dwelling on Rákóczi Avenue. It is Seder, the family meal and service on the evening of the first night of the Passover feast, but he did not wear a prayer shawl. The way Mother tells it, he would only don that for services on the Sabbath.

A dozen of us are seated at a big oval table, me opposite Grandfather, between Mother and Father; on the table are dishes filled with the food that will be involved in the ceremony.

Remember, Gizi says to my mother, who later tells me, how my little sister used to sweep her hair, which cascaded to her shoulders, behind her right ear when she lifted up her glass to take a sip of wine; her eyes would be sparkling, and she would place a kiss on my cheek, just like when my mother still lived, and it was her greatest pleasure to see her big daughter and the little one, sixteen years between them there were, exchange kisses. I remember that, Mother would tell me later on, and she asked if I could remember the Seder evenings. I was six or seven at the time. Yes, says Mother, I also remember the heaving plates and the crowd round the table. I don't remember Bőzsi's face, but I do somehow that gesture of the hand. As if it were self-contained, independent of the body. I don't say that to Mother, but I see the cascading of her hair as in a film loop, the play of the fingers, the gesture of slightly throwing back the head. I took just a single sip of wine, and even that made me tiddly. Mother leads me into my grandparents' bedroom to let me lie down on the divan which stands before the two beds. Meanwhile, I walk next to Bőzsi. I, too, get a peck on the cheek; I can smell her perfume. This comes back to me later. I tell Mother. It sets her mind at rest to have someone with whom she can chat about Gizi and Bőzsi, and I also learn from her that when Gizi's father found out who her fiancé was he said that it was out of the question for him to be an army officer, especially a Jew. That is no way to make a living in times like this, Gizi's father declared in the study. I know that in spite of this Józsi donned his first lieutenant's worsted uniform, pinned on the silver service medal and the regimental Karl Troop Cross, polished his parade boots and showed up none the less.

Before the chambermaid announced him to Father, Gizi told my mother, before announcing that the first lieutenant was here, I went in to plead with Father, but he did not so much as look up. He was reading in that big leather-upholstered armchair of his. He had on a tobacco-coloured silk dressing-gown; he did not even bother to put on a jacket. That was his way of making me understand that for him

Józsi was a nonentity, no big deal, a nonentity. I have no idea where Gizi got that 'no big deal' from, Mother added.

The door opened, in stepped Józsi, and he stood before Father as if he had been hauled up for a court martial, Gizi related to Mother. Józsi would have been thirty-four years old. Gizi could scarcely suppress her laughter as she recounted how Józsi had entered the room, says Mother, because her father, Uncle Siggie, didn't so much as look up from the armchair, but then he got to his feet after all. Józsi thought that at last he could speak, but Father only went over to his writing desk and noted something down; he did not even sit, Gizi related. Father squiggled down sentences that nobody else could read, but he would later make use of them in his lectures at the university. He made notes for two minutes on end, no big deal, with Józsi stiffly at attention in front of the desk, then Father finally put down his pencil, placed the palms of his hands on the edge of the desk as was his habit, leaned forward, and, just imagine, he didn't look at Józsi, just at his two medals, did not even say a word of greeting, even though Józsi had said, A very good day to you, Professor! He had practised that morning, Gizi told Mother, and Mother giggled when she told me, as if she were twenty and listening as Gizi described that when her father finally broke his silence he poked at Józsi's jacket and said, That's the regimental Karl Troop Cross, isn't it? Józsi immediately answered that next to it was the silver service medal, but her father broke in to say that he was only interested in the regimental Karl Troop Cross. He knew that anyone who received it must have put in decent service of the front line.

He studied Józsi for a long time, and not the regimental Karl Troop Cross but the way he was standing stiffly before him with his adorable little 'tache and pomaded hair. Look, first lieutenant, he said, I know my daughter loves you. I take no pleasure in the marriage. I have serious doubts as to your career prospects, but my daughter loves you. He gave a resigned wave of the hand and stepped over to the cocktail cabinet, took out a bottle of cognac and poured out a drink, not for me, just for Józsi and himself, clinked glasses with Józsi, although Józsi had not been able to get a word out since entering the room saying, A very good day to you, Professor, and that is the silver service medal next to it, just stood to attention in front of Father. No big deal, that's how the proposal of marriage went off, Gizi told Mother.

That was the point at which a coughing fit broke out, with Józsi unable to hold it back any longer.

Gizi's father had already heard that Józsi received a lung wound on front-line duty, but according to all the doctors he had recovered completely. Gizi implored her mother, and Gizi's mother implored her father, said Mother.

Ten years later, in the year Hitler came to power, Józsi was advised by the General Staff to ask to be discharged on the grounds of poor health. A captain tosses in the remark, You know, old chap, up at the top they aren't too fond of Jews.

Józsi challenged the officer to a duel, Mother related, asking two young cadets to stand as seconds. He duly appeared at the appointed time at the appointed place, a forest clearing in Kamaraerdő over by Budafok. Gizi knew nothing about it. The captain didn't show, sending a message by his batman that he would not fight a duel with a Jew. Józsi later recounted that the squaddie had stood before him, saluted and said, Beg to report that the first lieutenant should not hang on because the Captain sends word, by your leave, that if you happen to be Jewish, then he will not fight a duel.

Józsi suffers a coughing fit and is carted off to hospital, and when he comes out he asks for retirement on account of poor health.

That Seder evening was the last time I saw him. He poured a drink for himself the moment he sat down. By the time Grandfather had taken a sip, although convention prescribed that he should be first, Józsi was already on his third glass and asking the ladies, including Bőzsi, for kisses.

I kept the regimental Karl Troop Cross for a long time, along with the tiddlywinks for table-top soccer and my lead soldiers. I could see you were attracted by it, says Gizi a few weeks after Józsi's funeral. Have it. It's yours!

Black suits Gizi, says Mother to Father.

By the summer of 1944 we were already living in the Róbert family's dwelling, the yellow-star house at 78 Amerikai Road, when Gizi and Bőzsi rang the bell. Good grief! says Mother, why haven't you got a yellow star on your clothing? Aren't you afraid of running into an identification check? We're disappearing, says Gizi, we've just come to say goodbye; Károly is going to look after us. Károly is a second lieutenant in the artillery. He does not come into the house but takes a stroll in the street. He was one of the young cadets who were József's seconds for that duel, says Mother after Gizi and Bőzsi have left. The blonde hair looked good on them, didn't it? she says to Father, but Father doesn't reply.

On 12 November Károly was present at the residence of Captain Vilmos Tartsay when the military wing of the Liberation Committee of the Hungarian National Uprising was formed. A week later Gizi is waiting for him at their home in Óbuda to tell him she has no news of Bőzsi; she was worried and asked him to accompany her to Zugló, the XIVth District. They need to search for the kid: that's how she puts it, Gizi is still talking that way about her now 26-year-old younger sister. The first lieutenant obtains a car from a fellow officer. They don't find Bőzsi at Gyarmat Street; the acquaintance at whose place she had been living with false papers says that the caretaker for the block had informed on her. Two Arrow Crossers had come and taken her to the KISOK ground on Queen Erzsébet Avenue, says Bőzsi's landlord. He had heard that from there everyone was taken to the Óbuda Brickworks.

That afternoon is the first time Gizi saw Carl Lutz at the brickworks. She learned that the group Bőzsi ended up with has already been sent off towards Hegyeshalom.

Three days later Carl Lutz reads the report of Police Captain Batizfalvy about these marching columns:

> They follow the autobahn through Pilisvörösvár, Dorog and along the Danube past Süttő, Szőny and Gönyű to Mosonmagaróvár. Ten thousand Hungarians have already been handed over to the Germans at the frontier. As of now there are some 13,000 walking on the highway. Almost 10,000 have disappeared from the numbers who set off from the brickworks; some of them died because they were unable to walk the distance, some were shot and a few hundred escaped. Death ships are anchored at Gönyű; several hundred are lying on board suffering from dysentery. The barges are guarded by the gendarmerie.

Veesenmayer, the Reich Plenipotentiary in Hungary, communicates to Berlin that, according to Eichmann's figures, a further 40,000 needed to be readied for handover.

SS Obergruppenführer Hans Jüttner, with the military rank of General in the Waffen-SS, reports the same day that he is setting off to inspect the Waffen-SS divisions fighting in the Hungarian theatre, in the course of which he was going to meet SS Standartenführer Kurt Becher in Vienna. He did not wish to give credence to Becher's report about the state of those who were walking on the highway, which was why he was heading for Budapest. He encountered the marching columns halfway there. He can see that the escorts are Hungarian gendarmes and Arrow Crossers; he can see the corpses lying by the road. He returns to Vienna and reports to Becher that he now believes what he had heard from him, and once he got to Budapest he would immediately lodge a protest with Obergruppenführer Otto Winkelmann, the commander of the SS Police in Budapest.

Hans Jüttner never reaches Budapest, as he is posted elsewhere.

On that very same day Colonel-General Károly Beregfy, Szálasi's Minister of Defence, issues an instruction in which he bestows on unit commanders the right to massacre and decimate:

> Any commander who is unable to maintain discipline and order with the means at his disposal is not suited to command, and it is necessary to proceed accordingly. Military financial support will be withdrawn from the dependants of all deserters.

In an official report, the Swedish Legation in Budapest recounts that those who arrive alive in Hegyeshalom are handed over to Captain Péterfy, his immediate colleagues being Captain Kalotay and Captain Csepelka. Before being handed over to the Germans those who remain alive are quartered in barns in which the bedding litter is filthy and contagious and dysentery is rife.

The Opel Kadett turns on to the highway.

The first column is reached as they are approaching Gönyű.

The car creeps slowly past the marchers. Gizi scans every face. She gets out and checks the dead bodies in the ditch. She does not find Bőzsi among the living or the dead. The groups are separated by a distance of fifteen to twenty kilometres. When they reach the next one Gizi always gets out, always looks at the faces of the dead and dying. After the third column Károly will not let her get out of the car on her own. He has to present himself to the officer in charge of each column. He shows one of the blank safe-conduct permits that Batizfalvy gave Lutz on which his name and rank have been typed.

At Abda, just outside Győr, a German car approaches from the direction of Vienna. The two vehicles are unable to pass one another because of a passing column. They have to stop. Standartenführer Becher gets out; Károly likewise. He salutes and reports to the general that he is on an inspection tour, carrying orders for Captain Péterfy at Hegyeshalom. The general nods and gets back into his car.

He gave me a good once-over, Gizi later tells Mother.

The officer smiles and asks where the ladies are staying. He uses the plural but only has eyes for one, the tall blonde woman. Gizi smiles back. With her right hand she brushes aside the strands of hair fluttering over her eyes and tidies them behind her ear.

Strings of small red paprikas and bulbs of garlic are hanging outside the shop fronts by the side of the road at Abda. Glazed pottery plates, jugs, hand-woven fabric. Fords, Audis, Mazdas and Opels are coming from the direction of Vienna, tourists getting out and buying. They drink beers.

If just one of the stables had been preserved. One of the barns. Or a new building with plastic walls was standing there so that passing cars and the astonished faces looking from those cars could be reflected in it while the interior space was also visible, the composed piles of accessories – not blankets, sodden knapsacks, shoes with their soles come adrift and scraps of clothing, maybe, but jeans, casual jackets with zip fasteners, coloured knitted shirts, briefcases, Adidas bags and, tossed among them, a scattering of bloodied clumps of straw and a scattering of plastic human body parts as in a *Guernica*, from which those passing by in the cars would quickly avert their gaze.

The Opel Kadett turns off in front of an office for the commanding officer that has been set up in the frontier post. Károly hands over the safe-conduct pass to Captain Péterfy and a list of the twenty-five names of people he has to transport back to Budapest. Captain Péterfy establishes that signature and stamp are authentic.

Three ICRC ambulances draw up and park behind the Opel Kadett.

Gizi proceeds alongside Károly. They enter the first shed.

White-gowned young men get down from the three Red Cross vans. They belong to the He-Halutz.

Several hundred people are stretched out in the shed. Gizi calls out Bőzsi's name.

The He-Halutzim had been ordered not to bother about the list of names but to stretcher those who are in the worst condition to the ambulances.

Gizi now calls out Bőzsi's name in the second shed.

She goes into the third.

This time she hears her own name.

Not a shout but a whisper.

Good God! Rosie!

Gizi . . . Gizi whispers, Mother.

Right away . . . at once . . . just a sec . . . hang on . . .

Gizi! Gizi! . . . The Róberts are also here . . .

The white-gowned lads come with stretchers.

The ambulances motor back towards Budapest, the Opel Kadett in front. Gizi is seated in the ambulance where my own mother and father are lying with ten others in a vehicle designed for six. She is clasping Mother's hand, Mother Father's. It's possible Bőzsi has already been handed over at the border, but I hope she managed to escape on the way, says Gizi; heavens above, her hair is bound to be full of lice. Father is not right in his head. He looks up once and says, We shall work, dearest. Even in Germany.

We were lying on a barge at Szőny, Mother says later, quite close to the water. All at once I sensed that your father was slipping on the wet planking on the deck, and I make a grab for him, but I was no longer able to reach him, although I dreamed that in the ambulance, says my mother for the umpteenth time. We are sitting in front of the television, and Zsuzsa Koncz is singing, throwing back her head, tidying her hair from her brow with that familiar gesture of the hand. My God! says Mother, although not because the gesture has reminded her, more because she has now forgotten what it is that the hand gesture reminds her of.

Three days later the leaders of the Hungarian army officers' resistance are arrested. The next day, Gizi later tells Mother, when the generals were being escorted to prison, Károly was shot in the neck in the street by an Arrow Crosser for attempting to escape.

It is morning.

We are standing in the yard of the Great Synagogue on Dohány Street. We line up to orders given by a sergeant with an Arrow Cross armband. Two men with Red Cross armbands are standing behind us.

We are marching again.

III

Our procession is guided across the yard of the Dohány Street Synagogue.

I am unaware that my grandmother, whom I last saw sitting on her bedside searching for her slippers with her feet, is now in the cellar of one of the houses in the ghetto here, barely a couple of hundred metres away. Nor can I know that later she will be lying under a pile of earth just a few centimetres deep where ten bodies are buried in the places where I am now planting my footsteps. I learn that six weeks later, as Mother clutches my hand while she leans over the grave and reads the names off a piece of card attached to a stick. There will be at least fifty similar graves in the temple's yard. At least thirty of us will read out at least three hundred names until we find Grandmother's name. I don't look back because under the archway through which I am passing, holding Vera's hand, is a pile of ice-cold corpses heaped on top of one another.

Mother's spectacles got broken on the highway; she has to lean right over to read out the names. She, too, is wearing boots and has difficulty walking in the mud.

There must be about thirty of us as the column turns on to Kaiser Wilhelm Avenue. Our pace is set by the sergeant with the Arrow Cross armband; sometimes we have to run.

It's early in the morning but seems more like night.

We leave Andrássy Avenue.

I'm not familiar with these streets. It is as if we were moving along in a tunnel or a channel. Some light is on at the side. A curtain is drawn aside behind a ground-floor window of one of the houses. It is a young boy who might be seven or eight but who has the face of an old man. Wrinkled. He is not watching us but the sergeant at the head of the line. A hand also draws aside the curtain of the next window. The young boy now watches from there and, as if he were walking with us, he also glances at us from a third window.

Fifty-eight years later I set off from the Dohány Street Synagogue along the same route. I recognize the house on Vadász Street in which I saw the young boy; the windows of the ground-floor apartment are curtained today as well. Maybe an elderly man lives there – with his children; maybe the children with his grandchildren.

On the left is the old building of a market hall.

I am not familiar with these streets.

I am familiar with the streets in the Zugló District and Baross Square at the end of Rákóczi Avenue, in front of Keleti Railway Terminus. That's where my grandmother lives, the one to whom I have no idea what is happening as our column reaches Vadász Street. I'm familiar with Andrássy Avenue; Gizi lives at the corner of Andrássy Avenue with Laudon Street. Six years before we had looked out from one of the windows in that second-floor apartment at the procession of guests for the Eucharistic World Congress on their way to Hősök Square at the far end of Andrássy Avenue. Józsi is drinking schnapps while Bőzsi brings raspberry cordial for the children; I marvel at the purple, scarlet and gold colours of the procession.

I have not been in Vadász Street before. My knapsack is lighter than it was a few days ago: the cans of preserves have run out, and I am wearing my spare pullover. Vera's little case hardly weighs anything, as she has thrown away her dirty underwear.

According to the 1943 map, where there is now an exit for the number 3 metro line in present-day Podmaniczky Square, it was then built up. In all likelihood the procession turned left to go down János Arany Street with Vadász Street the first on the right.

I don't make a halt at the metro stop but go further to the Burger King outlet on the corner; in the next house is a Crystal dry cleaner's then the John Bull Pub on Vadász Street.

I walk in, but I don't sit down or order a beer at first.

On 22 November Carl Lutz issued an order that all *Schutzbriefe* had to be filled out at the Glass House for every person applying for protection.

The John Bull Pub is near the Glass House, and I decide to drink a glass of beer after all.

There are several hundred people blocking our way. The two men with Red Cross armbands explain that we shall have to wait.

As not enough safe-conduct letters were available to meet the needs of the vast rescue operation, they had to be secretly printed at Budapest Press, Lutz recollects, thereby overstepping the authorization he had been granted by Berne. Expecting Berne to be of any assistance was hopeless, he wrote, as a wire at the very beginning had warned that under no circumstances should diplomatic immunity be extended to foreign nationals in premises belonging to the legation. Meanwhile several hundred Jews had already pushed their way into the Glass House, and they could not be sent out on the street even by force, because Arrow Crossers were seizing anyone wearing a yellow star, hustling them to the Danube bank and executing them there.

The sergeant reports to an Arrow Cross officer that he has brought our group here.

Mádi pushes her way forward in the crowd and reels off the names of the three of us to a man who is taking down details by the gate. Someone says that there are fifty typists at work in the building issuing Swiss safe-conduct letters. Curious faces in the windows of the next-door building. One man is taking photographs, some people are covering their faces, others looking up as if they thought it was important for them to feature in the picture.

Fifty-eight years later I come across the faces of a few children in photographs that have been published in various books. If I were in one of them, would I recognize myself? Next to the captions to the pictures is an attribution to the Swiss Federal Institute of Technology Archive of Contemporary History (ETH). Most of the men in the photographs are wearing trilbies; the women have no hats or scarves on.

Vera is swept from my side. I pay no more attention to the photographer but try to locate her.

There are three men entering details by the gateway; these are immediately passed on. It is possible to get a brief glimpse of the yard inside each time the entrance is opened: the outer glass roofing carries on past the entrance. A man in a peaked cap brings out the *Schutzbriefe* that have already been filled in; he reads out the names. The many hundreds of people fall quiet; names are passed on by word of mouth. Anyone whose name is mentioned is allowed through. Someone says how good it would be to make it into the house; someone else points out that there are already several thousand inside, on every floor and even down in the cellar.

The outer glass roof no longer exists; the old main beams are still visible, however. A woman comes out through the entrance. She opens the door wide in order to be able to drive out the Opel that is parked there. I ask her if she lives in the building. No, she parks there during the day by permission of the caretaker. She is not even sure if anyone lives in the house. There is a workshop in the corner; I should ask there.

She is around thirty and is wearing a three-quarter-length car coat and brightly coloured silk scarf. She has blonde hair, wears frameless eyeglasses and has recently applied lipstick. I get an impression of there being an air of pity in her expression as she looks me over. She points the ignition key at her car, which bleeps back in response. She would like to shut the gate after I have gone in, saying, I'm late, I'm rushing to pick my little girl up from nursery school, Lord, this eternal rush. By now it is not pity that I detect in her gaze, more power-lessness. Perhaps the compassion was not directed at me in the first place; maybe towards herself. Still, if she is rushing, why does she spend so long looking at me? She asks if she should shut the gate or not.

The man with the peaked cap at the gate says they cannot issue any more *Schutzbriefe*; those whose details have been registered should come back at eight o'clock tomorrow morning.

It has now gone four o'clock in the afternoon, and it is forbidden to be out on the streets wearing a yellow star, a boy next to me yells. Everyone pushes towards the gate. I put an arm round Vera and grab Mádi's hand. The crowd swept us into the courtyard; the gate is slammed shut behind us. I mention a name to a man standing by the stairs. Just then it comes to mind: Father had shouted it in the Óbuda Brickworks from his departing column. The man asks how come I know the name. He's a friend of my father's, I say. The man asks who my father is and where is he? I tell him who my father is and that our parents were taken away from the brickworks five days ago. I use the plural; the man looks at Vera and Mádi. Vera is shivering. One of the lenses in Mádi's glasses is broken.

Go upstairs, all three of you. First floor, second door on the left. *Schutzbriefe* Section.

On the nameplate: Dr E. Beregi, Dr M. Bleu, D. Friedmann, V. Geiger, Dr E. Gellért.

Fifty-eight years later I find the names in the archives as well as the fact that nineteen sections operated there.

We go past the first door. The nameplate: Relations Section.

In the documentation I read: 'Relations with legations of neutral powers, with ICRC organizations, with underground movements, with parties, with children's homes.'

We enter the second door. There are maybe twenty or twenty-five people waiting in front of four desks. Antique furniture, chests of drawers, armchairs. Women, both older and younger, in white blouses at work on Remington typewriters, with which I am familiar as I learned to type on that make of machine in Father's workshop. A balding man searches his notes for a long time but doesn't find our names. He says that they will be able to provide a *Schutzbrief* tomorrow; all they have is as many as the number of names on their lists. We should look for a place in the attic or in the garage.

Mádi also does not remember which of us it was who, having found no place even to sit after looking up in the attic and down in the cellar, said that we were not going to stay. Again, holding her by the hand, I have Vera in tow behind me. She slips in the mud in the yard. She weeps. I'm covered in mud, she cries. I've never before heard her talk this way. I mop her coat with my handkerchief.

So are you going to shut the gate now or not? the woman in the car coat repeats.

Maybe, I replied. Yes, maybe. No. She leans closer. She wears Givenchy perfume. She scrutinizes my face. It's as if now she had something even more important than getting somewhere on time. If I could establish what that is, I have the feeling I could arrive at some deeper insight. She has a small wart over her right eye. She is stroking her chin; silver fingernails. She goes back to the car, picks up two crammed shopping-bags on top of one of which is a head of cauliflower, in the other a plaited loaf of challah and baked cakes that she slings on to the rear seat. Screw all of you, she mutters to herself. She starts the car. Tyres squeal as she speeds out through the gate. She doesn't stop, doesn't get out, doesn't shut the gate after her.

I take another look the old photographs through a magnifying glass. I spot a boy in a school cap. He is about my age, but he's wearing 'specs. He is pressed against a wall in the crush.

I also head for a wall with Vera. A woman asks us what we saw inside the house.

K., a former classmate, writes from Jerusalem in the autumn of 2003:

> Rumours had spread that the inmates of children's homes were going to be moved to the ghetto. The Zionist movement, He-Halutz, decided that they were going to save four youngsters, bringing us to the Vadász Street Glass House. A massive uproar broke out among the crowd at the entrance. They were not in a mood to let us in at all, but after protracted arguments the gate finally opened. The sight was indescribable – a mass of people swarming wherever you looked. A place was designated for us in the attic. I came across more than one acquaintance. They were sitting or stretched out lethargically on enormous plank beds, spooning up other people's leftover scraps of food from a mess tin. I asked where I could bunk down. Here, they replied. There were hardly any toilets in the house, and there were long queues for them. The other three boys and I decided we were not going to stay. We told the guard we had been given an errand. They let us out.

I place the photograph of the crowd milling at the gate in a folder, as I also do with a photograph bearing the caption 'Discovery of bodies in yard of Dohány Street Synagogue'. On that can be seen five elderly men in hats stepping round the graves. They are wearing Red Cross armbands. Behind them are a Red Army officer and a policeman; in the background small piles covered with rags from under which legs poke out all tangled up with one another.

The people who can be seen in the picture perhaps passed by on the very same day Mother and I discovered my grandmother's name on one of the graves. Maybe we were treading in their footsteps, maybe they in ours, but the spectacle of the mound of bodies in the picture is certainly similar to what we saw.

I close both parts of the gate after the woman's Opel, cutting a hand on the bolt that fastens it. Next to the gate is a commemorative plaque: 'This was the legendary Glass House. Those who lived to see liberation here cherish the memory of Arthur Weiss, who was its hero and fell victim of the rescue action for thousands on 1 January 1945.'

I place documentation of the Glass House's organization, which lists the names of the heads, secretaries and chairmen of the nineteen committees. Arthur Weiss is one of the four members of the overall board of management.

I also file away a photograph of the office that I went to, now the Archives of the Museum of Contemporary History. First floor, second door on the left. In the picture, standing in front of floral-patterned wallpaper is an antique German cabinet and on it a pendulum clock. Four vases. On the right is a bentwood table and armchairs. A besuited, bow-tied man of about forty-five is reading papers and probably dictating to a woman in her twenties next to him in a white blouse and suit, who is at work, fountain pen in hand. Another woman, holding identification papers, maybe a registration form, judging from her open mouth and the posture of her upper body, seems to be dictating to a white-bloused colleague operating one of the typewriters. Another typist can also be seen who is copying details from a sheet of paper placed on the table. Behind her a fifth is writing on the table with a fountain pen.

In the file I place a picture with the caption 'Wedding of Carl Lutz and Gertrud Frankhauser', also from the ETH. They are passing before a whitewashed building, almost certainly a chapel; only the windowsill can be seen, the wedding guests in the background. The sun is shining. Lutz is in a black suit with a white bow-tie; he's holding a top hat in his left hand. Gertrud's dress, a string of pearls and veil are all white; she is carrying a bridal bouquet in her right hand.

The file is filled within a few days.

The fountain between the Lukács Baths and the Danube promenade near the Buda side of Margit Bridge. Lush vegetation. I took the snap in the autumn of 1943 with an Adox Sport folding camera which had a 1:4.5/105 lens. I was given it as a birthday present by one of Father's friends. There are bright lights on the little pool around the fountain; the luxuriant tropical vegetation hides the building of the baths, but a few of the balconies are visible. I am among those who tied for third position in a national photographic competition for secondary-school students. I accept the certificate for that fourteen months before the crowd pins Vera and me to the side wall of 29 Vadász Street.

I put that photograph in the file as well.

Scissors, folds.

I buy some more files.

I clear a shelf for them and clear another one for still more.

I buy a photocopier.

I make a pile of books from which I have yet to cut out photographs.

I work carefully in libraries, checking before cutting a picture out from a book. One afternoon I can't escape the gaze of a little boy. I hastily thrust what I had snipped out into my folder, but I see that he has caught me in the act. I put an index finger to my lips. He grins and stands up. Could it be that he is going to report me?

I don't leave home without a folder.

After a while I also start to carry a briefcase.

I nick photographic picture books from bookshops, a different store each time.

I clear a whole room so that the document folders piled on top of each other will fit in.

I begin to be selective with my material.

My memories are blurring together with the secure sights.

I make sketches from memory.

I make photographs of earlier sites that can be seen in documentary photographs.

I learn how to scan.

I place the more recent photographs on top of the old ones, the old on top of the newer.

I want to spy on the woman with the Opel I saw at 29 Vadász Street. I have to wait for days. In the meantime, while waiting, I drink beer in the John Bull Pub on Podmaniczky Square.

Finally I spot the Opel. I catch it with my camera. The woman leaves the gate open this time, too.

I find an archive photograph of the yard of the Glass House, jammed full of people, and superimpose the Opel on it.

I make my way to the first floor of the building directly opposite it. I ring the doorbell of one of the apartments overlooking the street and say I'm a Belgian photojournalist and ask if they will permit me to take a photograph from the window of the façade of number 29. There's a taxi parked in front of the house. I superimpose the taxi on the crowd that can be seen in the archive pictures.

I have no need of memory.

I have no need of forgetting.

I clear out another room for the folders.

It runs through my mind that there is no difference between the old and the new photographs; the two belong together. The one cannot exist without the other. By dint of years of labour I have produced a special pair of glasses that frees me of the need to actually take photographs: the glasses allow me to see the present streetscape in old photographs and the old views in recent pictures. I test what happens if I concentrate all my efforts on making everything old vanish both from the pictures and from my memory. That doesn't work, so I'm on the right track is my thinking. On files containing old material I write today's date, whereas as on more recent ones I write the dates of former times, and by the next day the original year adorns the files, I read Schopenhauer's *The World as Will and Representation*, cutting up the pages with scissors, putting each leaf in a file. I still have to superimpose the maps on each other – 1903, 1943 and 2003 – but my table is not big enough for that. I get a new one made, which means I shall have to empty a room; in a continuation of my dreams I dream that perhaps I shall have room in the Óbuda Brickworks for the new files, but then that is where the Praktiker Store is standing.

Vera's lips are blue, her face white. She always took care that a lock or two of her blonde hair should flutter free from under her beret, even when going to school, and she would adjust the beret that way even in the brickworks, but now she pulls it down over her ears like a helmet. There is a cold sore on her chapped lower lip. She links arms with me, snuggles up to me. Her body does not warm me.

I don't see Mádi. She said she had come across an acquaintance, a friend of her parents.

It is snowing again. The man in front of me says that he, too, must wait till tomorrow morning for his *Schutzbrief*. We are going to head off. Where? Home. You'll have to stay here, he says. The two-hour period for which the curfew is lifted each day has passed. If you try to cross the city wearing a yellow star a patrol is going to catch you; you'll be taken to the banks of the Danube and shot.

We back our way out of the scrum. I take my knapsack off and we cram it into Vera's little suitcase. I rip the yellow star off both of our overcoats, with Vera picking out any threads of the stitching that remain. We set off on the route along which we were taken that morning to bring us here from the yard of the synagogue. We do not hurry – that would be too noticeable – nor do we go slowly, as that, too, might draw attention. We don't look at anyone.

Everyone is clutching something, including those coming towards us and those who hurry past. It's as if everyone were afraid something could be taken off them; as if everyone saw in the other a person who is tracking their steps and checking out what they can steal from them, whereas, in fact, it's the other way round. On one of the posters:

> Fear of being punished by summary courts is holding some individuals back from answering the call to present themselves to join up. In order to facilitate the return in a manly fashion of those who are inclined to fulfil their duty, without causing loss of honour to the military personnel who have been deeply offended by this absenteeism, I assure total exemption from punishment to those who present themselves by 24:00 hours on 2 December 1944.
>
> Minister of Defence Beregfy

We get on a number 44 tram at the corner of Rákóczi Avenue. I have tokens to use on public transport. We don't go inside, but embrace each other on the platform, keeping our gazes outwards from the tram. The sole illumination in the carriage is provided by a single blue-painted bulb. The platform becomes crowded, and I'm squeezed between two youths wearing caps of the Levente movement; I can't see their faces, only feel their bodies pressed up against me in the crush. The passengers inside sit mutely on the wooden seats with the blue lamplight on their faces making them look like wraiths. A Home Guard officer is sitting among them. His face is also blue; he, too, is hunched up with a bandage wound round his head under his shako. What is presumably blood that has congealed on his left temple looks dark blue. At the corner of Stefánia Road a sentry with a submachine gun is standing guard in front of the Arrow Cross's district HQ. The street lights had still been on in Baross Square before we reached there, but only a few are on after Aréna Road,[1] between the two, then from Hermina Road onwards the tram proceeds in darkness. At the corner of Hermina Road I can no longer see the board of Mr Zsilka's hairdressing salon, nor do I see the barrier at Francia Road. No one gets on or off. The tram driver speeds up, the conductor shouts out the stops and before we know it we are at Amerikai Road, and I call out hoarsely, as if it was important that nobody should recognize my voice, This stop.

We stand at the tram stop.

The tram rattles off, leaving the darkness behind it, and disappears into the even darker distance.

Snow is covering the ice of the Erzsébet Ice Rink. The loudspeaker is dead. There are no street lamps shining on Amerikai Road either. It's as if we were not stepping ahead but downwards to a place where the darkness is even greater still. Maybe we'll move on if we see anything suspicious, I say to Vera. What do you mean suspicious? she asks. Well, suspicious, like something that could get us into trouble. So where shall we go then? she asks.

Carl Lutz checks how things are going with issuing *Schutzbriefe* at Vadász Street. The previous day or the next day?

The typists watch him as he makes telephone calls. He lists the houses in József Katona Street, Tátra Street and Pannónia Street on the front door of which a sign has to be set up to state that the occupants of the house are under the protection of the Swiss Legation. He takes over numbers 4, 15/a, 15/n and 14–16, Tátra Street, hands over numbers 7/a and 7/b Hollár Street to the Swedish Consulate and in return asks that on the front door of number 36 Pannónia Street a letter declaring that it enjoys Swiss diplomatic immunity should also be put up alongside the note testifying to its Swedish protection.

I can find no photograph of Lutz standing, telephone in hand, in front of the ladies.

He goes out and opens the door with the sign 'Supplies for Protected Houses'. He confers with the secretaries. He then leaves the house, forcing a way through the scrum at the gate.

I am standing at the corner of János Arany Street. I set off because I want not only to retrace my own steps but also follow the traces of

Carl Lutz's footsteps, covered over as they are by many hundred of steps at the time and many hundreds of thousands of steps since then.

Next to the old photograph recording the typists at work I place one of Father András Kun. He is not standing on the bank of the Danube where a few days later he will shoot bursts of submachine-gun fire but speaking at an open-air meeting. On one page is a stern-faced, shaven-headed man in a black uniform; on the other a raincoated young man with a necktie and an ardent look on his face. Father András Kun, a former Minorite friar, has a masculine look with thick, chiselled eyebrows. His right hand is raised in a Nazi salute, the wide sleeve of his cassock slipping back over the arm; he is sporting an obvious Arrow Cross insignia.

Lutz reaches his embassy, housed in the former US Legation in Szabadság Square, and goes upstairs into his office. Gertrud hastens to meet him. They kiss. There is a blonde woman seated in one of the armchairs. Familiar, it crosses Lutz's mind. On the table are a bottle of cognac and two brandy glasses. Gertrud takes out another and pours for all three of them. They clink glasses. Gertrud refreshes the drinks. Frau Gizella, do you remember her? She was travelling with the officers along the road to Vienna.

The officers in the Hungarian Army resistance had been arrested and mostly shot in the back of the head; those who were still alive were awaiting sentencing – that much Lutz already knows. He puts in a telephone call and meanwhile sinks into the depths of a leather armchair, leans back and stretches both legs before him. At the other end of the line is Ambassador Carl Ivan Danielsson, head of the Swedish mission to Budapest. Lutz asks if he has been called back to Stockholm or whether he is travelling and what was the thinking in the Swedish Ministry of Foreign Affairs about Szálasi's call on the ambassadors in Budapest to join the Hungarian government in moving to Sopron? Gertrud lights up a Darling and blows smoke rings. Gizi is amazed, as if she were a little girl sitting in the circus, with everyone around her, similarly pigtailed little girls and close-cropped little boys, clapping the stunt. Carl Lutz dials another number and after a few sentences replaces the receiver. Both Daniels-son and Angelo Rotta are staying, he says. So, will we? Gertrud asks. We'll stay.

He did not seem tense or uncertain, just tired, Gizi tells Mother later. I didn't pay much attention to him. I was looking at a photograph on the wall – just imagine, there was a stag looking back at me, standing in a meadow and making a magnificent show, in glorious colours with sunlit mountains behind it. It turned out the photograph had been taken in the Swiss Alps. Mother later told me, we were out there with your grandfather – just a moment, in '23 perhaps.

Gertrud tells Gizi that twenty years before Carl Lutz had taken photographs; some had even appeared in newspapers. He had photographed not only in Switzerland but also Sweden, Germany and, naturally, Palestine, where after the outbreak of the war, as an employee of the Swiss Ministry for Foreign Affairs, he had represented German interests with the UK, the mandated power. There were around a couple of dozen of his photographs on the walls, Gizi told Mother, including some he had shot in Budapest, among them one showing two Arrow Crossers with submachine guns dragging a women by the hair – and you could see the street sign of the wall behind them: Pannónia Street – and I asked Gertrud when that had been, and she said he'd taken it only last week. That was when Carl had travelled along the road to Vienna.

Gizi gets up and looks more closely all along the photographs on the walls. He develops most of them himself, says Gertrud. Gizi would never have thought that for Lutz a glance cast at the pictures was the simplest form of approaching what I call a crime scene, nor can she know that Mother would later recount in just as much detail what she had heard from her.

The rocky promontory of the Meldegg is a splendid vantage point from which it is rewarding to take a picture at any time of day. Lutz is particularly fond of sunset: in the back-lighting at this hour the distant snake of the Rhine has a silvery sheen, but the light appears to come to a standstill, with the eastern part of Lake Constance already grey. The tranquil green villages take shelter in the folds of the hillsides. Indiscernible to other eyes, he knows exactly which among the many steeples is the church steeple of Walzenhausen, his native village. Wherever he is sent, to his postings in Palestine, Berlin and Budapest, the photographs are always there on the walls of his various offices, the sights making the foreign environment more homely, even though they do not do away with the sense of homelessness – as for that, he thinks that is because of a deeper matter he has no chance of resolving.

It could be, he says to Gertrud, five years before they arrived in Budapest, while he was pinning up two newer photographs on the wall of his office in Haifa, that these conflicts never can be reconciled. In one of the photographs Arabs are throwing stones at a lorry full of Jews, and two of them are grabbing one of the truck's passengers; alongside them is a third who has a dagger in one hand. In the other photograph armed Jewish men are breaking into an Arab hovel, a little Arab boy watching on with curiosity. By the end Carl had begun to loath the Arabs, Gertrud tells Gizi in front of the picture, and he began to detest the Jews and British officials as well.

Lutz's notes suggest that he doesn't tell Gertrud everything. There are many times when he believes he has understood something from what he has experienced in different countries, but then he comes across events at the sight of which, he senses, the rational mind balks and the suspicion arises that he will never rid himself of that sense of unease. There are things he would like to say and discuss. But over and over again he comes up against the problem of their inexpressibility. Not because of the rules of diplomatic work, no, but because he does not wish to unsettle Gertrud. Even he himself is unsure about his sentiments and suspicions.

He has a Leica camera with an f/2.8 lens. After years of service in Palestine he finally gets back home. If it were up to him, it would be to have a good long rest.

He makes his way to the church in Walzenhausen. Flowering almond trees in the April light. The cluster of buildings of the Lachen farmstead stands slightly to the left, behind the church, in the bend of the little street leading to St Margarethen. One of those houses is where he was born. Behind is the elevation of the Meldegg.

He takes several photographs, waiting so he can catch exactly the same shot in the light of the morning, the afternoon and at sunset. He positions the shot so that a blossoming branch of an almond tree should always be seen bending into one of the upper corners of the picture. He arrives in Berlin in May 1941. In the Ministry of Foreign Affairs in Zürich he had been charged with representing Yugoslavia's interests. On the night he arrives the city was bombed by Allied planes. The day after his arrival the newspapers carry stories about the defeat of the Yugoslav army opposed to the Nazis. Lutz gets the message that his assignment is not going to last very long.

He was received by the Chief of Protocol of the Office of Foreign Affairs of the Grossdeutsches Reich, who tells him that they well remember how successfully he had represented German interests in Palestine. He meets several officials whom, in the days immediately after the outbreak of war, he had personally accompanied in an armoured car with a police escort to Haifa, whence they had been able to return to Germany. He could have no idea, given Yugoslavia's collapse, how long he would have any business in Berlin, but he had set to work in the manner expected of a disciplined official. In his spare time he would rove around Berlin's environs. He pays a visit to the garrison church of Potsdam. The sacristan, an angel-faced sixteen-year-old, proudly tells him that this is where, on 23 March 1933, Hitler, following the Reichstag fire one month earlier and his own electoral gains soon after, reconvened the new Reichstag in the presence of President Hindenburg. He adds that Johann Sebastian Bach also played there and transported his admirers, so he says, to higher spheres.

He gets to see the forests of Spreewald, with its maze of inter-weaving canals, many people rowing and paddling on the water, some propelling punt-like craft with long poles.

This is his favourite picture, Gertrud indicates to Gizi, not that I snapped it. Nor did Lutz, thinks Gizi, because he can be seen in the picture.

The punt glides noiselessly through Spreewald. Lutz is sitting in the prow; in the bows is the boatman, who operates with deft pushes of his long pole. Flutters of birds' wings, shadows of overhanging trees. In Lutz's hands is his Leica. They step ashore by a line of poplars. It is then that Lutz notices the boatman is dragging his left foot, so he helps him on the damp bank. The man is in his forties. Lutz imagines that it is because of his crippled leg that he has not been called up into the army, although it might also be that he had received a war wound. I could ask him how he ended up here; he could ask me the same. He has a feeling of being fenced in by a common fate in which there are many more together than hitherto.

My foot, are you asking what happened to my foot?

I didn't ask, Lutz thinks; he feels vulnerable because the man read from his expression what he wanted to ask.

Some bastard, chopping into me with a spade, the bastard.

For Lutz space now expands; the time is unidentifiable. The meadow, the canals, it's as if behind the line of poplars he could see the man's foot as a spade digs into the ankle, but there is nothing to go by as to who raised the spade, why, where and when.

Students approach. Lutz asks one of them to take a photograph of the two of them. He sets distance, the light and the shutter time on the Leica and steps over next to the man.

Gizi looks at the picture. The scenery was really pretty, tranquil, she says later to Mother. Lutz smiled at the camera, but it was evident that it was a forced smile; the other man drew himself up, wellington boots, knee-britches, hunting jacket, military bearing, a good deal taller than Lutz.

The Poles are worse than the Jews, says the man when the student hands the Leica back to Lutz. That's what springs to mind when I think about my foot, even though the Jews are nevertheless worse than the Poles, and the worst of all are the Polish Jews if they get hold of a spade.

Lutz understands. That's all there is to the story. He scarcely knows anything, but still it's as if simply on account of that slight knowledge he was party to it.

I used to guard the gravediggers. Eight hours on duty, eight hours on stand-by, eight hours off duty to start with. But later fourteen hours on duty, six on stand-by, four hours off. Chopped into me with a spade, the bastard.

When he looks at the picture later on with Gertrud, it occurs to Lutz that the German may also have sensed there was some sort of bond between them now, the way he held his body, standing shoulder to shoulder, the way he had looked not straight into the lens of the Leica but at him when the lad had taken the shot. You see, he tells Gertrud later, it's as if he was waiting for me to enquire about how the spade had chopped into him; he was waiting for me have at least one question. When he talked about it, Gertrude tells Gizi, I felt that I, too, had become a party to the same thing he was. That I don't understand, Gizi chimes in. No wonder, dearest, because I don't understand it either, but that's the way I felt then and still feel now.

I think the reason I did not ask, Lutz says to Gertrud in front of the photograph, was not because I didn't want to get to know his story, but because I was scared of what I might learn. You said much the same thing when you escorted the Germans from Haifa to the border, Gertrud says. Lutz can't remember having said anything of the sort at the time. Back then everything had been clear. Berlin had recalled its officials. They had travelled in an armoured car to the border; he had a very clear memory of confinement, boiling heat, a stench of sweat mixed with petrol fumes. He had talked with Gerhart Feine, the German Vice-Consul, about how none of them knew what their next posting was going to be. At the border Feine had shaken his hand at great length and made him give his word of honour to pass on his humble regards to Frau Lutz.

It was on New Year's Eve 1941 that we set out from Zürich to Budapest, Gertrud says to Gizi. Well, I mean, expecting one to board a train on New Year's Eve – tell me, dear, do you recall where you passed New Year's Eve going into 1941?

Gizi does not say that by then it had already been three years since her husband had been laid to rest, does not say that she had sat by herself listening to the radio when Károly, bearing a bottle of champagne, rang the doorbell. She does not say that the first lieutenant had for the first time stayed the night there, because she knew that Gertrud would immediately ask, Oh, darling, is he the one who yesterday in the street . . . maybe not completing the question because she would not dare say *was gunned down*. Gizi remains quiet. Gertrud takes Lutz into the next room, returns and pours herself a drink. Gizi places a hand over her own glass. She wonders what Gertrud must have been through in previous years, whether even before that her wrist had shown such a practised tipping gesture when downing her drink. Our train left St Margarethen punctually at midnight, says Gertrud. We looked at our watches, and I said, 1941. Carl waited a few seconds before bursting into laughter. Your watch is running late again; we are already in 1942.

The night was pitch black on both sides of the Swiss–Austrian border, Lutz was to note later, because the government had yielded to German pressure in ordering a blackout of the country. The Germans were seeking thereby to make it harder for British bombers to navigate over the occupied territories, including Austria. The route was Munich, Linz, Vienna. The next night everything was shrouded in the darkness of the war. We travelled first class, Gertrud said to Gizi, among high-ranking officers and Party leaders. We could see through the windows that at every station there were patrols and security people checking papers; many were the times when we had to wait on an open track to give priority to military transports. We could see they were moving guns, supplies of every description, tanks. It was all as if the war had burst its banks and covered everything. Carl said that at one point he started up and looked out of the window just as a train transporting tanks was passing by. I could never have put it so well. The train jolted, I'll never forget it. Carl jumped up. Perhaps he had been dreaming. His look was one of alarm; that's when he said it.

They chatted, Mother said, as if they had long been friends.

Lutz was standing by the train window. Alongside the train of carriages, now bumping together from the sudden braking, was another train with a cargo of tanks. On the tanks were soldiers, wordlessly smoking cigarettes. Lutz sat back down, says nothing to Gertrud, merely notes it down, decades later, that before being woken by the braking he had been dreaming that the two of them were standing on the canal bank, the German punt man and he, and the German kept repeating, With the blade of the spade, the bastard! By the time he had noted that down he had found an explanation for the dream, but at the point he had glimpsed the grim-faced, grey-uniformed soldiers smoking on top of the tanks he did not know as yet why he had been dreaming what he dreamed, but that filled him with such uncertainty it was as if not only was a spectre pressing on him but also everything he seemed to know and take in yet was baffling and unknowable, a feeling of uncertainty which verged on fear, and he wanted to protect Gertrud, who had been puffing on her Darling as she lay tucked up on the lilac velvet upholstery of the seat, from that feeling. We'll see who receives us in Budapest, he says. It will be clear from that whether we can achieve anything or whether it's just the coolie work customarily referred to as official duties that awaits again. Carl had already had experience of that, Gertrud says to Gizi, if they were looking for officials who would always conscientiously discharge official duties, then someone would utter his name, but he had had enough of that, enough, *enough*, says Gertrud altering her voice to a high pitch as if only now were she taking it on board that he had already long had enough of it.

She fell silent, Gizi says to Mother, virtually buttoned up, then she leaned over, even though there were only the two of us in the room at the time, and she whispered, You know there are times when he is unbearably sensitive? He feels so offended that others are always being appointed to positions that should rightfully have been his long before, but he calmed down when it was Ambassador Jaeger who met us off the train at Keleti Railway Terminus.

Gertrud is thinking: I talk too much to this Jewish woman, but the fact is I feel at ease with her. You're very different, she says, from other Jews. In Palestine we were leery of the Arabs but also of the Jews – no offence meant – but Carl always said that he came out best with the Germans.

Gizi says nothing; now Gertrud also says nothing. Gizi finally says, We are very grateful for everything. She kisses Gertrud on the cheek and asks which perfume she wears.

Ambassador Jaeger waits for the train arriving at Keleti Railway Terminus. Also there was Kilchmann, the Consul, such an agreeable chap he is, says Gertrud; he'll made a play at anyone in a skirt. What you Hungarians would say, hang on a tick, *csápta a szélt* (raises a storm). Gizi corrects her Hungarian, *csapta a szelet* – the brandy was making her sleepy, you see, she says later to Mother; both Józsi and Károly always laughed at how any time I have a drink I immediately feel sleepy.

In December 1942 Ambassador Jaeger writes to the Marcel Pilet-Golaz, a member of the Swiss Federal Department of Foreign Affairs who was made head of the Political Department and thus in effect the Foreign Minister:

> The government here is exposed to sustained and ever-greater pressure to rid Hungary completely of Jews. The Germans are demanding that the Hungarians should assemble all Jews and hand them over. These people should be delivered by train. The Germans assert that they will transport the able-bodied to the eastern territories; those who are not able-bodied will be disposed of 'in a manner not specified in more detail'. To what extent the Germans will be able to fulfil their demands in the future depends on the outcome of the war.

Six months later Pilet-Golaz warns Carl Lutz by letter to refrain from assisting the escape of groups of children to Palestine. Actions of that nature were overstepping his authority and were not among his duties as a representative of foreign interests.

Gizi would like to sleep. Ever since, in searching for Bőzsi, she had peered into the faces of those dying in the ditches on the road to Vienna, Mother tells me later, she had been able to get little sleep; ever since she learned that Károly had been shot in the back of the neck, all she wanted was to sleep. Gizi listens to Gertrud, the leather sofa is deep, now she would be able to sleep, but she waits and drinks because she needs to ask Lutz for ten unfilled Swiss safe-conduct letters. That was when I wanted to get them for you, too, she says to Mother.

The telephone rings, and Lutz comes back in. He grasps the receiver in such a way, Gizi sees, that the fingers clenched round it turn white; that was how they looked on the bodies she had seen by the sides of the ditches. With fingers like that how was he going to sign the *Schutzbriefe*?

At the other end of the line Gerhart Feine repeats that an order has come in from Berlin that as long as Carl Lutz is in Budapest he should not consent to the Arrow Cross attacking the ghetto and Jews in protected houses. Lutz knows that in view of the current strategic situation in the war Berlin considered it to be important that relations with Berne should not deteriorate. Lutz does not advise Feine that, following Ambassador Jaeger, Sub-Consul Kilchmann had already left Budapest, and Berne did not care what the Arrow Cross did, nor did they regard as important whether he, the current chargé d'affaires, stayed or returned home to Switzerland.

Two young men bring in a large bundle of printed material. They place it carefully on the writing desk. Lutz takes a look at the freshly printed letters, checking his own forged signature on them. He finds it satisfactory.

Gizi pulls on a Red Cross armband. She asks Lutz for ten unfilled letters. She hides them under her blouse. She says farewell and hurries out with the two young men. In the stairwell one of them asks her whether she has anywhere to stay that night. She gives a name and address. On foot it's an hour's walk across town, says Gizi; it's gone ten o'clock, so the general curfew is in force.

The lads seat her in a Red Cross car. Not a soul is to be seen on Andrássy Avenue. No lights filter out from behind blacked-out curtains. The city is a dark mass, consisting not of houses nor of streets but of darkness.

That night the military spokesman at Wilhelmstrasse relays to Hitler the news that Budapest is considered indefensible; even the generals would find it acceptable if it were declared an open city. Hitler flies into a rage and yells that if he had no regrets about sacrificing German cities, then why should there be any regret about a foreign one? Vessenmayer, who is also present, adds, We are not worried about Budapest being destroyed if that means Vienna can be defended. For the wired order to Budapest, Ferenc Fiala, Szálasi's deputy and press officer, calls a press conference. The only thing that can save Budapest and its inhabitants from destruction is to fight, and by common consent the Hungarian and German leaderships and the Hungarian and German armies will undertake to do that.

Hitler personally puts Obergruppenführer Winkelmann, commander of the SS Police in Budapest, in charge with the defence of the city. Four days later he gives a personal order to replace him when Winkelmann also reports that, militarily speaking, defence of the city is hopeless. Szálasi accepts a German instruction whereby bridges and public utilities on any ground that is surrendered should be blown up.

Gizi gets out of the Red Cross car at the corner of Andrássy Avenue and Mihály Munkácsy Street. The three-storey house is one of the city's most modern buildings: clean lines, closed balconies, a Red Cross sign on the gate. The lads have been given to understand that they need to give four rings on the door bell. In the corridors of the upper floors there are doors on both sides, some of them open. The faces of curious boys; on the second floor there are young girls.

She is led into a cabin-like room by the rear staircase. Divan, wardrobe, two seats, a washbasin. She is told where the toilet is at the end of the corridor. She may not switch the light on as the blackout measures were not perfect; she is given a pocket torch. On the seat are books and newspapers; she looks through the magazines under the bedclothes. One announcement is for a Levente alert that will be at seven o'clock on Thursday morning:

> The enthusiastic army of our Levente sons will have to fulfil a most important task, which calls for many industrious young hands. The chief treasure of a Levente is his honour, says the Levente law. Now

our Leventes are again being called on to prove that they are the staunchest guards and defenders of the nation's fortune.

She does not know what day it is; she does not know when it will be Thursday.

Carl Lutz, attaché case in hand, gets out from the Packard in front of Keleti Railway Terminus. He goes up the eight steps leading to the platform.

It is Thursday morning. He is taking the 7.30 train to Vienna, where he will have to wait two hours for the connection to Zürich.

This is same time that Gizi wakes up in the Red Cross home on Mihály Munkácsy Street. She takes a clean set of underwear from her grip, washes the dirty items in the washbasin, rolls the knickers and cotton stockings up in a clean handkerchief.

The escalator takes me up from the Baross Square metro station. On the right is a Princess Patisserie; on the left they are selling kebabs, and there is a Pizza Hut. A table offers espresso coffee made from Omnia beans for sixty forint a cup. Five rows of steps lead from the subways to the platforms. I go up.

Lutz looks back at the statue of Gábor Baross – the revered Hungarian Minister of Ways and Communications in the latter part of the nineteenth century – which was standing at the head of Rákóczi Avenue, Budapest's main street. Open trucks, packed with Levente youths of sixteen or seventeen, are turning into Baross Square from Rottenbiller Street in front of the Fillér Store. On the platform papers are being checked by two men with Arrow Cross armbands; behind them a sickle-plumed military policeman is standing.

I look at the Arrivals and Departures indicator boards. Two homeless people are sitting on a bench fishing lumps of preserved meat from a can with their fingers. A third is lying on the ground next to them in a dirty quilted coverlet.

Lutz looks for the service for Vienna. The vaulted glass roof of the station is showing bomb damage in a number of places. It is starting to snow through the gaps on to the platforms. He reaches the first-class compartments. Another Arrow Cross patrol passes by. He again has to show his diplomatic passport. Two MPs, rifles trained on him, are leading off a young man in Home Guard uniform. A porter arrives with elegant luggage on his trolley; a women in an astrakhan coat is on the arm of a Home Guard major. Two other Arrow Crossers are kicking a yellow-armbanded forced-labour serviceman who is stretched out on the ground. Lutz takes photographs, and he tries to get a shot of the smoke plume of one of the in-coming engines.

I am standing by the buffers of platform 4. The Wiener Walzer service from Vienna is due and arrives on platform 5. Passengers flood out. Jeans, jazzy shirts, Adidas bags, suitcases with zippers. The asphalt surface of the platform has no doubt been renovated a good few times in the past sixty years, but all the same it is like a find at Pompeii. The two homeless are well mannered enough to take their empty cans to the bin; the third does not budge from the filthy coverlet.

Lutz hears gunfire.

He also hears the sound of a violin.

He still has time before the train departs and goes over to the arrivals side of the platform.

When he first arrived in Budapest this was where Ambassador Jaeger had waited for him in the hall which leads out on to Kerepesi Road.

The bursts of gunfire he heard are coming from the trotting racetrack slightly further up Kerepesi Road and on the right; he can hear the difference between a short and a long burst. The music is coming from close at hand: Schubert. Lutz used to play the violin when he was young, and later on he even played Palestrina occasionally in an impromptu quartet. He recognizes Schubert's *String Quintet in C*. He can hear the first violin and one of the two cello parts, but both are being played on violins. MPs are standing guard on the doors to and from Kerepesi Road.

The second movement of the string quintet. It's so boundless, he said to Gertrud after a concert performance of it in Zürich. Boundlessly sad, Gertrud had said. No, Lutz had protested, just boundless, boundless.

Even sixty years later there are still four chandeliers of five lamps each hanging from the ceiling of the waiting-room. The two violinists are standing on the left by the wall. One is in a worn-out raincoat, the other is in a black overcoat with fraying sleeves. Both are unshaven and wearing checked peaked caps. Both have dark glasses; two white canes are propped against the wall.

They finish the movement, and immediately they start to replay it from the beginning. Lutz has the feeling that they have been doing this for a long time. Maybe that is why they are not conspicuous to the Arrow Crossers and the MPs. Lutz takes out a banknote and drops it into the tin plate by their feet. They don't thank him, but he has a feeling that they can see him even from behind the black lenses. Their violin bows are threadbare; the cello line sounds almost scraped out.

I steer clear of the cars waiting by the exits on to Kerepesi Road and walk back to Baross Square. I count the number of steps leading up to the station. Opposite, where the former Fillér Store used to be, is the Grand Hotel Hungária. On the left, next to the Golden Park Hotel, the vacant site of a building destroyed by bombing during the war is fenced off. On the right are unplugged bullet holes on the uppermost floor of the house at the corner of Gábor Bethlen Street.

Once more I go up the same eight steps on which Carl Lutz made his way up to the platform, then I stroll off to the right into the waiting-room which leads to Kerepesi Road. I count the number of chandeliers again. I find it hard to credit Lutz's idea that the two men with black-lensed glasses and white canes could have been playing for days. It is impossible that Arrow Cross patrols would have neglected to check their papers and realized that both the dark glasses and white canes were covers. It seems impossible that they would play their violins with such worn-out bows – and the cello part on one at that – and meanwhile around them army deserters were being captured and forced-labour serviceman kicked around while MPs are checking the papers of anyone who goes near any platform. Lutz no doubt hid from the spectacle behind music that might be conjured up in this context and stopped his ears with what he felt to be the boundless sounds of the Adagio of the *String Quintet in C*.

But he writes that he saw them.

Do I have to accept that notwithstanding?

I look at the left-hand wall of the entrance hall. The corners are fairly mucky.

Could this have been where they played?

I am not in a position to learn anything about them and, as for

Carl Lutz, merely that he listened to them playing their music. That's not much, but the minute during which I think of that not-knowing-much is time experienced, possessed. It is likely that the two faces, the black-lensed glasses, the white canes, the ripped raincoat, the black overcoat with its fraying sleeves were lost as far as Carl Lutz was concerned, but the sound had remained, and this evoked these memories in him, feelings he wanted to cling to.

He arrives at Westbahnhof. He sees no soldiers at the station. He strolls along Mariahilfer Strasse; at the Ring he turns left. He looks dumbfounded at the passers-by.

He walks on to Heldenplatz. He knows that this was where the Jews, elderly people, women and children, were assembled before deportation. Now schoolboys are throwing snowballs, and one even hits Lutz.

Following his steps I, too, saunter across the square. I don't know where he stood, but I can be quite sure that he would not have seen the Holocaust memorial opposite.

Across the way is a statue of Lessing.

I am strolling among tourists with coloured skins.

We are progressing in the same story, the layers of time slip by each other, propelled by their own energies.

That evening he arrives in Berne. At eight o'clock the next morning he enters the office of the head of the Federal Department of Foreign Affairs, who hears him out then nods. He offers him a drink. He is also listened to in two other offices. We all read your reports, says Dr Edmund Rothmand, who is in charge of Police Services, as he, too, offers a drink. Gertrud will ask me later, Lutz thinks to himself, why I travelled to Berne when I knew I could not count on getting any attention? Already the couriers were bringing the same message to Budapest that I am hearing in these offices. Wait a while. The situation is confused now. I watched them, he tells Gertrud later, and I felt relieved. Gertrud does not understand. The reason Lutz smiles at his wife is that I am on the other side of the glass wall that they have pulled in front of themselves.

His notes break off.

I shall pick up from where they continue later on.

The morning after that he is back in Keleti Railway Terminus. There is still the same confusion on the platform. This is not Berne or Zürich, not even Vienna, he thinks as Arrow Cross patrols check his papers twice over.

The two musicians are not in the entrance hall leading to Kerepesi Road. Next to the wall where they had been standing two MPs are carrying out checks. Lutz shows his diplomatic passport for third time.

They were almost certainly not blind, says Gertrud, almost certainly . . .

What do you mean by if we see anything suspicious we'll move on? Vera asks a second time on Amerikai Road . . . Where to?

IV

Numbers 74, 76 and 78 Amerikai Road were all built in 1927. Number 74 is a two-storey villa, number 76 four-storeyed and number 78 single-storeyed; big rear gardens and trim front gardens. Number 76 was designed by Lajos Róbert, a friend of my parents, and the villa at number 78 he had built for his own family. We moved into one of the rooms there in June 1944, when we had to hand over our own home at number 74 to those in charge of the German military hospital opposite.

A common night descends on the three houses. Vera and I stand in front of the gate of number 76. The windows of the apartments are blacked out with blue paper; behind us, on the ramp up to the hospital, is a machine-gun post.

Five months earlier two white-gloved Wehrmacht officers had rung on the bell of our home. They were accompanied by an NCO with a tommy-gun. We saw them as they strode with slow steps across the road. Mother speaks German.

The officers raised their hands to their service caps in salute. They inspected the rooms and found the house suitable for use as an office. They instructed the concierge and the caretaker and his wife to prepare an inventory; we were given twenty-four hours to move out. The Róberts are already waiting for us, says Father when they leave.

I still preserve that inventory in an old file. I have read through it many times over in the course of the past sixty years, and now I read it over three times more. I can move around my old home using my mental picture of the listed objects. By the third read-through I can smell our things; everything is palpable. The Adox folding camera with its f/2.8 45-mm lens, which I keep in my writing desk, is on the list. It was fixed in position by a learner's violin – that was my elder brother's. I also have a clear memory of the bookcase, and it can also be discovered from the inventory that we had 250 books, and the next line records that there were 250 kilograms of kindling wood and coal in the house. Surprisingly, my father had a tailcoat, although I never saw him wear it. Then the wedding photograph flashes into my mind. In that case, right . . . a tailcoat. Six cooking pots . . . six saucepans . . .

Everything cleared out of the cupboards.

Mother types on her Olympia portable what the warden of the house dictates. The concierge stands behind him with hands thrust in the pockets of her apron.

I hardly ever use the Olympia portable typewriter, but it's still close to my writing desk.

Let's wait, I say to Vera at the gate.

It would have been better not to come here after all.

But we had nowhere else to go.

After sixty years I pick one of the unknown names from those listed with the doorbells.

I would like to get a view of the stairwell, I say. But why? . . . Sometime, anyway.

We are let in.

The old lilac tiling.

I'll ring, I tell Vera, but I hesitate.

We hear steps coming from the basement. Vera lets go of my hand.

Mrs Linnert, the concierge. If we happen to bump into her we address her as 'Auntie' Linnert, and if we speak about her we use 'Mrs' Linnert, just as we have heard our parents do.

Lord above . . . Can it be you . . . ?

She was more scared than we were, says Mádi sixty-nine years later; everyone was afraid of everyone else, of the bombing, of the front, of getting into trouble for helping.

Mádi was no longer with us by then, so how could she have any recollection of Mrs Linnert's trepidation? Is it possible that all three of us stood at the gate after all? Or perhaps she recalls my telling her once about our return? Or had I perhaps once told her about the fear that I had seen written on Mrs Linnert's face? Yes, perhaps she recalls my memory, but it cannot be completely discounted that her memory is more accurate. At any rate, the fear written on Mrs Linnert's face is not a small matter. Her face is not a single monolithic face; it's not a face, really, but a feeling. It hides in objects, conceals itself in the depths of homes. It's as if the arc of the valley around the Óbuda

Brickworks is encompassing the whole city, and thus the city itself is all part of one big crime scene.

Yes, she was more afraid than us; even Vera was not afraid when we got back home.

Mrs Linnert steers Vera into the caretaker's dwelling.

I set off on a voyage of discovery. I avoid number 78, the single-storey villa where we spent the summer and autumn. The back-door opening into the kitchen is open. Bed linen strewn about all over the Róberts' bedroom, window-shutters lowered, a single wall light left on to provide illumination. It sends light over the decades.

The bookcase is open. A few volumes are lying on the floor. I pick up a copy of the 1927 *Literary Encyclopaedia* that Marcell Benedek edited. While we were living here I used to read it every day. A brown cloth binding with the lettering of the title picked out in gold. I wanted to read the lot, from A to Z; by 15 November I got as far as K. I stow the copy in my knapsack. I hear a soft whooshing from over by the cherrywood cabinet. A pink light. An enormous opalescent seashell. It belongs to Uncle Róbert. One is not permitted to touch it, but once I was allowed to hold it to my ear. Among the fingerprints on it must be my own. His grandfather had willed it to his father, his father to him, said Uncle Lajos. It preserves a century and a half of sounds; deep-sea shells like that absorb the sounds into them. Speak into it if you want. I said my name; nothing else sprang to mind.

I am holding it right now. I say my name into it this time as well. Is the one voice on top of the other?

When last week I described Carl Lutz's steps at Keleti Railway Terminus I put on the record-player the 'Adagio' of Schubert's *String Quintet in C*, which he had preserved from the playing of the two blind beggars standing by one of the exit doors that time he travelled to Berne to make his report in December 1944. Now I place the seashell close to the record-player; the music starts; I would like it to preserve the 'Adagio', the sound of which Lutz could never shake off.

It is dark. I carefully put the shell into my knapsack between the spare pullover and the warm socks.

I sneak out of the house.

I go across to number 76. The lilac tiles of its stairwell glitter in the dark. The door to the first apartment on the mezzanine floor is shut; that belongs to Vera's family. The other door can be pushed open.

I find myself standing in the Beifelds' hall. In one corner is the card table; Mother and Father used to play here, although in the case of the ladies it was more a matter of playing rummy in one of the rooms inside. One of the cane chairs is placed exactly where, seated next to Father, I used to watch the slippery switching of cards in the deal.

The Persian wall hangings are missing from the dining-room, the paintings, too.

The second floor. The door to the Hirschs' apartment opens if you push on the handle.

All the rooms here as well are familiar to me. I could almost taste the birthday cakes, but what now catches my attention is that a wall light has been left on. The curtains have been torn down, the doors on the wardrobes are wide-open, the chairs flung about; they must have stamped on the crockery in the kitchen and on the games in the children's playroom, although a little figure of a cavalryman, my favourite, has remained intact, so I tuck that, too, in my knapsack.

I open the windows in the lounge. There is a full moon. The green velvet cover with the golden tassels has been swept off the piano; I set it back.

A flush door opens into the spare room. I find bed linen in the drawers of the divan bed. I tear the blackout paper off the window and don't put the light on. I never did have a room of my own. I shall be able to read once it grows light: a good job I took the *Encyclopaedia*.

Bursts of submachine-gun fire are heard from close at hand from the corner of Korong and Kolumbusz Streets.

In the morning I wash in cold water. I choose one of the three coloured tooth mugs. I find half a tube of toothpaste, from which I squeeze some on to a finger. I give my socks and underpants a good wash and take clean ones from my knapsack. I go down to the mezzanine. Vera is drinking a cup of tea and eating bread and jam. The jam is cut off a block; I get some, too. I invite Vera to the Hirschs' dwelling and show her how I've set myself up. We clasp hands in the stairwell, but once in the apartment she draws away from me and sits at the other end of the divan. I try to reach for her hand, but she won't permit it. I ask her if she would like to move in here; I would relinquish my room – *just the way it is*, I say. I would find somewhere else to sleep. She says the Linnerts' place is good enough for her for the time being.

In the summer my parents enrolled me to study music: out of the two-hour lifting of the curfew that was five minutes there and the same back. The woman who was teaching advised against the violin or the piano – they call for prospects, she said to my parents. The word was new to me, but I sensed that I understood what she was driving at. I would suggest the piano accordion, she said. You can learn the basics with ten or twelve hours of practice. She taught me Viennese waltzes and 'Tango Bolero'.

I try to play 'Tango Bolero' for Vera on the piano. I hit the wrong key a few times.

She brings a chair, sits down, puts her elbows on the piano and cups her chin in the palm of her right hand. She is mimicking actresses such as Katalin Karády in *Halálos tavasz* (*Deadly Spring*) László Kalmár's 1939 film based on the book by Lajos Zilahy.[2] A good job she did not light up a cigarette. Her way of walking is just like Karády's. I leave off 'Tango Bolero', step behind her and bend down to her neck. She doesn't smell good; she can't have washed, probably not for days by this time. She darts off to the bathroom; I hear the sound of the WC flushing. She comes back but not stepping like the actress and singer Katalin Karády. She says she is hungry, she'll go downstairs; perhaps there's something to have for lunch there. She takes my hand and pulls me along.

We eat in the kitchen – a thick brown soup of roux then a stew of boiled beans, both from the same dish. Vera leaves half of the beans in the dish. 'Uncle' Linnert is in his fifties; he has a silvery moustache, which droops into the spoon when he eats. He says they're drawing closer, by which I suppose he means the Russians, although I can't hear any guns. His voice is just like that farmer at Szilasliget, just to the north-east of Budapest, almost at Gödöllő, at whose house we spent a summer holiday when I was six. He would look up at the sky over the walnut tree and say, It's going to rain, sod it! even when there wasn't a cloud in the sky. Even when there was absolutely no danger of hail knocking down his orchard; even when he was waiting for a storm to break the long dry spell.

That afternoon I find blackout paper and drawing pins. I place the paper over the window, and by night I read by the light of a table lamp. I can hear bursts of submachine-gun fire from the same direction as yesterday. I switch the light off and open the window. Flames are shooting up from over by Kolumbusz Street.

I place in one of my folders a copy of the documentation:

One of the actions by Arrow Cross shocktroops which sought the greatest number of victims was directed against the Kolumbusz Street camp, which was under protection of the International Committee of the Red Cross. They broke into the camp despite the protests of the ICRC representatives who were present. The camp's doctor was also shot dead when he protested in defence of the patients. The elderly were lined up and sent off to the ghetto; those aged between sixteen and sixty were herded off to Józsefváros railway station and packed into trains that were going to Bergen-Belsen.

I lean out of the window.

I can hear the bursts of gunfire.

I do not know what is happening.

Every day I pass the plaque that was unveiled twelve years ago in memory of Dr Kanizsai, the commandant and the other victims.

For supper we are given bread and a mug of tea. Mr Vespi says that the children cannot stay here because they will endanger the lives of the residents of the house. He doesn't say that to us but to Uncle Linnert, Mr Vespi being the warden for the block. He has gingery hair and blue eyes and was a sergeant in the First World War. He was wounded in one leg and walks with a limp.

I go up into my room and make the bed. I take off my boots and britches, drape my shirt round the back of a chair.

Friedrich Born, the authorized ICRC representative, reaches Józsefváros railway station at a time when he is no longer able to prevent the loading into cattle trucks of those dragged away from the Kolumbusz Street camp.

I am freezing under the coverlet, so I put my shirt on anyway. I later find out that Mr Vespi has reminded Mrs Linnert a second time of her duty to report shirkers, as he puts it. What business does Mr Vespi have with the two kids, says Auntie Linnert, adding that she is well aware what the law says, and she'll take care of it tomorrow. She doesn't know what she and her husband ought to do, and what is the sergeant going to tell the Russians, she asks?

I warm up under the coverlet. I think of Vera. In the brickworks and the Dohány Street Synagogue, though, despite curling up tightly pressed to each other, what was happening as I was thinking of her just now had not happened then. I leave it to my hand to gratify the urge. The first time it had happened had been last summer on the night of an afternoon when we had kissed while sitting on a pile of bricks in the garden. I had in my nose still the smell of the perfume she had been wearing in the summer.

The night passed by.

The next day passed by.

Vera says that she saw their coffee service in the Linnerts' kitchen cupboard.

On the third day Auntie Linnert opens the door.

Quick . . . !

I dress hurriedly. She leads me to the cellar. Vera is already there.

Through the grating over the window I can see a truck pull into the yard. Boys of about my age and wearing Levente caps jump down from it; a few older boys. Mrs Linnert calls out for us through the window. We have to go out. All the residents are made to stand outside the door to their apartments. Anyone not Jewish is allowed to go back inside. Wearing a fur cap, Mr Vespi salutes and reports that he has carried out all orders.

He reports to a Home Guard leader with an Arrow Cross armband.

The lads, I can see, are still sleepy. It's 6.30, and it's snowing. Vera lets me put an arm round her. The lads are ordered by the lance-corporal of the patrol to strip the contents of any apartments that are not occupied. Mrs Linnert is obliged to dig out a trunk to hold the more valuable items. One of the lads asks the lance-corporal what is deemed to be a more valuable item; he is tow-haired with brown eyes and is in a blue braided coat and, rather than a Levente cap, is wearing a grammar-school cap. He looks at me while he asks the question. Mr Vespi reports that there are still two Jews in the building. The boy in the grammar-school cap comes across to me and whispers, You should scarper.

What qualifies? I'll tell you what, the lance-corporal bawls.

Suits, women's dresses, hats, tablecloths are carried out to the truck; I even see two tennis racquets. One of the older youths asks if they should bring down a piano from the second floor. The boy in the grammar-school cap chips in, Don't bother; it'll put it out of tune.

The lance-corporal is tall. On his belt are two bulging ammunition pouches. His boots are worn; he is holding a bayoneted rifle.

I've heard that you know where they hid the soap. Somewhere here there are three crates of soap.

We are standing in the apartment where I have spent the last few days.

The cupboards have already been emptied. The lads are trampling articles that have been swept on the ground. In the playroom is large pile of board games, model cars and dolls; a few of the tin soldiers are slipped into their pockets. Two of them are tossing a big sleeping doll backwards and forwards.

The lance-corporal bawls, We haven't come here to play games, bugger it! Now then, my boy, let's be having those three crates of soap.

He tosses his peaked cap on to the piano – it's the sort of cap worn by border guards; the flash on his collar patch is green, which means he's infantry, whereas border guards also have a red stripe on the edge of the flash. My elder brother and I used to paint the insignias of rank and branch of service on our tin soldiers. My brother was called up for forced-labour service at nineteen years of age; he joined up at Bustyhaza, where they had to lug bags of cement on the military airfield. Two were allowed to carry a sack if an individual was unable to carry fifty kilograms on his own. We got the last postcard from him back in October, at which time they were on the march, heading for Germany.

This isn't where I live, I tell the lance-corporal. I haven't got a clue about any soap.

A likely story, squirt!

In my form at school there was a lad from Kőbánya, the Xth district, and he spoke the same way: Watch it, squirt! I'll box your ears!

Speak, or I'll smash your face in!

The boy in the grammar-school cap comes over. He observes the others. I've seen in films how the white-gloved footman gives that sort of snooty look to all the guests who are ignorant of the rules of etiquette. He sits down at the piano and plays.

The lance-corporal thumps me with his fist. It's a hard blow, but I don't feel much pain – it's more as if I were watching him thump someone else.

He thumps with the other fist.

I want to say again that I know nothing about any soap, but the sound just won't come out, and I just flail with my hands.

He goes out. He has a word with Mr Vespi in the corridor.

The youths just gawp at me; two of them sidle off. The lance-corporal returns. I hope you've come to your senses, he says quietly, or shall we begin again from the beginning?

He does not wait for me to protest but kicks me in the groin. I crumple slowly to the floor.

Give it a rest, boy . . .

I am able to get back to my feet.

Schnell! Schnell! he yells at the boys. They no doubt have lots still to do.

Who will remember, as time passes, this particular house on Amerikai Road when there are many just like it?

The lads will get back home after a full day's work: one brags, another forgets where they had been, some stay silent when their parents ask, one complains of having a headache, another sits down to play the piano, yet another reads the newspaper:

Levente Alert Across All Greater Budapest. The enthusiastic army of our Levente sons will have to fulfil a most important task which calls for many industrious young hands. The chief treasure of a Levente is his honour, says the Levente law. Now our Leventes are again being called on to prove that they are the staunchest guards and defenders of the nation's fortune.

I am standing in the stairwell; the tiles are the same as they were, although several are missing and the gaps have been painted over with lilac oil paint. Three generations have left their fingerprints on them since then. My own were also left there that time I fell against it.

Vera is in the cellar now, squatting in a corner, a black scarf covering her face.

They are vacuuming carpets in the lobby of the Hotel Astoria. There is a group of Japanese tourists at the reception desk.

This is the first time I have been here in something like fifty years.

The location of the swing door is unchanged. The hotel's coffee room on the right – which has a view on to both Lajos Kossuth Street, the continuation of Rákóczi Avenue inside the Inner Outer Circle, and Magyar Street, the first turning on the left – as well as the restaurant on the left are similar to what they had been fifty years before, and on the evidence of contemporary photographs that was also the case before the war.

Carl Lutz waits at one of the tables in the middle of the restaurant. The head waiter steps over: he's in a white tuxedo, white bow-tie; his brilliantined hair is parted in the middle. He does not speak, does not nod; he waits. He spots that Lutz can catch in his eyes a stringency not in keeping with his occupation.

Lutz is sitting with his back to the entrance. He can read off the head waiter's face that Gerhart Feine has just walked into the restaurant. The head waiter snaps to full height, the carriage of his head being much as if he were saluting the major with an eyes-left.

Lutz has not yet seen Feine in uniform. Next to the Iron Cross are two rows of decorations; in Palestine he went around in light linen suits and coloured jumpers.

The head waiter takes his service cap; he does not write the order down but makes a mental note of it. When they are on the second course Feine slips across a copy of a wire concealed in a damask serviette. Lutz is able to decode it by placing it in a prepared newspaper. The newspaper is for that day, 30 September:

Number 65, dateline Budapest, 3 April 1944, Reich Ministry for Foreign Affairs. The reaction of the inhabitants of Budapest to the two air raids has led to a strengthening of anti-Jewish dispositions in wide circles. Yesterday handbills were also distributed which demanded taking the lives of 100 Jews for every Magyar killed. Even if this is unrealizable as it means that we would need to kill at least 30,000–40,000 Jews. A huge opportunity for propaganda lies in the principle of retribution by acing as a deterrent. In the course of my discussion with Ministers Jenő Rátz and Antal Kunder I perceived that a measure of this nature may be implemented without any further ado. I request instructions as to whether I may embark on such measures after the next air raid.

Veesenmayer

After dessert Feine suggests they stroll over to the coffee room. The head waiter accompanies them. Through the window Lutz can see that the Fórum Cinema House is screening the 1944 hit film *Az afrikai vőlegény* (*The African Fiancé*) with Kálmán Latabár in the lead role.

Feine asks for coffee with milk. Raising the saucer to his lips he asks Lutz in a whisper to give his word of honour that he will not breathe a word about their conversation to his superior Ambassador Jaeger or even his spouse, *die gnädige Frau* Gertrud, as he puts it, because if the briefing should leak out it could not be ruled out that he might the victim of an unfortunate accident.

Lutz asks him how long he has been aware that people are being gassed at Auschwitz. We are engaged in a war, says Feine. He said that with a run-of-the-mill air, Lutz was later to recollect. I've been photographed together with a murderer, he says. Feine's expression immediately changes. He was a discharged SS officer, Lutz adds hastily; on the picture we are standing next to each other, and I have an arm around his shoulders. Feine can't take in what he is driving at. He pays for both of them. The head waiter glides in front of them in order to open the swing door.

Once back in his office Lutz takes down from the wall the picture in which he is posing with the German punt man. That evening Gertrud notices the gap on the wall and after some rummaging comes across the photograph in one of the drawers of the writing desk. She pins it back up. You were fond of it, she says to Lutz the next day.

It crosses Lutz's mind that it should have been ripped in two long ago. That student to whom I handed the Leica to make the shot did a good job. He had not known then that the limping flatboat man had been a guard at Auschwitz.

Tell me, do you understand why the Jews want to be Hungarian at any cost? Gertrud asks. Lutz is glad to have got off the subject of the photograph. No, he doesn't understand, he says. Not that he doesn't understand that either, although that is what he would like to say. He has a lot of things to say, but those matters it would be good to speak about are unsayable – but not because they were things he had given his word to Feine that he would keep quiet about.

He was to write later:

When, in May 1942, three young members of the Czech resistance fatally wounded Reinhard Heydrich, one of the most brutal tyrants in history, I was in Budapest. We all knew about the reprisal action, the way the entire village of Lidice was razed to the ground, obliterated, the men brutally executed and the womenfolk and children deported. When the news first came through that the Germans had annihilated millions of people in Auschwitz and other concentration camps at first I, too, sitting in my study in Budapest, found it hard to believe. When I made enquiries at the German Embassy an acquaintance of mine would only say in a whisper that one was not supposed to know about that and it was better not to. Then in April 1943 we learned about the Warsaw Ghetto uprising; we knew the Germans had sent in armed trucks and tanks, and the last 40,000–60,000 Jews were literally burned to ashes . . .

I see Gizi's steps, despite only being able to see Mother's look as she tells me what she had later learned from Gizi.

Mother seems not to be relating something she had heard from her aunt but telling some ancient story, as if she were hearing Gizi's voice from the dim and distant past and not just a few months after the things she was talking about had happened, in a voice that was already husky when she was young. You know, Gizi says to Mother, I may have been seen with Károly before he was arrested with the resisting officers. When those animals gunned him down at the street corner, someone could well have squealed on me. I suspected the situation could be dicey in that neighbourhood, so I went back to Lutz at the Swiss Embassy. His wife is a nice woman, a bit flirtatious, but that's part of it. Of what? I asked Gizi, Mother says with a face as innocent as it could be. When she asked Gizi what was it a part of, Well, a part of the whole mess of war, dear, said Gizi, giggling at the innocent face Mother had put on in asking the question.

The looks in people's eyes, on their faces, are more important than events. Perhaps that's a frivolous thing to say, but then again perhaps it isn't. For me the memory of looks is more important because events make their way into them, and one has only to move forward from the look to the sense and from the sense to the events. The shits squealed, Gizi says to Mother, and Mother pronounces 'the shits' with some embarrassment when she tells me.

Gizi could not have stayed at the Swiss Legation, but then she did not want to, I learn from Mother. She only wanted to glean information on how she might get in touch with those of Károly's fellow officers who had survived, although it was also important for her to wait until the freshly printed *Schutzbriefe* were brought from the printer. When she had got hold of those she went over to the ICRC home on Munkácsy Mihály Street. I sent a message from there to one of the He-Halutz groups, she told Mother, that I had the safe-conduct passes. The sleuths who might have seen me with Károly had sniffed out where I was, it might even be that one of those who had me nabbed was somewhere in the chain, but anyway that same evening two plainclothes men came for me. Follow us, madam, that's all. No big deal. Grey trilbies, overcoats with black velvet collars, I didn't have the slightest idea where they were taking me, and they sat me in a taxi, which must be heading for 60 Andrássy Avenue,[3] or so I thought, but we get out in front of the Astoria, go across the entrance lobby, down the staircase, and that's when it springs to Gizi's mind that in the past it had been possible to go down those stairs to a basement wine bar. The four of us once went there with your father and Gizi's husband when he was still alive, so Gizi asks the two trilbies – you know what she's like, everything no sweat – she asks, I don't suppose you gentlemen are inviting me out for a dance?

Gizi is being held in a Gestapo slammer.

A major is interrogating her.

Gizi does not ask for an interpreter. The major is clean-shaven, and when he leans forward Gizi catches the whiff of his aftershave. He had conspicuously long fingers, Gizi says later. Just imagine, says Mother, she even asked the major if he was a pianist.

The major is so astonished that he promptly responds. No, an electrical engineer.

I just thought your fingers have such graceful lines, but, of course, an electrical engineer may need his hands for equally delicate tasks.

Averting his gaze from Gizi's provocative glances the major poses his questions. The things you imagine, Gizi laughs. My tasks are set by no less than Herr Friedrich Born, the head of the International Committee of the Red Cross himself. You must be acquainted with him, Herr Major. And how had she come into contact with Herr

Born? Oh, at a reception! He was pointed out to me. He was looking to take somebody on who spoke perfect German and had nursing experience.

The major leans back as he extinguishes the flames of the match with a delicate flick of the wrist.

At whose reception did that meeting take place?

Gizi is well aware what is hanging on her answer.

Herr Gerhart Feine was throwing a delightful party at the German Embassy. I had already had the pleasure of meeting him earlier.

Gizi knows from Gertrud Lutz that Feine is no longer in Budapest. She also knows that, although Feine had been in close communication with Carl Lutz and Friedrich Born, he had easy access to the Gestapo. She also knows that Born had left Budapest in recent days in order to report in person.

The Gestapo major is also aware that Born is not in the city.

Who can confirm all these things, madam?

It would be simplest, Herr Major, if you were to put in a telephone call to my friend, Frau Gertrud Lutz, the Vice-Consul's wife, at the Swiss Embassy.

The major is in a tricky position. Not only does he have precise details of Lutz's activities, he is also in possession of a copy of the secret declaration in which Feine, on behalf of the Reich's Ministry for Foreign Affairs, guarantees Lutz inviolability in return for the assistance he had provided before in Palestine.

He dials the embassy's number and asks for Gertrud Lutz.

She even knows that the Lutzes happen not to be spending that night in their own home because the way to Buda was no longer safe in the dark, Gizi will tell Mother later. He turned away when he spoke into the receiver, so I didn't hear what he asked; when he put the telephone down he made a sign to the two detectives that I could go.

The Gestapo men accompanied Gizi up to the lobby. Lounging on the leather couches are callow young men with Arrow Cross armbands and submachine guns. At the exit two men saluted them as if they had been in uniform. Gizi blows them a kiss, crosses the road and stands outside the cinema, looking at Kálmán Latabár in the photographs. She hitches up her Red Cross armband and sets off down Lajos Kossuth Street towards the Danube.

*

Mrs Manntz lives in the basement of number 74 Amerikai Road; two rooms and a kitchen. They can't stay at my place, says Auntie Linnert. Vespi also saw them come over.

Auntie Linnert mutters something to her. Fine, says Mrs Manntz, but only up to 7.30 in the evening, you know, Helmut comes out of the hospital at eight o'clock.

When your husband gets home from the front he's going to shoot your Helmut dead, Mrs Linnert says.

Mrs Manntz's husband is a carpenter. He's been gone a year on the Eastern Front. Since May Major Dr Baron Helmut von Friedenburg, deputy commandant of the hospital opposite, has been spending his nights with Mrs Manntz. She was born in the Jászság, is tall, and she wiggles her hips when she walks. In the mornings she works as a cleaner at the hospital; in the evenings she waits for the major. If István gets back home Helmut will shoot him first, she says.

God Almighty! You're such a tramp, Hel, says Mrs Linnert. She sounds as though there were a touch of envy in her voice. Have you got any potatoes? Mrs Manntz asks her as she is departing. Just enough for what we need . . . Come over if it's onions you're after . . .

It's six o'clock, and I'm arranging the things in my knapsack. Mrs Manntz sees the seashell. Yours, is it? I don't tell her I got it from the Róberts' place. She likes it a lot; she'd give me a can of preserved meat for it, even two . . .

In any case you're not going to need it any more.

I won't give it to you, I say.

Vera asks me to turn away because she wants to change her knickers.

I don't wait till 7.30. Vera does not understand where we're setting off for. The streets are dark. German guards are on sentry duty at a machine-gun post in front of the hospital. The rain does not bother me; I am glad I can hold Vera's hand.

Gyarmat Street, Kolumbusz Street, Thököly Road. A number 44 tram with the blue-painted light bulb inside the carriages draws near with two Party functionaries on the rear platform. They look at us when the carriage rattles by beside us.

Father's paper-processing workshop was off the courtyard of 41 Francia Road. In front of the hut of József Rübner's timber shop it springs to mind that it was here that Dr Ernő Fogas, in his first lieutenant's uniform, saluted my father on that day when he first went out on the street wearing a yellow star on his coat.

The window of the caretaker's flat is beside the gate. It is opened at the third knock. I can hear Mrs Ulbert calling out behind her for her husband.

Mr Ulbert is a postman. They are fond of us, I say to Vera; my parents did a lot to help them, and they did a lot to help my parents. He cautiously comes out to meet us. To his question I say that I don't know what has happened to my parents. We'd like to lie doggo in Father's workshop, but I have no keys with me. He goes to fetch a wrench and hammer; he uses the wrench to hold the padlock and then hits it. The ringing carries a long way in the night. The lock gives at the seventh or eighth blow.

In the workshop is a small machine with which texts can be printed on paper bags; at its back a paper cutter. A partition wall separated the adhesive binder from the office. In the middle there is a big trestle table with benches around it. The gumming shop has no window, so we can turn the light on. During the summer Father hid two trunks among the bales of paper; in these I find warm clothes and behind them there are blankets.

We make a bed on the gumming table. We don't have any supper as we are not hungry. We lie down on the table, embracing each other under the blankets.

A mouse scurries in the corner.

Vera is able to sleep even with my hugging her. We are in our underwear; I ease my underpants down. With one hand under her back, I grope with the other under the front of Vera's knickers. She gives no sign of having woken up.

There must be more than one mouse in the corner; it seems that it is their noise which wakes Vera with a start, and she is now alarmed to see what I am doing with my hand. I switch on the light. I find a broom and beat about with it in the corner. Vera watches from above, pretending she has not noticed she is not wearing knickers. I scramble back beside her. Did you scare them away? Yes. That's good, she says and slowly lies back down.

Between her thighs it is like a split plum, except its pulp is pink and not green; around it fluff with a golden shimmer. I prop myself on my left elbow; the places in which I had been kicked that morning are aching. Arousal lifts my abdomen on to her thigh, with her skin caressing my skin. That scares both of us rigid. I turn on to my side and cover my groin with my hand; I would be ashamed if she were to see what has happened to me. I pull her knickers back up. Her look now is like the one at the piano when she was mimicking Karády. I try to kiss her. Her eyes are full of tears; she quickly turns her back on me. I tuck her up and switch off the light. A short while later she is pressing her backside into my lap and quietly snoring as if she were asleep. I don't know what she might be feeling; she tells me twenty years later.

I dream about crossing the stairwell and ringing the first doorbell. I ring the bell once but hear six hammer blows. I ring the bell once at each, and after each ring I hear the six hammer blows resound. The doors are immediately locked, but in the second it takes I recognize the faces that have been seen so many times. I don't understand how Auntie Linnert and Mrs Manntz could have ended up in one of the apartments, and I can see from the looks they give me that they, for their part, don't understand how I come to be standing before their door. The spyholes in the doors are quickly shut, but I can nevertheless still see into the apartments. Everyone woke up to the rings on the doors, now everyone goes back to bed. Everyone is sleeping on the same sort of trestle table as Vera and me; mice scurry round each of the tables.

We cannot stay long here either, I say to Vera in my dream.

It is still dark when I put my clothes on. I stow the blankets back behind the bales of paper. I don't know whether or not the women will come into work in the morning; I don't know if anyone has spare keys, but if they do come at least they will not find us undressed. Vera is shivering in the cold. I ask her at least to wash her face, there's a tap at the back. There is no toilet; there is one next to the caretaker's flat, but we can't cross the yard at this time of day. I tell Vera that next to the tap there is a drain – she can use that if she wants to pee.

Maybe it was here, at the windows of the Astoria coffee room over-looking Magyar Street, that Lutz and Feine drank their coffee. I order a cappuccino. The waitress, who must be about twenty-five years old, has a slim waist that does not fit her otherwise ample looks, nor do the marked features and jutting chin fit her rounded face. Rather, it looks as if she had been moulded from discordant components.

Would it help me, I wonder, if I knew what the layout had been like sixty years ago? Perhaps there are photographs from that time. Who should I ask?

I could have spoken to the manager or enquired at the reception desk, but more important than any plan of how it looked at the time is the look on a young woman's face when I pose that question.

She is eager, just as if I had given a further order: I cannot think of a blue to which I could compare the blueness of her eyes. There probably is one, if nowhere else than one mixed on an artist's palette from a great range of blues, maybe with a dash of yellow, or maybe black, or both. Perhaps both, as her look grows both darker and lighter.

I ask her, Tell me, all I have heard is hearsay, but it is said that in '44 the Gestapo had a set-up in the cellars. Had you heard that? She's not rightly sure . . . it rings a bell . . .

Five minutes later she brings a glossy brochure, published not long ago to mark the ninetieth anniversary of the hotel. I ask her again how she came to know about the Gestapo. Instead of an answer she says that's where Katalin Karády and the actor Pál Jávor were brought; she'd heard that from her father. Her father must have been a little boy when the war was on, perhaps he was not yet born, I say. Her father had heard that from his father, she says, because he used to work here. There is pride in her eyes, confusion as well, as if her smile, too, were coaxed from disparate sentiments. It's a family occupation. Her father started here and is now head waiter at the Palace Hotel on Rákóczi Avenue.

Katalin Karády and Pál Jávor were not brought here but to the Gestapo's HQ on Swabian Hill, I say. The smile vanishes, but she is still disposed to chat: then her dad had got it wrong, although perhaps it was her grandfather who had misremembered it.

You should ask him.

That is a mean thing to say. I daren't look her in the eyes.

I didn't know him; I think he was already dead when I was born. The regulation smile afresh. I am familiar with a great variety of such smiles, but this one I had not come across before. I see a mask for infinite boredom.

Twice a week I drink coffee at the same table; I don't ask the waitress any questions. Sometimes I also have a Cabinet brandy. I want her to get used to me. On one occasion I mention that Mother's aunt was among those brought to the cellar here in 1944. After a while I get to learn that her father was born in 1951. I write up notes at home. Her father began working in the profession as a boy; her grandfather also started working in the Astoria. He was also there during the Second World War, but she doesn't know what post he held – it could have been as a porter or a waiter; it might even have been as a head waiter. Her father says it's all so shrouded in obscurity that he might even have carried a weapon. He was gaoled in 1945 and was given five years, although for what is 'a total mystery'. In 1956 he defected, and they never heard from him again. It's of no interest, she says.

I note down that when she speaks about this the black is more intense in her eyes than the yellow. I note down that I don't believe what she tells me – neither what she says about her father and grandfather nor that she really thinks it's of no interest. But I note down that, nevertheless, that may be how she feels. I note also that by the time we are talking like old acquaintances she replies in answer to a question that she does not know if her father said nothing more about her grandfather because he, possibly, knew that what he happened to know needed to be kept secret – or maybe he just did not understand what she was questioning him about. I note down that, none the less, she had asked. Yes, she says, I think he genuinely did not understand, so there was nothing to talk about.

When she says that she is standing by as if she had had just realized something and felt obliged to ponder on that.

Maybe she was imagining her father's glazed look of indifference.

She shrugs her shoulders, perhaps in the same way her father did when she questioned him.

As I see it, she would be glad if I do not trouble her with further questions.

For the first time since I have been following the trail of my old footsteps I feel that anything that sinks into oblivion when it happens is lost for good.

She looks back from another table; she can see that I am getting down to work.

There was a time when I used to work in the Astoria, so why not now . . . ?

By the time I reach the end of the paragraph, I write, I shall have to confront something for which so far I have lacked the nerve: I have reached a detour. But I have not yet reached the end of the paragraph. How might I get further on in a story about which even someone to whom it happened knows nothing? That woman was going nowhere, the same as her father; even her grandfather may have sleepwalked into his own fate without having any idea of where he was going. Am I supposed to know something about which they themselves knew nothing? I am caught in a trap, I write. I could only extricate myself if I were able to understand what gives birth to what I have called indifference by descending into that nocturnal world through which I wandered, yet the price would be that I have to see myself through their eyes. It's just that I cannot get to the bottom of their stories in their place. All the same I would like to, I write. I dread contradictions like this. I need to consider that perhaps it was the waitress's grandfather who took the coffee to the German major who had interrogated Gizi, and I should see him as the head waiter who keeps under observation the meeting between Carl Lutz and Gerhart Feine before Carl Lutz's telephone had rung a second time on a later night.

The first telephone call, coming at nine o'clock, is about how up around St István Park, on the Pest bank of the Danube opposite Margit Island, the occupants of one of the houses under Swiss protection are being lined up by Arrow Crossers. Lutz and his wife get into a car. When they draw up before the building the Arrow Crossers level weapons at them. At the Hungarian Ministry of Foreign Affairs Lutz delivers a verbal memorandum to Baron Gábor Kemény. The Foreign Minister instructs the district commander of the Arrow Crossers that his men must withdraw from a house which is under diplomatic protection. The commander in turn proceeds to the site and authorizes that the action be continued. Lutz arrives back at St István Park with the minister's chef de cabinet. The Arrow Cross commander and the chef de cabinet draw guns on one another; Gertrud takes a picture. The chef de cabinet pays no attention to the weapon being levelled at him and has the people who have been lined up led back into the house.

Is this how it's going to be every evening? Gertrud asks when they get back.

The telephone rings again one hour later. Gertrud picks up the receiver. Of course, I know her, she says in answer to the Gestapo major's question, she is an esteemed friend of ours, to me personally, and a colleague of Herr Friedrich Born's at the ICRC, who is charged with looking after sick children.

It was quite simple, says Gertrud to Lutz, I would quite fancy the Jewish woman myself if I were in your shoes, dearest.

That night Károly Beregfy, the Minister of Defence, issues a summons:

Anyone who is still sitting at home unarmed should come and fight! Enlist at the district branch of the Arrow Cross Party. Hungarian women, skivers must be held in contempt! Shame and a calling to account will be the fate of those who do not take part in the defence of our capital city!

The military high command adopted a plan drawn up by the joint Hungarian–German committee concerning the actions that are to be implemented in the event of a withdrawal from Budapest, which includes a list of factories, public buildings, railway intersections and bridges that are to be blown up. Sándor Csia, Szálasi's deputy, opens the session with a quotation from the great Reformist Liberal Count István Széchenyi: 'We are lost if we confer when the time has come for action.'

An announcement appears under the joint signatures of SS Obergruppenführer Karl Pfeffer-Wildenbruch, commander of the German force defending Budapest, and Colonel-General Iván Hindy de Kishind, holder of a hereditary knighthood of the Vitéz Order and at the time commander of Hungarian I Corps:

Joint German–Hungarian martial law is coming into force in the area of Greater Budapest. Capital punishment awaits all traitors who, by committing acts of sabotage and incitement, whether by word of mouth or written, or by actual sedition, endangers the lives of fighting forces.

A few days later Ferenc Szálasi proclaims that in the interests of the Great European Project he is willing to accede to the view that the German high command should not declare Budapest an open city. It is therefore necessary forthwith, and accepting all sacrifices, to make a start on organizing the defence of Budapest at all costs.

I don't recall when Gizi next visited us in the Alice Weiss Hospital, says Mother, but we had certainly been there for several days. The only places for those who were brought back from Hegyeshalom were on palliasses placed on the floor in the basement. Undoubtedly we asked her to look for Jolán Bors, you know, she was the one who . . .

I know, I interrupt. Mother has already told me many times over that she got Gizi to look for Jolán Bors, and I've already told her many times over that I remember Jolán Bors bringing a large bag of apples for us in the brickworks. We gave her address to Gizi, and Gizi found her. Jolán set about looking for you, she went first to Amerikai Road and only after that did she go over to the workshop.

I tell Mother yet again that we did not let anyone on Amerikai Road know that we were going to Francia Road. I don't know why I repeat it so often. Maybe because I see in her face the joy it gives her to be able to say anew that Jolán Bors found us.

It would be nice to be able to ask Jolán Bors herself. She must have been around twenty-five years old then, so perhaps she is still alive. She used to live in the south-eastern suburbs, in Kispest, the XIXth District. She wore a headscarf. Oval face, big brown eyes, a basket invariably on her arm. A defrocked nun, says Father. Why, though? No one asks her. Bent over the gumming table, she spreads the paste with mechanical whisks of the gluing brush on the pre-cut paper of the bag, folds it, turns the half-finished bag and pastes its edges again, smoothes it down and stacks it in the pile beside her 25-year-old self.

Mother no longer seeks to evoke memories of her but what she herself said about her memories.

I listen to the story behind the words.

The Ukrainian third front had reached the town of Vác, north of Pest on the Danube. Units of the second and third fronts joined forces at Ercsi, just south of Budapest on the Buda side of the Danube: 'The Hungarian theatre of war in a 150-mile arc is in flames,' reports the war correspondent of the *Völkische Beobachter* from Budapest. 'It is now not just a matter of the Hungarian capital city but also about how Vienna and south-eastern Germany may be defended at the cost of defending Budapest.'

When the ring of the siege tightens from the east to reach the districts of Újpest (IV), Sashalom (XVI), Rákospalota and Pestújhely (XV), Zugló (XIV) and Kispest (XIX), the Arrow Cross chiefs of staff ask General Otto Wöhler, leading the German 8th Army and the city's new commanding officer, to guarantee the chance of breaking out for the garrison stranded in Budapest. There could be no question of this, however. An order has arrived from Hitler to say that the battle front must be maintained at all costs, declares the general.

Jolán Bors hurries through the streets of Kispest. Trams rarely run, and there is only room on the steps on to the carriages. She reaches Boráros Square on the southern Pest bank of the Danube then walks north to Rákóczi Avenue. There are long queues in front of the food shops; she joins one of them and buys two kilograms of apples. She clambers on to a number 44 tram. An air-raid warning is sounded; all traffic comes to a halt. Armed Arrow Crossers herd people into the public air-raid shelters on Baross Square. One hour later she resumes her journey towards Zugló on foot.

Vera is freezing cold. I am unable to persuade her to rub herself down with cold water from the tap at the back.

Mrs Ulbert arrives with Jolán Bors shortly behind. Her brown headscarf with the pink pattern is pulled right down to her eyes. Sweet Jesus! she cries, I don't know whether out of happiness at finding us or from horror at the way we look. She puts the big bag of apples on the big trestle table. She gives both of us a smacker. Vera draws back not knowing who is giving the kiss.

Jolán Bors recounts what she has heard from Gizi. My parents are still alive. Only now does it occur to me to think for the first time what it would mean if they were not alive. Since our column set off from the brickworks and they disappeared in the fog on the highway it had never once struck me that I might not see them again.

Then we'll go to where they are.

That's not possible, she says. They only admitted those who were sick. There are five times as many people as there are places, and the

Arrow Cross are taking away the walking wounded every day. The head physician, Dr Temesvái, has had the gates closed. Aunt Gizi says that you are to go to number 4 Munkácsy Mihály Street. There's a Red Cross home there, and if you give them her name they will take you in for sure.

Vera asks, What has happened to my mummy?

I haven't heard anything about her, says Jolán Bors.

She shows us where another trunk is hidden behind the bales of paper. I find a pair of warmer britches and thick socks. For Vera we search among Mother's warm knickers: they are too big for her, but they don't slip down if she puts on two pairs. She is most pleased by the ladies' handkerchiefs.

You can't stay, Mrs Ulbert says. Her husband is an army deserter, so for the night he went to his younger brother's place in Pestújhely, but they'll be out looking for him and will search the house, so you can't stay.

I go into the office behind the partition wall and type a letter to my parents on the Remington. Jolán Bors says that when she next meets Aunt Gizi she will pass it on to her, but if they don't meet up she'll go to the Alice Weiss Hospital. The guards might let her hand in a letter.

We wait until evening, when we open one of the cans of meat. We still have some dry bread. At dusk I put on the knapsack. Vera is carrying her little suitcase. Mrs Ulbert says farewell, making a sign of the cross.

On Francia Road there is only a pavement on the side with housing; on the other side is a railway embankment. A single street lamp is the only lighting. Coming the other way, from Thököly Road, a pair of Arrow Cross men on patrol is approaching. We cannot turn back now. We have no papers; I grip Vera by the hand. They are twenty metres away. I put an arm round her; from the way she snuggles up to me I can sense that she had understood we had to go straight ahead. Ten metres. The street lamp is now shining from behind the two men with their submachine guns, so I was unable to get a clear view of their faces. Their hands are on the stocks of their guns; they are walking in step. I press Vera to the wall, press close against her and throw my right hand up high, shouting, Long live Szálasi!

There is no lamp behind us, so it could be that only now do they notice us. Vera embraces me, thrusting her head to my neck. Can't you find a better place to snog, boy? He can only be just two or three years older than me, but he chuckles immoderately at his own wit.

We reach the lamp.

Vera is unable to go any further, but I can't allow her to stop.

In the distance is the rattling of a tram. The iron grille over the front of Mr Zsilka's hairdressing salon, on the corner of Thököly Road and Hermina Road, has been pulled down. I had not seen the spire of St Domonkos Church look so high before; the entrance to the Glória Cinema is dark as there is no late-night showing.

I turn into St Domonkos Street on Thököly Road. On the corner of Abonyi Street, which runs parallel to Thököly Road, and András Cházár Street is the Budapest Jewish Grammar School. The school-yard lies beyond the cast-iron gate of the driveway. I point out to Vera from the street where the nets and backboards for the basketball court are. We used to go into the gym along a corridor in the basement, but there is also a door opening on to the yard, and when the weather was fine we would run about outside, plimsolls, satin shorts and a white or blue singlet. I tell Vera that the gym floor had sawdust sprinkled over it, so if anyone fell over they did not hurt themselves, but on the other hand balls did not bounce very well.

At the St Domonkos Street Grammar School they attempted to provide protection for two thousand persons. It was barely possible to move around. There were eighty of us confined in the cellar; we slept on the floors without any blankets. On one occasion the Arrow Crossers dragged off 150 people and vowed that we would be next. Each and every time we heard footsteps approaching we thought it was our turn. Mother could take it no longer; one day she went out in order to find a hiding place somewhere else. Arrow Crossers gunned her down in the street in front of the school.

This letter of recollections I put in one of my folders.

I am unaware that behind the locked gates the men who can be seen in the dim light in the hall are member of a guard organized after the 150 persons had been dragged away the previous day.

The park is covered in snow.

Nearby bursts of submachine-gun fire can be heard, with cannons in the distance.

We reach Aréna Road. German tanks are rattling towards Hősök Square.

I later find out that Mrs Manntz's husband deserted from his unit and he gets home the very night that Vera and I are slinking along Aréna Road.

Sergeant-Major Manntz throws off his sopping-wet overcoat and steps into the bedroom. He goes back into the kitchen and is just reaching for the big carving knife when Major Dr Baron Helmut von Friedenburg shoots twice through the open kitchen doorway. They bury the sergeant-major in the garden. There are many bodies buried in gardens.

V

Submachine-gun bursts can be heard from the direction of Hősök Square.

Vera does not dare come out from the cover of the trees in City Park.

We wait.

A cloud floats across the moon.

Not one streetlight is shining in Délibáb Street, just off to the right near the top of Andrássy Avenue. There is a Red Cross sign on the gate of number 4 Mihály Munkácsy Street. The door is opened after three raps. An enormous hallway with staircases winding upwards on either side to the mezzanine. We are led into one of the rooms. A writing desk, cabinet, three chairs. A woman of around forty in a dressing-gown comes in. She writes down our names, dates of birth, parents, home addresses. On being asked I say that I last saw my parents at the Óbuda Brickworks, but I had been told that the Red Cross had brought them back from Hegyeshalom, that they were in Alice Weiss Hospital and they got a message to me that we should come here.

Vera stays quiet. Her mother had been taken away in the same column as my parents, I say, but we had heard nothing about her; her father was in a forced-labour brigade, and nothing had been heard about him either.

The woman, holding her by the hand, takes her away. She returns five minutes later and we go up to the first floor. The corridor is deserted. I ask where Vera went: to the girls on the second floor. I shouldn't worry, she's in a comfortable spot. She tries two doors. At the third she is told there are eleven there. This is fine, she says. I should try to get some sleep; don't pay attention to anyone. You'll have time tomorrow to see who to make friends with.

The room is dark and stinks. No one budges. The woman repeats sharply that a palliasse is to be freed up for me. She runs a torch beam over the floor. The boys are sleeping tightly packed next to each other.

I don't know how I shall be able to find a place. She orders two of the boys to shove up closer to each other. I find a blanket under the window and wedge myself between two bodies. I hear a voice every hour and later I learn that was the room's senior. Left! Right! Everyone turn together! There are some who only wake up if the boy next to them is breathing in their face.

I wake up to a rattling of mess tins. There is a long queue in the corridor. A ladleful of tea poured into the mess tin and a round of bread. Some of the boys go back into the room and have their breakfast sitting on their palliasse, but most of them squat in the corridor or lean on the wall. I choose to sit on my palliasse. I tell the boy next to me my name and ask him how I might be able to meet Vera. He says that there is a glass door at this end of the second-floor corridor; I can rap on that, but it won't do any good; they'll not let me in. I go upstairs and knock on the door. A young woman with a white headscarf opens the locked door. It's not allowed, she says gently, meanwhile scanning me at length; you know, not all the boys are as decent as you are. She will tell Vera that I came. Come back just before supper time.

There are twelve of us in the room, which must be about five by three metres in size. One of the boys is sewing his trousers, which have split along one of the seams; a second is collecting dirty underclothes, shoving them into a white linen bag. I had a similar sports bag, containing my gym shoes and kit, which was tied to my school satchel. A stubble-jawed, lanky, cross-eyed boy is slumped against one of the walls, yelling and giving every appearance of masturbating, one of his hands clutched over the buttoned-up fly of his trousers, his tongue hanging and panting, but he is more likely laughing. A little boy of six or seven is watching him engrossed, as it he were gazing at a clown in a circus.

A bespectacled boy comes over, perhaps older than me. He tells me his name and puts his hand out. The name is familiar; I seem to remember hearing it from Father. His father was also a paperman (that's the word he uses) with a workshop in the VIth District, a few streets away in Szív Street. He introduces me to his younger brother. We agree that I should carry my blanket and headrest (my haversack) across next to where they are lying; they, too, reckon our parents must know each other – they're the Riegler boys.

Before supper I make another trip up to the second floor. It's the same person as yesterday who opens the door. I have to wait. Vera comes along in a posse of girls. She has let down her hair and has had it tied up with a white ribbon. I tell her I've come across a person I vaguely know; she has, too, a classmate, an awfully nice girl. She says that so deliberately as if she were years older. She puts an arm around me – I think just so the others can see. The corridor takes a turning beyond the glass door, and there are some armchairs at the turning. The woman with the white headscarf has a little girl with very long hair sitting in her lap; the women is raking through the hair with a fine-toothed comb, hunting on her scalp between the hair strands. She's got lice, Vera whispers and asks when I can come again. Tomorrow just before suppertime.

Supper consists of powdered soup – BB packet soup it was called. Along with the bread this time we get a slice of Hitler lard; a thin slice of jam from a block is also dispensed. The grandparents of the Riegler boys are in the ghetto; I tell them my grandma is probably also there. One can see the top end of Andrássy Avenue from the window at the end of the corridor. There are few people on it; mostly Arrow Cross patrols. The boys say it's likely they are coming from number 60 because that's their GHQ.

I sit on the palliasse. A tall boy comes in; he is eighteen or so. Did you come yesterday? We go out into the corridor. He introduces himself: Soproni he is called. He doesn't give a first name. He has a little toothbrush moustache. He asks if I have any forged papers. I haven't. If I have five pengő he can get me some, not that he needs the money, but the movement does, paper has to be obtained, stamps have to be made and the printing also costs. For the time being they can do identification papers for messengers in the Levente Youth Army Corps, the sort of thing that would pass muster during an air-raid alert. I count out the money. He asks me for my personal details, getting me to choose a new name. I also alter the final letter of my mother's maiden surname from 'i' to 'y', and I choose my father's birthplace of Kiskunhalas as my own. What about your religion, he asks; we agree on Roman Catholic. Vera ought to get papers as well. That's tougher, he says. For the time being we only have the stamps for Levente messengers, which can't really be used for a girl.

Someone is always running in the corridor. There must be small children somewhere because one can hear the sound of their cries. The elder of the Rieglers is standing by the window. He says nothing; neither do I. In one corner of the room one of the lads kicks a smaller boy, who tries to kick back, but the bigger boy catches his leg and starts dragging him along with the smaller boy now hopping on one leg and yelling. Riegler quietly tells the older boy, Stop that! He doesn't, so Riegler socks him one on the jaw. The lad is thrown back against the wall and in getting to his feet squares up for a fight. Everyone is paying attention. Before the lad can lay a hand on him, Riegler lands a second blow and just says, Stop it! Back to your place!

We again take up positions next to each other at the window, again saying nothing. Riegler has a strong jaw, bowed lips and a straight nose. Not Jewish-looking, I reckon. Nor is my nose, I believe. Last year when one of the senior boys wearing a Levente cap spat at me in the street, he said you don't even look like a sheeny, you little shit. Riegler has a head of thick brown back-combed hair. My own is brown as well. Once after washing it I pegged my mother's hair-grips into it so that it would dry wavy. My parents had guests staying, and Mother's woman friend went to the bathroom. I heard her asking her, Rosie, do you let your little boy use your hair-grips? Mother chuckled. I would never have been able to thump that boy for mistreating the younger one. I'm pleased Riegler did it.

He asks how my parents managed to get from Hegyeshalom to the Alice Weiss Hospital, and I tell him what I have learned from Jolán Bors. He had given the office false personal information, he whispers; he was actually seventeen. At the brickworks he had arranged to join the under-sixteens in such a way that his younger brother had gone over first, then their father – the old man is the term he uses – had slipped over to the brother and told him, and an Arrow Crosser started beating him back into place and the old man put on a huge act about only wanting to say goodbye to his little boy. He embraced my brother and whispered that he should pass him his registration form – the old man was pretty savvy to working tricks like that. He brought the registration form for me and started pushing me over towards the under-sixteens' group, making sure the date of birth would not be checked by the same Arrow Crosser that had already seen my brother's form. With us no one had looked at our registration forms, I tell him; we were simply allowed to go over to the Red Cross group. That's just it, he says, sometimes they do and then again sometimes they don't. It all depends on that, but don't tell anybody that I'm over seventeen. His glasses have steamed up; he takes them off and wipes them. He's got long fingers. He notices I am looking at them. I play the piano. His voice is different from the one in which he recounted the scene his father had staged at the brickworks. Tell you what, I'm not half going to miss the practice!

I would like to repay the confidence, so I tell him it's also possible to get papers from Soproni for five pengő. I know, we've got one, too; it counts for fuck-all if they really check, although it's still worth five pengő.

I ask him what happens if there is a proper identification check, and I hand over the one that's worth shit. There's no telling with a bloke who's set on murder. I spoke about that with my old man, and he said that in such a case you had to try to look the fellow straight in the eye and just stick it out. I don't see him as being any older now; it's even almost as if he were younger than me. I don't get it, I tell him. What the hell has getting it to do with anything? I don't get what makes someone want to kill. You being a Jew, that's what. That's what I don't get. Let's leave it, mate; there's no way of getting to understand that. I tell him that on Francia Road, which Vera and I had gone down on our way to Thököly Road, there had been a pair of Arrow Cross men coming the other way and I had greeted them with Persevere! That's what I mean: look them straight in the eye. Then they don't shoot? Maybe they will, maybe they won't; that will come out in the wash after they have either shot or not shot.

I ask him how long, in his view, is it worth staying here in the home. He doesn't know. This is a good trolley bus to ride, he says, but you have to get off it while you still can. And how can one tell when it's time to get off? He doesn't answer.

The cross-eyed lad, who's slumped against the wall, once more starts the game of pretending he is masturbating. He again begins clutching the air in front of his buttoned-up fly. Howls of laughter. Forget him, says Riegler; that prick has never had a real orgasm in his life, you can take it from me.

We sit back down on my palliasse. I slowly start to unpack my haversack. At the bottom of it is the shell that I took from the Róbert family's apartment. I show it to him; he takes it and presses it to an ear. Nice, he says. Is that yours? It is now that it sinks in for the first time that I have actually appropriated the shell, although I feel that is not of very much significance, given that everyone is swiping stuff, and I had simply borrowed it and would give it back to 'Uncle' Róbert after the war was over. Every sound is there in the shell, I say, including what we are saying right now. He gives it back then ruffles my head like adults do. Watch out that none of the lads pinches it. Does that happen often? There have been some cases, not here but in the other room. That's when a shake-down is ordered. And what's that? Two of the orderlies for the floor come in, and you have to lay all your stuff on the palliasse. They search everything, and if they come across anything that's been stolen they take it away and you're punished by being given so many days on bread and water.

After breakfast Soproni says that I should go next door. There are still two there, the seniors. It's possible they don't even live in the home. One of them takes leave of Soproni after giving him my papers. Soproni lifts up one of the pieces in the parquet floor; a hollowed-out area contains a stamp and an ink pad. He stamps the papers, puts the ink pad back in its tin box, the stamp is wrapped again in greaseproof paper and put back in the hollow, and the parquet piece is replaced. The messenger's papers state that Iván Károly Seres, RC by religion, born at Kiskunhalas on 11 March 1930, mother's maiden name Rosa Imrey, is authorized to remain on the streets during air-raid warnings. Signed József Bakos, ARP Commander for VIth District.

I hear my name being called from the corridor. I have a visitor; go into the hall.

Jolán Bors's big black headscarf also covers her shoulders. I had not noticed before now that there are sentries at the gate – a policeman with a sidearm and a man with an ICRC armband. I am asked if I know the visitor. Jolán unpacks from a shopping basket; she has brought me a clean shirt, clean socks, two bars of chocolate, a link of savoury sausage, a kilogram of apples. She says she'll take way my dirty clothes. She is pleased to be able to sit in the hall on a bench by the wall; she has a long journey ahead of her. My parents are better. I'll be able to pay them a visit at the Alice Weiss Hospital in a week or two, so I should stay where I am. I am not clear on whether that is a message from my parents or her advice.

I go up to the office, ask for two sheets of letter paper and write with them resting on my knee. I've kept a pencil in the back pocket of my trousers, although there's only a stump and it is blunt, so I keep digging into the paper. It would have been better to ask for a pencil as well, but I haven't the nerve to go back. Jolán's face is white. Presumably it is always is, but now it is markedly so. She says that she was with my parents yesterday, and she set off from Kispest, on the outer south-eastern fringe of the city this morning. Now she will take my letter to my parents before she gets back home this evening. Had I met up with Aunt Gizi? I don't understand why I ought to have done. It's just that she is also there if needs be.

He takes her leave; she has to press on. She wraps herself up in her black scarf. I take my things upstairs, breaking off two squares of chocolate on the way up the stairs; I shall give the other bar to Vera in the evening. I give the two Riegler boys two squares each. Every time I go to the office there is somebody else there. This time it's a young woman in her twenties. I tell her that I've heard my aunt is here somewhere (Aunt Gizi is Mother's aunt, but I don't feel this is the place to go into details). She is back five minutes later and, leading me by the hand, takes me up to the third floor. She indicates one of the doors and tells me to knock.

There is no response. I count up to fifty before carefully turning the handle. There is a dense pall of grey cigarette smoke over everything – purplish rather. The curtains, too, and also the figure standing in front of the curtains in her dressing-gown. It's lilac silk with a white floral pattern. The figure does not turn round. I don't recognize her from the voice, which is hoarse. The figure turns round. Her face has also changed. Maybe she has spread cream all over the skin; it's glistening. Lots of blood vessels are showing in the whites of her eyes. The last time I saw her she was not blonde. The dressing-gown is not buttoned. She has a black brassiere. It would be good manners to avert my gaze, but in the brickworks men and women had to relieve themselves in front of one another and no one turned away. Her voice is like a soldier's. She recognizes me and gives me a hug. She doesn't smell of cigarettes. It's not a sweaty smell, more a body odour. A smell of eau de cologne. She says my parents were very weak but starting to pick themselves up. She asks if Jolán Bors had been to see me yet. This was a good place; I needed to be patient. Did I want to send a letter to my parents? I tell her I have just written one, and Jolán Bors was taking it.

She combs and asks me to turn the other way. I sense from the swishing sounds that she must be taking off the dressing-gown. I take a cautious peek at her. She is sitting with her back to me. She has black panties. She stands in front of me in a twill skirt and green blouse. Her hair has been smoothed down with a parting in the middle. She asks whether I have encountered her younger sister Bőzsi anywhere. Her voice is again husky, like when she called out after my entry. She must be somewhere here, surely somewhere. The network of capillaries in her eyes again dilates. I say that from what I've been told there are only children in this building. I know, sweetheart, but promise me that if you chance to see her you'll tell her that I am well and she can leave a message for me here, at the home. I try to pick words that I think will be of reassurance. She kisses my brow. Come tomorrow. Knock three times so I know it's you. Where is she going? She says she has lots of things to attend to. She puts on her fur jacket, white headscarf, Red Cross armband. We go along the corridor together, all the boys staring in wonderment at her – at me, too, for walking with her. I ask her what the date is: 8 December.

I go over the glass door. I have to knock there, too. General János Kiss, Lieutenant-Colonel Jenő Nagy and Captain Vilmos Tartsay, who were among a group of General Staff officers leading the army sector of the Committee for National Uprising and Liberation, the Independence Front, were executed on 8 December 1944. The head of the committee, Endre Bajcsy-Zsilinszky of the Smallholders' Party, had his immunity as a Member of Parliament suspended by Parliament, and on Christmas Eve he, too, was he was hanged at in the Sopronkőhida prison on 23 December.

On 8 December the total forces available to General Karl Pfeffer-Wildenbruch number only seventy thousand men, with Hungarian units comprising the regular army, reserve troops and the police force. The worst bloodshed is that inflicted by Eichmann's Sonderkommando and the SS units of mainly ethnic-German Hungarians.

*

Where, I wonder, could Mother, sitting on a mattress in the basement of the Alice Weiss Hospital, have put my letter after she was given it by Jolán Bors? In her haversack? Under the blankets? She read it out to Father. She folded the sheets in four. Grown thin with age, sixty years later the paper is still crossed by the folds.

She hands it to me. I hold the letter in my hands something like twenty or thirty years after I wrote it. No, it can't be as much as thirty; Mother was no longer alive then.

Gizi came in that day, Mother says, leaning back in the brazil-wood easy chair. That brazilwood easy chair no longer has gold silk upholstery; that got ripped during the war. Now she is sitting in a brazilwood easy chair with pea-green upholstery two or three years before she died. She hands me my letters. She had said nothing about them for quarter of a century. Which drawer did she keep them in? Most likely the cherrywood chest of drawers which used to belong to my grandparents. Did she take them out from time to time? Unfold them, fold them back again? As she hands them over my fingers touch hers. On the day that Jolán Bors brought me the letter in the hospital Gizi also showed up. The reason she can remember what happened on that particular day is that Gizi had also gone to the hospital to report on her meeting with me. You've grown up so much, Gizi said about me.

She was nicely made up and looked very swish in her fur coat, Mother said. Gizi had style in what she wore, she learned that from being with Józsi – my word, how smart Józsi looked in his first-lieutenant's uniform with his First World War medals. That was when Gizi learned how to carry herself off so well. When she was young she had been a daddy's girl, and Uncle Henrik left everything just lying all over his study, flicked his ash on the carpet, and he would look for his notes with his wife and with Gizi when all the time they would be on his writing table. So there was Gizi in her fur coat, Mother tells me twenty-five years later. She was wearing a Red Cross armband and had on bright-red lipstick. But that day she was as scatterbrained as she had been as a girl – she parked her handbag on the mattress and a minute later could not find it. She began asking us about Bőzsi. Your father and I just looked at each other, didn't say a word, when she mentioned Bőzsi a second time, that she was going to see if Dr Temesváry, the head physician, if he knew anything about her, so I said that we had already asked that earlier that day and he had heard nothing about her – although actually we hadn't asked, we were just worried about Gizi throwing a fit. We didn't want that to happen there; there were people who were dying on the mattresses, even some who were dead only they hadn't been taken away because the morgue was full. That was when they started digging graves in the hospital courtyard. It was a slow business because there were hardly any men around, and those who were there were so weak they were barely able to lift a spade.

The whites of Mother's eyes seem damp even though she was not crying. It's of no significance, says the doctor; it's the sort of thing that comes with age, you know, says Mother, after Józsi's death and even more so after little Eva's death, Gizi really had only Bőzsi left, what with Uncle Henrik and her mother already having died before the war.

When Mother was speaking about Gizi that's what she always called him, Uncle Henrik, but she never mentions Gizi's mother by name. Is that because she didn't like her? Did Gizi, too, dote on her father? I had forgotten that Gizi's daughter, little Eva, died two years after Józsi was buried.

I unfold the squared paper of the letter:

Dearest Mother and Father,

We took our leave thinking that day we would going to the Red Cross with the children, but we had to stay in the brickworks another two days, and after that in the Dohány Street Synagogue. We went from there to Vadász Street, but we didn't want to stay there. Vera and I went back home without wearing a yellow star. We had to leave Amerikai Road, we were in the workshop for two days, and from there we came here. Girls and boys are kept separated. At first I was very bitter about ending up in a pig-awful place, but then it turned out fine. I have two friends as well, the sons of Riegler the paperman.

I describe the daily fare.

Breakfast: awful BB packet soup and a dried-up slice of sour bread.
Lunch: BB soup or some crummy soup with pasta or, if we get lucky, hard beans.

Supper: BB soup or unsugared tea.

We were originally allowed to defer return to the ghetto until 15 December, which has now been postponed to the 20th.

Next the most important of all:

The thing is, we are not going to the ghetto. It was rumoured that everyone between fourteen and fifty years of age was to be taken to the ghetto. But where to? I heard from Jolán Bors that you are trying to acquire papers. It's not just a birth certificate but Levente papers, an identification card and maybe a registration or deregistration form as well. If you can, send blank papers urgently with Jolán, because I have now acquired a Levente messenger's pass.

If possible, please get hold of papers for Vera as well. For her a birth certificate will be enough. She has had no news of her mother; it is said that Uncle Seidel has been taken off to Germany. She doesn't want to be left alone, and I don't want to leave her here either.

Dearest Mother and Father, write in detail what the situation is. Are you going to leave or stay? How long can you stay? Where would you go? Can you send me the papers? Write to tell me how you are. If you can send Jolán, she should bring a shirt, socks and underpants from the workshop.

Send food if it's possible and most urgently of all send as much money as you can. I am now down to 20 pengő.

I have received the things you sent so far. Many thanks for those! I hope you are both well, dearest Mother and Father.

Many kisses, Iván.

PS If there is any way of doing so, please send papers for Vera as well!! Try to get Jolán to have a look what can be retrieved from 76 Amerikai Road.

I tap on the glass door to the second-floor corridor. I open the door. There are girls sitting at the bend in the corridor. Vera does not come up to me; just waves. She has a tot holding on to both hands. I recognize them as her cousins. I wasn't aware they were already here, nor was Vera. Edo has passed his sixth birthday, Judy is going on five.

They don't know what has happened to their parents, says Vera. They met yesterday evening. They were permitted to go into the room I'm in, she says, so we were able to sleep together.

She's telling a fairy story. Judy has an oval head; her features follow the story. She blushes and knits her brow.

I have to get back to my room.

Soproni comes.

Could I lend him my windcheater? He is going to disappear for a day or two, but I shouldn't tell anybody. His overcoat is long and heavy; it would be easier to move about in a windcheater. You're taller than me; it will be tight for you. He tries it on. Yes, it's bit of a squeeze, but no matter, he says. It's good because it has four pockets. He'll give me his own coat to keep until he gets back. He brings a Halina duffel coat the colour of milky coffee. That appeals a lot as I never had a coat with fancy braiding. He says it came from Transylvania. It's a shame it is so heavy and just a bit too long for me.

We check that the spot where the yellow star on my windcheater used to be is no longer visible. It's fine, he says. He can wear it safely on the street. Don't worry. I've got really good papers. I'll bring one for you when I come back.

It is cold in the room, so at night I spread the coat over the blanket. The older Riegler says that Soproni also has some hand-grenades.

I dream that I'm walking in the street wearing the duffel coat. An Arrow Cross patrol is coming the other way. They admire the coat. We hail each other with the fascist greeting 'Kitartás!'[4] They are driving along a yellow-star group, and I turn away in case I am recognized by anyone in the column. On the pavement two men and a woman break out laughing. The laughter echoes louder and louder as if the whole city were resounding, as if it were not just three people but many thousands. Vera steps beside me, bringing Edo and Judy, and we are going to our workshop on Francia Road; Vera does not ask where they are but takes off her knickers. We lie down on the big trestle table. She sits up, leans forward and cups her chin in the palm of one hand before lighting up a cigarette, exhaling blue smoke through her nostrils, spreading her naked thighs apart, well aware that I can see. She blows the smoke, and I am startled awake by the sound of the window being opened. I can see the moon from where I am on the palliasse. The lad who pretended to be wanking is standing by the window. I get up and also go over. I don't know what he is called, but in the moonlight his face looks like that of a clown covered in flour. A policeman is strolling in the snow at the front entrance, hands in the pockets of his cape, the collar turned up.

It has to be at least ten below freezing, says the boy. Do you reckon the grub round here is edible? I reckon it's uneatable. I don't answer, instead I go back to bed, break off two squares from the bar of chocolate hidden in my haversack and give one to him. I can't do a swap. I've got nothing. Take it, I say, let's try to get some sleep.

Perhaps it wasn't snowing; perhaps the moonlight was not that intense.

The sad clown's face.

As I recall, I said to Mother when I took over the letters from her, at six o'clock the next morning there was a pounding on the door to the room.

Six o'clock in the morning. They are banging with fists on the doors along the corridors of the Red Cross home on Mihály Munkácsy Street. The room seniors are holding a meeting. Now then, lads, the older Riegler returns to the room, the brothers are waiting for us, next it's either the ghetto or the banks of the Danube.

Seated on our palliasses, we pack our haversacks. We are given five minutes. I am practised in doing that by now. A gendarme on the landing of the staircase is issuing orders. The girls are sent off from the second floor. I stand on tiptoe but cannot spot Vera. The supervisors have put on Red Cross armbands. The Arrow Crossers shove them, too, among us.

We line up in threes facing Délibáb Street. I discover Vera is standing fifteen to twenty metres in front of me. She has Judy holding her left hand and in her right hand is the little case, with Edo hanging on to the handle of that. Vera is wearing a shawl under her beret to keep her ears warm.

Gizi rushes out of the building. She is wearing a Red Cross armband and a man with a submachine gun pushes her into the line. Gizi loudly demands to speak to the commanding officer. Another Arrow Crosser comes over. Gizi shows him her papers, and she is led to the front of the line. A regular army second lieutenant lets her return to the building.

The Arrow Crossers split us up into three groups. Vera and the two children are in the second group; I am in the third. At the head of each group are two men with submachine guns. Gendarmes form the rearguard. Gizi reappears and confers with the second lieutenant. As she passes by I call out her name sotto voce. Try to be patient she whispers back, even when the order is given to march off. Tell the others; try to be patient. Riegler snorts with laughter. And what if your arse is getting shot at? Are you still supposed to try to be patient?

Several of the supervisors step out of line and gather with the group of infants and girls to discuss things with Gizi.

The first group is sent off. Bayonets are set on the rifles, right hands on the stocks of submachine guns. Commands ring out with the second group. Vera is hidden from view by taller girls. A black Packard turns in off Andrássy Avenue. It brakes. I have already seen the bespectacled man who gets out of the car, the woman who is with him, too.

Gizi runs towards the car.

A lieutenant-colonel has also arrived in the car. He orders the regular army second lieutenant over. The lieutenant stands to attention in front of him and says he must execute the order given by a superior officer. Two Arrow Crossers step up and point their submachine guns at the lieutenant-colonel. The woman produces a camera, and one of the machine gunners yanks it out of her hands. The bespectacled man displays his identity papers. The lieutenant-colonel says that he has just come from the Ministry for Foreign Affairs, the higher order is valid. Individuals of all military marks are obliged to discharge diplomatic agreements. He rips the camera out of the hands of the Arrow Crosser with the submachine gun and hands it back to the woman.

The lieutenant salutes. The woman takes the photograph. She tells Gizi to stand in front, darling, let me have at last have a picture of you. Gizi does not move. The woman takes a photograph of her where she is standing. Maybe I also got into the frame.

We troop back in threes. The first group could not be caught up with. A man with a Red Cross armband runs up; they have already been marched through the ghetto's wooden gate, he says.

Leader of the nation Szálasi takes cognisance of the International Committee of the Red Cross's memorandum on the protection to be accorded to Jewish children's homes and other Jewish charitable institutions only to the extent that they are able to continue their operations within the ghetto.

The Packard sets off with Gizi sitting in the car. In the vestibule the man who brought the news that the first group could no longer be reached comes over to me. He inspects the duffel coat. Are you the one who lent the windcheater to Soproni? He asked me to pass on the message that he's sorry but it won't be possible to swap back for the time being. But this is too big for me, and it's heavy. I can see that, but he can't do it. Why not? There is an assertive edge to my voice. Look, kiddo, he was taking part in an action, and first of all they need to extract a bullet from him and wash off the blood from the windcheater.

Frau Lutz was a decent stick, Gizi reckoned, said Mother, only she took to the bottle a bit more than she should, but then Gizi herself hit the bottle quite often. By then it must have become clear that she was not going to find Bőzsi, but she still asked around when she came in every other day to visit us in the hospital.

We go back to our rooms. Vera waves from the bend in the corridor, holding on to Judy with the other hand.

Carl Lutz tries again to establish contact with Berne. He then looks for Friedrich Born, the authorized representative of the ICRC but does not find him in his office. In one of the rooms that is used as a darkroom Gertrud herself develops the roll of film she took of the Arrow Cross assignment. She pins up the new series of shots next to the pictures that are already on the wall.

In the first picture Gizi is to be seen with, behind her, the two Arrow Crossers with submachine guns who were on duty at the entrance to the Red Cross home on Mihály Munkácsy Street. In the next shot Gizi is standing next to three boys in the column which is ready to set off. The boys are around fourteen or fifteen years old; one of them is wearing a conspicuously long overcoat. This was the first time Gertrud had seen a coat decorated with that sort of braiding.

On a loggia of the building opposite the children's home an elderly women is leaning over. She has a bread roll in one hand and is taking a bite out of it.

Gertrud also took pictures when she was in the Packard as it was driven towards the embassy on Szabadság Square. In this next series are bombed-out buildings. The Arrow Cross sentries in front of number 60 Andrássy Avenue. A group of children wearing yellow stars in Hitler Place.[5] A boy on a bicycle next to the column. He cannot be more than fourteen. He is wearing the uniform of one of the cadet schools: green collar patch without any insignia of rank, something like an officer's cap with two brass buttons. Gertrud took the shot when he was passing them, keeping his eye on the car with diplomatic number plates. She gazes at the boy pinned up on the wall. The cap has slipped down to his left eyebrow; stern; there is an expression on the face.

That day the front line reached Gödöllő, just to the north-east of Pest. The battalion of troops that was left from the routed Hungarian 18th and 10th infantry divisions were pulled into the German formations. Somewhat further east a large part of the badly trained reserves deserts at the village of Tápiósgyörgy on 12 December. To replace them two thousand Arrow Cross volunteers. Colonel Pál Prónay, a hussar who formed a company of officers during the White Terror in 1919, prepares the force for deployment. László Vannay, who had also been in the officers' company in 1919, organized a battalion formed mostly of youths between the ages of fifteen and eighteen and using drill sergeants from the SS 22nd Cavalry Division. On the same day that Gertrud had a prolonged view of the cadet-school cyclist, Vannay's detail murdered several dozen people in the cellars of the Toldy Gymnasium in Buda and by the bank of the Danube, executing army deserters and Soviet soldiers who had been taken prisoner. Ferenc Szálasi bestowed the rank of major on Vannay, who made good the losses in his battalion by staging round-ups in cellars, thrusting rifles into the hands of anyone considered able to fight and, without training, pitching them straight into active service.

'Ervin Gálantay, volunteer dispatch rider for the Vannay battalion, as a pupil at the Kőszeg cadet school' – a photograph signed Krisztián Ungváry on page 91 of a book entitled *Budapest ostroma* (*The Siege of Budapest*) published in 1998. Oval head, military cap pulled down to the right eyebrow. Stern expression on the face.

Carl Lutz comes out of the other room and views the photographs that have been pinned up on the wall. Most particularly that in which Lieutenant-Colonel Bagossy, who is accompanying him, is pointing his revolver at the lieutenant wearing the Arrow Cross armband. I can't make Bagossy out, says Carl Lutz. He's a wild beast. He imagined that the secrets within the pictures were beyond his knowledge. Lutz takes photographs in order to capture things that other people would not discover; Gertrud likewise. Could it be there is something to be discovered in the picture but not what he had thought? Many of the details are for him unidentifiable, even though he thought he had remembered everything. The looks, the place, the weather . . . Apparently not . . . He tries to conjure up his earlier self on earlier pictures, in which he, too, can be seen. Everything can be seen, yet it's still as if something were missing. Two weeks earlier he had taken a picture of the entrance to the Foreign Ministry in Berne. He had felt like taking a few photographs of the city; he had sought something in the entrance to the building, but he only now woke up to what that was while looking at the photographs pinned up on the wall. In the Foreign Ministry the response to all of his questions was that they had received his reports and collated them, whereas the truth was they had kept quiet about them and let them rot at the bottom of desk drawers.

Gertrud pours herself a glass of cognac. She does not pour one for Carl Lutz. She is surprised that he asks for one.

You were also not fond of the Jews in Palestine, says Gertrud. They are all lying. Lutz reconstructs years later what he replies to this. Who? In Berne, of course, everybody in the Foreign Ministry. Of course, Gertrud said, he is later to write. Yet it was with them that you wanted to make a career, you do now as well . . .

Lutz puts down the full glass of cognac on the table. Gertrud turns away. Maybe she thought, Lutz writes later, that she ought not to have said what she said.

All he says by way of a response to his wife is that it was a happy chance coming across Feine in Palestine.

But you didn't tell me everything you knew even then, did you, darling, any more than you are doing now.

No, I didn't.

Do you think that is proper?

It's an official secret.

Also what you learned from Feine . . .

He made me swear not to tell . . .

They all lie, so it doesn't matter if he made you swear.

With that I just spread my arms, Lutz was to write.

He goes back into the other room.

I also did not tell you that his parting words were, You cannot understand, Carl, that we know what the future will be. It just hasn't happened yet.

Gertrud is sitting in one of the armchairs waggling a foot in small circles. She breathes in deeply, pulling in and tensing her abdominal muscles. She twists her head, gets up, fills the coffee percolator, lights the gas flame under it. The water comes to the boil three times in the flask. She cautiously opens the door to the other room. Lutz has already fallen asleep on the double bed in the office that had not long ago been converted into a sleeping place. The standard lamp had not been switched off, which was unusual. The light of a lamp on the small round table. A file lay on the table – orange with a green cord to fasten it. The knot was undone, and the file was open.

Gertrud had not seen the orange file before. There was no question that her husband had readied it for her. She switches off the standard lamp and goes back into the office.

It was 11.35 in the evening.

At the top were Carl Lutz's notes. He had written the first in Budapest.

On 30 July 1942 Dr Jezler had reported in top-secret code to the central security authorities the atrocious events in the east that had been the product of the decisions reached at the Wannsee Conference. The reaction of the centre in Berne: the mutual mudslinging should be treated critically.

Gertrud lights up a cigarette. Who is this Dr Jezler? What is this mutual mudslinging?

Why do they not take minutes of sessions of the Federal Council? Lutz writes on the following page. Do they not want the Swiss population to learn about what they themselves already know?

Photostats: 'In France children are brutally separated from their parents. We were eyewitnesses to scenes which reawaken memories of the massacres in Bethlehem. All the signs are that there is a single main goal: the total annihilation of Jewry.' From the 27 August 1942 issue of the *Schweizerische Kirchenzeitung* of Lucerne.

In October 1942 National Councillor Albert Oeri appeals to the first session of the Swiss Assembly on Refugee Affairs: 'It is not possible to make everything we know public. I am able to state, however, that what awaits those who are caught at our borders while trying to escape is far worse than death.'

In Vilnius 60,000 Jews have been slaughtered, reports a Swiss newspaper in February 1943.

In March 1943 the Work Relief Society of Zürich draws attention to the fact that every refusal of entry at the border is, in practice, tantamount to a death sentence.

On 27 July 1943 it is reported in one of the synagogues in Zürich that hundreds of thousands of families have been exterminated.

Gertrud can hear bursts of submachine-gun fire from the street.

It is five past midnight.

Instruction of 29 December 1942 by Dr Heinrich Rothmund, head of the Swiss Central Police Bodies, to border units: 'All possible care must be taken that refugees who are to be refused are not allowed to come into telephone contact with anybody, whether directly or through intermediaries.'

Gertrud would like to have another cognac, but she senses that she would be sick.

She takes a drink.

She does not vomit.

When I returned to Berne last week I upbraided them for everything, writes Lutz.

Gertrud can see from the date that the note was written two weeks before. They nodded, he writes, then started to talk about other things.

Not only were they humiliating themselves but me as well; nevertheless, I do not regret making the trip. I can see more clearly the sin of which I have no part, but I might as well have had, and I must bear the shame of that. Yesterday I found in the library that the American Legation left here a copy of an English translation of *The Brothers Karamazov*. I have been reading it at night. Gertrud, thank goodness, sleeps very soundly. I read Alyosha's words: We are good, good . . . When did I last go to church?

Gertrud spits out some yellowish vomit on to the carpet and treads it in with the soles of her shoes.

Yesterday Friedrich Born handed over the German translation of the Auschwitz Protocol. I was told by him that on 7 April 1942 the camp's resistance organization smuggled out two young Slovak Jews, Walter Rosenberger and Alfred Wetzler, who adopted the pseudonyms of Rudolf Vrba and Josef Lanik. They presented evidence, plans of the camp and data about the mass killings and the use of Zyklon B, a hydrogen cyanide preparation. They had signalled that preparations were already under way to receive and destroy the Jews of Hungary. The Protocol took up thirty-eight pages and 1,130 typewritten lines in Hungarian. The camp's location, its equipment, the guard system, the methods by which selections were carried out for the condemned to be gassed were set forth.

The Protocol is being circulated in a restricted circle in Hungary, writes Lutz.

I am given a copy in June. To the best of my knowledge Jewish organizations in Geneva received it at the same time and handed it on to the press; the press does not even communicate details. To the best of my knowledge the Vatican also received copies. In Hungary copies went to the papal nuncio, Angelo Rotta, to the Prince-Primate, Cardinal Jusztinián Serédi, to Bishop László Révész of the Reformed Church and to Regent Miklós Horthy.

The next bundle of papers is fastened with a large paper clip: a separate sheaf within the file.

Gertrud reads the top page then impatiently pulls off the clip so that she can turn the pages more easily. The movement causes the bundle to slip from her hands and – seemingly there is a draught in the room – the papers are blown around.

She gets up. First of all she wishes to establish which window or door could have opened, but she finds them all closed. She kneels down but feels giddy from making the movement. She clambers to her feet and sets off for the bathroom, not noticing that she is trampling on pages from the protocol. She washes her face with cold water. She thinks that perhaps her blood pressure has again dropped sharply, so she lies down on the bench for dirty linen and dangles her head down. She waits before going back to the room. She had read beforehand that the Auschwitz Protocol was thirty-eight pages long, but she does not dare bend down for the scattered pages for fear of another giddy spell. She slowly gets down on to her hands and knees and starts to collect the pages.

She has no notion of how long she had been reading, how long she spent in the bathroom or how long she has been collecting pages.

She goes to bring a jug of water but first gargles over the wash-basin, using a mouth wash and a Swiss toothpaste, then dabs a few drops of Givenchy scent on her temples before resuming her seat in the armchair. It's as if time were passing which is not her own but of which she is nevertheless a part. She is outside of this time yet unable to extricate herself from it; it is impossible to determine whether real time is the duration of reading or the time of what she is reading.

The prisoners' actual living quarters . . . inside the camp proper covers an area of approximately 500 by 300 metres, surrounded by a double row of concrete posts about 3 metres high, which are connected (both inside and outside) with one another by a dense netting of high-tension wires fixed into the posts by insulators. Between these two rows of posts, at intervals of 150 metres, there are 5-metre-high watchtowers equipped with machine guns and searchlights.

At 2.15 a.m. she reads:

Twice weekly, Mondays and Thursdays, the camp doctor indicated the number of prisoners who were to be gassed and then burned.

For ten minutes she attempts to add up the total of those who were to be gassed from the numbers of incoming transports that are detailed, and the number is so large that she is unable to cope with this, and around three o'clock she reads:

At the end of February 1943 a new modern crematorium and gassing plant was inaugurated at Birkenau. The gassing and burning of the bodies in the birch forest was discontinued, the whole job being taken over by the four specially built crematoria, with the ashes being used as before for fertilizer at the farm labour camp of Hermannsee.

A huge chimney rises from the furnace room around which are grouped nine furnaces, each having four openings. Each opening can take three normal corpses at once, and after an hour and a half the bodies are completely burned. This corresponds to a daily capacity of about 2,000 bodies. At the inauguration of the first crematorium prominent guests from Berlin were present. The 'programme' consisted of the gassing and burning of 8,000 Krakow Jews. The guests . . . were extremely satisfied with the results, and the special peephole fitted into the door of the gas chamber was in constant use. They were lavish in their praise of this newly erected installation.

While she is reading she becomes very conscious of the fact that, just a few months ago, 400,000 people from the country in the capital city of which she is now reading had come to this very fate; she reflects that those who were made to line up just a few metres away in the Óbuda Brickworks and who marched along the road through the hills of Buda had, in all certainty, met that same end. At around half past three she stops reading, tries to fasten the pages of the protocol together with the unusually large paper clip, puts it back in the file, during which process one sheet drops out – it so happens right on to the section of carpet that is slippery from vomit. She picks it up, carefully mops it with a handkerchief, closes the file, notices the still-full glass of cognac, reaches for it but does not raise it to her lips, although that had been the intention and does not understand why, if she wants a drink, the hand holding the glass does not move towards her lips and squeezes the glass so tightly that it breaks. So she hurls it at one of the pieces of furniture. After the noise has died away she does not dare turn round in case she were to come eye to eye with Carl Lutz.

One of the secretaries is standing in the doorway in her dressing-gown. Can I be of assistance, madam? she asks. No, it's nothing, says Gertrud. But your hand is bleeding, says the secretary and takes her to the washbasin, washes the hand that was cut by the shards of glass and bandages it with gauze. Gertrud gives her a kiss on the cheek and sends her back to bed, clutches the file and enters the office that is now being used as a bedroom. She switches on the standard lamp. Carl Lutz is lying there with his eyes open. Gertrud can see that he sees her putting the file back on the small table. Like a corpse, the thought runs through her mind. She switches the lamp off, takes off her dressing-gown and puts on a nightdress on top of her underwear before snuggling up to Lutz under the shared blanket. She feels closer to the man than she has ever felt before. She would like to embrace him but suspects that he would not welcome that, even if he knew that she did not want to make love.

They awaken at half past six and make breakfast together in the bedsitter kitchen.

They do no talk.

They walk to the sleeping area together.

Gertrud puts the file that was left on the small table into the bottom drawer of Carl Lutz's desk.

Mother shows me the shot in which Gizi can be seen in Mihály Munkácsy Street. She told me, Mother says, that another one was also taken of her, but she would give me this one because you are in it, too, there at the end of the row.

Also visible behind those who have lined up, on the loggia of the house opposite, is the woman who is biting into her roll.

VI

The post brings two photographs with no letter enclosed and no sender's name on the envelope.

In one of my truly old files I find a few lines about a time I visited Luca Wallesz in 1976, and there was a young girl there:

> She hopes to be able to learn from me something about what happened to her family in 1944. According to Luca, my mother and grandmother were taken in together to the brickworks on the same day as her mother, to whom I apparently spoke, advising her to join the same line of people over sixty and under sixteen years old that I was standing in. According to Luca, a woman friend of the girl's mother was also with them, and later the girl's mother married the fiancé of the by-then-dead woman friend, but in the late fifties they had parted . . . I have forgotten the girl's name, and anyway Luca asked me to keep it strictly confidential . . .

I had forgotten all about that note. The file had slipped behind the accumulation of other files and had become crumpled. It did not come to mind when that teacher had followed me, not even when she said that we had left Luca's together.

Maybe I did have a tendency, let me put it like this, in the recesses of my self, to take refuge from things that Luca said, although I am certainly not the sort of person who wishes to endorse the wiping of memories.

I was always ashamed whenever anyone gave me to understand that they would like to forget certain events, while I assured them that I understood.

I was ashamed even when anyone gave me to understand that they were unable to free themselves of the memory of certain events, and I assured them that I understood.

The teacher speaks softly – not timidly or even cautiously. It's rather as if her declarative sentences were to come out as interrogatives. I sense an edge of hopefulness in her voice, notwithstanding the fact that her words seem to be building protective walls. She does not wish to let the person with whom she is talking get close to her yet she is ready to supply answers to inquisitive questions.

When did I feel that way about her voice? During that first encounter? When we got off the number 1 tram together?

Will it be possible for me, with the assistance of the voice that I conjure, to get to the roots of the story about which she would have liked to interrogate me?

I put Schubert's *String Quintet in C Major* on the record-player.

Ever since I learned from Carl Lutz's diary that he felt a sense of infinity in its sound I always listen to it when I reach a hairpin bend while working.

I place a telephone call to the Zsuzsa Kossuth Health Gymnasium and ask what the surname is of one of their teachers with a given name of Györgyi. I am put through to the head. I start by clarifying the reasons for my request. I make a note of the address in Abonyi Street, look up the telephone number in the phonebook then dial.

Is it she who picks up the receiver?

Do I hear a man's voice?

At least it becomes clear she has a husband or partner; I am bound to admit that I am curious.

She herself wanted to call, she says. She wanted to ask if I had received the two photographs. I thought it was you, I want to say, but she does not permit me to respond. You know, she cuts in, sometimes he does not even come to mind. How did she recognize me in front of the school, remember me from more than twenty years before, I ask. It's such so long a time as all that, she says. Do you really think it's been such a long time? Really, when you stood there, by the memorial column, it all started over again. What do you mean by 'all'? I ask. Well, that I really ought to know everything; that's why I sent the two pictures, on the off-chance. What off-chance? I ask. So why did you not even add a sender's name on the envelope? She has no answer to that, and I also run out of things to say. I listen to the silence. Neither of us wanted to spell out what we were actually talking about; perhaps it's precisely on that account that it is clear to me what she may be thinking, and I sense that for her, too, it is clear what I am thinking.

I have a few questions about the photographs, I finally say. Fine, that's all right, she says, not mentioning that she ought to be accompanying her child to a special class, not mentioning that they are expecting guests. She just says, Half a mo', while she checks her schedule.

We agree on a time.

Where, though?

I say.

Oh, there . . .

I arrive at the Andrássy Hotel a quarter of an hour before the time we have agreed.

I walked across the City Park along roughly the path I took with Vera.

It is not December; there is no Aréna Road. It is late winter, and it is now named György Dózsa Avenue.

In my imagination I chalk a circle on the pavement of the corner of Mihály Munkácsy Street and Délibáb Street. That is where Soproni lay in my bloodied windcheater. Since we were able to return to the Red Cross home, I had slipped out with the supervisor, who had given me to understand that now it was all right for me to wear the ankle-length duffel coat, and he showed me where the two bullets had hit Soproni. I wonder if they had been taken out.

What had been the Red Cross home during the war is now the five-star Andrássy Hotel. On the façade I can make out only a few minor alterations; even the entrance is where it used to be. There was a time when the door that opened on to the hall was not a glass door. On the right is the reception; to the left a passage to the dining-room and coffee room.

Györgyi cannot imagine why I suggested we meet here. I shall not tell her straight away; I want to watch her face as she comes to discover the hotel's past.

A young man at reception greets me. I have to disclose why I wish to look about upstairs.

Which newspaper are you from?

He does not wait for an answer but introduces himself and tells me, without being asked, what his duties are, how long he has been working at the hotel; he asks that in my report, that is what he calls it, I should mention his name as it would assist him in his professional career, as he calls it.

The red carpet in the corridors is held down with brass rods. The wallpaper is cream-coloured. Hanging on the wall are reproductions of Impressionist paintings. I go up to the second floor with the young man courteously coming with me. The doors are where they used to be. I come to a stop at the second door to the left of the stairs. In response to a request from me the young man hurries off downstairs to fetch a door key. Fortunately it is not booked, he says; trade is only moderate, but by Christmas it will, with luck, be full.

Ash furniture. On the double bed is an azure silk coverlet; the curtains are cream-coloured with a pattern of a colour similar to that of the coverlet.

On the wall is a reproduction of a Klee painting. *The Playground.* I say, one of his most interesting arabesque traceries. The young man's expression changes. I think it's from the late twenties, he says. I take photographs, sir, and I also draw, although I'm probably not talented enough as I was not accepted for art school, but I'll try again next year.

There was a time when I happened to be staying here. I tell him. I'm not a newspaper reporter, I'm not writing an article, so I can't write your name in anything, I'm sorry to say. That's no matter, sir, I'm glad to hear that you stayed here. Klee is extraordinary, isn't he? I think you share that view; there are times when he leads me to make connections where I seem to identify something which lies beyond the picture.

I tell him that I have an old document which carries a signature, the lettering of which resembles the squiggles of arabesques that can be seen in the print.

Would that be some kind of work card?

I tell him that it is a forged identification document which was produced in this very room during the war. The stamp was brought out from a hiding place under the parquet flooring here, and this was where somebody wrote in a name that was not the real name . . . and that lettering was like the arabesques . . .

The houses opposite and the front gardens are as they were. The roadway is clear. I try to make out the spot where I stood in the column as it was about to set off.

On 18 December 1944 the ICRC moves the occupants of the Jewish boy's orphanage into the empty rooms. An agreement is reached with the commander of the 1st Battalion 13th Regiment Military Police that it will provide defence if that becomes necessary.

I was left alone in the room. My companion wanted to leave me to myself. I go down into the coffee room, draw up notes and order a Cabinet brandy.

I wait twenty minutes. A waitress then approaches me to ask what my name is; there is a telephone call for me at reception.

It's a madhouse here, says Györgyi. I'm dreadfully sorry, but one hour ago I was told that I would have to replace a colleague who has fallen sick and should have been on a study tour with one of the classes. The train leaves this evening for Germany, so right at the moment I don't know whether I'm coming or going, and I am packing right now. They knew that I have a valid passport. Madhouse, or what? I shall get in touch as soon as we arrive.

I order a coffee and ask the waitress if she could bring me a few sheets of writing paper. The request comes as a surprise, but she is accommodating. She comes back after a long delay, apologizing that she had to go up to the office to fetch the paper.

Above, on the second floor, is the former room from the window of which I would be able to see the section of the road where Vera lines up with Edo and Judy.

I write down that on one of the two photographs Györgyi sent me two sixteen-year-old girls are standing in the gate of a two-storey villa with a front garden. Each has an arm around the other's waist. One of them is fair-haired, slim, long-faced, freckled and is smiling; the other is dark, the hair shoulder-length, the face oval and with a serious expression. They are not familiar to me, but the house is – I don't know how, but I have a feeling that I once went there. It has big balconies and large corner windows, a wrought-iron garden gate, a house gate most likely of brown oak, with a glittering brass door handle clearly visible. There is a kennel in the front garden with an enormous watchful retriever.

The dog is my handhold.

For several weeks during the summer of 1944 I used to visit this house to play the accordion. Five minutes from number 74 Amerikai Road, the second building along from Erzsébet Királyné Road also in the XIVth District. That is where I learned 'Tango Bolero', which I had also played for Vera.

The message of the photograph is a renewed attempt by Györgyi to try to rescue something from a fading time. This opens the way for me to recall deeply buried memories, because recognition of the house located the two girls in front of the garden gate to the tram stop at the corner. A number 67 is approaching from Róna Street. I am coming from Amerikai Road, the two girls from the opposite direction. The number 67 has already set off from the stop at Uzsoki Street, and we take our places. I always get on by the back platform, they get on by the front platform, and we travel to St Domonkos Street, get off together at the church, me trailing behind and marvelling at them. I am thirteen; they are around sixteen. I enter the gates of the Boys' Gymnasium building as they proceed further to the Abonyi Street entrance of Girls' Gymnasium.

Sometimes I am able to find a seat on the tram, sometimes they do. They talk. After a while we exchange greetings. They usually converse in such a way that the slim, fair-haired freckled girl does most of the talking, and the serious-looking brunette nods. As if she were meanwhile thinking of something other than what they are speaking about and only stirring when the freckled girl laughs. The laughter is provocative, and the other girl looks around to see who heard it; I snatch my own gaze away so that she doesn't see I am looking at them.

I recognize them from the window in the corridor at school when there is a girls' handball match in the schoolyard for their PT class; they are in the same team. The freckled girl is the nimbler and has a more powerful throw; the serious-looking girl draws her eyes together in seeking out her playing partner, and she passes the ball accurately. Quite a lot of my classmates are standing by the window when one of the players in the opposing team hits the fair-haired freckled girl below the stomach, and one boy says that for her that must have felt as if she were being screwed. You dopey twit, says another classmate, that's quite a different feeling; it hurts her in exactly the same way as it would you if a ball accidentally hit you in the same place.

She has to stretch out on the ground. Her friend runs across, bends over her, massages the spot and makes her exercise.

The next day the boy who had been ticked off arrives panting to report that he has found a hole in the wall of the shower room next to the gym hall. He had stacked one jumping board on to another and stood on those, and the fair-haired freckled girl and the serious-looking brunette were in there naked, scrubbing each other's backs, and when they turned their behinds had been touching. Get lost, says the other classmate, who had reproved him the previous day. Your arse would touch mine if there were a number of us taking showers.

I order a second glass of cognac. If Györgyi has set me off on a track she will have to deal with the consequences, although every-thing had made me unsure of myself; the bodies of the two girls under the shower, in a tight space, squeezed against one another. Ági, the freckled girl, liked to run cold water immediately after the hot. Klári opens the door. The aisle is empty. She pulls a towel off the bench she had put there previously and begins to rub herself dry. Her skin is flushed from the change of temperature, and unexpectedly she starts whispering about her boyfriend. Both dry themselves. Ági, prompted by an urge incomprehensible to Klári, spreads her arms. They have often taken a shower together, even compared breasts, but Klári still feels Ági's body has changed, and she does not understand why Ági is looking so intently at her breasts. Both feel embarrassed and would rather not look one another in the eye, but they are driven by some unknown feeling. Ági speaks, and her breast swells. It happened yesterday evening, she says. What? Klári asks, even though she has no doubt what happened. You know – *that*, Ági whispers, with Miklós. But where? At his place. They had never used the kinds of words by which some of the other girls in the class liked pro-vocatively to speak about it, so it had always been *that*. Ági stretches, her breasts quiver. Klári pats her hair and kisses her shoulder and both giggle.

All the people from yellow-star houses in the XIVth District were assembled at the KISOK football ground. Maybe Ági, too, as well as Klári's mother and grandmother had been sent to the brickworks in the same column as us, but, being over sixteen and the grandmother nowhere near sixty, in which batch had they been dispatched towards Hegyeshalom? Luca even told me that Klári had seen when Ági and her mother lined up in the group headed for the gas chamber and had run after them, but a German kicked her back. I had seen photographs of skeleton-thin naked bodies queuing up and setting off for the whitewashed rectangular buildings between armed men and dogs; maybe that was why I had suppressed in myself what Luca told me about it, the reason she was recounting it to me. But now I have to make an effort to see through Klári's eyes the shaven heads and napes of the neck and then later recall the nape of Ági's neck, the nape of her mother's neck, the spectacle of the two chimneys of the crematorium. It's rather as if the roll of film had been exposed to light: they vanish, but the memory of the necks, the armed men and the dogs remains. The picture may be of even poorer quality with the passage of years, but there are times when everything is sharply visible, usually while dreaming. And, on waking, the Christmas tree on the Appellplatz, the soldiers are kicking two escapees. The gallows have been erected next to the Christmas tree, and everyone is driven out of the barracks. While the hanging is in progress the candles are lit on the tree. Ági's body was as filthy and smelly as her own; she did not want to smell her mother's body. The stools are kicked away from under the legs of those on the gallows.

I go to the toilet.

On my return I ask for fresh sheets of paper from the waitress. She rushes off, no doubt again to the office, but this time she returns more speedily, and later I give her a double tip.

On the back of the two pictures Györgyi sent are captions. On the first is 'Klári and Ági in 1943'; on the second 'Mother and Father in 1945, not yet married'.

The setting of the second picture is easily identified as the terrace by the lake in the City Park. In the background is the flight of steps in front of the Műcsarnok, the Art Gallery, and the person taking the photograph must have had their back to the lake. One can readily discern a chequered tablecloth and two glasses of beer. Klári has quite short hair; not long before she would have still had a shaved head was my first thought on seeing the picture. Her face is angular, not oval as in the other picture. The shape of the chin is also changed, having slipped forwards and become more pointed. She has thrown herself back on the seat as if she wants to keep herself far away from the man sitting opposite her.

The man is tall and broad-shouldered. Short-sleeved shirt; taut arm muscles on display. He has a thick head of hair, dark and combed back with a wave at the front. The two are not looking into the lens of the camera nor at one another. I wonder who they asked to take the picture and, having asked that person, who they are not looking at, the camera or one another?

According to a note I made in the depths of one of my files, which has been hiding on the lowest shelf for nearly a quarter of a century, Luca said that Miklós was a very decent young man. Klári had brought him round once to meet her but that had been after they got married, maybe in 1956 or 1957.

In other words, something like ten years after the photograph was snapped.

'Miklós is tall, athletic, black hair, used to live on the corner of Kolumbusz Street and Erzsébet Királyné Road,' I noted. What I did not make a note of was that maybe around twenty-five years before I may have seen Miklós when we travelled together with the girls on a number 67 tram to the school because he was dating Ági at the time, so he would be bound to have known Klári as well. He must have known they were friends. He must have had a good idea that Ági had told her they had made love, even though both she and he had sworn that *that* would remain a secret. He must have had a good idea that Ági had shown Klári the letter he had sent when doing labour service at Bustyaháza, because on the cards he got in reply there was always written 'Klári sends greetings'.

How could he have known that they were taken away together on 15 November 1944, first to the KISOK football ground then the Óbuda Brickworks? At that time he himself was being marched somewhere near Kassa on the way to Germany.

Forty kilometres a day.

The dead and dying in ditches at the roadside.

Luca told me a number of things about Miklós – not at times Györgyi had been present, perhaps later. She needed to talk to someone about things that had suddenly come to mind.

Years after that photograph of the two of them on the terrace at the lake had been taken, Klári asks Luca if she thinks it would be permissible for her to marry Miklós. All Luca says is that she had read – in my own notes that had been dug out to prepare for the meeting with Györgyi – that it was OK. This has very little relevance nearly quarter of a century after that note was made, I wrote a few days ago in fibre-tip pen next to my old note.

That was probably an error on my part.

From what I am trying to put together from the shards of the mosaic, one may presume the man and woman in the photograph do not just *happen* to be looking mutely at the same indeterminate point, where they see the same thing, but presumably they keep quiet about it because they had already discovered what, on studying their faces a half-century later, I would call an acquiescence to incommunicability. One cannot read from the looks that that man would for years attempt to carry off the unspeakable spectacle and moreover that the woman knows this. And she also knows it when they embrace one another as a married couple and even at night she is unable to free herself from wondering whether the man, now her husband, made love just as vigorously with Ági. The spectacle of the shaven napes of both Ági and her mother still looms before her, and the man senses something of that; he is acquainted with what it is like to take silent leave of someone who has started on the death march. He carries on hugging his wife and meanwhile sees in his mind's eye a pair of dead eyeballs. He is also familiar with the laborious process of straightening out a body with rigor mortis. On the farmstead near Kassa, while the front line sweeps over, he looks for a spade so he can dig a grave for his friend who has died of dysentery, but all he can find is a crowbar with which he spends a day scraping out a shallow pit then gathers a few handfuls of earth to sprinkle over the corpse.

For years after the first meeting, which is preserved by the photograph, Klári had no wish to meet Miklós again, nor he to meet her. Later Klári asks Luca whether it would be all right to marry Miklós.

She dare not ask her husband while they are lying with fingers clasped whether he had lain the same way with Ági; from the man's silence she senses it was just the same. Had Ági also wanted to make love again as quickly as she did, and had he done so with her just as he had with Ági? That is something they never speak about. Klári stifles the question that is about to slip from her lips. Miklós senses what she must be thinking and is grateful that she says nothing, and nine months after this evening Györgyi is born. When Klári and Györgyi are wheeled out of the labour ward and Miklós bends over them their shared thought is that they have avenged themselves for everything by giving life to their daughter, and the fact that this is what they think about in the hospital corridor also means that, although both of them are well aware it is not a 'normal state' (they speak about it later in just those words), they are unable to suppress it, but still it is better not to keep on torturing one another with it.

Klári could not have claimed that the reason she was unable to discuss what happened in the camp with Györgyi was because she would then have had to say why her father and she could not stay together – or rather, the reason she could not speak about why they had been unable to stay together was because then she would have to speak about what happened in the camp.

She did not want to talk about dreams.

I thank the waitress for her assistance and leave her 300 forints as a tip.

This story is like good literature, I note down, full of doubts and uncertainties. I have lived the greater part of the years of my existence, and I can see that the reason I have devoted my life to writing is that I am trying to counter transience. I have to see things with the eyes of many in order that my own should remain sharp.

At reception the young man comes to meet me. He gives me two photographs. One is a shot he took of the second-floor room, the other from the window. He says he noticed to which part of the street I was paying particular attention.

So quick?

I did say that I'm a photographer, sir. There is a handy room and equipment here.

I thank him and say nothing about the fact that everything in the pictures is bright and sunny, in contrast to my memories.

I stand for a while at the entrance.

Where could Györgyi have travelled to so unexpectedly?

I read the prices on the menu displayed next to the entrance.

On the wall is a marble plaque:

To the memory of Lajos Gidófalvy, 1901–1945, and men of the 1st Battalion 13th Regiment Military Police, saviours of the Jewish boys' orphanage which stood on this site under the International Committee of the Red Cross and on 24 December 1944 came under Arrow Cross attack.

Vera and I were no longer there by that time.

Three or four days after we had been lined up the Red Cross admitted a new group into the building. The Arrow Crossers and gendarmes came for them, too, on that Christmas Eve.

I read through the text on the plaque once again.

I set off along the route that our own procession had started along: Délibáb Street, Bajza Street then turn right along the Alley towards Lövölde Square and the city centre.

VII

At Lövölde Square I tell Vera that we'll skip off when we get the chance. Right now we are not required to run; we are not being forced so much as herded into the square. From time to time there is a shout of 'Close ranks!' as the column spreads out and the smaller ones become detached. Our escorts seem to be less vigilant, taking care only that those who cannot keep up and are left at the back do not get behind the two gendarmes who form the rearguard.

The third person in our line is the boy with the clown face. He has latched on to me ever since I gave him the square of chocolate.

In Lövölde Square I see no signs of interest in the looks of the passers-by watching us. They must have got used to seeing columns like ours. Clown-face does not have a knapsack nor a suitcase or satchel; he dangles a small bag in which there are handkerchiefs, a scarf and a pair of socks.

Vera, standing on tiptoe, tries to make out where Edo and Judy are. The smallest children are walking in a separate group in front of us; there must be about twenty of them, surrounded by carers with Red Cross armbands, some of them resting as they are carried in their arms. I spot Edo and Judy and wave to them.

Vera seems to be getting ever smaller and more pallid. I don't know where her beret is; maybe it's in her little suitcase. She has pulled the warm headscarf right down to her eyes – that is what is making her head look smaller.

Clown-face woke up every night and went to the window. The first time I got up and went over to him, but then I contented myself with watching from under my blanket. I have no idea why he stood by the window, nor do I know why I woke up each time he woke up.

Ack-ack guns in Lövölde Square. Barbed-wire obstacles have also been positioned, and children are jumping about around them. A squad of gunners to man the guns; a pile of bayonets and rifles. The soldiers allowed the children to throw snowballs at them, and one of the bigger boys can scramble on to one of the guns. The others would like to do the same, but the commanding officer, a sergeant, forbids that.

Clown-face steps out of line, seemingly just drifting, but he looks back at me and winks. He is swinging his bag as if his mother had sent him to do some shopping. By now he is by the pavement, behind the back of the Arrow Cross lance-corporal on the left flank. He needs to pass between two men at the edge of the pavement, but one of them catches him by the arm and calls out to the lance-corporal. The lance-corporal beckons to the gendarmes, and from now on he has to walk between them. He grins and pulls himself up straight, although even so he only reaches their shoulders, and the gendarmes occasionally jostle him.

The Riegler boys are two rows in front. The bigger one looks back as if to urge caution; he may have guessed what I am preparing to do. It is necessary to keep an eye not only on the armed men but also on those standing about on the pavement. I put an arm round Vera and try to help her straighten up and again stand on tiptoe. She says she can see her cousins among the little ones, but I don't think they can see us even though they have turned several times to look back. Edo is walking in the middle of the row; Judy has one hand being held by a Red Cross lady who is carrying a very small girl in her other arm.

We reach Rózsa Street. Then Izabella Street. A burst of noise. Riegler calls back to say that over there is the gate of the ghetto.

I stop after Hársfa Street, from where, to the best of my recollection, I caught a glimpse of the gate.

Vera's steps are more determined, which is encouraging; she will need to be self-reliant. Again I catch a warning look from Riegler. The column is bunching up; the armed men are directed to positions by their commanding officers; Clown-face is pushed by the gendarmes into the back row. A policeman is stationed next to our row on the right; before us and on the left is an Arrow Crosser with a submachine gun. We close up to the group of tots. Another group is now marching at the front of ours. We are so close to the Outer Circle that I can now see on the far side the huge entrance gate; the guards level their weapons at the approaching procession.

The officer at the front shouts out orders. We march. I clutch Vera's hand. Edo and Judy are now quite close, and Vera calls out their names. They look back, and Judy would like to stop but is not allowed.

I shall have to backtrack a lot in order to recapture the look on her face. A description acquires gravity if it allows something beyond what can be expressed or preserved to materialize in it. If I try to conjure up Judy's face to myself I need to move beyond the stretch between Király Street, Hársfa Street and the Outer Circle, where she turns round on hearing Vera's call, and go back to a summer afternoon in 1944 when, sitting on a pile of bricks in the yard of number 78 Amerikai Road – at the time littered with building materials – Vera and I first exchanged a kiss and instantly separated. Judy was tottering towards us from over by the spot where the sacks of cement were lying, clutching a pinwheel, the paper vanes of which the two of us had cut out with scissors, and our arms touched while we were pinning it to a sausage stick. Judy had raced with the vanes of the pinwheel spinning in the breeze, her cheeks flushed with delight. Vera had snatched her up and hugged her, then the two of them, hand in hand, had resumed running. Judy's delight, therefore, was part and parcel of the kiss and also of the thrill which went through me afterwards while they, laughing merrily, had raced around. It was decades later that Judy's face first appeared among my memories, bidden by another face, also that of a little girl, albeit a slightly older little girl, a face not unlike the close-up shots of the face of a young girl in Ingmar Bergman's film of *The Magic Flute* as she intently watches, happy and excited, conveying the changing moods of the music with which both Mozart and Bergman express a knowledge of *something* more than itself, of wonderment over the many aspects of life it is possible to know. I squeeze Vera's hand and watch the armed escort and so have to withdraw my attention from Judy. I have no choice, and I cannot be aware that it is for that reason her look becomes imprinted in my memory.

The first lieutenant marching at the head of the column reaches the other side of the Outer Circle and comes to a halt at the gate. The two gendarmes bringing up the rear were, at that point, near Hársfa Street. The children at the front had also crossed the Outer Circle by then. A number 6 tram was approaching from Wesselényi Street. The policeman who had been marching on the right-hand side hurried to the front, stopping where Király Street crosses the Outer Circle to take over directing the traffic. With a raised hand he warns pedestrians to halt. With the rails being slippery from slush the driver is unable to brake, so the policeman beckons that he should carry on, as, with the other hand, he bids the group of children in front of us to halt. The column is split in two.

It takes eight to ten seconds for the tram to rattle over the crossing, covering as it does so the figure of the first lieutenant on the far side of the Outer Circle and the policeman who is directing the traffic. Vera is still waving to Judy, and I am holding the other hand. I yank her after me and we step out of line.

I cannot see the Riegler brothers even past Hársfa Street.

I need to find a gap between the people standing on the pavement.

The air-raid siren starts up.

Suddenly everyone is running.

The tram had passed the crossing. The policeman directing the traffic snatches at his rifle. The pedestrians who had been standing on the pavement scatter. No one is paying any attention to us. By now we are on the pavement. We carry on towards Mussolini Square.[6] I get the feeling that a man in a fur coat was thinking of setting off after us.

I stop in the middle where Király Street crosses Erzsébet Outer Circle, waiting until the traffic signal has turned red and the traffic coming from Lövölde Square has come to a standstill. I bend down for a few seconds to chalk out in my mind the spot where we stepped out of the column fifty-eight years ago. I pass my hand over the paving stones. Several pedestrians stare at me. A student even tries to help me up. Thanks, I say. I'm fine. Another boy hoots with laughter, meanwhile the traffic light has changed and a car driver is honking at me. Behind me is the shop front of a KFC outlet, in front a branch of the K & H Bank of the Kredietbank of Belgium, to my right the violet lights of an erotic show.

I often alighted from a trolley bus here in the seventies. There used to be a coffee bar where I would drink a coffee standing up; there were always several women at the tables, and I later learned that I was drinking in a place that prostitutes used to use. Some of the women were well into their forties, but they still cut good figures. It may have been that those working in the erotic show were daughters of those women. During the war they could well have been much the same age as me, and it's not impossible their mothers had also been prostitutes. I have heard tell that there were a lot of men who had been called up for forced-labour service and deserters from the regular army who found a hideaway in the bordellos of Conti Street and Ó Street on the other side of Andrássy Avenue in the VIth District.

It is fourteen steps from here to number 5 Theresa Outer Circle. I look at the entrance and the stairs. I am not sure that this is where we came while the air-raid siren was sounding and everyone sought cover at a run. At number 7, though, everything is familiar: the entrance, round arch leading to the staircase, the wrought-iron banisters on the steps.

The man in a fur coat who has been keeping us under observation from the moment we stepped out of the column is coming after us. I do not fancy testing how well my ARP messenger papers will stand up. The gate to the house is open with whitewash arrows to indicate where the air-raid shelter is located. I wait until the man in the fur coat is caught up in the crowd before hastily moving further on.

The entrance to the next house is wide, and there are stairs leading in two directions. A man is shouting and directing women and children down towards the cellar while men stay there, sitting on the steps, so we edge our way in among them.

I want to stay near the exit.

Vera is freezing. Wiggle your toes! She can't, she replies. Everyone there is a stranger to one another, which is to our advantage as we do not seem conspicuous. Bomb blasts can be heard in the distance; the sound of ack-ack guns is closer. A woman is sitting next to me and asks where we live. Zugló, I say. Have the Russians got there yet? No, I say, not so far. I spot behind a column the man who followed us from Király Street. It's not a fur coat he s wearing but a hunting coat; his peaked cap is not an army one. He is setting off towards the man directing the flow of people, who is presumably the warden for the building.

Vera cannot grasp why I am pulling her after me, and I don't have time to explain. I shoulder two men out of the way, which prompts one of them to take my mother's name in vain. Once we reach the street I don't look back, and we reach Mussolini Square. The air-raid alarm is still sounding; others are hurrying, some running. There are two ack-ack batteries in the square. Commands are bellowed. There are some people gawping from the pavement as the cannons attempt to keep track of the aircraft as they swoop down and unload their bombs over the Western Railway Terminus not far away. We turn into Andrássy Avenue.

A woman is lying on the ground in front of one of the houses. She seems to have slipped in the snow, so we help her to her feet. Vera hands her back her shopping-bag, which contains about half a kilogram of potatoes and a few apples. We lead her under the nearest doorway. She expresses her gratitude as we take shelter next to her. We wait there until the siren sounds the all-clear, and the woman takes her leave. We are standing at the corner of Eötvös Street; further up and on the other side of the road we can see the Arrow Cross sentries in front of number 60 Andrássy Avenue. We can't go that way, I say; we can't go back in the direction we came from so let's head for Western Railway Terminus. Perhaps as an alternative we could go down the continuation of Eötvös Street to the right, but in two blocks that would bring us back to Király Street. With one hand Vera sweeps the snow off a bench at the corner and sits down. I tell her to get up, it's cold. Which way shall we go? I don't know, but get up, please. No, I shan't, she says and says it quietly. I'm not getting up, and I'm not going anywhere. I sit down beside her.

The bench which is standing on the pedestrian precinct in front of the post office on Eötvös Street nowadays cannot be the old bench. I go down to the Király Street end of Eötvös Street. Last year I bought a black hat in the corner shop, and I said to the hatter that for my fourteenth birthday I was given a brown boys' hat with a green band on it, since when I have never had one. They haven't made a line of boys' hats for a long time, he said.

In Király Street I try to find the exact spot from which I last glimpsed Judy's face, which would mean that she had accomplished her task inasmuch as it is the business of the dead to find their way to those who have remained alive.

The tiny place that Vera and I occupy on the bench is ours. It is snowing more heavily. I stand up and ask, but she does not move, so I start off. Yet even now she will not come, so I stop.

I ought to pin down the date. I try to find points of reference. Mother has kept three of my letters, and I put in a call to Mádi in Paris. I try to match up dates. Where can the lost traces be leading?

Back to Amerikai Road? Francia Road? Back to Mihály Munkácsy Street?

One of the letters bears a date from six days later.

We could not have sat on the bench on Andrássy Avenue for six days.

I go back to Vera and give her a hug. We set off.

We hear a burst of submachine-gun fire from number 60 Andrássy Avenue. An ack-ack gun behind us barks again; searchlights sweep the sky.

On 8 December Soviet troops reach the town of Vác on the Danube bend, some thirty kilometres to the north. By 9 December the north-eastern perimeter of Pest is being pounded. Father Kun's order to shoot a group who have been made to strip naked on the Pest bank of the Danube: 'In Christ' name – Fire!' Captain Imre Morlin of the Artillery deploys the fourteen–eighteen-year-old military cadets who have been placed under his command, and they are joined by young men from the Ludovika Military Academy: 'In accordance with your military-school training, every man will fight to the last bullet!' Plenipotentiary Veesenmayer receives instructions from Berlin that all possible assistance should be given to facilitate the harshest procedures against the Jews. On 12 December those possessing Swiss or Swedish safe-conduct letters who have been detained in custody up until then are set off in columns marching west towards Komárom. Lieutenant József Klima's unit breaks into the Divine Love Girls' Institution. The women and young girls who had been hiding there are loaded on to trucks waiting at the Buda foot of the cog-wheel railway, taken over the river to the Arrow Cross building in Újpest, then from there to the bank of the Danube where they are shot. On 14 December Anton Kilchmann, having left Carl Lutz as the sole Swiss representative, arrives in Berne. During a subsequent administrative juridical investigation on 31 August 1945 he rebukes Chief Justice Otto Kehrli that on his arrival there was nobody to debrief him; the Ministry of Foreign Affairs was completely indifferent to what was happening to its officials in Budapest. From 15 December onwards Arrow Cross patrols constantly circle Carl Lutz's office. That same day Pioneer Battalion 751 of the German regular army is deployed in battle.

I search for the words to help me to fill that void of six days in which I have lost my tracks. They may be somewhere in the blind spots of my memory but, sad to say, untraceable.

Vera never called me to account for leaving Edo and Judy on their own. She knew that before she could she would have had to call herself to account.

Vera was then three months past her twelfth birthday.

Dearest Father and Mother,

We are well! Misi was here and told us you are thinking we ought to gain admission to the Red Cross, which was granted an extension until the 22nd. We would rather stay where we are, as we don't want to have to plan any more escapes, seeing that it's already the 14th. If you are able, speak to Dr Temesváry, maybe we can join you at the hospital. Ask what the position is with Mihály Munkácsy Street! Don't worry, we're fine; we have food to eat. Misi said that you should not complete your registration forms but wait, because perhaps we can write in our actual home address soon! Write to say whether I should wait or should I send those too with Jolán Bors, as I'm right now expecting her to return. It would be good if she were to bring our registration forms; if you can get hold of papers without fail!!! We will be waiting here!!! For the time being we will not go there.

All my kisses.

Where could Misi have gone on 14 December? Where was it that we would rather have stayed than again having to avoid being herded into the ghetto? Did Misi bring registration forms for us? Then why was I asking to be sent some with Jolán Bors? It is quite certain, therefore, that we did not go back to Mihály Munkácsy Street.

I wrote that letter on a typewriter. Fourteen lines. Signed at the bottom with my name and Vera's in ink. The typewriter lettering is recognizably that of the Remington in the workshop; that was also the only place there would have been any ink. Also the letter is on printed stationery bearing the letterhead MANUFACTURER OF STATIONERY AND SPECIALITY PAPER BAGS, with the address and telephone number: Budapest XIV, 41 Francia Road. Tel.: 297-826.

I ought to ask Misi. I put in another call to Mádi in Paris. Good timing, she says; my brothers will be paying a visit this evening. Misi has no recollection of where he met me, but the next day he says he is sure he went to the Alice Weiss Hospital, where my parents and yours were, and he also went to Amerikai Road, but he is quite sure that he did not go to Francia Road.

Mother reads my letter, sitting on a mattress in the basement of the hospital. She has to screw up her eyes to read, her glasses having broken long ago. Jolán Bors is standing beside her. Father bends forward as he looks at Mother; he is also sitting on the mattress and has to bend close in order to hear what Mother is reading because a dying patent next to them is wheezing stertorously. Nurses are racing about between those lying on the mattresses on the ground. There are no bedpans, they are yelling, they are not able to set up infusions for anyone. The head physician, Dr Temesváry, arrives by way of the steps; he is podgy, and his white gown is tight on him. He pays a call to everyone in turn, assistants – two plump nurses – in trail. Mother folds my letter; in her knapsack is a small pocket, which is where she hides it next to the letter I sent from Mihály Munkácsy Street.

It never occurred to me what my parents thought about what would become of me when their column left the Óbuda Brickworks. What did they think about, I wonder, when the ambulance brought them to the hospital and they were lying among the dying? These are not the sorts of things one can ask about, in just the same way as they never asked me what I had thought about them when I was left on my own.

On 15 December Carl Lutz gets news that Giorgio Perlasca, passing himself off as the Spanish Consul-General, had taken part in the rescue work and called upon the papal nuncio, Angelo Rotta, to threaten Hungary's Arrow Cross government that diplomatic relations would be broken off if they did not abandon the mass murder. I cannot do that without instructions from the Vatican, he says.

Rákóczi Square, in the VIIIth District just off the main ring of the Outer Circle, is covered in litter. It is February, and the temperature is 5 degrees below freezing; the time is eight o'clock in the evening. I set off from the square down Miksa Déri Street. The entrances to the houses are barricaded behind dustbins. The reek of refuse and rust is pervasive. At the end of the block, at the junction with Víg Street, a man in a jacket is in discussion with a whore. Greasy locks of greying hair sprout from under his ski cap; the whore's look is sympathetic. That was a long time ago, the man is saying, and the whore, seemingly remembering what was a long time ago, is nodding. Of course, it is possible that she is not a whore; maybe they are not holding a discussion, and it could be pure chance which has brought them together at this junction after decades. They are stamping their feet to keep warm; my feet are also cold, and the slush is splashing on to my trousers. On Nagyfuvaros Street, a few streets further on, a bus is in service and cars are being parked, yet, despite this being the city centre, it has the feeling of an outlying part of the world, a world of basements, a world of cellars.

I step into a house doorway. Six overflowing dustbins and enough rubbish all around them to fill a seventh. A child darts out of the stairwell and slips on the rubbish. Two young Roma men in their twenties come out wearing shabby but clean Adidas jackets. They wish me good evening and ask if they can be of any help. I tell them I'm just looking; there was a time when I lived around here. They would be glad to help, the taller man says. I thank them, but I can see that they are disappointed that I rejected their offer. They have sad looks on their faces. Come on, the taller one says, let's get going.

The yard is tidier than the doorway. Three floors of outside corridors, gaps in the plaster. On the right is an unlit stairwell. Opposite is the back staircase, which in days past would have been used by servant girls, porters and postmen. The third floor has a vaulted passage, only the passage leads nowhere; all that can be seen is sky.

I note down the number of rubbish bins, the flight of stairs which leads nowhere, the grilled basement windows.

Nothing at all about the building seems to have changed over the past fifty-eight years.

We have to go up to the second floor. Vera stops at the landing on the first floor. It's a good thing we are wearing two pullovers under our overcoats; it would have been even better if we could have had two pairs of hiking socks to put in our boots. It must be 10 degrees below. We keep beating our palms together.

On the second floor one has to knock on the door as the bell is not working. The stairwell is unlit, as is the apartment that we enter. We have to pass through two rooms in both of which are six iron bedsteads with another six fitted on top of them, all empty. In the third room a woman is sitting next to a standard lamp with a green lampshade. A man in a black hat and a scruffy raincoat is standing next to her. They introduce themselves, and the man moves to shake hands. He says he runs the home, and we must obey his instructions; there are times when these will be orders, he says; that is unavoidable. There are no girls here, he says to Vera; you will sleep with my wife. It's best you go through next door straight away. The woman drags one leg. She leads Vera away.

They asked what we are called, nothing else. The boys are downstairs in the cellar, says the man. Everyone went down when an air-raid warning is in progress. The all-clear has already been given, I say. He did not hear it. Anyway it was better if they stayed in the cellar, he says; you'll see what I mean when they come up. He points to one of the upper beds. I clamber up. Don't unpack your haversack, he says. Why not? Are you parents still living? Yes. His parents are no longer alive. Can we stay here? Anyone will be able to get a place here as long as he and his wife are here. And how long will you be here? That I don't know, he says.

The boys come up from the cellar, ten or a dozen of them. They are different from the ones I was with at Munkácsy Mihály Street, although it could be that the only reason I see it that way is that there is just a single candle to light the room, so I see their shadows rather than them. One of the boys is such a beanpole that when he is standing by my bed his head was above my palliasse. Empty it, he says. Why? Shut it! Just empty it out! I lie back and try to stuff my haversack under the blanket. He reaches for it, socks me on the jaw and snatches the haversack from under the blanket. I turn round and as I do so kick his head. That was not my intention, but I don't regret it. He falls on his back. He picks himself up and yanks me off the bed. You're best advised to clear your bloody haversack, one of the boys says. I can't see their faces in the dark; the candle has almost burned out. He twists one arm behind my back and pushes the haversack into my free hand. Tip it out here. His is the lower bed. I raise the haversack, turn it upside down and shake it. When all my things are on his blanket he says put them back, one item at a time. Let go of my arm, I say. He does not let it go but does loosen his grip. I pack everything back. When I reach the shell he says leave that on the bed. The head of the home brings a new candle and lights it. I reach for the shell, but the boy is quicker. That's mine, I say. What can it do to make it so important to you? It doesn't matter, I say. It's up to me to say what matters and what doesn't. It carries voices, I say. What voices? Those of my parents, my parents' friends, including what we are saying right now. There you are, that's exactly the sort of thing I needed. But it's mine. I need it, he says, again reaching for my arm. I let fly at his face with an elbow. He staggers against the bed. I snatch hold of the shell and step to the side. His punch hits me on the shoulder; I put the shell down on the bed so I have both hands free to defend myself.

The head of the home left the room with the candle guttering in the draught, which allowed me to observe the boy's face. He was as tall as I had thought and older than me, although perhaps only by a year, maybe not even that. I saw no anger on his face; I am surprised that I seem to see sadness or, rather, obstinacy. He throws a fresh punch, but that, too, seems to lack passion but is powerful none the less. I duck away, just as he ducks away from my punch. I do not leap at him as yet, although I sense that this will be the next move. I can see that he has it in mind to leap on me. Arms hold me back; him, too. I wrest myself from the hold, as does he. A stick whistles down between us, not touching either of us, rather as if a sword blade had slashed in two the few centimetres that separate us; we do not cling to each other, but now I scent his sweat more strongly, although maybe it is my own body odour. My arm is twisted behind me; his, too.

The head of the home is standing near the candle.

He shoves us in front of two men; they say nothing, neither does the head of the home.

I return to the bed and again start packing my things back into my rucksack.

One of the men picks up the stick which had whistled down between us. The stick is white. The other boys are sitting on their beds. I don't know where the two men came from. One is wearing a raincoat, the other a frayed black winter topcoat. The head of the home says to the raincoated man that they should play something; all the gentlemen here appreciate music. One boy in the corner guffaws. The raincoated man leaves the room and comes back with a fiddle, plucking the strings. I do not climb on to the top bunk but sit on the lower one. The lanky boy takes a seat next to me.

The head of the home snuffs the candle's flame between two moistened fingers and leaves the room. I ask Beanpole why, of all things, he needed my shell. He does not answer. I ask him how he got to the home, but he does not answer. I ought to clamber on to the top bunk and try to get some sleep.

Beanpole had been in the Kolumbusz Street home in the XIVth District. He tells me that after we have been sitting on the bed for ten minutes. That time the Kolumbusz Street home was fired on I could hear from number 76 Amerikai Road, I say. That was us, old chap, although I didn't come from there but from Józsefváros Station. In Kolumbusz Street the camp leader was shot, the camp physician was also shot and the young and elderly were hauled off to the ghetto, whereas I was taken with the other physically fit men to the goods yard.

I ask how he managed to get away. It was dark; the Arrow Crossers and soldiers could barely see anything. They would fire off a burst every five minutes so that everyone would shit themselves, but after the fourth burst I knew when the fifth would be coming, so I had a few minutes to do a bunk.

There was a shell like it on my father's writing desk, he says. My father was the camp doctor on Kolumbusz Street. I can give you the shell if you want, I say. Give over, he says. It's not even mine, actually, but belongs to a friend of my father's; I'm going to give it back. When will that be? I ask him whether he has heard anything about being sent from here to the ghetto. No, doesn't know anything. Do you reckon the head of the home knows? The rabbi, you mean? I didn't know he is a rabbi; it's Friday evening, but I haven't seen him praying. He doesn't pray, he says. What about you? I don't pray. But you said he's a rabbi. I asked him, he says, and he replied that he doesn't pray; he has looked up at the sky and saw it was empty – there's nobody to pray to. Good, huh? Got you, I say. He used to have a long beard, he says, but he cut it off with scissors as he doesn't own a razor. He said it was for health reasons, but I don't reckon that was the real reason.

Your father was the doctor at the Kolumbusz Street camp? Let's get some sleep, he says. I'm freezing, I say. Take your blanket down from the upper bunk and lie down next to me, he says. You won't freeze so much under two blankets. Who is the girl? he asks once I am lying down next to him. You saw her? I saw her. She's a cousin. That's crap! Cousins don't behave that way. Well, she's called Vera. Vera? That's right.

I am not able to fall asleep. Nor can he. I still don't get it, I say. What? That the rabbi doesn't pray. He told me he doesn't want to lie. To whom? To the Everlasting Father. I don't understand that either. He said he doesn't want to lie to the Everlasting Father that he places his trust in Him. I understand that even less. I don't understand it either, though . . . Though what? All the same I understand it a little. What? Let's go to sleep, he says. A person needs sleep. At least try. A person needs to eat and needs sleep. Is there any food here? No, no food. Two boys go to the Teleki Square market and nick whatever they can, and we share that out. They're good at it; two others were caught, though, so they'll go out instead until they get nabbed. What happens then? We'll draw lots to see who the next couple will be. Could it be you? Sure it could, he says; it could be you, it could even be the two us together. And if the person who draws the lot doesn't want to go? There's no option. Try and get some shut-eye.

I thought things would become clearer in the morning. That one could choose between darkness and opening the window with its blue-paper shades. The stairwell is lit by a dim electric bulb. Jolán Bors is at the front door; she has brought two pairs of warm socks. One of these I pull on over the socks I am already wearing, the other pair I shall hand over to Vera.

That was when you sent the third letter, Mother says. Jolán said you were all right; she was always seeking to put my mind at rest.

Where did I lay hands on these small folding letter cards? I wrote on both sections inside, numbering the pages. They are hard to read, with one line slipping into another.

Did I go back to the room and write it there?

Maybe I sat down on the top of the stairs and wrote on my knees.

The pencil was almost certainly what was still left of the stub from Mihály Munkácsy Street; the point must have been totally blunt by then.

Jolán Bors stands behind me on the landing and waits until I have finished the letter.

Mother tells me that they asked Dr Temesváry where we might go if we could not go to the hospital yet, and the head physician may have said that the children in the Nagyfuvaros Street home had not been sent to the ghetto yet.

Mother gets up from the brazilwood easy chair and takes her medicine for the evening. Stay, she entreats, but says nothing more. I say nothing more and just take a seat in one of the armchairs, which used to be Grandfather's. Mother feels comfortable among old furniture, so do I, and I am sitting in one of Grandfather's chairs as, thirty-five years later, I write that Mother, having handed over the third of my letters, entreats me to stay.

Dearest Mother and Father,

We are well. Don't worry about us. We still don't know exactly but it looks likely we can stay here. If we cannot go to you tomorrow or the day after, then we shall stay or else go to another Red Cross home. If we have to leave after the 22nd but before the 31st (I don't think it will come to that), will we be able to go to your place? I am hoping that the police don't show up suddenly and so we get a chance to sneak off again. It would be good if Jolán comes here every day; I can then send a letter every day. Ask her to drop in on you straight after here, so she can bring your letter the next day!! She should bring any grub that she can!!! If you can, send a cap, gloves, shirt, underpants with her and for Vera stockings and any underwear that's available. Of course, only send them once it is certain that we can stay here until at least 31 December. Write to say whether you will be staying there. If so, until when? If we were to go there, where could you put us up? How long could we stay at your place? Perhaps by tomorrow we shall have something sure to report on, so Jolán should come. It is maybe not too late if we only find out tomorrow that we have to leave by the day after! If it is at all possible, we would go after it is dark!! (That's because of the police raids on Teleki Square.) If that's impossible, of course, we shall go in daylight; in any event speak to all the doormen, so that if we should turn up looking for you they let us in without any trouble. It could be that all the preparations are pointless because we can stay here.

Send things only if it is sure that we can remain here, because we have very little room to store anything!

Don't worry! Look after yourselves! Hoping to see you soon and until then all my love.

PS. We would like to get away from here. Is it possible with papers to rent a room? It's not very nice here, but if there is nothing else we'll put up with it, of course.

The standard lamp in the third room is on. The green lampshade gives the impression of everything being in an underwater world. I have covered one of the couches with a striped prayer shawl.

Jolán Bors comes in behind me. I dare not say to her that it would be better if she stayed outside. I want to find Vera. As I enter the rabbi's wife raises her hand in a warding-off gesture with the look of someone preparing for the door to be burst open, but then she spots Jolán Bors behind me. Jolán is wearing a headscarf; so is she. They are the same height and both have black headscarves. I tell her that I have written a letter to my parents, and I would like Vera to sign it as well. Vera comes forward from the corner and asks Jolán Bors if she knows where her mummy is. Jolán does not answer. I hand the pencil stub over, and Vera signs the letter under my name.

We go through the rooms with Jolán. Before we step out into the outside corridor we are joined by the man in the raincoat who plucked a tune for us on the violin the evening before. I would have liked to ask him what tune it was that he played and to say that I could play the piano accordion a little and that it was one of the tunes I had learned, but I don't dare ask because I can see he is in a hurry. We let him go ahead with Jolán Bors. He stops on the corridor; he has the white stick now. He puts on a pair of dark glasses.

Jolán Bors unexpectedly gives me a kiss. It is something she would not have dared to do before as it would have been odd to give the boss's son a kiss, although admittedly they did not call my father boss in the workshop: he said they should address him as Mr Béla. Her face has a strange odour – not unpleasant, mind you, more like it had been sprinkled with flour.

Jolán Bors proceeds down the outside corridor and reaches the man with the dark glasses and the white stick who is carrying his violin under one arm. The man waits and puts his free arm round her, and they proceed in that fashion.

One of the boys says news has come through that people who live in homes will not be taken into the ghetto. I can't find my bed companion of the previous night and don't feel like discussing this with the others. One broad-shouldered lad in a pullover and peaked cap comes over to me. Are you the new kid? What's it to you? I say in reply. He whispers in my ear that they're shooting a line, you'll see, they're coming to get us.

I go out on to the corridor. Beanpole is slumped against the railings smoking a cigarette butt. He asks if I want a drag; I decline. The sleet which fell last night has frozen to the banisters in long icicles. The sky is invisible, being covered by black clouds, so it's barely lighter than inside in the rooms. The windowpanes are broken. My duffel coat appeals to Beanpole. It's not mine to give, I say. What do you mean not yours? I tell him the story of how the coats were swapped. I can't imagine how he is still managing to get a puff out of the dog-end which has already burned down to his fingernails. Had Soproni bought it? It could be, I say, but maybe they managed to extract the bullet. You did well out of the swap, he says, this one's a lot warmer.

I seek out the rabbi. I'm told he's down in the basement with the sick. I go down there but can't find him. I wait for him on the landings. It's a way of passing the time, and it's better there than in the rooms or the cellar. The rabbi comes that evening with a basket on his arm. We go upstairs together. He has brought bread and carrots. Can I help with serving it out? We go into the room where his wife is with Vera. Green light again, as if mould were covering the walls, the furniture, the wife's headscarf, Vera's face and the rabbi's hat.

The woman calls the boys in individually; they each get a slice of bread and a carrot. I don't know how I should address the rabbi. He tells his wife that perhaps it was a mistake to share out the carrots as well that day; they ought to have been put aside for the following day. His wife says that we were down to praying to the Everlasting with all the fasting.

The rabbi takes a prayer robe or shawl out of the cupboard and wrapped it over his head. The black stripes of the robe glitter in the light; I see the white silk as green. He takes the robe off, folds it and puts it back in the cupboard. We are not fasting out of any wish to adhere to the Teaching, he says; we are fasting because we have no option, and we do not partake of any assistance from the Everlasting. Is it always up to us to act in order that the Book of the Law is adhered to, I wonder, or is everything not the other way round? That He ought to behold us and build the Teaching in accordance with what He sees. Is everything the other way round?

Vera is paying attention.

Dearie me, she presses the palms of her hands together, that's going too far.

The Zohar, the rabbi replies, says that all our wishes will be accomplished when the heavens are rent. The heavens were rent, and we have been left on our own. We have followed the Book of the Law, and despite that are unable to see our own shadow. Joshua consoled those wandering in the wilderness when they trembled that they could not see the shadows of their pursuers, for a man who casts no shadow is not a man, the Book of the Law says, there is no man. But can our shadows be seen in the dark, I ask myself.

Vera is crying, so, too, the woman. They embrace each other.

I ask if everyone from here is to be taken into the ghetto. He says, I don't know, son. I've heard people say they will, but I've also heard that an extension permit is due to come out, I say. He had heard the same two bits of news. He asks if there is a place we might go to. My parents are in the Alice Weiss Hospital, and supposedly we shall not be allowed in there, though, of course, we can try if needs must. When I said that Vera came over to me. What did she think? I ask. Should we make a start? She says, It's not up to me. I don't have the authority – not from the Everlasting or from anyone else. You lot need to decide. Is there a chance that we won't be taken in? Maybe there is and maybe there isn't.

I go through the rooms tapping on the iron frames of the beds. I only check if the shell is still in my haversack. Then I go back. I tell Vera to pack it away in her small suitcase. The rabbi and his wife are sitting under the green lampshade. The woman gets up; she hugs Vera and also hugs me to her. She looks questioningly at her husband, and the rabbi also gets to his feet. He makes a deep bow before her, then steps over to Vera and places the palms of both hands on her head. He then places his palms on my head before making another deep bow to his wife.

Rifle shots can be heard from Teleki Square; from the Outer Circle it is more in the way of machine-gun bursts. I walk a few steps in front of Vera. At road junctions I wait and only signal if I see no one around. We reach Teleki Square. I feel easier in the dark streets than in the dark rooms. I don't know if Jolán Bors has reached my parents. I don't know if my parents have read my last letter and warned the doormen that we might be coming. I can see people hanging around the market stalls. They are not armed. One of them has just forced a wooden door. Come on, he says. It's a bit warmer here.

We walk on. The cemetery wall is lit up by the moonlight. German army trucks hurtle next to us along the main road from the direction of Orczy Square a bit further out of town. Vera says she doesn't mind if we hurry because it will warm up her feet. Baross Square in front of the Keleti Railway Terminus. No doubt there are patrols around the station.

From Nagyfuvaros Street it takes me twenty-four minutes to reach Baross Square via Teleki Square.

My steps of old and of now trace the same path, although it seems as if I am not standing at the mouth of the square but, as it were, on the bank of a wide river where the traces again vanish and the paths of long ago can no longer be tracked.

We needed to avoid Baross Square because of the patrols around Keleti Station, so we had to take Rottenbiller Road, going in a north-easterly direction.

What now takes me twenty-four minutes was probably twice that back then.

In the post-war subway in the square two homeless people are reclining on the ground under grubby coverlets, their heads covered by ripped sacks. A young man of about twenty is sitting on a folding chair; in front of him there is a scattering of coins in the open lid of a violin case and a few 200-forint banknotes. The moment he glimpses me he starts to play: Vivaldi. I wonder what makes him think that classics are what the old codger needs. He's a student at the Conservatoire, he says when I ask. Some of his fellow students have pitches nearer the centre, but he likes it here and even more in the outer suburbs. He has a wavy mop of blond hair, frameless glasses, a black Adidas jacket and white Adidas trainers. His belongings are all worn, but he clearly looks after them, so he is not playing because he is broke. He asks me what I'm looking for in this neighbourhood so late in the day, so I ask him what makes him think I'm looking for something. Why does he rule out the possibility that I'm simply heading for somewhere? I don't want to be nosy, sir, but I just had the impression you are looking for something, he smiles. I beg your pardon. If I would like he would play a request of mine.

It's as if there were another city under this city, and it was sounds from there that I was hearing. Not just familiar sounds but unfamiliar ones as well; or, to be more precise, sounds that were once unfamiliar yet at the same time are part of me in much the way, perhaps, that everything which happens to me also belongs to others, maybe even the young man gripping his violin under his chin, in just the same way as the moments are part of me during which I was once able to avoid Baross Square, in just the same way as the many millions, or even hundreds of millions, of footprints that others have left on my traces from long ago. Stepping into the unknown I also proceed in the unknown left to me by others; the boy who was little older than fourteen knew the way and chose well, the proof of that being that I am able to be here now. That fourteen-year-old took upon his own shoulders the possibility that I would search for him in vain.

The young man plays some Schubert at my request. I earned three thousand today, he says when he finishes, but that's exceptional; there are some days when it's only two or three hundred. He makes it crystal clear, with a dismissive gesture of his bowing hand, that he will not accept money from me. He packs up his things. That was a good note to end on; thank you, sir, for giving me the opportunity. We shake hands.

I go further along Rottenbiller Road to Damjanich Street, crossing it midway, then on to the Körönd roundabout on Andrássy Avenue. I must have stood around for about ten minutes in the subway, which I will need to deduct from the time taken for my route from Nagyfuvaros Street in the VIIIth District to Szabolcs Street in the VIth.

I had to tell my parents what route we took; there was no way they would not have asked. I tried to read from Mother's look what she might have retained of it all, but I don't know when that was exactly. Probably at least quarter of a century later. She mostly does crocheting in the brazilwood easy chair; little place mats and gloves in beige thread. She's paid buttons for them from some inner-city wide-boy. Now I come to think of it, she says, which way did you come? She lowers the crochet needles. I am afraid my silence over the matter is disappointing to her, as I can't say which way we went after avoiding Baross Square.

When she was at Nagyfuvaros Street Jolán Bors said that if we were forced to go after all we should avoid Hősök Square.

How is it possible to reach Szabolcs Street but avoid Hősök Square?

One has to go left down Bajza Road off Andrássy Avenue, because the next crossroads is Mihály Munkácsy Street, so it is not advisable to go down there as there may be armed patrols around the vacated Red Cross home. So I go left down Bajza Road, turn right up Lendvay Street and then, after crossing Dózsa Avenue, along past the terrarium of the Zoological Gardens.

The photograph on my ARP papers shows me standing by the terrarium of the zoo. Over the white short trousers is a somewhat darker linen jacket and open-collared white shirt. My hair is parted on the left. The photograph was almost certainly taken in the summer; one can tell from my squint that I was facing into the sun. There is no yellow star on my jacket, so one can suppose that the photograph must have been taken the year before it was stuck into the identification papers. Under the photograph is the personal description:

Face: long
Nose: regular
Hair: brown
Eyes: hazel/green
Height 172 cm
Distinguishing marks: *crossed off*

The pavement dips into the subway under György Dózsa Avenue then rises again on the other side.

I turn into Szabolcs Street. The hospital is made up of three huge blocks. It has gone six o'clock, and visiting hours finish at seven. I raise two fingers to my cap in a salute to the doorman; I have no wish to be drawn into giving an explanation as to why I have come or where I'm going – it's visiting hours. In the lobby there are staircases going in all directions, passages, openings, tables and, on the left, directions to Basement 1.

There are five steps down. The basement is the same one as fifty-eight years ago, except now it contains no mattresses, palliasses or stretchers. The walls are the same and the network of pipes under the low ceiling. There is a single wheelchair to the right, like a symbolic element in an art installation.

I walk the length of the corridor, counting the steps: 120. I walk back.

I saw the two of you immediately as you came down the stairs, says Mother.

VIII

We do not stop at the main gate to the hospital. I'll take a look and see if there is a side door, I tell Vera, and set off towards the second building. I give three knocks on the door but get no response, so I went back to the main building where the door is opened when I knock.

Three men are standing in the hallway. One has a white smock on; the other two are wearing ICRC armbands. They pull me in. Quick, says the man in the white smock, they're firing. Didn't you hear? There's shooting going on all over, I say, adding that our parents are here in the hospital.

A night nurse is called who leads us upstairs. I tell her my parents' names, but she does not know all the patients by name, so she accompanies me as I look through all the wards.

Vera stands in the corridor, slumped against the wall and shivering. I make a sign that she should say there and set off.

Two years before, in the Amerikai Road Hospice, I saw my grandfather a few hours before he died. Mother would only allow me to come as far as the door to the ward, and it was from there I glimpsed him. Mother embraced me and covered my eyes before leading me out to the corridor.

I open the door to the first ward. Then the door to the second.

In twos and threes, patients are lying on the beds and on mattresses laid on the floor between beds. Where there are three those are dead, and in places there is one dying patient next to two dead ones. In places there are even small children sitting between the beds. Night nurses are doing their rounds. Men with stretchers arrive to take out the corpses.

I cannot find my parents, even after having looked in the fourth ward.

A fat man arrives. Behind him are, no doubt, doctors.

He asks me who I am and how I managed to get into the building. Have I got a permit or some kind of safe-conduct paperwork?

I show him my ARP messenger's papers.

You came here with that?

That's right.

He says something to one of the men in white smocks to take a note of my name. I also dictate Vera's name. The man says that the people who were brought in from Hegyeshalom may be in the basement corridor.

We go back to the entrance. One of those with a Red Cross armband takes us across to the basement. Vera stumbles on the steps in the dark.

We move about deep down with only a flickering candle.

I have to bend forward in order not to bump my head against the pipes that run under the ceiling.

I keep bumping into into beds and mattresses on the floor.

There is not room for us to go side by side, so Vera follows behind me, and I reach back to hold her hand.

I only spot Mother when she is standing right in front of me. She hugs me tightly to her. She is terribly thin, but I never felt her hug me more fiercely. The skin of her face is burning. She does not smell sweet or of cigarette smoke like sometimes, and she does not smell sweaty; it's more as if she were bringing it from very far away, from a very great depth, as if she herself were the mysterious smell. She embraces me at such great length that I am able to identify the odour wafting from her body; it is like the smell I sensed a few minutes ago from the corpses in the wards.

Vera stands forlornly behind me.

Mother takes me by the hand and pulls me after her, while I, in turn, pull Vera.

By now I can see quite well in the dark.

Beds on both sides with mattresses between them. The many bodies seem to become one enormous body trailing off into the dark infinitude of the corridor.

I lean over Father. His smell is familiar; it's rather as if the skin of his face had preserved something of the sharply fresh aroma of his shaving soap, even though my lips touch a bristly stubble. He finds it difficult to raise his arms from under the blanket, which is pulled up to his chin; his embrace is feeble. I sit on the edge of the bed and watch Mother help him to struggle up. He is in his winter coat and

Mother in a warm housecoat. Jolán Bors brought it, she says. Father grins. I can't see much of his face, but I can see the grin and the grey of his stubble. It's not at me but Mother that he is smiling. A foot fishes for his shoes; suddenly he gets up with ease. He takes a few steps and sees Vera, takes her by the hand, leads her to his bed, sits her on it and wraps his blanket round her. A white-smocked man comes, shining a flashlight. He hands out doses of medicine. Already all the better for seeing your son, aren't you, Uncle Béla, he says to Father. For an instant the torch flashes light on his features. He's an elderly man; he must be at least ten years older than Father.

Vera enquires what became of her mother; she knows she isn't here, in the hospital, but where might she be? We are given some bread from Mother's haversack on to which she spreads margarine. That, too, was brought by Jolán Bors. Police raid, it is announced by the guards at the entrance. I get into bed next to Father, Vera next to Mother. Beams of light sweep over the basement. Men in black uniforms are holding a flashlight in one hand and a submachine gun pointed at us in the other. Making his way ahead of them is the same podgy white-coated man that I saw in the corridor on the first floor. Father pulls me down further under the blanket. That's Dr Temesváry, the head physician, he whispers. They stop at each bed. At each the head physician takes the pulse, and in each case he reports that the patient is not in a fit condition to walk. Marasmus. Moribund. Pneumonia. Plenty of Latin terms. Thrombophlebitis, he says as he leans over Father. I can see from his look that he has recognized me. Severe infective hepatitis; he indicates me. I feel hot. I am probably running a fever. Maybe I had picked it up on the road or even back at Nagyfuvaros Street.

The armed men come back from the far end of the corridor, three men jostling before them. There are rats scuttling under the beds.

The dead were carried out on stretchers in the morning.

Father struggles to his feet and takes me by the hand; we set off. We leave our outer garments on the bed. He wraps himself in a blanket, I in the duffel coat. Ten minutes we get to wash, he says, we have to hurry, and it takes three or four of the ten minutes for us to reach the ground-floor showers. There is soap and a towel. He washes his groin, his chest and armpits; he says I should do the same. I had never seen him undressed before. He had lost so much weight that the skin on his arms and legs is wrinkled. He scrubs my back and I scrub his.

Vera is sitting on Mother's bed, and Mother is cutting her hair with a pair of scissors. Vera looks at me, and I say that short hair suits her. She says she had wanted for ages to have it cut in the French fashion, like a boy, but her mummy had never allowed her. Mother reports that while we were taking the shower Gizi had popped in on a visit, and she had asked her to get Vera's name added to our Swiss safe-conduct pass under our family name, saying it quietly so that Vera does not hear. Gizi had said she would try.

That was already the third or fourth visit Gizi had made to the hospital, says Mother. The first time she came she, too, had searched for us by torchlight, and the second time she knew where we were. The first time she came, I remember, she had a photograph of Bőzsi, and she was shining the torch on it, going over to each bed and asking if they had seen her. She brought bread and she brought apples, and after she had gone right along the whole corridor with Bőzsi's photograph she came back to us, and your father sat her down beside him and tried to set her mind at rest. So I just let it be; there are times when a few words from a man can have more effect, says Mother.

That evening I have to gather my things together and make tracks. Dr Temesváry says that an Arrow Cross patrol can drop by at any moment, and he cannot give any guarantees for the safety of anyone who cannot prove he is incapacitated. Vera can stay as maybe they are not after young girls, but you, he adds, are tall enough to look older.

I am pleased that he treats me as a grown-up, using the polite form of 'you'; maybe that's down to the duffel coat. He says I can hide in the nurses' home, the single-storey block out at the back, next to the fence. I pack my haversack, and we take leave of each other. It's not far away, Dr Temesváry tells Mother.

The yard is dark. A nurse leads me by the hand; we dodge around the heaps of snow. Just show me the way, I say, and I'll find it by myself. So she points it out. There are several single-storey buildings in the yard; it's the last of those I need to aim for. Corpses are lying by the wall of the first building. When will they be buried?

Yesterday I leafed through some old books. It was at one of the lines of the Passover Haggadah that the features of the rabbi on

Nagyfuvaros Street flashed through my mind: 'As for the one who does not know how to ask, you must initiate him.'

The nurses' home is dark. There are six beds on each on side. I pick one. No, that one, says a young nurse who is undressing by the last bed – not telling me to turn around. She's in a white petticoat. It is from under the blanket that she then tells me to try to get some sleep; she will have to get up at midnight, which is when her relief comes. Are you cold? I am. Me, too, she says. Rub your feet together under the blanket, she advises. The duffel coat helps. I wonder if Soproni survived his wound. If he didn't then was he buried in my windcheater?

There is a pine tree standing in the corner with a few burned-down candles on it. Could it be that the nurses were celebrating Christmas that evening?

At midnight I am awakened to find all around us is shaking. I guess it is midnight from the fact that another nurse is undressing in the corner and slipping into the place of the one I saw earlier. It's started, she says. The thunder of the cannon fire can be heard from Pestújhely, the XVth District, out to the north-east. They have started. Are you Jewish? she asks. Why? Does it matter to you? I'm not, she says, but nothing matters.

I would like to have a chat with her, and I get a sense that she, too, would quite like that. But then I also want to get some sleep.

Continuous gunfire.

On 23 December Soviet troops from Transdanubia, which are now surrounding Budapest, occupy Érd, the village lying just beyond the south-eastern outskirts of Buda. Hitler, having declared Budapest a fortress city which has to be defended to the last man, rejects a request from General Karl Pfeffer-Wildenbruch, the commander of IX Waffen-SS Alpine Corps, to regroup the 8th SS Cavalry Division Florian Geyer from the bridgehead in Pest, but Colonel-General Guderian, Chief of Staff of the General Army, consents to this on his own responsibility. On 24 December at 4.15 Guderian and General Hermann Balck, then in command of the German 6th Army, request permission to surrender Budapest in order to withdraw the troops to western Hungary, but Hitler rejects that proposal, too.

In the Opera House in Pest a performance of *Aïda* was given. Before the start of Act 2 an actor in military uniform appeared on stage in front of the curtain to pass on to the audience the frontline's greeting. I can reassure you all with a clear conscience that Budapest remains in Hungarian hands, he says.

A memorandum prepared at the Swedish Embassy reports that some twenty-five Arrow Cross soldiers broke into the Red Cross home at number 7–11 Mihály Munkácsy Street, where, the children having earlier been removed to the ghetto, a further group had been placed under protection. Two sick elderly women who were in the building were shot out of hand, and two three-year-olds in room 8 on the second floor were also shot dead.

Men of the University 1st Assault Battalion are placed on alert on the orders of Emil Kovarcz, Arrow Cross commander and a minister without portfolio in the Hungarian Government of National Unity. István Zakó, the Arrow Cross Party youth leader, proposes that university students may leave the capital with the fleeing Arrow Cross militiamen, but the decision is taken to stay and fight. Our action will help the Hungarian cause, declares Gyula Fischer, the battalion commander.

General Iván Hindy, commander of the remnant of the Hungarian forces defending the city, delivers a radio appeal to the inhabitants of Budapest. The situation is serious, but the capital will be relieved speedily. He submits a report to the Minister of Defence and the Chief of the General Staff:

> The great mass of people may not await the Russians as liberators, but they are in such a mental state that they await Soviet occupation with resignation. People are weeping and in despair that the city will be destroyed. They think with horror of the possibility that all the bridges will be blown up.

By near daybreak I have got used to the continuous thunder.

The nurse is also awake. She smiles, and I try to smile back. She is very young. Her clothes rustle as she dresses. I turn my back, although it would be good to take a peek. But now she is already by my bed and gives me a peck on the brow.

The black Packard whisks through villages. Gertrud Lutz is sitting beside the chauffeur with Gizi in the back seat. Gertrud has been this way before; the legation rented a holiday house at Bicske, around thirty kilometres due west of Buda. Gizi has also been here. The time they had gone to Hegyeshalom they had driven along the highway passing through Gönyű by the Danube, just before Győr. This time, too, she has a white headscarf and an ICRC armband.

They do not talk, although Gertrud occasionally says a few words to the chauffeur, and he himself occasionally enquires if they should drive further. The sounds of tank guns and machine guns can be picked up from the thunder; they are travelling near the front line. Gertrud tells him to drive on; she wants to buy potatoes, flour and fat. She had recently come to an agreement with a farmer living next to the rented house that he would slaughter a pig. Gertrud has the feeling that for all that they are constantly running across soldiers marching or fleeing westwards and having to stop because German panzers are cutting across the highway. But being in the ravaged countryside is better than staying in the blacked-out city.

In place of the spectacle of marching soldiers Gizi sees the column marching towards Hegyeshalom, the dead bodies in the ditches and her own self bending over them in search of Bőzsi. And she also sees Károly's face as he takes her hand and sits her in the car. He had laughed, Mother says. Gizi had told her that Gertrud laughed. Perhaps it was because of that, said Gizi, he took me on the trip to ease my depression. Gizi had been in a terrible state when he visited the hospital, says Mother, she was so worn out that your father and I agreed that the best thing for her would be for her to stay with us. Dr Temesváry would have permitted it. She just sat on my bed and cried. I don't remember that, I say, and Mother glances at me but does not respond, although it would be nice to know what is running through her mind, but I don't ask. Memories stay fresher if they are tucked away, and undoubtedly we share that awareness. Maybe she's thinking what a good job it is that I don't remember everything that she remembers. But Gertrud laughed, Gizi tells Mother while sitting on the hospital bed. She wanted to shake me up a bit, the dear, brave lady with those 'no big deals' she picked up from me. In the twilight, coming up to Bicske, we almost collided with a Russian tank, then we got caught up in an attack by a low-altitude plane, so the chauffeur slammed on the brakes and yelled at us to take cover in the ditch – we dropped flat on our stomachs among the soldiers. And when the attack was over Gertrud said, There you have it, darling, no big deal; let's carry on, I want to take that slaughtered pig back home. But then it didn't work out because the farmer with whom she had made the agreement had done a runner, although fortunately his neighbour, who you could tell just by looking at him was completely broke, gave her some potatoes, fat and even honey. And Gertrud said in the car on the way back, There you are, poor people are different, both here and back in Switzerland, and they can allow themselves to have a heart, whereas anyone who owns anything just grins like a hamster. And Gizi said that 'grins-like-a-hamster' to herself several times over, says Mother. She spoke very good German, but she didn't know expressions like that, so Gertrud had to explain it, and when Gizi got the drift she finally burst out laughing, and both of them laughed on the way back, not at what could be seen through the car windows but at the way Gertrud tried to imitate a grinning hamster by pursing her lips, and that was something Gizi herself acted out at the hospital, says Mother. I don't recall that, I say, nor that she went into a weeping fit. She sat on my bed, says Mother. I don't recall that either, I say. For heaven's sake, here's me crying my eyes out to you, says Gizi, me crying my eyes out to you, and she made a fresh trip between the beds. She had a snapshot of Bőzsi, which she lit up with her torch and asked everyone all over again whether they had seen her. One of the women, barely able to speak, snatched at the photograph. My dearest, she whispered, and Gizi had trouble plucking it out of her grip.

Maybe Gizi never did come back and sit on the bed; maybe she did not talk about Bőzsi. Mother's gaze may be switching between what actually happened and the imagined; such uncertainty is familiar ground for a gaze, and it guides my own, too. I do not visualize Gizi sitting on the hospital bed, but the hand gesture that Bőzsi makes comes to mind, only the hand gesture. I don't see her, so that flutter doesn't seem to be her hair. Might that change over time into a gesture?

Gizi went not long after that, says Mother. She had to get Vera's name written into our papers. The only way of doing that is put it under yours as if she was your younger sister; so Vera was given our family name. Do you remember what she said when I told her that now she had to behave accordingly and say that we are her parents and you're her elder brother?

I couldn't remember.

She said, Mother says, But that would only be until my real parents returned, wouldn't it?

Perhaps what Mother is thinking of is that Vera's parents never did return.

But she couldn't have known that then.

Gizi brought a new safe-conduct letter, she says. Lutz's signature on it was genuine. That was on Christmas Eve. She also brought chocolates and recounted that Lutz had met a very high-ranking German officer at the Gellért Hotel. She and the Lutzes had dined in the restaurant because Gertrud had insisted that Gizi eat dinner with them. That's something you weren't in a position to remember, says Mother. There was a time your father and I had dinner at the Gellért with Gizi and Józsi. At that time Józsi could not wear his officer's uniform, and Gizi had not as yet dyed her hair; it was dark brown and was shoulder-length; she had a tobacco-coloured evening dress, which she chose to go with Józsi's worsted; mine was mauve to go with your father's dinner jacket. We got the money from your grandfather, although your grandmother could not have known about that, of course.

Whatever happened, and however it happened, Mother's gaze vanquished time. For her, whether I was approaching the fifteenth year of my life or three decades older, I was and always remained her little boy. When she was lying tucked up in the intensive-care unit with drips in her arm and sheets up to her chin, I bent over her and pressed the palms of my hands together – not the way Grandmother pressed them together during prayers but in order to move them left and right in front of her open eyes to see whether her eyelids would quiver, but they didn't. She had only hours left, and I understood that I now had to take on the full weight of her look, which could no longer respond itself.

This assumption of responsibility was one of a number of occasions when I attempted to will myself across an unbridgeable gulf in unconscious preparation for my investigation.

It could be that there weren't four of us at the Gellért; maybe it was more, maybe Bőzsi was there and others as well.

*

Gizi is sitting in the Gellért Hotel restaurant. Carl Lutz and Gertrud are seated opposite each other. A waiter brings in bowls of bouillon, having first, with a ceremonial flourish, placed on his tray the soup plates that had been set out on the table. Gizi is seated opposite the window, so she can see the barbed-wire barriers on the square in front of the hotel and the gun placed at the Buda end of the Franz Joseph Bridge. The food was brought in on silver platters. What time is he coming? Gertrud asks Carl Lutz. Soon, says Lutz. Gizi does not ask who they are talking about; because they were not sitting opposite a window that overlooked the Danube they were unable to see that armed men were shepherding a small group across the square.

Gizi smiles and tactfully glances at Gertrud; the two women can share the reason why she is glancing at her and not at Carl Lutz, and Gizi even bursts out laughing when Gertrud breaks into a laugh. Of course, darling, it's no big deal. If you've got to go, you've got to go. As if they were laughing over the fact that Gertrud can now say 'it's no big deal' flawlessly in Hungarian, she gets up airily and heads off towards the ladies. There are military officers seated among the guests, the younger of them giving Gizi conspicuous glances, so when she feels that nobody is looking she races down from the mezzanine and, as she leaves the entrance, almost stumbles into a barbed-wire barrier. By now the group has crossed Gellért Square. There is a young woman walking in the back row, beside her a policemen with rifle; the woman's hair is ruffling and she smoothes it down. Gizi reaches her and grabs her by the arm. The young woman breaks into a smile; there is understanding in the smile, dignity. Gizi smoothes down her hair and plants a kiss on her forehead, the policemen pulls her away and the procession carries on. Gizi would like to accompany them, but already as much time has passed as would have been necessary to hurry off to the toilet, so she returns to the restaurant and, as she again passes the officers' table, she notices a general is arriving in great haste and giving instructions to the colonel seated at the head of the table.

The colonel salutes and sets off to the neighbouring wing of the dining hall.

Gizi had not noticed before, but now it strikes her eye that sitting at the corner table is a writer whom she knows by sight; indeed, she obtained a signature from him a few years before at one of the Book

Week tents. The writer has just finished his dinner and has taken out a notebook in which he starts to write.

'I pick my way between trestles carrying coils of barbed wire to dine at the Gellért Hotel,' writes Sándor Márai in his *Diary*.

The saloon bar was destroyed a few days ago by a bomb from an intruder aircraft; more than a few guests died, but nobody speaks about the death toll; in the grand upper restaurant tables are laid with immaculate linen tablecloths and napkins, tasty and not all that expensive dishes are served noiselessly on silver platters by superbly trained waiters. For twelve pengő I can dine in a peacetime setting with electric lighting; well-dressed people are seated at the tables, the waiters' dickies are dazzlingly white. From the window I can see a big gun guarding the bridge and the hotel's entrance along with several barbed-wire thickets, which will be used to defend Gellért Hill when it comes to close combat. A group approaches in the street: older and younger women with headscarves, children – Jews being sent to some site for deportation. Two policemen with rifles are steering the group; not one word of comment from anybody in the splendid, warm, well-lit dining-room.

Gizi watches the writer making notes and sees that he is about to leave. She also sees an SS colonel enter the dining-room, halt in front of a Hungarian general and salute with a raised arm, although the general seems not to notice that the colonel misses out Hitler's name with the *Heil!* but hurries on and extends a hand to greet Carl Lutz.

Gizi always got out of the old Opel Kadett when they encountered a column on the highway to Hegyeshalom.

SS Obergruppenführer Hans Jüttner, coming from Vienna, got out from his car the first time at Abda, just outside Győr. When he glanced in the Opel's window and with a smile enquired after Gizi's accommodation, standing beside him had been SS Standartenführer Kurt Becher.

Becher is waiting at Carl Lutz's table. Smiling. He has thick, dark eyebrows, thick lips. He kisses the hand first of Gertrud then Gizi. Although she recognizes him, Gizi cannot tell whether he recognizes her.

On the highway Gizi had on a Red Cross armband and a starched white cap. The Colonel takes a long look at her. Gizi tidies her hair behind the ear with a single gesture.

Becher links arms with Carl Lutz and they set off towards the adjoining room.

Gertrud tells Gizi, says Mother, that the Colonel had behaved as if something were gong on between you, and you yourself looked flirtatiously at him as if there had been something on which to look back – rather exciting, I must say, darling.

We did meet, Gizi says to Gertrud but she does not say where or that when SS-Obergruppenführer Hans Jüttner and SS Standarten-führer Kurt Becher got back into the military Adler on the highway from Hegyeshalom she had got out of the car to look along the ditches to see whether one of the bodies might be Bőzsi, and Károly had to pull her back to the car.

SS Obersturmbannführer Adolf Eichmann steps down from his armoured automobile at the gate to the ghetto in Dohány Street in the city centre. The sentries – two policemen with rifles and two Arrow Crossers with submachine guns – salute.

He passes by the synagogue garden, casting a glance at the dead bodies piled on top of each other at the foot of the iron railings. It is sleeting. He turns up the collar of his cloak and sets off for the parallel road, Wesselényi Street, turning down the connecting road of Síp Street. He checks the readiness of the tanks parked in front of the Jewish Council's building. A first lieutenant with an Arrow Cross armband presents himself, awaiting instructions. Eichmann gives orders that within a few hours, at a time-point to be communicated by the Reich's Chancellery, they should make a start on liquidating any survivors. Nothing is lost, he says; the Führer's new weapon is being readied for deployment. The first lieutenant reports that he has been given orders to attack the Swedish and Swiss Embassies at six o'clock the next morning. He accompanies Eichmann back to the ghetto gate. The SS Rottenführer who is the driver of the armoured car is smoking and chatting with the sentries. On the arrival of the first lieutenant they stub out their cigarettes on the palms of their hands.

The car is driven back to headquarters. In the Majestic Hotel Eichmann calls Joseph Goebbels, Reich Minister of Propaganda and Plenipotentiary for Total Mobilization, on a direct line. Himmler is sojourning at some unknown place; a deputy relays his order that the planned action in Budapest should be agreed with Eichmann's immediate superior, SS Standartenführer Kurt Becher. Eichmann seeks Becher by telephone and is informed that he cannot be reached; he is in discussions at the Gellért Hotel.

I walk past the railings of the garden of the Dohány Street synagogue, reading on the memorial plaques the list of names of those who perished. I step into the yard.

Whose tracks am I following up?

My own? Adolf Eichmann's?

I walk to Dob Street, the next block on from Síp Street. The entrance to number 4 now looks exactly the same as it did ten years ago at the time I learned from the Register of Births, Marriages and Deaths that my maternal grandfather was born there in 1871 and took a walk round the area. Back then the vaulted entrance had given me the impression that in the nineteenth century a horse and cart might well have been able to stop in the gateway, and I get the same impression now, although the dustbins would probably have got in the way.

I find among old family photographs a small advertisement, clipped from a newspaper, about the dedication of Grandfather's gravestone. I don't know which newspaper that would have been, perhaps the *Esti Kurir* (*Evening Courier*), as that was what Grandfather used to read. That black-framed announcement was all Mother kept.

Last year I had a stone cover made for my grandparents' grave, as we had always had to weed it once a year, and I don't want my daughter to be left with that chore. The gravestone itself is a fine marble block, and Mother had Grandmother's name incised under Grandfather's, with other names being added since.

I file away in the appropriate folder the newspaper announcement about the dedication of the gravestone. I clip out of a documentation volume a portrait shot of Adolf Eichmann and slip that, too, into the same file. I note that Eichmann was born on 19 March 1906, so that in 1944 he was thirty-eight years old and an SS Obersturmbannführer. His line of duty was the racial purification of Europe, the total eradication of Europe's Jewry. In the photograph his right eye is squinting slightly, the left one even more, the way he holds his head not exactly military.

I take a number 49 tram to Gellért Square. I had arranged to meet Györgyi in the hotel's tearoom.

I get there half an hour early, which gives me enough time to walk around the ground which, while it was not my footsteps that have left traces there, I still regard as being part of my exploratory journey.

The hotel's hall is neutral yet dignified; foreigners talking at reception. In the restaurant on the mezzanine I am met by a waiter in a lilac-coloured dinner jacket. Thank you, I say, all I'm doing is having a look. I am satisfied with that 'all I'm doing', which corresponds with my sense that, Oh, sir, all I'm curious about is what could those few steps have been like that Adolf Eichmann – accessory to the murder of many millions of people, as well as an accessory to reducing Budapest to ruins – took. That's all, as well as the fact that there was a time when he passed this way just like I am just passing by this way. What, I wonder, could he have seen when casting a glance through the enormous windows at the Danube, the ruined buildings, not to say the tank traps and trestles, the big guns guarding the head of the bridge, which it is quite certain were standing there, because an esteemed colleague, who, by the way, ate dinner here, recorded as much in his diary. That's all, sir, that what it's about, that's all . . .

The furnishings in the conference room are salmon pink.

Györgyi called yesterday. I'm back, she said in a voice that did not seem to be stating that she was back but was asking whether I was back, as if she knew that I was travelling and, furthermore, knew precisely where I was and whether I was there or already here; as if she were familiar with the feeling of uncertainty that, for me, is the everyday state of the zone between not remembering and not forgetting, and she had similar feelings; yes, as if she had also not got back from an obligatory trip on which she had substituted for a teacher colleague but from a journey that was real enough but nevertheless could not be called that.

It has been obvious for quite a while that Györgyi is following me and that is how she is trying to find a way into the past, yet the way she said I'm back was that by way of her voice she implied that I, too, wanted her to follow me.

Adolf Eichmann enters the restaurant. The army officers with Arrow Cross armbands jump up just as before when Kurt Becher arrived. Eichmann does not deign to greet them.

Gizi, Gertrud and Lutz are drinking their coffees. Another SS officer, thinks Gizi. Gertrud has her back to the newcomer. Gizi raises the coffee cup to her lips. She has a vague recollection of having seen the high-ranking officer before. He's not a hardened soldier; his look speaks more of an intellectual and as if he was not seeing what he was looking at. Gizi supposes, He's not looking at me but at something behind me, not the Danube, though. Maybe he's thinking of his family; he's around forty, so no doubt he has a wife and maybe children.

'I did not understand Becher,' Carl Lutz will write in his diary.

Why would he want to meet me another time? I have learned since then that for the sake of his business transactions he was in direct contact with Himmler, who wished to receive a cut of the pickings from the Manfred Weiss industrial conglomerate in Hungary. Becher placed himself at his service and in return Himmler had suggested that the Budapest ghetto ought not to be reduced to ashes, which was what Eichmann was ready to do. With an eye to the future, Himmler had already started to distance himself from Hitler, and he exploited the fact that although the extermination of Europe's Jews was Eichmann's particular province, he ranked merely as an Obersturmbannführer and therefore had to treat Standartenführer Becher as a superior officer.

And,

The two of them fought each other like jackals, but when Eichmann stepped into the hall he was sweet-tempered and acknowledged without comment what it was that Becher was to keep him posted about. Becher gave him no instructions, stressed that he was informing him of an order coming from staff headquarters, and meanwhile acted as if it was not Eichmann he was speaking with but turned to me, as if what was most important for him was that I take note of his intervention, and when it was possible I should pass that on to the appropriate authority. Even many years later I have no wish to imagine what Eichmann's expression must have been like. All the same . . . The look lacked any feature that would have allowed one to deduce what I knew about him. That is was what remains most memorable. Yesterday, while writing my diary, I read that the Hamburg-based 101 Reserve Police Battalion of the Order Police (Ordnungspolizei), which included middle-class professionals, officials and skilled workers, without being given any specific order and acknowledging no political standards or moral norms other than those of the Nazis (that's what it says), massacred several thousand Polish Jews in 1942. Might it be that taking action without thinking can result in more evil than the evil instincts that reside in man anyway? Everything that is happening here is all so ordinary, is what I read from Eichmann's face, this Becher and this Swiss as well, which is to say me. Gertrud once said that Eichmann is proof of what man is capable of, and at the time I agreed with her. Now I hold a different view, but I am not in a position to discuss it with Gertrud. I don't think he is proof of what man is *capable* of but what man *is*.

He underlines the two words then gets up from the writing desk. Through the window he can see the far shore of the lake and the green hills of the Appenzeller Vorderland. If he were to step over to the window opposite he would be able to see the church spire of Walzenhausen and that favourite rocky peak of the Meldegg. He returns to the desk, Not long ago at the bottom of a crate he had found his first diary: 'Today I made a decision to keep a diary, and with God's assistance I shall carry it on so as long as I am able to.' The entry is dated 16 June 1914.

After some more rummaging he comes across two communications from the Consular Service of the Ministry of Foreign Affairs in Berne:

We draw to attention once more that your correspondence should always be circulated with a copy to the head of the legation. We are firmly convinced that if you had kept Herr Kuebler, the Consul, fully informed he would have stopped you from committing professional mistakes.

That communication is dated 3 May 1938. Lutz could not remember what the professional mistakes in question had been; all he recalls is that in 1938 Kuebler was Consul-General of the Swiss Legation in Palestine.

The second communication is dated 17 September 1938:

> It has come to our notice that you are preparing copies of official communications for your own private collection. As you are probably well aware, under no circumstances may federal officials lay claim to materials that they have committed to writing in their official capacity.

Carl Lutz wonders how many drawers at home must be filled with his diaries and files.

> I muse that my country's policy was not to extend recognition to Stalin, and how right it was, but to recognize Hitler and Mussolini. Those who reminisce often pose the question, what kind of people were those diplomats? I posed similar questions myself in 1944 in Budapest: what kind of people were the Hungarians who cooperated with Hitler? Exactly what? What kind of Hungarians? And what kinds of Swiss are my superiors?"

He puts down his pen. Who, he wonders, poses questions like that? He supposes that everything vanished even for him, despite all his efforts; to no avail the reminders of his diaries and photographs.

He steps over to the window once more.

The look-out on the Meldegg is easy to spot, but the emotion that he felt when he first glimpsed the rocks is irretrievable.

The story has been lost, he writes, but why should it have been brought home to me on that particular day; that I didn't know then, and I don't know now either, he notes down five years later, when he reads what he wrote on 19 September 1962.

Eichmann takes leave of Kurt Becher with a salute and *Heil Hitler!* He does not go out through the door leading to the restaurant. A smaller door leads to a staircase going down to the hall. A few minutes later Becher also departs by those stairs.

Carl Lutz returns to the restaurant. A cognac or coffee? Gertrud asks. Gertrud and Gizi take cognac, Lutz a coffee.

Two hours later Adolf Eichmann climbs into the armoured car that is waiting for him in front of the Hotel Majestic. In a photograph preserved by the Military Archives Division of the German Federal Archives he is smiling as he leans on the vehicle. The caption states this is the last photograph of him to be taken in Hungary.

Three hours later Kurt Becher left Budapest in another armoured car.

Gizi was watching television yesterday, says Mother; she rang me up to pick her up at Ruszwurm. Once a month she takes her afternoon cup of coffee at Ruszwurm Confectionery on Szentháromság Street on Castle Hill in Buda. Gizi is the deputy manageress, and she brings my mother a coffee, sits down with her and they chat for half an hour every month.

She was looking peaky, says Mother. Which means she herself is looking peaky, if she says that Gizi was looking peaky, and she needs to moisten her cracked lips. She covers her mouth with the palm of one hand so that no one should see her as she gathers her spittle then passes her tongue first over the upper lip then the lower lip. I'm sitting in front of the television, Gizi tells Mother, and it is showing pictures from the Eichmann trial in Jerusalem. You'll never believe it, but I once saw him; I had a brush with him in the Gellért when I was with the Lutzes and he walked past the table. Mother takes the hand from in front of her mouth, her lips still cracked as far as I can see. I had to grasp Gizi's hand and press it against the marble table; she was trembling, repeating over and over, you know, he walked right by me, right by me. Carl Lutz was pale-faced when he got back from the other room, says Gizi I don't know who he'd been speaking to – with Kurt Becher, that much I knew, because Gertrud recognized Becher – but neither of us had known who Eichmann was.

After the coffee Gizi had served herself a glass of cognac, although it was forbidden to drink any alcohol while on duty, says Mother.

Adolf Eichmann was hanged in Jerusalem in 1962. He had maintained his innocence throughout the trial. Hannah Arendt wrote of the judgement that was handed down:

And just as you supported and carried out a policy of not wanting to share the earth with the Jewish people and the people of a number of other nations – as though you and your superiors had any right to determine who should and who should not inhabit the world – we find that no one, that is, no member of the human race, can be expected to want to share the earth with you.

With a report of what my investigation has uncovered tucked under one arm I walk down to the hotel lobby. The corridor off to my left leads to the tearoom. I pay a visit to the gents. After washing my hands I comb my hair. I then sit at one of the windows that looks on to the Danube, waiting for Györgyi.

IX

At the next table they are speaking in German – businessmen, no doubt. Grey and brown jackets – small-chequed and large-chequed – buttoned shirt collars, cross-striped light necktie, plain azure necktie, black leather folders. Hennessy brandy, plum brandy.

Györgyi called yesterday. In the hour since she arrived she has said not a word about where she had been, so we can meet now; she did not ask so much as state it, although I did catch a sense of familiarity in her voice that I had not on previous occasions. There was also a hint of restlessness hovering behind the personal manner of addressing me at the same time as there was determination.

Her voice thereby was as if it were a story in itself, or rather it expressed the influence that a story had exercised on her.

The German businessmen were just sipping their drinks when she reached their table.

Both of them paid attention.

Her white blouse was the same as she had been wearing when we alighted from the number 1 tram at Thököly Road. Yet maybe a new one, all the same; perhaps she bought it while on the trip, as the girls would have been travelling in brand-new gear, and she would not wish to be outshone.

She does not wait for me to get up but pulls out another seat with a vigorous tug and sits down. As if she were being pursued and had just managed to pull up the drawbridge in the gateway of the castle walls.

The two Germans now pay attention to me; Györgyi's appearance has added to my stock in their eyes.

She asks for a coffee.

I get the impression she senses the looks she is attracting from the next table.

She drinks her coffee.

She fishes out a photograph from a minuscule straw purse and slips it in front of me on the table. A girl of about sixteen and a woman of about forty. Györgyi more closely resembles the older woman. A stretch of rainy street; both of them in raincoats, both with yellow stars. Both are looking into the lens of the camera. The girl is wearing a beret; the woman a knitted cap that can be pulled down to the ears. On both there is a curl of hair on the temple. They do not look sad. Or listless. There is no fear on their faces. It's as if a prying eye were examining them through the camera lens, probing who you are, what you feel, what you are thinking, and they had decided that they were not going to give anything away. Let the person looking at them see they are as they are. They have nothing to own up to, nothing to hide. They would like to move on, it's true, but they have no objection to having a record made of them.

Didn't you see her?

No, I didn't, I say. How would I have done?

On one of the display cases that have been installed in the recently renovated stations of the original underground line. The one by the Opera House on Andrássy Avenue. She had discovered it there by pure chance on the day her train was leaving. Her mother and grandmother in the autumn of 1944. She had made enquiries this afternoon as to where it had been found, who found it and how come it ended up in the display. It was found in some archive, the official in charge had said; one of several dozen photographs of its kind, and it was pure chance that this one been picked. All the same, you ought to have asked me. There were no names on the pictures, no text to refer to, the only guides being the yellow stars and the bare branches of the trees and rainy pavement. A huge number of photographs had been accumulated, all the people who could be seen in them anonymous; I'm sorry, we are terribly sorry, the official had said.

I ask if I can order her a drink.

No, thank you . . . Well, maybe a dry Martini.

I ask for a glass of vodka.

On one of the pictures that she had sent in the anonymous envelope one could see a house in Amerikai Road, I say. Was that why she had followed me on the tram?

I've already said that I recognized you.

She downs the Martini. She is past thinking back.

Thinking back to what?

She searches for the words. Well, the past, she says finally, saying it as if she were ashamed to designate all the things about which she had not thought for a long time with such a banal word. But now she was incapable of anything else, she adds. Already, quite a long time ago, a gap – that is how she puts it – had been left inside her; but, despite this, what, for a very long time may have filled that gap, were memories that she had thought of as hers but were actually those of her mother. But let's not bother with explanations, she says in a frosty tone.

I think something must have happened, and it was not just that she had come across this new photograph.

I tell her that I had discovered, at the Opera metro station, a composite photograph of the class at the Israelite Gymnasium which passed the school-leaving examination in 1944, and among the portraits was one of an acquaintance who has long been living in Paris.

Her fellow teacher had not been sick; she did not have to substitute for anyone. She had merely taken time off and joined the class excursion at her own expense. Twenty-two students had travelled to Ravensbrück – fifteen girls and seven boys – with two teachers to lead the group. Where are you off to, her fellow teachers had asked at the railway station? That's brilliant, at least you'll be able to keep the kids in order.

She had had no expectations of the trip, she says. What could I have expected? But she had had a feeling that there was some business she was holding inside her that had to be attended to, and I did not dare ask what that was because, although her voice is cool, I reckon I can see in her look a plea for me not to ask her what business had to be attended to, as if her look was saying that she could not explain it anyway.

The Germans watch as we down our drinks. As far as I can tell they are satisfied with us – we were getting on pretty well, they must have thought.

Before her mother died she had asked that if a gravestone were to be ordered she should also have engraved on it her own mother's name with the date and place of her birth and the date and place of her death, which was Ravensbrück.

Her mother had never before disclosed the name of the camp. She did not hide the number tattooed on her arm, but she not willing to mention the name of the camp.

When we got near the gates to the camp the other two teachers stood at the back of the group and behaved as if I were the leader, even though they, too, could speak German well.

The students had made their way towards a whitewashed building.

On the left there is a memorial column and an artificial lake, I say to Györgyi, the glass of vodka in my hand.

On the left there is a memorial column and artificial lake, Györgyi says.

The crematorium is not far from the entrance, on the right, I say.

The crematorium is on the right, she says.

Two chimneys, five viewing apertures with shutters over them.

That's right, she says.

I see that she would now attempt to set off in the direction of my gaze.

Two lines of a dozen barracks facing each other, between them the Appellplatz. Six ten-metre posts, each carrying two floodlights, I say.

They must have lined up on the Appellplatz I don't know how many times each day, she says, so when I was standing there what went through my head was that I could have paid a visit long ago, but I did not want to.

She stands on the Appellplatz, takes a few steps. She is walking in the footsteps of her mother, her grandmother and her mother's friend, I muse. I do not tell her that I too have stood on the Appellplatz in the footsteps of her mother, grandmother and mother's friend when I still had no idea that among the many thousands and tens of thousands of traces were some belonging to someone I would one day come to know. I did not stand between armed guards and students there but between two faceless GDR officials. They hesitantly allowed us to leave the prescribed route and to enter the former camp, accompanied us silently to the Appellplatz. Because Györgyi had stood there it was now her story; as I stood there at that time I had the feeling that it was rather the story of the two faceless East Germans.

I don't tell Györgyi that no more than fifteen years after the crematorium had been in operation I had asked a young woman of twenty-five – who was selling small collections of photographs labelled

'Acht Fotos KHZ Ravensbrück' ('Eight Photographs of Ravensbrück') for two marks at the entrance to the camp – where she lived, and she said in the next village.

That village was 800 metres from the camp.

Did your parents live here during the war?

Yes, they did.

What did they say about you getting a job here?

Nothing.

Did you ever ask them what they recall of how the camp operated?

They knew nothing about it.

Have you heard about it from other people?

Nobody.

But it's only half a mile away.

No, nothing from anybody.

Didn't they see the smoke from the crematorium chimneys?

I've already said, they knew nothing . . .

Eight photographs:

A transport to Auschwitz
Prisoners at work
Women building roads
A view of the camp
The Appellplatz
The crematorium
A firing squad
The memorial by the lake

I bought a packet of the eight photographs.

We might have spent an hour inside there, Györgyi says. The Appellplatz was muddy. It was drizzling, and anyone whose coat was hooded pulled that over their head. One of my colleagues said we should go because the kids were freezing. As we were heading for the memorial, past the artificial lake, one of the girls came over to me and linked arms with me, tears in her eyes. I didn't know what to say to her, Györgyi says. It wasn't easy to stay quiet, but it would have been even more difficult to say something. We set off the two of us to walk round the lake, and when we were far enough from the others she stopped. Miss, one of the boys said that this was only put up at a later date, that there's no truth in the whole story.

Györgyi is speaking in an icy voice. I cannot imagine the tone in which she replied to the teary-eyed girl. Her look is the same as Mádi Róbert's when she said what, on the morning of 15 November 1944, I could not have seen from the other room. Yes, Györgyi's look is familiar, like the look of those who speak about rationally incomprehensible events in similarly frosty tones. I told the girl that my mother and grandmother had been brought here, and my grandmother and a woman friend of my mother's had been incinerated in the small whitewashed building with its two chimneys and five viewing apertures with shutters over them.

The group sets off towards the waiting special coach.

Go, says Györgyi to the girl, or you'll miss the coach.

She waits until everybody has boarded.

She waits in order to keep the others waiting.

The two Germans at the next table pay their bill.

Would I relate to her my recollections of the camp?

My hosts, or rather my East German escorts it would be more accurate to call them, did not budge from my side. I would have liked to have been left alone for at least a few minutes, but they did not budge while I measured the span of the opening to the furnace of the crematorium. It was just wide enough to swallow up a body lying horizontally. The Appellplatz was muddy on that occasion, too. It had been raining then as well, and I caught a bit of a cold.

And did you write about it?

No. What I felt at the time was so insignificant. I caught a slight cold, my throat tickled. It may well be that if I had not coughed and worried about not being able to change my sodden socks until the evening I would not have written about it even then, because I could not find the right words in which to record it. Although I did write down that much.

What do you mean, that much?

The fact that I could not find the right words in which to record it.

This is the right moment for me to slip across the table a folder in which I have placed a typescript. It is a novel, I say, the chapters that have been completed so far.

Her look is that of an accomplice; she feels she has become a part of something to which it may be hard to pin a name but involves the two of us.

We leave the Gellért's tearoom – I'll write up what happened next later – we then go out in front of the entrance to the hotel.

We start to walk in step with one another. When we reach the pedestrian crossing to Szabadság Bridge I look back. Before my eyes there appear trestles, barriers made of rolls of barbed wire, the cannon guarding the head of the bridge and the hotel.

Györgyi also looks back. I make no mention of what I had just imagined, as I sense from her look that something is being brought to mind for her as well, albeit something different. We owe each other the courtesy of at least leaving the past the way in which it lives on.

At the Erzsébet Bridge, the next bridge upriver, I remark that it was across here that the column we were in was driven – I deliberately choose the word, smiling meanwhile – to the Óbuda Brickworks. It's possible that her mother and grandmother were also in it. This was where Father had ticked me off for looking right because the Arrow Crossers were bawling at us not to look, meaning not to look at the blown-up statue of Gyula Gömbös.

The Danube is grey; there are no lights. Still, the Parliament building is easily visible upriver on the opposite bank, looking like a piece of the décor, as does the string of hotels on the Pest riverbank. Their roofs slip on to the roofs of the houses behind, the city being concentrated on a single spot as if the buildings were their own replicas. As if I were not seeing the city in which I have lived my whole life, a city whose streets and squares are well known to me, but a stage set, one viewed from the wings rather than the auditorium. Maybe my eyesight is changing, as not long ago I was knocked down near here by a cyclist, I say. Györgyi is clutching the file that I passed to her in the tearoom under one arm. When she starts to read it at home she will get to the part that describes that it was exactly where we were standing, perhaps fifty metres from the Buda end of Margit Bridge, that the procession from the brickworks that was destined for the Dohány Street Synagogue was driven on to the footbridge erected over the swirling river after the old bridge had been blown up. Perhaps she will think about where her mother and grandmother and mother's friend can have been in the column at the time when it was sent off towards Hegyeshalom.

She remarked during the walk that she still meant to drop into school, but already two number 17 trams had departed from the terminus without her getting on.

Was it a good idea for me to make that journey?

It is almost as if that was the question she were posing to herself, but it seems to me that it is important she does so in my presence.

She prepares to say farewell and yet allows a third tram to depart.

She was ashamed that when they came away from the Appell-platz she was preoccupied more with her umbrella, because it chose there, of all places, to misbehave, is the way she puts it.

I quite understand, I say; it was also rainy when I went there.

We are standing quite close to one another at the tram stop. She gives me a grateful look for also speaking about the rain.

In a dream the packet of snaps bought many years ago at the entrance to Ravensbrück is stolen from my room, which I had locked myself from the inside. Györgyi shows up and together we search my drawers, together open and close my accumulated files. Györgyi mean-while reads a number of my notes in an old letter; we cannot find the pictures, and their loss makes me see the freshly whitewashed walls and two chimneys of the crematorium more sharply.

I write the dream down after waking up at dawn. I continue that I am standing with Györgyi at the terminus of the number 17 tram. She will later read the typescript I passed her and go out to her mother's grave in the cemetery where she had also had her grand-mother's name inscribed on the gravestone. Her mother, I write, had not wanted her mother's name to be preserved on the memorial to the martyrs, and she had never explained to Györgyi why not, but before she died she had asked that when it came to setting up a gravestone for herself then let her grandmother's name also appear on it. She had specified: 'Here is preserved the memory of Mariann Rajna, 1906–1944, killed at Ravensbrück'. Györgyi does not, however, have her father's name carved on the gravestone, as she knows nothing about him, and he might still be alive somewhere abroad.

I hope that what she reads about herself will not be without interest to her. I sense that she wished to have herself seen by another's gaze. While she reads about herself, I write, she will also encounter another story.

For weeks I have been looking in music shops and secondhand bookshops in search of a book on or guide to Schubert's chamber music. Unsuccessfully. I listen to the 'Allegro' passage of the *C major Quintet*. The music is also a story. I am seeking a similarity between the story that can be voiced and the story that lives in me. It is not to be found in the sublime, although the more times I hear it the more strongly I doubt as to whether this is really true. The radiant sorrow of the 'Allegro' can master an inability to remember, gliding over the crevasse of the past by filling it with a sense of boundlessness, and it comes to mind that Carl Lutz noted down something similar.

I shall make a trip to the cemetery and look for the grave of Györgyi's mother. Does it resemble my description?

It is possible Györgyi was present at Luca's funeral, although I didn't recognize her. Four, five years ago, would that have been?

Ten degrees below zero. January. There would have been around twenty of us in the unheated mortuary. It is quite a long walk in deep snow to the freshly dug grave. I can't see any familiar faces; she might have been there. Warm shawls and black fake-fur coats; hats pulled down over foreheads. Luca's daughter looks older than her mother had done.

We stand speechless in the snow. I see everyone looking as lonely as Luca had been. The bare trees are lonely, the snow-bound gravestones, too.

I walk across to my parents' grave. I don't normally come out to the cemetery in winter. I sweep the snow off the gravestone with one hand; I would like to clear the lettering at least. Two steps away is the grave of my maternal grandparents. Black marble with gold letters. Under my grandfather's that of Grandmother: 1874–1945. It does not say that it was January. The date, too, I was told by Mother. My grandmother died on 6 January in the ghetto, in the cellar of a house on Dob Street, maybe a hundred metres from the house where my grandfather was born in 1871. Next to their grave is Gizi's. There are many inscriptions on the stone. Alongside Józsi's rank as a military officer it is also inscribed that he died of poor health following an injury during the First World War. After my father died Mother used to bring flowers for all three graves; now, since Mother's death, I also place a stem on my grandparents' and Gizi's gravestones.

The three graves are within six paces of each other. I step into the footsteps of those stepping in the footsteps of Grandmother, Father, Mother, Gizi.

How many times have I made those six paces?

Gizi left nobody. Mother had her name incised on her gravestone.

She would now be one hundred years old, if she were alive. Her husband was young when he died, her daughter was young when she died, her lover and her friends were young when they died, Bőzsi was young when she died. Apart from me, there is now no one who can remember Gizi. As regards her story, the story of others on the basis of her story, the once-fourteen-year-old boy is the only one who has any knowledge, only he is able to write such words.

I can see in the way Mother looks that she is unable to separate in her own mind Gizi's various expressions.

The two young girls are strolling in Kálmán Tisza Square.[7] One is six years old, the other seven. Both are wearing white lace gloves as they stroll. A third girl, no older than them, is coming from the direction of the Városi Színház.[8] Hey, do you want to come and play with us? Gizi hails her. Mother repeats the question. The young girl sets off to play with them.

Decades later they can still giggle about it.

Even in her old age she combed her hair like . . . says Mother.

Like who? I ask Mother severely. I am trying to get her to realize that she is not finishing her sentences.

Gizi, of course.

And how did she comb it?

Why, the same way as Bőzsi, she says, and saying it as if she did not understand why she has to repeat herself. Did you never notice that the hand gesture she made when she swept her hair aside was the same as Bőzsi's? You know, I think that what was important to Gizi later on was not what she said but having someone to say it to. Once I sat with her up in the café on Castle Hill, and she said, You know, Rosie, I ought to take a trip to Switzerland to see Gertrud or Carl Lutz – she said Gertrud or Carl because they had divorced by then; Gizi had heard about it. I ought to take a trip and have a talk with them. And when she said it, says Mother, her look was just like that of someone who had no interest in what had happened to Gertrud or Carl Lutz, and she was not interested what she was saying, just in talking about it with someone.

It was not hard for me to picture Gizi's face when she says this to Mother, because Mother's expression was also like that of someone for whom, similarly, it was more important just to be able to talk with me than what was actually said.

Gertrud places the gifts she has prepared for colleagues and staff of the legation under the Christmas tree. Continuous din of weaponry from the Pest side. She had managed to bring back a Christmas tree from Bicske, and she had thought about candles well before. She would not allow Gizi to leave. Not long before, a barrage of mortar shells had hit the neighbouring building. Carl Lutz helps to light the candles and joins in the singing of 'Silent Night'. He records that in his diary, as well as the fact that he had been informed that both Adolf Eichmann and Kurt Becher had left Budapest.

The cannon fire dies down around midnight. Just two of them are left by the Christmas tree, Gertrud and Gizi. Gertrud relights one of the candles. They remain wordless until it has burned down. Darling, does it matter if I ask you about your husband? No, why would it matter? You never spoke about him; you only mentioned Karol. Károly, Gizi corrects her. Admittedly, I never said anything to you about my husband. Oh yes you did, says Gizi, about your travels, about Palestine, you did. Gertrud laughs. More intimate things, I meant, darling.

Józsi was always very plucky, says Gizi. It took pluck just to dare to ask my father for my hand in marriage. It was also pluck that he was willing to fight a duel when my honour was insulted.

Gizi senses, though, that Gertrud is not interested in what Józsi said when stood to attention, his officer's shako in hand, in front of his future father-in-law or when he named his seconds for a duel. It is pleasing to recall her father's cigar smoke, pleasing to think of Józsi at the family banquet of Seder, drinking his third glass of wine and trying to peck Bőzsi on the cheek.

Gertrud, too, must clearly sense what Gizi feels, as she does not enquire about things that Gizi obviously does not wish to talk about. You know, darling, she says, Carl was never plucky. He lacks those masculine traits. Gizi nods, finding what Gertrud is saying interesting, but right now nothing comes to mind about Carl Lutz other than that before lighting the candles on the Christmas tree he signed the family's safe-conduct papers covering four names, with which, if possible, she will set off to the Alice Weiss Hospital at cockcrow.

Not that I can complain, says Gertrud. My life with Carl is certainly interesting, but I do envy you a little, darling, for being able, no-big-deal, to gain more experience in the sphere of men. Gizi muses that she does not know how much of that pluck would have remained with Józsi if he had been faced with the situations that Carl Lutz had faced. And I am envious of you for not having had to gain more experience in the sphere of men, she says.

Gertrud laughs. All is not lost yet, darling.

They exchange a kiss.

X

Another nurse comes into the sleeping quarters. I had not seen her before; she can be only two or three years older than me. Red hair in a long ponytail; she is freckled and has luminous green eyes.

Dress! Make it snappy!

Should I make the bed?

Oh, just leave it! Come quickly!

Snow had fallen during the night, covering footprints and also the corpses that had been stacked beside the building.

The head physician is standing in the doorway of the main building, which lets on to the yard. Dr Temesváry is stout and very bulky, blocking the entrance. The small nurse snatches at my arm and hauls me back; the head physician had given a sign that we should wait. I did not see him make a sign.

Two Arrow Crossers try to tug Dr Temesváry out of the doorway. He holds fast. They are grasping submachine guns. Temesváry says something to them and does not budge. A third Arrow Crosser comes, and they manage to haul him aside. Men are shoved out of the building. The little nurse puts an arm round my shoulder. The men with submachine guns lead the men away. Maybe they'll content themselves with those eight, the nurse says.

Should we wait?

You can be sure the director will signal when we can go.

I don't see him make any sign, but the nurse says, Now. We run.

Gizi emerges from the building, and, while running, I see that she, too, breaks into a run to the front and towards the main entrance. We reach the door on to the corridor. Temesváry grabs me by the arm and the sister runs inside.

Gizi comes back. They've just taken them away, she says to Temesváry.

I can see nothing in the dark of the basement, only seeing Father when he is standing right in front of me, behind him Mother and

Vera. My parents are carrying haversacks, Vera her little suitcase. Gizi produces from her handbag the new Swiss letter. She shines a torch on it. It's got all of your names on it. Your family name has changed, she says to Vera, and you must practise using it. And when my parents return . . . it's only till then, isn't it? Yes, says my mother. She last saw Vera's mother in the marching column as it neared Hegyeshalom.

We step over people lying on mattresses. Gizi spots the yellow stars on Mother's and Father's winter coats. Heavens, Rosie, she says as if scolding a child. Rip those off immediately!

They tear the yellow stars off their coats. I am about to take Vera's hands, which I have got used to doing – that's how we set off on our journeys – but instead step over to Father and help him pick out the ends of cotton threads that have been left where the star had been sewn on. Gizi says, Well done; good job. She then turns to Vera. You go first to the main gate, and you have to act as if you'd just dropped by to visit someone. That job appeals to Vera, and so, getting into her role, she sets off. I'm raring to go after her, but Gizi says, Wait a bit. You've got a haversack; that's different.

Behind me is the dark bend of the basement corridor. The old people are shouting the loudest, not so much the women as the men.

The ginger-haired ponytailed young nurse pops up from the inner depths. It's time for your rounds, Doctor, she says. Temesváry stretches a hand out to Gizi. The nurse pecks me on the cheek. Vera looks back, but Gizi gestures that she should keep going. At the main gate we should turn right straight away, says Gizi. I will keep twenty or thirty metres ahead, so if I stop and signal look for a doorway, step into it and wait. You come after me, she says to Father, after you Rosie and the girl. You stay at least twenty to thirty metres behind me and keep a look out behind. If you notice anything, tell your father, and you, Béla, pass it on to me.

It's time to make your rounds, Doctor, says the ginger-haired nurse, who I can see is looking at me.

Godspeed, says Dr Temesváry.

General Karl Pfeffer-Wildenbruch of the Waffen-SS, commander of the forces charged with defending Budapest, reports to Hitler by radio from his headquarters blown into the rock of Castle Hill that he has been obliged to pull back his forces from the north and east of Pest, because the front line is approaching Újpest and Rákospalota, and he requests permission to allow the remaining forces to break out of the encircling ring.

The general has all motor vehicles seized and orders that the troops be concentrated to make a breakout. Budapest must be defended at all costs, Hitler directs anew, and those who disobey orders and break out will face instant court martial when they reach German lines.

Vannay's paramilitary shock-troop battalion, still comprising mainly officer cadets aged between fifteen and eighteen, recaptures positions the Germans had lost at the village of Csömör on the north-eastern fringes of Pest. Soviet tanks, however, draw up in an unstoppable battle array on the flat terrain between Fót and Rákos-palota, near the Danube, in the north-easternmost part of Pest. SS anti-tank gunners dig themselves in between Angyalföld in the XIIIth District and Újpest in the IVth.

We're heading towards Angyalföld, says Gizi, and goes in front. Father follows a minute later. Mother takes Vera by the hand. I wait and count. Then I, too, set off. There are constant mortar blasts.

It may be that Gizi set off more to the left after all.

On a 1943 street map the block of the Albrecht Barracks lies to the right-hand side of Lehel Road. Past the Aba Street turn-off, on the right, are the buildings of the No. 1 Army Catering Unit, while behind the Albrecht Barracks on Lehel Road are the barracks of the Army Transport Corps and further on the Vilmos Barracks.

On that 1943 map only the sites of barracks, other military premises and railway stations are specially marked. The Albrecht Barracks are similarly marked on a 1903 map; the No. 1 Army Catering Unit is here called Military Catering Store; the barracks of the Army Transport Corps the Szekerész Barracks; and the Vilmos Barracks are the Tüzér Barracks.

It is unlikely that we passed in front of these barracks, so most likely we had set off more to the left.

I can see an army squad a couple of hundred metres behind us. They are leaning forwards as they run across a broad road, and on reaching the other side they throw themselves on to the snow. They are not firing but probably taking cover from mortar bombs, and we are far enough from where it strikes, although one can still feel the shock wave from the explosion.

The broad street was presumably Lehel Road.

It would be no bad thing to make it snappy, sonny boy, says a man next to me. I don't know where he came from. He is in a black winter coat and has wrapped his head in a rag. No bad thing at all before they start peppering our arses. What are you doing wandering the streets at this time? Where are your mother and father?

Father is keeping his distance behind Gizi and I behind Mother and Vera. A growing number of people are wedging themselves in between. Everyone is in a hurry; some are running and some, like the soldiers, throw themselves on the snow when mortars impact.

The last time I saw so many faces was when we had soldiers escorting us and people stared at us from the pavement. Now no one stares at anybody; everyone minds their own business. Those damn fools still want to fight, pants a man who is pushing ahead beside me. Aren't you in a Levente troop? Sure, I say, I'm a Levente. Make yourself scarce, because Leventes are also being pulled in. Yes, sir, I say. One can tell you're a Levente, he says. You get trained to say, Yes, sir, Yes, sir. Take care no one mistakes you for a Jew. Yes, sir, I'll take care, I say. Those bloody fools even took me to be a Jew. Now tell me straight. Do I look like a Jew?

He stops and rips the rag from round his head.

Father and Vera are drawing further away, but still I can see them better when I am stopped.

No, sir, you don't look anything like one.

It's all the same to them. If they're in the mood they just bring out the submachine gun and pop! That's a nice duffel coat. Are you from Transylvania? Yes, I say.

I can't see Gizi, can't see Father; Mother and Vera are now turning at the corner.

Nice to have met you! This is where I turn off.

Father's steps are increasingly secure. Since we started he seems to have regained his strength. He waits for Mother and takes the haversack off her while Mother takes over Vera's little suitcase.

Gizi is waiting for us on one of the corners. When I get there I can see there is an anti-tank gun no more than thirty metres away; around it eight to ten German solders are stamping in the cold. Their NCO is smoking a cigarette. The five of us walk on together with Gizi blowing kisses to the soldiers. The NCO salutes. One young soldier looks Vera up and down.

Gizi makes a sign, so I drop back again.

I have no idea where we are going, but maybe we have now covered about half the distance. Everyone is watching out for mortars, which are landing all round, and everyone is carrying something, whether a sack or a bag or a suitcase – some are even carrying boxes tied up with string.

Do you remember that route we took from Szabolcs Street? I ask Mother.

She reels off a list of street names. There were two air-raid warnings, she says; twice we had to go down into cellars.

I remember one air-raid shelter.

People got used to the wailing of the sirens, like bursts of submachine-gun fire or the crumps of mortars.

Collapsed walls of houses. Seeing houses in ruins.

Gizi stops again, Father as well, and he signals to Mother and Vera. If Gizi decides that we must turn back it will be my job to keep track of what is going on behind me. Perhaps she spotted an Arrow Cross patrol, maybe a patrol of Germans or regular Hungarian Army or policemen.

It only matters to us what she saw; the rest carry on as before.

A mortar hits near by.

Aircraft are coming over from the direction of Rákospalota.

Gizi beckons from a gateway. Down into the cellar, quick!

It's like stumbling into the basement of the hospital once more. Pocket torches provide light. Women, children and some men. We press against the wall, Vera next to me, Mother hand in hand with Father. Gizi was carried further along by the jostling. It's a good job she has a torch and can shine the light on herself.

It is rather as if we had not got this far across snowy squares and streets but along a lengthy tunnel that the sprinters, haulers, fugitives and those seeking a hiding place have cut deep underground. The yelling, the darkness and the pushing do not bother me; I have got used to it. Opening one's mouth is not a good idea–I've learned that. The person next to me might be no threat, but then again they might. I still do not know precisely where we are headed, although I suppose Gizi must. According to our Swiss paperwork, Vera and I are sister and brother, and Gizi has warned Father that under no circumstances should he produce the letter if an Arrow Cross patrol, policemen or gendarme stops us to check our papers, because that letter requires us to wear a yellow star.

What am I supposed to say if we have to identify ourselves, Father asks.

That's why I'm going first, Béla. That's why you come behind. That's why your son is keeping an eye out behind. To avoid anyone who might ask for our papers.

We are standing among men, pinned to the wall. I'm from Zugló. I hear this is the fourth air-raid warning since this morning. He is standing with his back to me, so I can't see his face. He lists the streets where he had to take cover in air-raid shelters.

Vera wants to sit down on the concrete, but I don't allow her. She might catch a cold and she could be trampled on if the crowd were to get going.

I said four years ago that it would come to this, says the man from Zugló. Even Napoleon came to grief. I said at the time, when that crazy painter roped us in, he was right about the Jews. Fair enough, that's acceptable, but why did he bring this war on us? Put a sock in it, someone else says. I don't give a shit about putting a sock in it, understand? Don't you or anybody else tell me to put a sock in it. My son was shot before my own eyes for legging it from his company, before my own eyes, understand? Now that shut *you* up sharpish, didn't it.

And I was there at the Russian breakthrough at Uriv, says someone in the corner in a dispassionate tone of voice. I got a shrapnel wound in my leg.

From the Russians?

Listen, the dispassionate tone continues, I fought up to the Don Bend, and I saw the shtetls being burned down, how every crappy little shack was looted, and that was sweet FA compared with what we're getting now.

Stop stirring it, will you? Just be thankful the residents put up with you lot, someone shouts.

I find it impossible to tell which voice is which.

I was with a Jewish labour-service brigade. Are you a Jew? A sergeant, I was, deputy commander of a squadron. Have you any idea of the order I had to issue? No leave for anyone in the crew while a single Jew lives. The Jews did mine clearance. At least that was one useful thing they could do.

The man with his head wrapped in a rag who has been walking beside me is boring his way through the crowd, trying to get near me. You keep your trap shut it and push your way in, I hear from one of the earlier voices. Why the shush now? Got some secret to hide? And who are you anyway?

Pocket torches are switched on. A hand grabs the rag from off his head. I suppose he is around Father's age, but he is already grey-haired. He has prominent features. Why shouldn't I keep quiet? His voice is firm. That's it, says the man next to him. He's keeping very quiet, trying hard not to say anything. Who are you? What do you do for a living? I'm a physicist. What sort of physicist? A professor of physics at the university, sir, if it's all the same to you. That's no reason not to speak up. There isn't anything I have to say, sir. You and your kind talk as if this was all one country; you talk as if the country had been destroyed by others, the bridges, the city; you don't even notice that this has not been one country for ages. What, then? There you are, sir. That is why I keep quiet, or shut it, as you so quaintly term it, because I have no wish to say certain things out loud.

By now Gizi is standing next to me and tells me it is time to move on.

Again there are lots of people around us, all carrying something. One elderly woman is clasping a dachshund.

The physics professor is again pressing his way forward among us in the snow.

There is a long line standing in front of a bakery. We have no bread, so it would be a good idea to join the queue, but we have to keep going or we shall lose sight of Gizi. A woman rushes out of a house, her face bleeding. Someone shouts, and Gizi stops. Her expression is as it was when I entered her room at the Red Cross home on Mihály Munkácsy Street. She was looking similarly confused then. Father steps over to her and wants to take cover, takes the Red Cross armband off her then walks on without her. You've got to go, son, says the physicist.

The carcass of a horse amid the ruins, one side stripped down to the bones. A man in an army jacket, hat on head, is carrying a watering can in one hand and an axe in the other.

On the 1943 map much of the area on the Pest side of Margit Island, down as far as Ipoly Street, is not built up, with the Transport Museum on the other corner. Possibly the house where we went into the cellar may today be situated a block further north, on Gogol Street. To the best of Mother's knowledge Gogol Street in those days was called Garam Street. She says it was in the cellar of number 38 that we took shelter. How does she remember that? Well, a classmate of hers lived at number 36; she had paid visits there. That's what I said to Gizi when the siren went off, that we should go to the house in which Tessa lived, but number 36 had been bombed out, and everyone was running to the house next door.

Number 38 Gogol Street is a newly repainted old building. The acid-green paint is awful. Beside it is a shop selling gold and silver jewellery and next to it a sign for a 'Wine-Beer-Restaurant'. On the 1943 map the nearby plots of undeveloped land are designated by pale-yellow areas.

The word in the column is that the weaving mills should be avoided. Artillery emplacements have been set up near by, and these are targets for the bombers; the carpet bombing is down to them. And also because of the Western Railway Terminus and Rákosren-dező Railway Station just to the north, says another man.

When the encirclement of Budapest was complete Hitler ordered the IVth SS Panzerkorps and the 96th and 711th Infantry Divisions, a total of two hundred tanks and sixty thousand men, to redeploy to Hungary. SS Gruppenführer Herbert Otto Gille was appointed commander. Himmler telegraphed Gille as follows:

> The Führer has appointed you, along with your corps to lead the relief forces for Budapest since you have experience of being encircled on several occasions and thus bear the greatest sympathy for the fate of the besieged formations, and your corps was the quickest to prove itself on the Eastern Front.

The daily bread ration for Budapest's inhabitants was 15 deca-grams, and for Christmas 1944 12 decagrams of meat was allowed. The water supply was at best fitful and in many places had ceased altogether. The command of the Hungarian 1st Army ordered that a special defensive campaign badge be made for those taking part in the fighting. From Sopron, on the western border of Hungary, Ferenc Szálasi rejected the assistance offered to Budapesters by the International Committee of the Red Cross because one condition was that food would have to be delivered to the ghetto.

Gizi pulls on the ICRC armband again, puts an arm round Father's waist and supports him; she must have said something, because Father then starts to limp.

There are five in the Arrow Cross group. They jostle a few men to a house wall and carry out an identification check on them. One of them cannot be much older than me; from the middle of the road he lets off two short bursts into the air from a submachine gun. Mother takes cover in a gateway and calls out to us. There is a store next to the entrance. The physicist is waiting on the lowest step. The Arrow Crosser who just fired two bursts at the sky hoicks him on to the pavement and levels his gun at him. I cannot hear what he says. The physicist bursts out laughing and looks at the boy in disgust. He unbuttons his winter coat. A gob of saliva appears on his lower lip; he does not spit but laughs and undoes his trouser fly. He glances at me. It is as if he were trying to warn me. That may be why he is still laughing. He reaches into the fly to show the submachine gunner what he is curious to see.

The Arrow Crossers select three men and direct them off towards Pozsonyi Road on the southern edge of the XIIIth District.

All five of us proceed side by side. Gizi does not go ahead; I do not drop back. We have been joined by the physicist.

Gizi later related, Mother says, that she had been given three addresses, but the protected houses were so crowded that she did not know which of them would accept us.

Avoid factories, a man shouts, that's where they're dropping the bombs. Even the Riegler boys do not head in that direction.

Gizi turns into Ipoly Street. We're going towards the factories, she says. Even the patrols give that part a miss. You heard it yourselves.

By now the physicist is in conversation with Father. Two anti-aircraft batteries in Gyapjúmosó Yard. The big market hall has been destroyed by bombs; the iron railings are now leaning out on to the pavement. The man in command is a German sergeant, but I can see Hungarian artillerymen in the gun crew, two of them carrying crates of ammunition, the rest scanning the skies. Gizi says that she and Mother will flank Father and the physicist, while we should walk on in such a way that the soldiers can only see women and us, the children, Vera asks her how far we still have to go. Not much further, says Gizi. When we get to the guns Father begins limping again.

We make a left turn into Pannónia Street towards the city centre. A block further south, at the junction with Csanády Street, a German panzer is approaching; behind it assault paratroopers are fanning out. I am familiar with the military terms. For years I've been reading in newspapers about what artillery emplacements, salvo fire, flexible disengagement, house-to-house combat and carpet bombing are. Previously I have only ever seen paratroopers behind tanks in cinema newsreels. The caterpillar tracks rattle two to three metres away from us; the soldiers, with their MP40 submachine guns ready to fire, pay us not the slightest attention.

What would have happened if it had been me and not the physicist who was made to unbutton his fly?

The older of the Riegler boys told me at the Red Cross home on Mihály Munkácsy Street that there was one occasion when he had once been ordered to unbutton his trousers. A kid no older than me, he said. He had never seen anyone's cock but his own. Maybe he had just heard that this was what had to be done when checking some-one's identification. What happened? What happened, Riegler guffawed, was that I told him, have a good look, Sonny Jim, because never before have you seen anything as fine as this. And then? I pulled it out. I'm right, aren't I? You've never seen anything as fine as this before? At which he told me to bugger off, said Riegler.

A corpse is lying on the ground at the corner of Pannónia Street and Károly Légrády Street. With one arm sticking out of the snow, it seems his last gesture was a wave.

Father tells the physicist that the Red Cross will guide us to a place of refuge. I don't understand why he is talking to a stranger. Admittedly the physicist did indicate caution with his look when the Arrow Crosser had made him unbutton his fly. And Father had told him I was his son. He introduced me while we were on the move, but I don't understand why this was important to him. He didn't intro-duce Vera, possibly because on the spur of the moment he is unable to say 'my daughter'. I do not hear what Father might have said, only that the physicist rejoins, That's the way it is, you see. They saw everything, knew about everything, but now they behave as if they knew nothing, if you please, as if they had been blind.

Maybe I noted the comment because of that 'as if they had been'.

Do you remember, I ask Vera twenty years later, what the physicist said about the people who were standing in doorways and on the pavement in Pannónia Street?

Vera only remembers the rats on the steps of the stores and the fact that she repeatedly asked Auntie Gizi (that's what she ended up calling her) where her mummy might be, and the third time she asked Gizi had replied that she had no idea where she might be either. And I didn't understand, says Vera, why she said it that way: she had no idea where she might be *either*.

Several blocks on, by now only a block away from the Grand Outer Circle, we reach József Katona Street.

I had never walked down Pannónia Street. It must have been near the Vígszínház comedy theatre on St István Outer Circle where I had been twice. Last year I went to see the musical *Fekete Péter* (*Black Peter*) with my parents, and we also saw Thornton Wilder's *Our Town*. In front of the red velvet stage curtain actor Artúr Somlay, playing the Stage Manager, introduced the story and its setting, and when the curtains opened he strolled in among the characters, who, some seated, some standing, were chatting among themselves. I later understood that they were playing dead people, and they were remembering their lives.

On the gateway to number 5/a Tátra Street, the next street leading off the Outer Circle, a Swiss letter of protection is framed next to a yellow star. A policeman is standing in front of the house. Gizi shows him her identification; the policeman salutes and calls for the warden of the house. He says he is not permitted to let anyone in. There is no more room and yesterday ten rooms had to be vacated because, in line with an agreement between legations, they were supposed to admit people under Swedish protection. Father shows him the family's letter. The warden spreads his arms and says there isn't room to fit anyone else in, even in the corridors. New people have been coming for hours; it's not just us he has had to refuse.

Vera says I should ask Mother if she has anything to eat. The warden closes the gate. Vera does not repeat that she is hungry but asks whether we have got to Buda. That would have to mean we crossed the Danube, I say. On those planks again?

The physicist says something to Gizi. We turn back for Pannónia Street. A German tank again approaches, probably the same one we met earlier, the soldiers behind it likewise holding their MP40 submachine guns ready to shoot.

Father reckons the physicist told Gizi that his cousin lives at number 36 Pannónia Street, and as far as he knows he is the warden there. Number 36 Pannónia Street also figured on Gizi's list, but according to the Swiss Legation we should only try there as a last resort, she says, as there were so many already there.

The physicist goes ahead and rings at the gate. On the pavement over on the far side of the road two Arrow Crossers are racing after the German tank. A tall woman comes out and embraces the physicist. They enter into a conversation with Gizi. The woman raises her hands in a declining gesture. The physicist unwinds the strip of sacking from round his head. The woman tells him, Laci, you would be best advised to go elsewhere because you'll be taken for a Jew, and you'll be taken away any time they line the people here up.

The physicist asks his cousin why they had stayed in the house if the situation was that risky. Gizi later recounted, says Mother, that the woman simply said that this was where they had lived for thirty years, and Berci had not wanted to move. He had become the warden, he had army contacts, you know, he was a sergeant in the Great War, at which the physicist said that he had wanted to be admitted to his university department, but it seems that had been impossible. There was just one bed for him, the woman responded loudly. One place can be found, Laci, but only one. This is a whole family here, good friends of mine, with two children, says the physicist. Gizi holds her papers under the woman's nose. They have a Swiss safe-conduct letter that's valid for all four of them, she says. Carl Lutz, the chargé d'affaires at the legation, referred them to this house.

The woman goes inside and comes back a little later. Gizi beckons. Father takes me by the hand; Mother takes Vera. Three soldiers are approaching from the corner, one of them an officer. They come to a halt in front of the gate. The woman pulls back into the stairwell while Gizi speaks with the officer. The soldiers hurry away. The stairwell is dark; the blue-painted electric bulb is providing light on the third or fourth floors. The entrance is spacious, with marble inside and wrought-iron banisters on the steps. The steps wind to the right in a semicircle to the first floor. We step over those sitting on the landings; children are asleep on mattresses. Father introduces himself to the warden, who is a tall man wearing a leather coat and an old-fashioned officer's cap. He looks at the fancy braiding on my coat and checks the paperwork. I've got two days of rations for 234 people, he tells Gizi. We've acquired two field kitchens and set them up in the yard. The womenfolk have to work around those. The menfolk have to chop wood, and every day a group of four goes out to fetch bread during the hours outside the curfew that are permitted for those wearing yellow stars. That's risky as they might get picked up by an Arrow Cross patrol looking to take people off to the bank of the Danube, as they so charmingly put it.

His wife is standing beside him. She is as tall as him with the same ashen features, her wrinkles just as deep.

You can count on us, Father declares. My wife cooks, my son will lend a hand with the wood chopping, and I'll go for bread when it's my turn.

Gizi says to Vera, And you'll do your bit to help as well, won't you, with washing the dishes and cleaning? Terrified, Vera nods.

I can't guarantee a bed, says the woman. Even the cellar is overcrowded. You can take your pick. Either you can go downstairs into the cellar corridor, where you can sit on a haversack or else you go up to the fourth floor where one of the apartments has been cleared out, but it's as cold as out on the street.

Father and Mother consult. I just hope they won't opt for the cellar corridor because Vera is afraid of the dark.

Gizi takes leave; we have no idea where she is going. She says something to the warden, and he raises a hand to his officer's cap in salute. I haven't seen the physicist since we entered the house. Gizi gives all four of us a kiss. Mother is crying, but why now of all times?

A four-room apartment on the fourth floor. The bathroom alone, tiled all the way up to the ceiling, is as big as one of the smaller rooms. All the windowpanes have been shattered by the bomb blasts. Father and Mother spend the night in easy chairs in the dining-room, Vera on a settee in the middle room, while I sleep in a corner room on a divan. Father rustles up two blankets and spreads one over Vera, the second over me.

The carpets must have been carried away; the cupboards are wide-open, the shelves are empty, clothes hangers are scattered all around. A bomb has torn a hole in the ceiling of the fourth room.

The next morning Mother finds a crust of dry bread, which she shares out, and opens one of our last remaining tins of liver pâté. Father goes downstairs, although I don't know where. He comes back then goes off to queue for drinking water. The duffel coat is wrapped round Vera's shoulders with the collar pulled up as well, so only her forehead and eyes can be seen. Father looks for the warden then comes back. He says he is going downstairs to chop firewood, so I go, too.

The yard is huge expanse of concrete – it must be about ten by fifteen metres in size. The inner balconies of the house next door can be seen from it. The two of us chop the wood, and two other men carry it away. The warden says that retreating soldiers had left their cauldrons in the street, and it was from there they had been brought in. The wood is green and only catches light with difficulty. Some women bring out cooking pots. At noon we stand in line for a helping of beans. There is a shortage of mess tins and mugs into which to serve it. Anyone who has eaten their ration wipes out the vessel with a sheet of newspaper before handing it on. Mother goes up to the fourth floor to wash plates and spoons in the bathroom, having been warned that even if the water is running it is not drinkable. Vera ate the beans now, whereas she left half of what was dished out to her by the Linnerts on Amerikai Road.

I rearrange the things in my haversack. My hand comes across the shell, but I don't pull it out, not wishing Father or Mother to spot it, as they would know it belongs to Uncle Róbert.

Despite that they do see it. Mother tells me to take care of it. Aunt Bőzsi was very fond of it and will be delighted that I have held on to it.

I have not seen the physicist since we arrived. I visit a few of the apartments. I recognize nobody and do not ask around. There are six to eight people in each room, with places for bedding down even in the kitchens and bath tubs. We prepare methodically for the second night. Mother and Father decide that they will lie on the settee where Vera slept and will take the blanket she had. Vera comes to lie next to me, and we spread my duffel coat and Vera's winter coat over the blanket for both of us.

We are used to the drone of aircraft, the detonating bombs and the sound of anti-aircraft batteries, and we no longer even notice the sirens sounding air-raid warnings and the all-clear.

Mother tidies the blanket on us and tucks the coats under me just as she used to do with my coverlet when I was a small boy. Vera, before she goes to bed, pulls on another pullover and an extra pair of warm knickers.

Mother says that tomorrow night we may go down into the cellar after all.

I have a dream about walking with Vera along Francia Road. Two men with submachine guns are coming the opposite way from Thököly Road and they fire a burst at us. I grasp her hand; she has been hit by at least three rounds, with holes as big as a fist in her winter coat, in mine, too, not the windcheater nor the braided duffel coat but a pale-grey herringbone spring coat of English cloth. My grandfather had a coat like it, and I am sorry that I have ruined it. Vera laughs as she looks at the holes. I am now moving along streets with Vera that I had not previously been in. There are many people on the pavements, some watching with interest, some unconcerned, some who follow us, and when that happens we disappear only to carry on somewhere else.

Vera turns so that now we are lying face to face, and she places her head on my shoulder.

Jolán Bors makes an appearance and gives me a square from a bar of chocolate; Mrs Ulbert then comes and guides us into a corner of a cellar, which is just like the workshop on Francia Road. We make our bed on the bag-gluing table, with Vera leaving only her petticoat and knickers on, breathing heavily on my shoulder. She pulls my hand down between her thighs and jiggles it while holding on to my wrist. Do that, she pants, more, now. Oh! Never before have I heard her give such a cry of dismay. I am scared that it will wake my parents up, and they will rush in from the next room. It wasn't so much that her voice was terrifying, more that it broke off. She sat up as if she were looking for someone, for the person who had stifled her cry.

In the morning we have a hard job disentangling ourselves from under the blanket and coats. Vera avoids my look. I stand in front of her. What's up, then? she asks. Did you sleep well? You didn't wake up even once?

Father says that we'll all freeze up here; it's better we go downstairs after all, so we pack.

In the stairwell there are shouts.

They're here! They're here! Line up!

XI

From Pannónia Street I started off by heading for the Comedy Theatre, Gizi told Mother, but there were guns down by the Outer Circle, one of them at the theatre's entrance, so I went back to Sziget Street.[9] Gizi wanted to cross the Outer Circle and get back to Szabadság Place by the Parliament building, says Mother.

No light was filtering out of windows. A few people were racing towards the Outer Circle, bursts of submachine-gun fire from Pozsonyi Road. At the corner with József Katona Street a group was being escorted by three Arrow Crossers with submachine guns. Gizi wants to cross to the other side of the road, but one of the Arrow Crossers grabs her by the arm and thrusts her into the line of captives. Gizi points to her ICRC armband and produces her papers. She is placed next to two elderly men; the others are herded away toward Pozsonyi Road, two streets closer to the Danube. One of the men gives a wave of exasperation and, on the orders of the Arrow Crosser, sets off after the group. Gizi tells the machine-gunner to take her to the officer in command; he has violated diplomatic identification papers and will be answerable for that. On the orders of Herr Carl Lutz, the Swiss Vice-Consul, the man standing beside her had to be taken to the Swiss Legation. That very afternoon Carl Lutz had negotiated with Major-General Gyula Sédey, the police commissioner for the city, she says to the young Arrow Crosser, and Herr Lutz's actions were taken with the commissioner's consent.

The Arrow Crosser hares off after his superior.

Gizi pushes the elderly man into the doorway of the yellow-star house from which he had been led. Two bursts of submachine-gun fire strike the wall next to her; the Arrow Crosser is racing back. Gizi says that she does not know what happened to the elderly man. The Arrow Crosser leads her off to the group walking to Pozsonyi Street. At the head is a first lieutenant with an Arrow Cross armband. Gizi shows him her papers, but the first lieutenant looks at her rather than at the papers. He is tall, slim and has a wound on his chin; his cape is immaculate, white kid gloves, holster on his belt. He salutes Gizi and gives her back the papers. Madam, if I am not mistaken, you are Jewish, aren't you? he says. Gizi protests with a laugh. Begging your pardon, madam, the first lieutenant says, don't play games with me. You are Jewish. In our family we can spot the racially pure at a glance.

Gizi is wearing a dark-blue beret. With her right hand she sweeps her shoulder-length hair behind her ear then again holds out her diplomatic identification card to him. Madam, I will say it once again, there are some things a person can sense. He makes a sign to the armed men, and the procession moves off. The first lieutenant then steers Gizi over to a nearby house, which has an Arrow Cross sign on the doorway. According to this the Party has an office in the basement. A small bedsit apartment. The officer leads her in and takes off the white kid gloves; he undoes the belt and places it on a chair. On the wall is a framed portrait of Ferenc Szálasi.

Would you be so kind as to take off your clothes, madam.

Gizi takes off her three-quarter-length fur coat, the first lieutenant his cape. He has six medals on his tunic. Gizi spots an Iron Cross.

If you wish, madam, I shall turn away until you have undressed. Don't worry, you will get to the Swiss Legation by midnight.

At that the first lieutenant turns away.

Gizi reaches for the pistol, but the first lieutenant senses that and throws himself at her. She shoots point-blank at his brow. She pulls the trigger twice. She puts on her fur coat and adjusts the armband. The street is empty. There are bursts of submachine-gun fire from the direction of the river. Ack-ack guns at Margit Bridge are firing at dive-bombing aircraft. Nearby houses are on fire. Sneaking from one doorway to the next Gizi reaches Szabadság Square. A police sentry has been posted to the entrance of the building of the Swiss Legation's Department of Foreign Interests. She finds just one typist in the office, about twenty-five years old and wearing heavy-framed spectacles. She is sitting terrified in one corner. Gizi recognizes her and knows that she had come to the country two years ago from a Swiss village and had learned to speak Hungarian fairly well, notwithstanding which she asks if she might talk in German. It may be because she's panicking, Gizi supposes. Herr Lutz was unable to get back from

Buda and had charged Herr Feller, the legation's first secretary, with taking over business, but his car had been held up by the Arrow Crossers. From the window she had seen them taking him away.

Gizi goes to the bathroom and moistens her temples. She finds a bottle of cognac in a writing desk and asks the typist if she would like a glass. The young woman shakes her head. Gizi swigs from the bottle. She sits down in an armchair, and they look at each other without saying anything. Gizi then gets up and dials the number of Lutz's quarters in Buda. A woman's voice announces that the Vice-Consul is unable to take telephone calls at the moment. Gizi asks for Gertrud. Darling, I'm so relieved to hear from you . . . Gizi interrupts to ask her to get a message to Carl that Arrow Cross assault units are taking people off to the Danube from houses under Swiss protection in the international ghetto, St István Park, Tátra Street and Pannónia Street. He needs to go there at once.

Gertrud says she will tell her husband. Gizi should stay by the telephone; she will be called back very soon.

But you are OK, aren't you, darling?

Never felt better.

You speak very good German, madam. The young woman finally gets some words out.

It seems to Gizi that she is calmer, possibly because she is not on her own. She explains that both she and her younger sister had a German governess. Our father took language skills very seriously and was always saying that without languages he would never have achieved what he achieved.

And what did he achieve?

He was a scholar.

Of the German language?

No, he was a classicist.

The typist said that Giselle was a pretty name, very exclusive. She laughs as she says the word exclusive. Gizi gets the feeling she is trying to prove that she is not unfamiliar with circles of that type, and she even asks if she has a younger sister with such a pretty name . . .

Erzsébet, but we all call her Bőzsi.

So where is Bőzsi now?

Gizi looks hard at the typist until she sees the terror reappearing on her features. She gets up and so does the young woman.

Gizi dials again and Gertrud picks up the telephone again. You'll have to wait a bit. Carl is in conference with Signor Giorgio Perlasca – you know, the Italian who is pretending to be the Spanish Consul-General – and Mr Daniellson, the head of the Swedish mission, is also here. They are putting together some sort of statement.

Gizi tells the secretary that the Herr Vice-Consul had instructed her that she should get into the legation's car and get over to him as soon as possible.

What about me?

You stay here. The building is under police protection. It will soon be at an end. Calm down!

Carl Lutz writes in his diary that evening:

The war has reached our house in Buda. All the windows of the British Embassy were smashed to bits by the detonations. For us the darkest period has commenced. For a start I instruct the men to clear away the shards of glass from the stairwell. My chauffeur Charles also sets to it. He has just arrived back from Szabadság Square, bringing that pretty blonde whose acquaintance we made in November. She is also helping. We fill one bucket after another with kilograms of glass fragments. Renewed explosions from near by. I order the women and children to take shelter in the cellar. Five policemen who were under orders to protect us had to lug carpets, upholstered furniture and a metal cupboard of food into the cellar. In case of emergency we also have to have access to a slop pail and a hand basin. The cellar was used to store wine, and the ceiling is reinforced concrete thirty-five centimetres thick.

He wants to be left alone in the room that has been set up as a study room. Gertrud and Gizi do not go down to the cellar, but Lutz asks his wife to leave him to himself. There is a mirror on the wall. The features he sees in that seem calm in contrast to his feelings. He places the thumb of his left hand on the pulse of his right hand, counts and measures a pulse of seventy-six, which also surprises him. Daniellson and Perlasca had been undaunted, conducting themselves like soldiers, he considered. Wallenberg was prudent, taking steps elegantly in even the most horrific situations. Lutz also envied his martial resoluteness and worldly aplomb. He inspects himself in the mirror. I'm just an ordinary official, he thinks; he sees his look behind the glasses as being expressionless, which makes him smile, and with the smile he looks more self-contented.

Gertrud comes in. Don't be angry, darling, but Walter Rüfenacht, the consul in Vienna, is on the line and wants to have a word with you.

As it is three days since anyone from Switzerland made any enquiry Lutz is surprised that anyone is at all curious about him. He thanks the Viennese Consul for his interest and says that he is as well as can be expected under the circumstances, but Budapest is experiencing a terrible time, with armed Arrow Crossers who were allied to the Germans murdering by the thousand Jews, military deserters and anyone at all whom they regard as unreliable. He had received a message that assault groups were preparing to set the ghetto alight. Even the German military command opposed that, but he did not know whether it could be prevented. We are in God's hands, says Walter Rüfenacht and hastily ends the call.

From the window Lutz can see that the city on the far bank of the Danube is alight. German tank columns can be tracked on the bridges that are still intact. He last paid a visit to Rüfenacht the previous year when he broke his journey back to Berne in Vienna. Walter used to compose poetry when he was young, he told Gertrud; he had become a superb official, but he always strove to turn the conversation on to art. Even with you, Gertrud had asked? Just imagine, even with me.

They had stood by the window in the consular office. Rüfenacht had shown him his bust of Lessing and said proudly, You see, Carl, German culture has given the world some great minds. Lutz had nodded, ashamed that all he knew of Lessing was just the name, he admitted, and you know, Walter, it has also given the world some great minds that were driven out of Germany. Rüfenacht had taken a newspaper out of a desk drawer. I understand who you are hinting at. Thomas Mann had declared that the age-old spirit of German art would help defeat the horror state that Germany had become.

Lutz is musing now that what had come to mind in Rüfenacht's office was not Thomas Mann, even though he had read two of his novels in his younger days.

He can also see from his window the burning cupola of Western Railway Station.

He fishes out from a desk drawer a tube of liniment. He takes off his socks, loosens his necktie, unbuttons his shirt, leaving only his left arm sticking out while with his right hand he rubs the liniment on to his left shoulder. He had pulled a muscle when he helped carrying the buckets of glass shards. He sits down on the one and only chair. He pulls open the lowest drawer of the desk. The movement again reminds him of Walter Rüfenacht when he pulled out the newspaper he had hidden there. It may well have been an English paper, as a German one would most certainly not print a statement by Thomas Mann.

He spreads out a map on the table. A young man who worked in the Swiss Legation's Department of Foreign Interests had sought him out during the weeks immediately following his arrival in Budapest. Not long after the man had unexpectedly been recalled to Zürich. On his farewell visit he had handed over a large envelope. In it was a map that he had drawn up, and he asked the Vice-Consul to study it if he got the time. Lutz had wanted to open the envelope straight away. No, not now, please, but wait a couple of days, he had said, because then I will no longer be in Budapest.

Is it an official report?

Oh no, Mr Vice-Consul! It's an appendix from the dissertation I submitted to Zürich University.

A likeable fellow, quiet and modest, mused Lutz. I'm sorry you are leaving, he had said. A few days later he had opened the envelope. In fact, it had been a map of the countries of Europe. The USSR was a big red blot, the other countries in various colours. On each country was inscribed a year.

He read the text appended to the map then hid it in the lowest desk drawer. He was to take it out every so often in the years that followed, always taking care to close the door.

Various dates had been written on the territories of the countries of Europe, with countries bearing the same date being coloured similarly. The first group of countries were dated 1950; the second, 1960; the third, 1980, the fourth, 2000. The first group consisted of the USSR, Poland, Czechoslovakia, Yugoslavia and Bulgaria; the second the Baltic states, Romania and Hungary; the third the Netherlands, Belgium, France and Greece; the fourth the Scandinavian countries, the southern countries and the French and Italian parts of Switzerland.

Lutz reads the notes.

One proponent of a theory of races in the nineteenth century had been the anthropologist Vacher de Lapouge. He argued that Europe would perish if the long-headed (or dolichocephalic) Germanic races were to be squeezed out by intruding short-headed (brachycephalic) non-Germanic races. He had written that in the twentieth century millions would destroy each other because of just fractional differences in their cephalic index. According to Gobineau the Aryan races had created European civilization; development always came to a halt when Aryan blood became exhausted. Racial purity was a guarantee of a successful history, which was why the Aryan race had a historic mission – a Germanic world empire. That was what Rosenberg propounded and what Hitler wanted to accomplish. The first step was the crushing of the anti-Germanic Judaic world conspiracy, the annihilation of the Jewish race. Race theory underpinned genocide. That is what had prepared the ground for the Wannsee Conference the previous month. The succeeding steps were slave status for the enemies of the Nordic–Germanic world empire and varying degrees of assimilation of non-hostiles.

Lutz recalls how surprised he had been by the unexpected transfer of his young colleague in the legation. Wavy fair hair, thick fair eyebrows, blue eyes, a slightly stooping posture. Lutz also recalls making enquiries about the young man in Zürich in 1942. All he was told was that he was no longer in the diplomatic service but had returned to his scientific career. Of his own accord? Lutz had asked. You will have to ask Dr Heinrich Rothmund, head of the Police Division of the Federal Department of Justice and Police, for the answer to that.

On the evidence of his diary, in February 1942, when he received the envelope, he noted that he should speak to no one about it, not even Gertrud. When he first heard about the Wannsee Conference he wrote in his diary: how long was I blind, how long have all of us been blind? The entry for 15 November 1944:

Today we again went out to visit the Óbuda Brickworks. I managed to place a lot of people under protection. It has been certain for quite some time that Hitler is going to lose the war and his plan for a German world empire cannot be realized. What if it had been?

There is a knock on the door. Lutz places both envelope and diary back in the lower desk drawer.

I would never have believed that I would be able to survive what happened to us, Mother said once, but I would definitely not have been able to deal with what fell to Gizi's lot, and yet I carried on without searching for words to endorse what Mother had said, that she covered the route to Hegyeshalom not on foot but by military car. The look on Gizi's face when she talked about it was as if she were relating a fairy-tale, although I would say it was rather that she looked like someone who knew full well that what she was speaking about could only happen in a fairy-tale.

In the houses of the international ghetto those in possession of a safe-conduct letter are being lined up, Gizi tells Carl Lutz, and then taken off either to the main ghetto or to the bank of the Danube. Darling, you ought to make a telephone call to Major General Sédey, Gertrud says. Lutz does not telephone but summons his chauffeur. Charles, if you don't mind, there is one more trip to make after all, and he puts on his fur coat, as do Gertrud and Gizi, while the chauffeur buckles on a holster and pistol.

Coming in from Buda the black Packard moves at walking pace over the Széchenyi Chain Bridge. People with haversacks or suitcases in their hands are crossing from the Pest side in among tanks, helmeted troops of the Waffen-SS and troops of the Hungarian Army. The Packard is stopped in the middle of the bridge by two men with Arrow Cross armbands. Charles indicates the Swiss flag on the car, and Carl Lutz has to produce his diplomatic pass as do Gertrud and Gizi. A bombing attack had raked the upper storeys of the Gresham Palace building on the Pest bank overlooking the Chain Bridge, the windows of the Academy of Sciences had been smashed. There are six tanks by the Parliament building. Another check. One of the machine-gunners cannot be more than fourteen years old. What a nice face he has, says Gertrud to Gizi on the rear seat. The youngster is wearing an officer's cap cocked over one ear. He demands the papers with his gun trained on Carl Lutz. Lutz asks him if he speaks German. He does. Where did he learn it? At cadet school in Kőszeg on the frontier with Austria, but anyway his parents had engaged a *Fraülein* as governess. Lutz asks him what is the point of the war. We are fighting for the homeland, the boy says. They leave Kossuth Square in front of the Parliament building by Alkotmány Street before taking a left turn into Honvéd Street.

Horses are standing motionless beside abandoned artillery carts.

By Margit Bridge two Hungarian Bofors guns are firing in the direction of Western Railway Terminus. There are two dead bodies by the wheels.

On ringing the bell at number 5/a Tátra Street a man in a leather coat opens the door. He is not wearing a yellow star and so is not a Jew; he is the warden for the house. An hour ago fifteen people were taken away in the direction of the river by Arrow Crossers, he says. I was able to conceal two small children; the fifteen were picked at random, and they included women.

Gertrud photographs the warden. She had also taken shots on the Chain Bridge and in front of the Parliament building.

Carl Lutz has the sense of having seen and heard before everything that he sees and hears; everything he feels and thinks repeats itself, the way Charles looks at him like a soldier at his commandant. He indicates to Charles with his eyes to turn into Pannónia Street, as directed by Gizi. Also repeating themselves are the way the street empties out around them, the way the bombers drone above them, always these repetitions: armed Arrow Crossers in front of 36 Pannónia Street allow people to enter; an army corporal with an Arrow Cross armband gives orders. He shoots into the air. A man with a military bearing in a short fleece-lined coat is standing in front of him. Also repeated is the way Lutz climbs out of the car, orders Charles to take care of the women and the way Gertrud reaches for the camera, but Gizi warns her that now is not a good time to take photographs. He had also seen these faces many times before, the faces of those who have been lined up, even if he had never before encountered these particular women, children and elderly men who are standing in lines of three between men carrying submachine guns, while one can clearly see through the open door that other women, children and elderly men are jostling on the stairs. He can hear shots coming from the third or fourth floor; the people are falling over one another – by now there must be fifty of them on the street and perhaps twice or three times that number on the stairs. What is happening right now might be repeated in an hour's time. He displays his diplomatic pass and commands the ensign to return the column to the house. The warden steps up to Lutz, salutes and says that under the regulations he is responsible for all the people who hold protective papers, so there are not only Jews living there.

Charles steps over next to Lutz and undoes his holster.

Despite Gizi's warning Gertrud takes photographs.

Lutz asks the warden whether there is a working telephone in the house. It is not working. Lutz tells the ensign that he is there with an order from the chief of the metropolitan police force that the residents of buildings that are under the protection of foreign embassies are subject to a higher authority. Let him be clear about that. At a time like this it can quickly become a case of holding people responsible, to say nothing of the retribution that will swiftly come with the changing fortunes of war.

Gizi interprets for him. Her voice is sharper than Lutz's. Lutz is astounded by the ensign's uncertainty. Gizi says to the ensign that the Herr Consul had told her that a photographic record was being made and if he did not allow people to return to the house they would go straight to the supreme command and show them the photographs, but if people were allowed to go back the Herr Consul was willing to destroy the film on the spot.

The people who had been stood in line returned silently to the house.

Gizi asks Gertrud for the camera, takes the film out and tramples it into the nearest gutter.

The people are directed by the warden.

Charles buttons up his holster.

Gizi tells Lutz that she wants to look for someone and will be back in five minutes. She presses through the crowd of people at the entrance. Gertrud links arms with Lutz.

After ten minutes Lutz goes after Gizi into the house.

On the right is a flight of steps to the upper floors; on the left steps down to the cellar. Children press up to the wall; old people are sitting on the steps. The warden orders everyone to return to where they were before. Those who had found places in the apartments should go back there; those who were in the cellar should return there. Lutz asks him to shout for Gizi. In response to the call others start to cry out other names. The warden attempts to clear a way for Lutz. They reach the first floor. Now Lutz also calls out Gizi's name and again on the second floor. They go up to the fourth floor and come back down again. Lutz every now and again gazes into a pair of eyes, sometimes strokes a child's head. They descend into the cellar, with the warden shining a pocket torch. Lutz grasps the stair rail. It is quiet in the cellar, and that helps to gain a sense of the expanse of the space. The silence seems to strike against the walls, to squeeze into the cracks. The cellar must be enormous. He treads on bodies. It crosses his mind that he had had to reach here, the very depths of existence, in order to understand where he had got to. 'It was as if the darkness had become the face of the world,' he would write in his diary. 'At the time I submerged myself into it I would not have been able to define it that way, but now I know that it was the face of the world that was staring at me from that invisibility.'

XII

There are no clouds over Lake Maggiore.

The yellowed leaves of plane trees fall on to the promenade beside the shore of the lake.

Luxury cars roll away from hotel parking lots.

Boats shipping tourists from Italy are putting into Locarno harbour from the south.

It is as if I were watching familiar pictures from travel films. The lake is pristine blue in the sunshine, the woods on the mountainsides emerald green, the peaks snow-white and there are flowerbeds of yellow, pink and lilac in front of the terraces.

Everything is slowed down – steps, the movement of cars, the drifting of boats on the water – as if the second hands on clocks in the windows of the shops in the bazaar were also running more slowly.

At that moment I was sitting in silence with Ágnes Hirschi, Carl Lutz's stepdaughter, on a terrace of the Muralto Hotel which overlooks the lake. The seats and the tables are white, the tablecloths and chair cushions striped white and blue.

I had received telephone messages in Budapest: there were several on the answering machine, some in foreign languages.

They raise questions, digging into shared locations, shared events.

Z, an editor from Swiss television, turns up at my residence and records a two-hour interview about what I remember of Carl Lutz. I consent to use being made of it only on condition that they do not skip over the parts about the times Swiss diplomacy left him to his own devices and on more than one occasion obstructed him in his work in Budapest and even after the end of the war censured him for overstepping the bounds of his authority.

A few months later I receive an invitation to attend the shooting in Locarno.

I am cited to appear, evidently along with others. I had not prepared for that when I set to work on the book.

I am in luck as I am holding a fresh strand in my hands.

It is well known that private eyes like to keep one step ahead of the official machinery of the police in order to uncover things that might be impeded, or even forbidden, by the 'higher powers'. In such cases an opportunity may present itself to discover how the barriers are constructed; how false minutes or reports come into existence; and how an investigation can be sidetracked. In such cases the wider context may become clear, and anyone inclined to search for the structure of universal order in individual cases may satisfy his ambition.

Let anyone who wishes to try come forward, a voice prompts me.

Enough of that. As we've already said, let us drop questions that relate to time.

I have also suspected all along that I am both following and being followed. Ever since I met Györgyi. This is not hard to spot if one looks back over one's shoulder at the right moment. More interestingly, I am following myself, the follower.

As if there were more than one me.

Without any of them I am not who I am. I am transformed. In all likelihood I live in the transformations brought about by encounters with the insoluble.

As if my own shadow were able to alter its shape. Sometimes that terrifies me, and the only thing that sets my mind at rest is that I try to follow my own alterations.

So then, who is it who is drinking a coffee now on a terrace of the Muralto Hotel?

From Ágnes Hirschi's look I see that at first that is precisely what she wishes to know, but since we have been talking for half an hour I start to get the feeling that she is curious about something else. About herself.

What would be the most natural is for me to be grilling her, but she keeps asking more questions. Her mother married Carl Lutz two years after the war was over, while she herself was just six years old in 1944. I had supposed that she knew about everything that I did, but it seems that again I was mistaken. The unfailing curiosity of her gaze betrays that she would like to hear about what was happening around her at the time because a six-year-old girl's memories are unable to retain it all.

She pulls the sleeves of her black pullover up to her elbows. Her forearms are suntanned – she and her husband go skiing at this time of the year. Her white blouse is open-collared; her auburn hair is flecked with many strands of grey and cropped short like a boy's.

It is then that I note that Carl Lutz's chauffeur was called Charles; he had a six-year-old son.

We used to play together a lot.

I think she is telling me that in order to get me to understand the sorts of memories she has mostly retained.

I came across a photograph, I say, of Carl Lutz sitting in a wicker armchair with you on one knee and a little boy on the other. I have that photograph, she says. You know, we used to play together a lot, but I can't recall the name of Charles's son.

A hundred people, or maybe more, line up at number 7 Szabadság Square in front of the non-functioning US Embassy building, where at present the Swiss Legation's Department of Foreign Interests has its offices. After a long wait a woman steps out of the queue; she is around thirty. It is November, it is raining, but she is not wearing a hat. She is strong and is sporting a thickly applied purple lipstick. A policeman standing in the entrance tells her to get back in line. My daughter is a British citizen, she says. We have the right to prompt treatment. She has shoulder-length black hair; her eyes are almond-shaped. She takes out some documents. She is towing a young girl by the hand after her.

A boat puts in to the harbour. Its passengers take photographs and buy postcards.

Ágnes asks for a tea.

In 1938 my parents decided to travel to relatives in London. It was my father's idea. Well, that was where I was born. I'm a British citizen. Not long after I was born we returned to Budapest.

The black-haired young woman leads the little girl by the hand up to the first floor.

Half an hour later they are able to step into Carl Lutz's office.

My mother later told me she felt that because she had managed to get Lutz's attention regarding the fact that I am a British citizen it no doubt helped, she said, and even if that hadn't been the case we were just on the point of returning home; my mother had packed; my father already had false papers and a place where he could hide away. We went back to Szabadság Square, and my mother was given a job, so when Lutz went to Buda we went with him. Then the house was hit by a bomb, and we moved down to the cellar – that was where we slept. I remember it. All that separated the sleeping areas at night was a sheet, with Lutz and Gertrud on one side and my mother and me on the other.

I have to tell her about my own meetings with Carl Lutz; she is gathering recollections about her stepfather. In return I learn that Carl and Gertrud said affectionate farewells to each other in 1946, which was also when Ágnes's mother and father likewise said their affectionate farewells.

I first saw him at the Óbuda Brickworks, I say, though, of course, I had no idea at the time who it was I saw.

Ágnes sits on Carl Lutz's knee.

She is playing with Charles's young son.

She is looking over the unruffled surface of the lake and asks for another cup of tea.

They lugged iron bedsteads down into the cellar. I didn't want to go down there. I kept bumping into beds– knocked my knee, I did. It was dark; I remember the darkness most of all. My mother washed our underclothes in a bucket.

She jots down everything she learns about her stepfather, I imagine in an attempt to populate the blank spaces in her memories.

I ask whether the things she is told awaken any memories – faces, maybe experiences? She says there was a time when that was so; something would flash into her mind, it but would vanish straight away. Many's the time she would read over what she had noted down about what others had said about her stepfather. That makes it easier for her to accept that it all really happened, and she was there as well, she played a part, that's how she puts it. I accept it, she says, but I can't understand it.

What can't you understand?

That what happened could have happened.

Her look is just like that of the little girl sitting on her stepfather's knee in the photograph. The little girl is alert and pouting.

The skin of Ágnes's face is bronzed even without any make-up.

Of course, what with all the mountain air.

I ought to make a note myself about her skin colour, the mountain air as well – that kind of thing I all too easily forget. Later, when I get back to my room.

My room on the first floor overlooks the lake. I learn that among the trees and bushes to be found in the natural park are comparative rarities such as the sweet gum, the Serbian spruce and the Atlas cedar. There is a flight of stairs on both the right and left of the lobby, the red carpet being held in place by glistening brass stair-rods. The central candelabra has eight arms; the one above it, at the level of the first floor, has six; and the wall lamps are all from the same family of light fittings. The flooring is of white-and-red marble tiling with a lily-ornamented pattern in the centre, the lettering of which says Hotel Locarno. Double-leafed glass doors lead into an inner hall, which gives on to conference rooms. Over the central door is a marble table. Under the caption 'Conférence de Locarno' is the date, 5–16 October 1925. Nations taking part in the conference: Belgium, Great Britain, France, Italy, Poland, Czechoslovakia.

I take a snap of the table.

Under that search term my Larousse encyclopaedia does not list Poland and Czechoslovakia as being among the signatories of the Locarno Treaties,[10] but it does list Germany.

The marble table therefore says something different from the historical record and the encyclopaedia entry something different from the historical record:

> The Locarno Pact was entered into with the object of bringing lasting peace to Europe. Great Britain and Italy undertook to act as guarantors of the mutual recognition and inviolability of the borders of France, Germany and Belgium and placed the prospect of armed intervention in the event that Germany were to occupy the demilitarized zone of the Rhineland. Germany was admitted into the League of Nations. Belgium's neutrality officially ceased.

During those very days Carl Lutz was working as a counsellor at the Swiss Legation in Washington, DC, and meanwhile acquiring a bachelor's degree at George Washington University. He is tormented by uncertainty and fearful of the future, he writes in his diary.

During that period my own mother and father were celebrating their first wedding anniversary. I place wedding photographs in the same folder where I keep copies of the photographs that Carl Lutz took as a young man. This is also the place for a photograph of Gizi as a young girl, a photograph of the black Packard that I have from my documentation and also the shot I took of the marble table in the hall of the Grand Hotel in Locarno that documents the treaties.

Ágnes is entering the hall as I take the photograph. Almost imperceptibly she drags one foot.

I was familiar with it, I say about the photograph in which she can be seen with the chauffeur's son, but I didn't know who the boy was or even that the chauffeur was called Charles. Well, it's of no interest how vivid my memories of Charles's son are. He always wanted to hold my hand. I liked playing with him, but I would not allow him to hold my hand. She says, The young girl who lay in hiding with you, how old was she then? She was in her thirteenth year, I reply.

What would those days have been like for me had Vera not been there?

We sit down in the main hall. This is where prime ministers must have sat; here where they signed the treaties. Ágnes lays out a series of photographs on the table as if she were playing out her life before me: pictures of her as a girl, family pictures, one photograph with Carl Lutz, again a picture together with the chauffeur's son, a portrait picture of her mother. The look on her face is as if she were seeing the snaps for the first time. Her left hand is placed close to the last of them. She runs her fingers over her mother's face almost as if touching it.

As if I were not there.

The two of us stay together.

Perhaps what I told her is helping guide her in fingering the features of the face.

Her index finger circumscribes the lines of her mouth then reaches further up along the nose to the eyes.

At times I see a portrait of Vera's mother as Vera ran her finger over the photograph in exactly the same way.

Ágnes says, Yes, it was good playing with Charles's son. It made it easier to get through those days – well, then again, we were very small, whereas you were a bit older.

She does not say that we had slept in the same bed, which is what I told her on the terrace of the Muralto Hotel. I don't suppose she was all that curious about what might happen during a night-time encounter between a boy who was in his fifteenth year and a girl in her thirteenth. Maybe a face from her own older girlhood comes to mind, maybe the touch of another's hand; the gestures that live inside us can copy on to each other as we sit wordlessly looking at the trees of the park beyond the big terrace, she resting her elbows on the table as she exhales smoke.

Vera is smoking Kossuth cigarettes, her chin resting on cupped hands. We are sitting on a terrace of the Duna Hotel. It is the summer of 1963.

We come face to face in Kigyó Street, just near where the central thoroughfare of Lajos Kossuth Avenue leads on to the Pest end of Erzsébet Bridge. We had not seen one another for eighteen years. She had on a sleeveless blouse with a floral pattern and a light-blue pleated skirt. Her hair was cut short with a sun-bleached wave at the front.

Her eyes were not always so very blue, nor were lips so sinuous. She is not wearing a bra – when she leans forward one can see her small but nicely shaped breasts. She has a son, who right now is at a summer camp. Her husband, an engineer, is away representing his firm in East Germany. She is a secretary at some institution with a lengthy name, and she tells me what it is known for short as if that were any concern of mine.

In Kigyó Street our steps synchronize. The sun is shining directly ahead of us. On the terrace she asks for a Coke. She sets her chin on her cupped hands in exactly the same way as she did sitting by the piano when I tried to play 'Tango Bolero' on the keyboard. She lights a cigarette, blows out the smoke, places her elbows on the railing then sets her chin back on her hands.

No, I don't smoke.

Your mother used to smoke, she says. Every morning in Pannónia Street when we read off a menu all the things we would like to eat and we got down to the Dobos torte at the end, she said that instead of the cake she would rather smoke two Miriam cigarettes.

I don't recollect that, I said. I asked whether she wanted a dessert now.

Dobos torte?

It was me who asked, wasn't it? runs through my mind. She exhales smoke and asks again. Dobos torte? That would be really good.

So, I'll order it, I say. But only if you also have it, she says.

You found it very hard to get used to being my sister, I say.

Yes, it was hard.

Her laugh is shrill, just like when she was a young girl.

Now she is bent forward, stiffening up. She is not looking at me; I can tell that she is aware I can see down the front of her dress as far as her nipples.

You always did read right through the menu, I say finally.

Your mum made me practise the name so that I wouldn't blurt out my own name if I was asked.

I was aware that Vera's mother did not survive the war. Nor her father. My parents last saw her mother at Hegyeshalom.

We eat Dobos torte.

Dark clouds are scudding over the Danube from Buda. The waiters are dashing around, collecting the tablecloths before it starts to rain. We go over to a patisserie. A duo is playing, a pianist and a drummer.

Ten years later the Duna Hotel was demolished, or maybe it was only five years. The Intercontinental Hotel is thirty years old and now goes under the name of the Marriott Hotel.

We drink two sibling cognacs.

I can't recollect which of us said that what we were drinking were sibling cognacs.

I do not dare take her by the hand; it is she who takes hold of mine. She guides it down under the table. Her thigh is skinny, her upper arm, too.

On the fourth floor at number 36 Pannónia Street we lie under the bedclothes in a cold room, the windows of which have been blown out. On the bedspread is Soproni's duffel coat. We are not hugging each other; there is no room for my left hand so I place it on her thigh. Under her tracksuit trousers are a pair of Mother's warm, long-legged knickers. Her mouth is by my ear. She is breathing heavily. The drone of an aircraft; it is in diving that the fighter-bombers let loose their bombs. The anti-aircraft batteries by the Comedy Theatre bark out their response.

We down the cognacs simultaneously. There's something I would like to talk over with you, she says.

I pay the bill, and we set off.

She takes a bottle of Lánchíd cognac out of the drinks cabinet. There is a standard lamp in the corner and two armchairs. We drink the glasses of cognac standing – I would like a sibling kiss, she says. What makes her so purposeful? I wonder. All I see in her eyes is a bright blue. Our lips brush each other's face.

Yes, Mother warned us to be careful. Someone had said that it was quite certain we were not brother and sister. While Mother was admonishing us I could not see her face in the dark cellar. Would it be better to stage rows? I retorted. Should we have a row twice a day? No, no, not that, Mother swiftly answered. She seemed to be at a loss. Already then she was ten years older than Vera is now.

She walks over to a chest of drawers, her steps Karády style. She lights up a cigarette. In a silver frame on the chest of drawers is a portrait of her mother and father and a young boy with a teddy bear. Herself and a man, possibly her husband. I don't stoop to take a closer look, I'm not interested in her husband, and Vera, for her part, did not ask me about anything. The two of us were the original couple, siblings in the depths of the cellar.

That was the time she ran an index finger over the portrait of her mother, from the lips to the eyes, in the way Ágnes Hirschi did in the lobby of the Grand Hotel. Slowly as if she were tracing its contours.

She sits down on the sofa, unbuttons the top button of her blouse, then the next. Lies back.

Undress me, she says.

I am not wearing a vest under my polo shirt. Wait, she says, sit next to me. Take my blouse off. Lie down next to me. Her breasts are plum-shaped; the two darkening nipples stand erect. Take off your underpants, my knickers.

She is clamping her legs together so I cannot get at them. She giggles. I was more adroit then.

On Francia Road, on the big table in the workshop where Jolán Bors glued bags. I reached the palm of one hand under Vera's bottom. I try. She shifts a little to assist. She reaches back and takes a tablet from the back of the sofa. Slip it in, she whispers. Is this the way the two of you do it? I lean over. There is no tenderness in her gaze. This is how we do it. I can see that she is already on the way; there will be a route ready for me to follow. I carefully push the tablet into her. More, she whispers as if it were not me but my fingers she was talking to. Leave them in a good long time, she says to my fingers, that's right, like that, for a long time, everywhere, more, more, now come.

Her eyes are again steely blue slits. We are negotiating separate paths while her body moves with mine. I am on the border, my face not yet pressed into her neck. Her cheeks blush, the features grow taut, the panting ever shriller, already squealing. Why does she open her eyes so wide? What is she searching for in my face? The screech is the same as of old and yet not the same, a quite different scream. My face cannot press into her neck. I am compelled to watch the fixed pupils, like those of a corpse, as if what they were looking at was beyond me, but she was only able to look into my face.

I later asked her what it was she was looking at. Or rather, I asked, What did you see?

Nothing, she says. When it comes down to it, nothing, thank you. She kissed me in sisterly fashion on the cheek, although in our lovemaking there had been nothing that could be considered sibling-like.

Some time was spent like this, with us lying next to each other without bedclothes. She placed one of my hands on a breast, she placed the palm of one hand lightly on my crotch. I should not be shocked by what she is about to say, but what had finally happened just now had never before happened to her; she had supposed many times before that she would be unable to find release without me, although she did not say from what. She had become resigned to the fact that it was futile, that moment could not arrive. She had tried with others, and not just her husband, but never before, you know . . . What was it like? Like never before . . . Now it had happened at last, she chuckled. Thank you, brother.

When the captain had yelled out at the head of our column, as it stood ready to move off in the yard of the Óbuda Brickworks, that those aged sixty and over and those who were under sixteen could quit the ranks, and when Father adjusted my cap and Mother wound my scarf once more round my neck and told me what food was to be found in my haversack, and Father enumerated what documents and banknotes he had slipped into the pockets of my windcheater, and when the Róberts similarly said their farewells to Mádi and the gendarme NCO was lining us up, and Father shouted out names and addresses, Mother was looking at me as though she wanted her smile to live on as my lasting memory of those moments. I see them grasping each other's hands and waving with their free hands as they reached the wooden gate and made a turn to the left. In all likelihood in the very last moment before the column disappeared Vera had spotted her mother's face in the last row – or at least so she says.

Mrs Seidel is thirty-nine years old. She is wearing a black winter coat with an imitation astrakhan collar, high-heeled shoes and a dark-grey beret. When Vera joins the line of the elderly and children, she tells her to beware of *you know what*. Vera would like more than anything not to hear the same old warning, and Mrs Seidel concerns herself with the buckle on the strap of her haversack. Perhaps after that she looked for Vera, perhaps wishing to say something different and even waved, but I was no longer able to see her, and she almost certainly did not see me because I had ended up in the middle of the column. Yes, you were standing next to me; you must have been in the middle of the column, I say with my hand still resting on her nipple. The column had already reached the gate, and you shouted out to her, shouted out her name twice. You didn't shout out Mummy, Mummy or Mother, Mother. Maybe that's why I remember what you shouted out was Klári, Seidel Klári. The reason I shouted out Klári, Seidel Klári, she says, was because I reckoned that there were so many who were shouting out Mummy or Mother. Like I say, that's what everyone was shouting. I saw her. She was walking in the last line, and she heard me calling out her name, says Vera. She turned round, I could see her face. I'm sure she saw me because she started waving, maybe even walked on tiptoe so that I should be able to see her. She had the look of someone who understood that they had to go whereas I would be staying. Her look was as if she had sensed that she would never see me again, and that was how I felt myself.

At the time even she could have no certainty about that, any more than you.

But that was what her expression was like, says Vera meekly. There was a postcoital satisfaction in her voice.

Maybe you felt like that only afterwards, I say. Maybe you only feel that way now that you have told me.

She draws her hand away from my crotch, and I draw mine away from her nipple. She embraces me.

I'm not saying while we embrace one another that I don't recall Auntie Seidel's look.

I let go of your hand and wanted to run to her.

Wanting to run to her mother but being unable to is a frequent subject of her dreams. She says that was what she dreamed about on the big table at Francia Road, and while in her dream she was helping me to pull down her knickers, she saw her mother as she was warning her to beware of *you know what* when she was thrilling from the touch of my hand. She had never felt it before, but she had heard about it from women friends; she had wanted the thrill to intensify. I was awake, she says, by the time I reached for your hand so you would keep it there, so it would be even better. But even then I still saw her, and that made everything which was good hurt so much.

I don't tell Vera that her cry of pain on the table at Francia Road, as I withdrew my hand in terror and pulled out my handkerchief to mop myself, that her cry of pain I do remember.

You never talked about that kind of thing, I say.

That kind of thing cannot be spoken about. Your parents were so good with me, and it was also so good to be a sister, I never dared tell anyone before. Ever since then it always pops into my head just short of reaching a climax. I went to a sex psychiatrist, and he said it was understandable, far from unique, even used some technical term for it.

And you never even said anything about it to your husband?

He does everything as it is. I don't want him to know why it is painful for me; he does not deserve that. It's not his concern, it's yours.

I stroke her eyelids with the palm of my hand and kiss her cheek.

That was a sibling peck, she says contentedly, eyelids closed. That was so nice, come on again, like that, more, more . . .

Ágnes occasionally makes notes while I talk about my memories of her stepfather, sometimes making notes even when I am not actually speaking. She takes it as natural for me also to make notes sometimes in the lobby on the diplomats' table.

I note down that Vera experienced the joy of being able to forget when she was finally freed of the memory of her mother's look. That's what I tell Ágnes; yes, Vera and I were older than you and the chauffeur's little boy. Vera was already having her periods.

She blushes.

Sorry, excuse me, I say. That truly does not belong to this discussion. Oh, goodness me! she says. Did her parents come back?

No, they didn't . . .

What became of you two?

We were children . . . we drifted apart . . .

Vera's only surviving relative was a great-aunt. She lived with her until she was twenty-one. I had to break free from her somehow, she says. She married her husband one week after meeting him.

She kneels on me. She moves slowly on me, then speeds up. She closes her eyes, I close mine.

Almost thirty years later Ágnes seems to be watching with interest as I make notes. After all, she is not exactly unfamiliar with what I am jotting down, how, at the time of meeting Vera again nearly twenty years after everything that had happened and sharing with one another what it was possible to share while we made love and clung to one another's lips, we inhaled time into ourselves and sucked it out of each other, negated it. After all, Ágnes with her gentle smile is also wrestling with time, although in no way showing that for her, too, that was a struggle.

Thank you, Vera said again when she was lying beside me. I was dying to tell her how I had seen her body when she was a girl. Little beads of saliva appeared at the corners of her lips while she listened. My memories became part of her memories, the way we talked was as if she really did have an older brother and I a younger sister. The roles that had formerly been adopted out of necessity became a playground, even though both of us knew it was not that. When saying goodbye we had the feeling that everything repeats itself, although the fact that her mother's gaze had robbed her of the chance of being able to find herself or that we should treat each other as siblings would not be repeated.

*

My first-floor room is in the left wing.

I stroll along red-carpeted corridors. In the hall are armchairs with plush blue covers, art deco mirrors and wall lamps.

The first shoot commences at ten o'clock tomorrow morning. There are seven of us from Budapest. Ágnes will be the last and would like to hear each interview from start to finish.

Without Carl Lutz those who will be recalling their memories in front of the cameras would not have been in a position to recall anything at all, although it would be wrong to keep the role of blind chance completely out of the picture – the unpredictable, perhaps the momentary hesitation of a black-jacketed submachine gunner. An example in my case is the fact that on seeing the two approaching submachine gunners on Francia Road I put my arms round Vera and pushed her against the wall as if there were no opportunity to snog anywhere else. What I gather from Ágnes's expression on the terrace is although she, too, had been invited to conjure up her recollections, for her that was the least important aspect – it was more as if she were on a pilgrimage in our company.

We are called *survivors*. That was how we were introduced to the recording crew. While roaming the corridors the conviction grows in me that, although I was briefed that the moderator of the discussion was going to use that term, I have to object to it. It is not a role in which I care to be cast. I am not a survivor, I am a witness, and perhaps my role when I am in front of the camera is to say a few words about the difference between the two. I have a certain acquaintance with the ways in which any story can be shaped, including what we refer to as history, with the cooperation of primped and war-painted, generally platinum-blond moderators, with their striped neckties or black polo-neck pullovers.

Dust and silence.

The plush blue covers have a rather faded hue; the frames of the mirrors and wings of the doors are drab. It gives an impression that the Grand Hotel has very much the look of the turn of the nineteenth and twentieth centuries. A pair of eyes staring uncomprehendingly at those coming in through the door. I wonder what sort of stories befell its new guests in that future, in relation to which diplomats' tables, ministerial fountain pens, dinner jackets, uniforms, ladies' fans and the waltzes struck up at soirées signified a by-now irrevocable past.

As I see it, Ágnes is stuck at the same junctions as I am. Maybe she also feels that at times like these one has to decide which way to take. She knew her stepfather as a kindly, bespectacled gentleman. As his stepdaughter she lived with him for decades in a cosy, secure atmosphere, yet she may well be wondering what he was really like. On the terrace of the hotel she had mentioned that his diaries might probably be most helpful to those who had not lived in close proximity with him, had not seen him in family surroundings as she had and thus were not compelled to confront the picture that emerges from the texts of the diaries.

I think Ágnes was alarmed by everything that Carl Lutz wrote about the indifference of Swiss diplomacy, the transgressions that he had recorded, and for decades she was unable to bring order, in speaking about it, to what was fact and what might, perhaps, be attributable to Carl Lutz's pique. Ágnes, as I see it, possesses moral readiness, and that spurs her to explore and preserve a past that might not be her own, it is true, but from which she cannot free herself, it being her fate to follow in its footsteps.

Carl Lutz cannot have been active at number 36 Pannónia Street at the end of December 1944, she says, because he was not in a position to undertake any trips to cross from his place in Buda to the Pest bank.

But he had to be there.

It is quite certain he could not have been there, she says.

Does Ágnes know about something else?

Was Gizi remembering something else?

I am standing on the first floor of number 36 Pannónia Street, haversack on my shoulders. Those who are forming up in lines before the house report back that a black Packard with a diplomatic licence plate from the Swiss Embassy had pulled up.

By then we were in the cellar, says Ágnes. Nor were the telephone lines working then.

I go back across the first-floor corridor of the Grand Hotel. At the time Ágnes was all of six years old, so how could she have such an accurate memory?

If I press the brass door handles down one at a time, step through the twin-leaved doors of each room and were to find no one in the rooms or the lobbies, the staterooms or perhaps even behind the reception desk, I seem to hear the noise of steps from all quarters, snatches of conversation, a humming coming through walls from left and right, up and down, that is similar to the roar from the old conch shell. I keep it on my bookcase, never did give it back to Uncle Róbert or even say a word to Mádi; indeed, it did not come to mind even when she visited my place last autumn, as it is now such an integral item among my belongings, its roar, even without lifting it to my ear, is like the noise of the city merging with that of the trees in the City Park, of the sound of the trees in our garden when covered for winter, not so much the sound, or even the sigh, that goes with my breathing – the noise I sense emanating from all sides is that kind of humming. There are eight of us guests, everyone with their own story, the members of the television crew handling them like Etruscan vases, finds stored in the depths of archives, fraying folios, with delicate movements of the hand, with the fingertips, eight of us out of the multimillions. I don't know what the others think. I am aware that only the director, the editor-reporter, the two interpreters translating from Italian to French, the diligent camera operators, the sound engineer and the assistants think that anything can be authentically invoked only in the question-and-answer game.

For me, however, that all-pervading roar is the authentic.

I don't have a pipe to fiddle with to help me ponder enigmas. I do not even have a full tumbler of whisky on which to sip as I launch off on the mysteries. Prints of marvellous Impressionist paintings are hanging on the walls of the corridors, but it is certain that behind them there are no hidden doors behind which I might find reference maps.

Time loses its measurability. There is no point looking at my watch; I am walking in a broader space–time. I can hear scraps of conversation from the ground floor, words from behind doors. I descend the stairs, and the young doorman next to the reception desk greets me in Hungarian. He knows a few words in ten languages in which he can guide the hotel's guests. Two cameras are being taken into the staterooms. Some people are carrying crates.

I go back to the first floor; someone steps out of each room, some complete strangers. Elderly ladies in straw hats, young men in jeans, polo-neck jumpers, two-pieces, Adidas trainers, stiletto heels. Ágnes appears in the doorway of room 10. My own is room 4, and I need to ask her when she first read Carl Lutz's diary. Was it while her step-father was still living, and if so did she ask any questions? If so what were his answers?

I can't see Ágnes, although only just now she was on her way downstairs.

I go back down the stairs and enter the main lobby.

On the left is some Flemish furniture. This may be where prime ministers drank their coffees in 1925. A piano near to a double glass door leading on to an enormous balcony. A twenty-something blonde girl in white shorts and a red jumper is standing in front like a statue. Two elderly gentlemen in armchairs covered with gold-coloured silk upholstery are in conversation, holding glasses full of mineral water, beside the huge oval negotiating table; one is wearing britches, the other white gaiters.

Ágnes is seated on a Thonet bentwood chair in the far corner; it is a long walk across the hall to reach her, with my path being blocked by a group of tourists that must have just arrived but already wish to see the historical paraphernalia and are obscuring Ágnes. By the time I reach the far corner I do not find her, so I go out and hurry along corridors, opening doors to look in rooms, imagining at each turning that I can see her in front of a door, but by the time I reach it she is nowhere to be found. It is as if I am wandering around a haunted castle, albeit one I'd been to before, although maybe I'd read about a castle like this, an enormous, incomprehensible building in which nothing is what it seems: the hotel's walls extend beyond the park, the gravelled paths, the lake, the mountain peaks, as if the location were appearing on a screen and is inaccessible. It is reflected. As if my presence has also been manufactured.

A door slams behind me, another opens in front. Writing pad in hand, a continuity girl arrives in jeans, white blouse, a black waistcoat, blonde hair cascading on to her shoulders. We agree in English that the recording won't be starting tomorrow morning but at two o'clock in the afternoon. Yes, of course, I can come in a leather jacket. Leone will pose the questions in French, Anna will translate my answers into Hungarian, and in the technical unit a Hungarian–Italian interpreter will relay a translation into Leone's earphone.

I ask why all that is necessary. The master copy will be in Italian, she says, but Anna only speaks Hungarian and French, which is why

Leone will pose the questions in French, which therefore – Understood, I say – Anna will translate for my benefit. The continuity girl takes me by the arm. There are now seven of those with whom I arrived sitting in the main hall and, of course, Ágnes. I don't understand why I ever looked for her on the first floor. Leone, the editor-reporter, offers me a seat and tells us what he is looking for from those who have been invited. He is polite and gives advice. A camera operator studies our faces; he is also preparing for us, as if we were actors following the director's instructions – as if everyone was obliged to re-enact what had happened to them, that's what they are expecting from us. I am the youngest. Among us there is an 83-year-old woman who met Carl Lutz and has recollections of the meeting yet still ended up being transported to Auschwitz. He is going to ask about Auschwitz, Leone says, as solicitously as it is customary to ask a star actress to produce her own wonderful, inimitable style out in front of the camera.

It is no longer the eight of us *survivors*, as we are being called, who are listening to the instructions, preparing to meet the crew's demands. I ask Anna straight away to go ahead and translate for Leone my interjection specifically that we not be considered survivors but witnesses. Leone nods and thanks me, but it seems as if he doesn't get the difference. It may have been obscured in translation; perhaps the ground between the two categories is unbridgeable. Anyone can be a survivor, I say, both the victim and the executioner, whereas a witness is one who preserves, does not remember, does not accuse, does not defend, does not forget. *Oui, oui, oui, oui*, Leone nods. The director of photography is moving about between us. One of the ladies starts talking about how she was shoved into the line of people who ended up in the gas chamber at Ravensbrück, that she was able to avoid being gassed, and Leone would like her to stop her – better tomorrow, in front of the camera – but the words are now tumbling out of her. Anna is forced to translate, and I feel I have already read something similar to what the old girl is telling us – another elderly lady, not the one who was in Auschwitz. The story is familiar, much as if I had written it myself, so this evening I will put in a telephone call to Györgyi. Now it was me who has had to travel, but I will be back in Pest in five days' time. Everyone is interrupting everyone else; everyone is recalling something from their own history; and Leone is forced to declare that we shall continue tomorrow in front of the cameras, but right now we have to move to the next room, where, one after another, we are sat in a big armchair: sound check; lighting check. We are puppet figures; it is not we who will be present with our fates, our stories, but what the moderator appearing on the screen will later refer to as history, and just as Leone is incapable of understanding the difference between a survivor and a witness it will also be left obscure to viewers. At Györgyi's number only the answering machine picks up. I'm phoning from Locarno, I say to the machine. I see the elderly lady who is speaking about Ravensbrück and can't be stopped, not even by Leone's gentle hint. I see her very slowly raising her right hand – the gesture seems to take hours – defensively before her eyes. Is that because she is being blinded by the light, or she does not wish to see what she is remembering? A hand-held camera is working without instructions; maybe the cameraman already sees the picture on his viewfinder: an old lady screening her face.

An hour later I redial, and now there is another prerecorded message on Györgyi's answering machine; perhaps she had come home in the meantime and heard mine. Thanks. I've read it. It'll wait is the outgoing message, which can only be intended for me. I must have given her the telephone number of my hotel room in Locarno, although I can't imagine why I would have bothered, as a telephone call would be expensive. I wonder where she has kept my manuscript – on a chest of drawers, next to her family snaps, or on the bedside table to be read before going to sleep, in nightshirt or pyjamas, or maybe she only keeps her knickers on, maybe she sleeps naked. Why do I suppose that she concerns herself with me at all? From the tone of her voice, I suppose, the recorded message she left was more than just those few words, as if they also denoted solidarity, curiosity, interest and not just the one to whom the text was addressed. Of course, why wouldn't she be preoccupied with how I describe her.

Ágnes protested, fearing she could not express herself well in Hungarian. She was eight years old when Carl Lutz married her mother and moved away from Hungary. As she listened to what I had to say to her it was like she was listening to an incredible story, since the recollections that had stayed with her from when she was six had been preserved more like a nightmare, an endless cellar gloom, an endless series of detonations, *an endless night* is what she called it, and although even as a young girl she had then heard from her mother and later from Carl Lutz many things *about what happened*, as she put it, that was a quite different matter to having a conversation on the terrace of the Muralto Hotel about fate and history, about the eternally recurrent phrase in Lutz's diary of *I never could comprehend how it happened*. Ágnes did not herself put it in this way; I helped her to find the words. She protested again, but it pleased me that I was able to find a way for her to express her own fate, having lost her Hungarian over the years. It was important for her to know what happened to me – as she put it, *I want to understand my life*. Simple words, I thought, and it was not just through lack of practice in Hungarian that she had been unable to say it that way – quite possibly she would be unable to express it so even in German – how she realized that she wanted to understand her life.

Anna must be in her forties: an oval face, harassed features, notebook and pen constantly in her hands. Although she rarely writes anything down, she translates fluently. Leone sits next to her, opposite me, near to the camera. Leone reads out his questions leaning towards her ear; she seldom asks him to repeat and concentrates on the questions that are to be interpreted, yet I still get a feeling she is more interested in what I say and as if what interests her more than my answers is how I look, just as I am more interested in the way Anna, and Leone behind her, look than in the questions that are being asked.

Anna's glance oscillates in the time that opens up during her task: it is too big a gap for it to be navigable without effort, as if she could see only what just happens to be being spoken about at the moment. Only what just happens to be being spoken about at the moment, I note down on the balcony in the afternoon light after the first shoot. The shadows are lengthening on the sward of the park. *Only* what just happens to be being spoken about, I write, underlining the *only* in retrospect.

I write speedily, not always employing all the accents and punctuation marks which are called for in Hungarian.

Two figures are strolling hand in hand on a path separating the tennis court from the park. The man has on a pair of ducks and a polo-neck jumper of flame red with blue stripes, the woman a white linen skirt and flame-red jumper; they are emerging from under the leafy boughs of the park. The woman opens her yellow-and-white-striped parasol; a gardener in a straw hat is sprinkling the lawn.

I ask Anna to repeat the last question once more, and that request throws her into confusion. She may think she did not translate it accurately as she looks back and consults with Leone, but the thing is I understood what she said perfectly well and simply wanted to gain time before answering. I can see the other members of the crew are paying attention; they sense that the sudden pause might be of significance, and the man with the hand-held camera sets off towards me. Anna repeats the question. In what way does the figure of Carl Lutz live on in me. Would I try to describe it?

Now the followed and follower swap places inside me.

In no way. I make an effort to ensure my facial muscles do not betray the fact that I feel a degree of triumph.

Leone confers again with Anna. Anna says that Leone told her I mentioned earlier I had met Carl Lutz several times. That's true, I say, only at the time I did not know it was him; someone said he was an envoy from some neutral country, that was all that was said about him at the brickworks and also in front of children's home on Mihály Munkácsy Street and later at Pannónia Street. I also recalled his car as being a military Adler, but I had just now heard from Ágnes Hirschi that it was a Packard, and I would be correcting that in hindsight in the manuscript of my novel. What he is asking, says Anna, is that I try to evoke my recollections of the person about whom I found out in retrospect was Carl Lutz.

The game is now in my hands.

I pretend to be deliberating at length.

The hand-held camera is turning, no doubt trying to catch my features as I attempt to evoke the figure of Carl Lutz.

It is impossible to accomplish that, I say as I watch Leone's face, because I have seen such a great many photographs, and I am familiar with the descriptions of him, so inevitably my picture of him is built up on that basis. At times like this one's memories are also changed; the original is lost and what dominates is what others have fixed in position – it may resemble the original, but really it is a copy. I am taking care with my every word; that requires more concentration than is needed for the evocation of memories. I set out my position. One summons the private detective; one wants him to tell one what he knows. What has he found out that officialdom does not yet know? That is one of the problems, I say. One has to free oneself from the received image; one has to try to look into the unknown and find out what lies behind the obvious.

I sense that my tone, albeit involuntarily, is provocative. I hope the unseen synchronous interpreter who is speaking my words in Italian into Leone's ear is not driving that home with its emphases. Leone is nodding.

Anna says that Leone understands what I am saying, so let's move on. The next question, says Anna, is how do I imagine the final meeting between Carl Lutz and Adolf Eichmann went? A scene in the screenplay deals with that meeting, and actors will play Lutz and Eichmann.

For me, too, that posed an insoluble problem in writing the novel, I say. According to the information at my disposal it was years later when Lutz himself recalled the meeting, so in other words even his own diary cannot be considered a truly authentic point of reference, because even that diary was written by someone who was looking back; one has no idea of what sort of mood he was in or what he knew on the evening he wrote that entry, but as to who Adolf Eichmann was in reality, it is quite certain that when they met Lutz cannot have known about Eichmann's past record, no way. Eichmann had the advantage: he knew more about Lutz than Lutz did about him, but there is no doubt that it was a case of two thoroughly professional officials confronting each other.

Anna says that Leone does not understand this and asks me to explain it more fully.

There are a lot of people standing behind the crew, but who are they?

One is the official of death, another of life, I say, and both of them understood their jobs very well.

It is as if what we try to evoke always gets lost. As if everything ends up under the dominion of the present, and remembering is not remembering, the attempt to evoke something not an attempt to evoke something. As if everything that happened was annihilated by precisely the attempt to evoke it.

Leone gives up his grilling about the possibility of evoking the encounter between Lutz and Eichmann. Anna says he is curious to know if there are any memories that are very important to me – and Anna's look reveals that she at any rate, unlike Leone, is expecting me to say something. That hopeful, provocative gaze summons up a sound. It is a transient sound; I can hear it coming from very deep down; its shriek is rising. I remember a shriek best of all, I say. Leone is baffled. A cry, Anna translates but does not translate that as if questioning it but like someone who is repeating what I had said, as if she were trying to confirm it. And why is that so important to you? Leone asks in Anna's translation.

I do not speak French, but I can sense a difference in the way their words are weighted. The hand-held camera again moves in. I smile. Well, that is exactly what I would like to keep for myself, I say. An intimate detail perhaps, Anna translates. Not a bit of it, I declare, simply the key for my being able to remember at all, and I don't have multiple copies of that.

The following day I am asked if I would care to watch the shooting of the encounter between Lutz and Eichmann.

One of the first-storey apartments has been opened. Dilapidated furniture; lighting is used in an attempt to overcome the drabness of the place. The actors' costumes and make-up reminds one of all the clichés of war films seen a hundred times before. Leone explains to the actor playing Carl Lutz to look at Eichmann with an impassive face, under no circumstances to betray emotion. I would be curious what he thinks about Lutz's feelings, but he says nothing about them. The actor nods; he is willing and unhesitating. I've played that sort of role before, he says and mentions the title of a film – which rings a bell – an action film. I'm thinking of the scene when I know who the serial killer is, he says to Leone, but to be completely certain I have to make him show his hand – that's how Anna translates it for me. I take care that my features show nothing or he will slip through my fingers, the actor continues. It's something like that you have in mind, isn't it, though, of course, the figure has to be neatly turned out.

Leone turns away from him. That will be fine, you'll see, fine, he says.

Anna whispers in my ear. Leone also said it for my benefit, so he was sure that I knew that work with actors always requires compromises. They had wanted someone else for the role, but that actor was in the middle of shooting for another production.

I go outside into the park.

The couple I saw earlier are now strolling on the far side of the bushes. The skirt is now orange, the trousers cream-coloured, with one in a polo-neck sweater with a black diagonal stripe, the other in an orange blouse. They are holding hands.

Along the path I see posters about a Joseph Beuys exhibition in Ascona. I buy a return ticket for the boat and look for a seat on the outermost back row on the deck. In front I have the pristine blue lake, spread out among mountainsides clad in emerald-green forests, and behind me the fantastically colourful line of Locarno's hotels and, high above the buildings, the pristine sunlight-yellow Monastery of Madonna del Sasso from 1480 and snow-white peaks. I take a look at the exhibition in a pristine pink building on a slightly sloping, gently winding little road, and while I wait for the boat to make the return trip I drink a beer on the terrace opposite the harbour. Everyone is strolling or sitting, sunshades, white ducks, white Bermuda shorts, palm trees, the splashing of water.

I stood for a long time in each of the three exhibition rooms, reading all the captions. I was aware earlier but could now study how a work of art is produced from an object picked out of nature and, on being set back into nature, preserves its aesthetic objectness by dissolving into its infinitude. I am not particularly disposed to creative approaches of that kind, but on the way back I reflect on whether or not I do, in fact, work in this manner, and is not fate my natural material, which, after working on it, I then place back if not into nature but, as it were, into its natural medium of history.

Again I chose the bench on the outermost back row on the deck and have another look at Ancona's dream harbour, see the wicker chair in which I drank my beer. By now the colours of sunset dominate the pristine blue of the lake and emerald-green of the mountainsides as if a heavy metal gate had been lowered from the clouds. A layer of darkness is forming on the lake, as if the air were stratifying, one layer covering the other; all has been thrown into uncertainty; the line of Ancona's hotels in the distance seems both to be and not to be. The

Madonna del Sasso hovers, but it is impossible to tell whether that is above the city or below the clouds. The snow has perhaps melted off the peaks, the rocks float in the dusk, and when a farewell finally has to be taken from everything that was visible the light glimmers, quite from where is inexplicable – not at the base of the sky, not between the clouds as they open up, nor reflected from the calm surface of the lake; it glimmers and once more illumines everything.

A seagull is perched on the rail of the deck, an arm's length away, watching me, its body quivering.

After the sun has set the rose-tinted block of the Grand Hotel makes its appearance in its vespertine light. The huge terrace is out-lined. The walls become transparent; one can imagine black-coated ministers seated at diplomats' tables, lining up with ceremonial steps. Each takes his place in turn in the same armchair; secretaries hand each other pens to sign the agreements.

As if it were not the Madonna del Sasso which is many hundreds of years old but the Grand Hotel.

I had to come here in order to live to see the moment in which so much becomes transparent, to be able to glimpse even myself as I sit on a balcony of the first-floor room and note down that I had to come here, and so that after sunset I am able to participate once more in the illumining strength of the glimmering light, and it occurs to me that I encountered such a feeling a long time ago, but where was that and when . . . ?

The seagull takes wing from the railing. It circles around, its trajectory cannot be followed.

The string of market stalls, the cafés under the arcades, the hotel terraces that overlook the lake, shoppers. Ice-cream eaters, diners. Perambulators. Elderly women in jeans; young women in beribboned straw hats.

The couple is a few metres behind. Are they following me? They are in identical diamond-mosaic harlequin costumes, not holding hands, although their fingertips are touching each other.

A warning bell sounds in the distance. The sound is not shrill or soft; not quiet and not loud – I find it hard to say quite what the sound is like.

The lights of the Grand Hotel come on.

Every window is alight.

The big terrace overlooking the park is also floodlit; the walls, witnesses to history, are like backdrops. The boughs of the trees are fluttering in the wind as it picks up. Assistants are racing down the paths; make-up artists are at work on the steps leading to the terrace; camera operators arrive, cameras on shoulders. A young man in a white polo-neck sweater and white Bermuda shorts races towards the building with a military uniform over one arm; he has slapped an SS officer's cap with its death's-head badge on to his head.

The actors and the survivors gather on the terrace. Make-up artists are diligently at work on the faces. The actor playing the role of Eichmann feels the cap is too big for his head and is padding paper under the sweatband to make it fit better. My travelling companions are drinking coffee; the woman who was in Auschwitz asks for a tea.

The grounds slowly fill up with onlookers.

The two harlequins slip in not far from me, as if they really were under instructions to do so. Up till now I had always seen them as a couple moving about on a stage. Now they are watching as spectators.

Could it be that what I am seeing is two men? Or two women? Does it matter? In any case they are indistinguishable.

The tourists cannot have the slightest idea – even for me it is an insoluble task – who on the terrace is a survivor and who an actor. An assistant calls several of the spectators on to the terrace, as if the instruction did not come as a surprise to them, as if they had been waiting for it. A row of bushes in front of the terrace is hiding, like a fire screen, the legs of those waiting for the director's instructions, so that only the upper bodies, arms and heads can be seen as in a puppet show. As if the survivors were the actors and the actors the witnesses, an assistant with flowing blonde locks hurries towards me. *Schnell! Schnell!* I've been looking for you for ages, she calls out. I try to take cover; the two harlequins are considerately concealing me as if we had ended up in some shared scene. The assistant grabs me by the arm and repeats that people are being kept waiting. *Schnell! Schnell!* Dragging me behind her, wrestling me up the steps. I step among the performers with the gravity of my shame. I hear a cry of *Cameras roll!*

XIII

I know what I have to do when I have to line up.

Father does not fold the blanket up in military fashion – there is no time for that – he folds it in four and clamps it under one arm. Mother squeezes a pair of warm stockings into the pocket of my haversack. I carry Vera's little suitcase. Vera takes the blanket from Father, and he helps Mother put the haversack on her back.

Two Arrow Crossers are standing on the first-floor landing. We have to get into line; the front is already assembling in front of the gateway. Everyone is shouting out to husbands and wives, children try to stay beside their parents. Old people are helped down from the third-floor apartment. They are the last. Father says we should stand close together in line, to get into the same row at the front gate.

The warden is downstairs, a woman says.

How can you know that? You always know everything. You can't even see who is at the gate.

The gent came up just now. He said so.

The gent is the physicist. The warden is in negotiations about the house's residents being under the protection of the Swiss and Swedish legations, he tells Father.

Ghetto or the bank of the Danube? a man asks.

Don't . . . The warden is talking it over.

I'm telling you the warden won't have any say in the matter, and nor will you. In the end they'll make out they are in the same position as we are. If confronted, they'll pin yellow stars on; it would have been better if they had noticed earlier.

The physicist runs down to the gate then comes back up. People have arrived from the Swiss Legation he says. We are standing closely pressed together on the stairs. Listen here, people, the warden shouts out after a while. Everyone back to their places. Those who were in the cellar back to the cellar, and those who were in an apartment back to the apartment.

Gizi's call can also be heard shouting out Bőzsi's name. Mother wants to go down to her, but Father holds her back. He asks the warden if we might move down into the cellar because the apartment on the top floor is too cold.

The warden dishes out instructions: strident voice, short sentences. Do what I say. Calm down. There is no room in the cellar. Wait.

Mother attempts to push through the crush of people. She is calling out Gizi's name.

I've already said, no shouting.

But she's here. I can hear her voice.

I got used to everybody shouting all at once back at the brickworks. I can pick familiar voices out of the noise.

Father's voice is the same as months ago; he has regained his confidence. Your mother is freezing cold up there. We won't go back. I'm also freezing, says Vera. Better the cold than the dark, the crush, the shouting and whimpering all over again, is what I think. I can hear you, I can hear you, Mother keeps repeating, although I don't ask what she hears. Almost certainly Gizi's voice. It is difficult for two at once to pass through the doorway to the cellar. I am being shoved from behind – a man would like to bring out a little child in his arms, and we make room for him. Make way, air, he is calling out. Mother shouts out again that she can hear Gizi's voice, but she cannot find her. Someone says that a man was calling out Gizi's name a few minutes ago, but he wasn't unable to find her either.

The cellar is L-shaped. Two lamps provide the light. The walls are dank, the ceiling is supported by timber beams. There must be a ventilation slit somewhere, because the lights of the lamps are quivering in a draught.

The cries are more muffled. Names, instructions, calls for help blend into one. I say to Father, shouldn't Mother shout Gizi's name, but he says nothing to her. He would like to take off his haversack, but there is not enough room. I help him, with Vera taking her small suitcase.

Gizi shouts out Mother's name from the cellar doorway. She is wearing a black headscarf that has slipped over her eyes. She is gasping for breath, jostling the people around her. Mother embraces her; Vera, horrified, hangs on to me. I cannot hear what Mother is saying, but Gizi seems to be reassured.

Frau Gizella! Frau Gizella! Schnell! Schnell!

Mother says that we have rations for two days. Gizi says she will try to find some food, but she doesn't know where. The Arrow Cross Minister of the Interior has ordered that everyone must be taken into the ghetto from the protected houses as well. In return for dropping that plan, Raoul Wallenberg on behalf of the Swedish Attaché and Carl Lutz on behalf of the Swiss Legation had offered their stockpiles of food reserves for the protected houses. She would make every effort, but she had to dash now. Lutz had to see to things elsewhere. She was sticking with him; she would be back as soon as she could. She had two apples in her pockets and gave one to me, the other to Vera.

There is no longer an officer's cap on the warden's head. He raises one hand to his brow and salutes Gizi.

People are seated on mattresses; room has been made for the sick as well. Squeeze up to let this family in. The warden makes arrangements. Father gets Mother to sit down on the edge of a mattress; Mother pulls Vera over. Father also finds enough room to set down his haversack. Someone holds it. The physicist. He is seated on a sack and pulls me down next to him. As far as I can tell the sack contains potatoes. It has to be guarded. It's communal, belongs to the house – best if we sit on it.

I ask the physicist what his name is. He grins and offers his hand; he says only his Christian name, László. I also introduce myself by my given name. He has slender, bony fingers. The skin on the palm of the hand is warm and delicate; it is a pleasure to hold. I tell him that I have a pass as a Levente ARP messenger but have not yet had occasion to use it. Does he think it would be possible to go about on the streets with that? I dig it out of the inside pocket of the duffel coat while he fishes his spectacles out of his inner pocket. Wearing the glasses he really does look like a professor. He reminds me of my natural-history teacher. He also had glasses like those with thick black frames, and he looked over the skulls and the sponge models of human organs in his collection in just the same way before picking something, holding it in his hand so we would be able to see it better.

He squints and his features tighten up. He gives me the papers back. Don't use it. Put it away. It's good as a souvenir.

Is it a bad one?

It might be a pity to try it out.

From year 3 we had physics lessons, I tell him. I finished year 4 in May, but I wasn't able to go to back to school after this autumn. He asks if I liked physics. Not a lot; I preferred Hungarian and history. It doesn't matter if you don't like physics, but it will help you think clearly. I know that; the teacher said so as well. He asks who was our teacher, and I give him the name. He is great scientist; it's just that those idiots have not allowed him to teach at the university since the Jewish laws were brought in during the thirties. He carries on talking as though it was not me he was speaking to but quits his gesticulating as there is not enough room.

A call for a doctor can be heard from a corner at the back. A short man in a beret hurries over ; he has a Red Cross armband and is gripping a doctor's bag under one arm. The warden shouts out four names from the head of the cellar. Today's water-carrying brigade; they should be at the main gate in ten minutes' time. I'll go with them. I tell Father I'll take a quick look around and promise to be back in five minutes. Let him stretch his legs, the physicist says; he needs the exercise.

I try to tiptoe my way out and keep bumping into bodies. It is hardest of all to move forward in the shorter leg of the L-shape. When I get to the bend I am helped by the glimmer of light from the cellar head.

The warden's wife speaks in the same military voice as her husband. Just as tall, and she, too, goes around in a short fur-lined overcoat. She has a pointy nose; her chin is protuberant. They have a daughter whom I have not yet seen. She is said to be eighteen years old, ill and has to lie in bed, so maybe it was because they could not take her away that they stayed in a yellow-star house.

Three of the men who had been designated to carry water were standing at the gate. The warden is again wearing his old officer's cap. One of the men asks him where he acquired it. It's from the First World War, he says. One of the men in the cellar had been a first lieutenant in the First World War. He asked him for it. If he was a first lieutenant then he could also take a job on, the man comments. He's ill, says the warden. He has spells of amnesia.

I do not know what amnesia is, but fortunately neither does the man, because he asks. Loss of memory, says the warden. He remembers nothing? That I can't say; I can't concern myself with everything. Where's the fourth bloke who's been assigned?

The man with the Red Cross armband makes a hurried appearance. Sorry, he says, it was hard getting past the people. You stay here, says the warden; you are needed here. Today I'll be the fourth. We start in five minutes. Get the buckets ready.

Anyone who's curious about what amnesia is like can ask the doctor here, he says, but there are times when he himself cannot recall things. You're healthy, says the doctor; I've already taken your blood pressure.

From the front gate I can see that new anti-aircraft batteries have been placed in firing position by the Comedy Theatre. A caterpillar-tracked tank wheels out of Csanády Street, a couple of streets away, with a black-uniformed SS soldier in the turret scanning the road with binoculars. Two women, shopping baskets in hand, hasten to the far side of the road. An Arrow Crosser is approaching and changing the magazine in his submachine gun as he walks. An old man shouts to two children from the doorway of the house next door that they should clear off into the cellar.

Have you got a ciggy? A lanky boy, probably a couple of years older than me, has come up.

I don't smoke, I tell him. He has only recently got into the habit, but he hardly smokes because it ruins the voice. He is a singer with the chorus of OMIKE;[11] he has already had solo parts with them. I used to have a season ticket for OMIKE concerts, I say. That's where I heard baritone Andor Lendvai in *Faust* and Dezső Ernster, the bass, in *Aïda*. Did you enjoy *Aïda*? Yes, I did, but I thought they would put on a full performance; they just lined up in evening dress on the stage. There was no acting, only singing. That's what they call a concert performance, he says. When there is no money for costumes or scenery or time for rehearsals they sing from the score. Ernster knew his part anyway; he had the role at the Opera House until he was kicked out. Gabriella Relle sang the role of Aïda, do you remember? I remember. I was standing in the second row on the right as an understudy. It could have been another performance that I saw. But I may have seen you.

In my mind's eye I see a giant figure, his face like a statue. I have a seat in the eighth row on the right, and I am wearing brown corduroy trousers. Gabriella Relle is singing. But I am looking at the giant. In front of him is a short slim soprano so the giant's chest is also visible – as broad as if it were a papier-mâché structure designed to make him look so enormous. The others have little or no make-up, but his eyebrows are pencilled, his face is powdered white and his lips are very red.

I was heavily made up to make me look older, he says.

He does not have a winter coat on, just a rust-coloured pullover – his chest just as impressive as it had been on the stage, his eyebrows bushy even without any make-up.

Aren't you freezing without a coat?

No, my body temperature is fine. It's a genetic endowment, know what I mean?

I get it, I say, even though it's the first I've heard of it.

Did you see *Don Giovanni*? I did. Well, it could be you saw me in that, too, another role I understudied for. I was the Commendatore. They had to switch it to baritone range for me. Vilmos Komor conducted.

If you were the Commendatore, then I was a bit scared of you.

He has a recent wound on his chin, pink in colour.

Your chin was much the same as now only grey.

That was a fake scar. Your coat would suit my needs very well, though. Would you consider swapping? I can trade it for a revolver.

It's not up for a swap, I say, and I don't want a revolver anyway.

He says that he has two revolvers, and it could be he'll make use of them if that's how things work out.

I ask him if he had used them already.

He had wanted to, but his friends would not let him; that was why he had the wound on his chin.

At this juncture the German panzer squeaks in front of the house on its way to the Outer Circle. Aeroplanes are approaching again. I say, I'm going back into the cellar. It's senseless to cram in with all those shit-scared Jews, he says; it's safer here. Pannónia Street is narrow; any bombs are going to fall on the roofs. They crash through two or three storeys. Here on the street only the bomb blast is dangerous. It's best not to stand in the doorway. He asks where I had been holed up, like that, and I tell him in Red Cross homes, in the hospital and now here with my parents. After some reflection I add,

With my younger sister, too. They're downstairs in the cellar. He says he is an orphan. I don't say anything. He says his parents were taken away from his native town of Szolnok during the summer; he had been staying with relatives here in Budapest because of the singing.

Do you know where they died?

We got the news in from the Jewish Agency on Vadász Street. It's ninety-nine per cent sure that the Szolnokers bought it.

I was in Vadász Street myself, I say, but I left.

Bombs are falling.

He had stayed on there, even got a job. The day before yesterday Arrow Crossers broke in. We had organized armed resistance, he says, but they banned that. The leadership was terrified. Maybe they were right, because if we had started shooting the Arrow Crossers would have wiped out three thousand. As it was they only took away a couple of dozen men, although they shot Arthur Weiss on the spot, right in front of the main gateway.

I don't know who Arthur Weiss is.

The house belonged to him. It was he who kept in contact with the Swiss. He gave them the addresses of the houses to be put on the protected list, including this one.

When he heard that Arthur Weiss had been shot dead, he says, he stood at the front gate and took out the pistol, but the chief of the guards at the gate, who was a weightlifter, had grabbed hold of him and wrestled with him, causing him to fall and crack his chin against a sharp stone, which is how he had got the wound.

The anti-aircraft batteries by Margit Bridge were now in action, and bursts of fire could also be heard from over by the Comedy Theatre.

I ask him how he got over here from Vadász Street.

With difficulty, mate. There are now rolls of barbed wire on the Outer Circle as well.

He had gone through the sewer system.

There are some good hiding places down there. You'll see in two or three days when fighting starts in the sewers. Give me a shout if you have second thoughts about the pistol.

The sirens sound the all-clear.

When the war is over Vilmos Komor is sure to be engaged by the Opera House, he says, Ernster as well. It would be great to get in there.

Like I said, I'm going back to the cellar. My parents are probably starting to get anxious.

No wetting yourself, or you'll be done for.

He takes a deep breath, filling his lungs with air. He lifts his eyebrows and presses his lips together. He can see I find that terrifying and laughs out a scale, which is even scarier.

The water-carriers return.

Water that is boiled by women to use for cooking is kept in one of the barrels in the yard. The firewood is chopped by whoever is in the designated team; today crates are to be chopped up. Drinking water is poured from the buckets into pitchers. One person per family is allowed to queue up, and 200 millilitres per head is measured out, with the warden appointing those who keep check.

I am able to move along in the cellar without stepping on anyone in the dark. The flames of the lamps only throw light for a few metres; consequently that make the rest of the cellar even darker. I lead Mother out by the hand. She obtains a cooking pot from the warden's wife and queues up for water, the four of us getting almost three-quarters of a litre. Now, carrying a full vessel, the route back is trickier. I think I might have stepped on someone, and I expect to be yelled at, but there is no yell; of course. The person might be very ill, even dead, I suppose. I have a word with the doctor wearing the Red Cross armband who goes over to the place. There is, indeed, a corpse lying there. The warden is called for, and he makes arrangements. There is a team of corpse carriers; two of them lift up the dead person and carry the body away. One of the carriers is Baritone, and it now occurs to me that we had not even properly introduced ourselves.

As far I can tell Vera is in a good place between Mother and Father. The physicist waves, so I sit back down beside him on the sack of potatoes. He lights a candle and explains to those around us how much oxygen is consumed by a burning candle in a voice exactly like my physics tutor in our lessons at school, so the end result, he says raising a finger, is minimal oxygen consumption while helping with the lighting.

I ask him from where he got the candle. He leans over with a face just like Father's when he is going to crack a joke. Father's face is oval, although admittedly the skin on his neck and around his mouth is sagging a bit. The physicist has a long face, and when he grins every wrinkle quivers. His expression is picaresque – that's a word I had learned in Hungarian literature lessons – I had even read some picaresque novels, and thinking about that helped take my mind off the dead person who had just now been carried away. If you must know, I pinched it, says the physicist. It wasn't easy, but I found a way. He chortles soundlessly and gently pokes me with an elbow. He then produces a pocket chess set, notebook and pencil and by the light of the candle starts jotting things down. There's a combination that he's puzzling over, he says.

Do you play chess?

Ruy Lopez, the Spanish opening?

Are you familiar with the big Maróti book?

Yes, I am.

He is jotting down the positions in an end-game. He says it's much more interesting to figure out the moves backwards, to work out how a checkmate has been reached. In that way you can see what moves should have been avoided, and it may be that even with a Spanish opening one ought not to make the most conventional sequence of opening moves. Understood?

Vera comes across, so I give her my seat on the sack of potatoes. The physicist closes his pocket chess table. We'll play a game sometime, he says. He extends a hand to Vera and introduces himself. Call me László, he says. All right, Uncle László, she says uneasily, and before introducing herself she glances at me. I can see her worrying about accidentally revealing her actual name, so I quickly drop in the family name. My younger sister, I say. She's called Vera. He takes a long look at me and then at Vera, as if he were weighing up how a brother and sister could look so different. Several people are now demanding that he douse the candle; there's enough light coming from the two lights at the back. He moistens the thumb and index finger of his right hand before snuffing the flame. Idiots, he says. They didn't take in a word of what I explained before.

Light the candle! Contact has been broken. It's impossible to see the map! Follow orders at the double!

I do not know who is shouting behind my back.

At ease, First Lieutenant, sir, says the man who just now had insisted that the physicist extinguish the candle, at ease; we'll busy ourselves with the maps later on, meanwhile we'll maintain contact in other ways.

A character is squatting beside me. Officer's cap, trenchcoat – the officer's cap seemingly the same as the one I had seen on the warden. The physicist stands up, and the man takes his place on the sack of potatoes. At times like this those who have stayed alive have to be placed back to back with each other in the trenches, he says, everyone has ten rounds, the squad's leader has a hand-grenade. On the Italian front we were completely surrounded; the section leader planned the break-out, but I passed out the order that the men should hold fire until the Eyeties showed up and were thirty metres from the trenches, then we fired a volley. Bam! Bam! Bam!

Vera goes back to Mother.

One has to prepare for all-out defence. My section leader was right about that; bought a bullet in the middle of his forehead. I was left with enough time to kiss the bullet's entry wound – it bloodied my lips – and then out with the hand-grenades! We surprised the Eyeties with the grenades. They were advancing on the left flank as well. Fix bayonets! I shouted from the trench.

The doctor brings a tablet and a glass of water and holds the man's head until he has swallowed the medicine.

A hush falls on the cellar like none I have ever previously experienced since coming there nor since. Even the warden talks quietly. May I have the cap, First Lieutenant? If it's for a sortie, son, then take it, the man says. How are you armed?

The physicist relights the candle. Listen, people, he says, for the next hour we are going to provide light here, so turn off the lamps at the back. The doctor is helping a man to lie down on a mattress. He's of no danger to anyone; it's just that he doesn't know where he is and what's happening to him.

I ask Mother if Gizi will come back. She will if she can, I'm sure, she says. She lays out a linen napkin then cuts four slices of bread and opens the last tin of liver pâté. We divide 200 millilitres of water between the four of us, with Mother wiping the rim of the mug after each of us has had a drink.

Vera is in the mood to play at compiling menus: let us order tomorrow's dinner. Father recommends fish soup rather than grilled bratwurst, and we go along with that. For me what springs to mind is schnitzel, and for the dessert all of us vote for Vera's choice, Dobos torte.

The next morning I search for Baritone and ask him his name.

Everyone is asleep. Every minute someone starts up, everyone is sighing or snoring or asking for water. Father goes out, saying he is off to the guard on the gate, although his stint is in the morning, and he is almost certainly doing it to give us more space. Mother also goes out, so we tuck Vera up. I can now stretch out and promptly fall asleep.

I awaken to the sound of shouting. One of the lamps is burning. The doctor is called for.

The physicist is asleep on his feet, his hands in his lap, chin on chest. He has a thick and wavy head of hair, which is greying. I stagger outside. Mother is seated on the steps at the front gate. I send her inside. There is room next to Vera. She should sleep.

The physicist is now awake and, prowling around, going up to the first floor then back down and outside into the yard. I tag along behind him. A patch of sky can be seen as it crossed by searchlight beams. An aircraft is caught, tracer fire roars up and hits it and it comes down somewhere near the Ferdinand Bridge, over the railway tracks just outside the Nyugati Railway Terminus.

The barrage of artillery fire from the north-east is continuous.

They're coming, says the physicist. Listen. From the interval between a bang and the shell striking you can work out roughly how far away they are. They must be just beyond the north-east of Pest near Rákospalota.

I ask him when he reckons they will get as far as here.

That depends partly on Guderian. I have an idea who Guderian is but don't know exactly, so I ask. He's a good soldier, smart, well equipped; he's already taken part in a fair few blitzkrieg campaigns. He says it as if he were explaining a mathematical equation and wants his listeners to follow what he is saying, so he speaks slowly and puts an emphasis on the word he considers to be the most important, and at that point rises his right arm; he does not lower his voice at the end of the sentence but drops his raised arm. The day before yesterday he had listened to the BBC from London; it's from there he has heard that Guderian sees no point in defending Budapest any further and has sent Major-General Walther Wenck to Hitler to ask that the German forces be permitted to break out. But Hitler, according to the

BBC, still refused to consent to this. It now depends on those smart generals whether another forty or fifty thousand lives will be sacrificed, ourselves included, he says.

We have water for two days, I say, and we also have two more days' bread rations.

That won't be enough, he says, because these clowns are going to carry out their orders.

So, how many days in that case?

It's impossible to predict, just as it is whether Wallenberg and Lutz will succeed in preventing everyone from being taken from the protected houses to the ghetto.

Us, too?

Us, too.

I ask who Wallenberg and Lutz are. I ask him if this is something else he has learned from the British radio broadcasts. He says they are diplomats, brave men. London says nothing about them; he has heard about them from friends, and there is also a young man here who is a singer in the OMIKE chorus, and he was close to Carl Lutz – he had heard about them from him, as well.

Baritone, I think to myself. I know the bloke myself. We had a chat yesterday. I went to the OMIKE concerts.

The physicist again resorts to waving his hands around. Superb, absolutely superb the performances they gave. What voices: Ernster, Lendvai, Gabi Relle, Annie Spiegel.

I thought Uncle Laci wasn't Jewish, I say.

Poppycock, he says. No one ever said that only Jews could attend.

The next morning two corpses were carried out. I stand in front of Vera so she should not see them.

Arrow Cross and German squads break into the Bethlen Place Hospital in District VII, a stone's throw away from the Keleti Railway Terminus. Most of the men are carted off to the bank of the Danube and executed. Arrow Cross shock troops were hauling off to the ghetto even non-Jewish British, American and Swedish citizens classified as hostiles. The daily ration allocated for the ghetto had a calorific value of between 150 and 800 calories. The food was cooked in five kitchens, and the deliverymen were regularly attacked, robbed and shot dead by Arrow Cross patrols. Officials working in the Jókai Street offices of the Swedish Legation, just off the Oktogon, were murdered. Arthur

Weiss – owner of the Glass House on Vadász Street, which was being used as an office by the Swiss Legation, and one of the men who had come up with the idea of using the privileges of diplomatic protection – was also one of the victims of the Arrow Cross bloodbath, as I read in documents of that period. According to the log kept by the Institute of Forensic Medicine the bodies of an average of around fifty to sixty people who had been shot in the back of the head were brought in daily. A group was snatched from the ghetto and finished off in Ferenc Liszt Square, again just off Andrássy Avenue by the Oktogon, with the bodies left lying in front of the Japan coffee house. In the streets of the ghetto thousands of bodies were left in the open, and epidemic disease appeared unavoidable.

The physicist is in discussion with Father. Father says we will get more room in one of the second-floor apartments. It's the warden's own apartment; they are going to clear out another room. There will be seven of us, which is still better than the cellar. There is lighting, and there is access via the hall as well as through the bathroom. We hand over our mattress. On the warden's instructions two men come to take away the sack of potatoes.

In the bathroom are empty cans of tinned food, empty sacks, brooms, Wellington boots. In the room are two couches, a divan and a mattress on the floor. The physicist helps Mother place the haversacks. He volunteers to be the one who sleeps on the mattress. On one of the couches a little girl is sleeping under a blanket – she must be about eight years old. Her mother is standing beside her, petrified. The young girl slips out from under the blanket, steps over to Vera, holds her hand out and introduces herself. Will you come and play? Vera is unhesitant in introducing herself by the name she is supposed to use, and the young girl's mother also introduces herself, saying that they, too, had come up from the cellar.

Mother allocates the sleeping places. Father and the physicist go downstairs to chop wood. Vera and I are given the spare couch; Mother and Father will sleep on the divan. Before leaving, the physicist says that if the empty sacks are brought in from the bath-room they will make a sleeping place, then he can pass the mattress on to someone else. Mother acquired some margarine, so she spreads it on one slice of bread each for Vera and me. Holding hands with Vera, the young girl gazes in astonishment at her eating. Mother spreads a slice of bread for her, too, at which the girl's mother produces a bag of peanuts from under her blanket and offers these around. She looks at Mother to check whether I can accept. Vera and I take two nuts each from the palm of her hand.

Mother boils water in the kitchen, which she pours into a bowl. I slip off my clothes and stand in the basin as she washes me from head to toe with a soapy rag; I don't ask where she acquired the soap. As there are no towels I dry myself on another rag. It may be a tea cloth, but it is clean. While Mother washes Vera in the bowl I go out into the hall. There are now several more sitting on mattresses than there had been before. We greet one another.

The door to one of the rooms opens, and the warden's wife hurries out, slamming the door shut behind her. I carefully open it. The room is very nicely fitted out with furniture of brown walnut: large and small sideboards, an oval table and six chairs. Our own dining-room was like this, except in a lighter colour. There is a glass cabinet on the wall between two windows; that is also reminiscent of our place, likewise at my grandparents' place – large and small sideboards, an oval table and six chairs there, too.

A girl is sitting in an armchair. She is maybe three or four years older than me and has a very pretty face. She is blonde and blue-eyed. Hi there, she says. And who are you? I dare not tread further into the room and give my name: we have just come up from the cellar and are staying in the room next door. That used to be my room, she says. The blanket slips off her. Her legs are very frail and held stiffly together; she is wearing a white skirt. I ask her if she is ill. No, she is unable to walk, not ill; spinal paralysis is all, she says. Do you know what paralysis is?

I do know, as it happens. Gizi's little girl had paralysis; she was also very pretty, but she died even before Uncle József died. I do not mention this to the girl. When I told her my name she introduced herself. She is called Éva.

Her mother returns. I can see she wants to bawl me out, but the girl says he's a decent young man. All we were doing was chatting a little, Mummy.

The warden's wife cleans with a feather duster. She goes out then comes back in; she is constantly doing something. She is tall, like her husband, and has a long bony face and long arms. You can stay if you want. She says it without so much as looking at me. Thank you, I say, but I think I ought to lend a hand to Mother or Father. The girl waves as I leave with a gesture as sweeping as if she were on a railway platform and waving goodbye to a departing train.

Vera had put on a clean blouse after her wash, possibly her last spare blouse, and also thoroughly combed her hair. She smells of soap. The two of us are in the bathroom. I lean over towards her; she holds her face still, and I press my lips to hers. She doesn't draw away. It feels good to hold my lips to hers, although it's not something I particularly want to do; I was just trying it out. I had not supposed she would permit it. I get the feeling that for her it doesn't feel good. Her lips are cold, and yet as if she did still want that she puts her arms round my neck.

We quickly go into the room.

By now I am aware that the physicist is an uncle of the warden's wife. It was he who had made the arrangements for us to be able to move upstairs.

I go out into the outside corridor. The firing from over by Nyugati Railway Terminus is audible. Sleet is falling. I lean on the railing from which I can see the back yard of the house next door, which is exactly the same as that of our house. There is a section of the yard next to the wall that has not been concreted over, and four people are digging a grave in the mud. The pit is now deep enough. Two corpses, wrapped in sacking, are brought, presumably the ones that were carried out of the cellar at dawn. The bodies are placed carefully in the grave. There are two women and a child standing by the pit; at the back, two rows of men, ten in all, with hats on their heads.

The sound of shelling grows more intense.

The gravediggers rest on their spades.

Baritone, at one side of the pit, sings the Kaddish. He has a beautiful voice and spreads his arms so that his chest seems even more robust, and his voice is powerful enough to be audible even as the detonations are going on.

The physicist is standing next to me; I hadn't noticed when he came out on to the balcony, but he, too, is leaning over the railing. He takes his glasses off and wipes them.

Aircraft again draw near.

Baritone repeats the Kaddish.

The members of the families are standing motionless in the sleet.

When the men start filling in the grave they each throw a fistful of soil into the pit. Baritone glances up, and I wave, but it's not me he is looking at – it's as if his gaze were boring through the clouds.

The physicist makes a sign of the cross. Come, he says, or we'll get soaked.

The news about the possible incineration of the ghetto got to the protected houses before I did. By the time I arrived there had already been a lot of suicides. In the house at number 35 St István Park a woman had thrown herself off the fourth floor. In other Spanish houses the men had decided to acquire arms. If I were certain that we had enough available weapons I myself would have given the order to attack. I think that the police might even fight on our side . . . I ran to see Ernő Vajna, the Minister of Internal Affairs, at the City Hall. Underground I found Wallenberg and Peter Zürcher of the Swiss Embassy. They had also come to ask Vajna to suspend the transfer of their protectees to the city ghetto. I asked them to let me speak first . . . I told him right away that further resistance made no sense and would only cause more death and the destruction of the city. I told him that an immediate capitulation would obligate the victors to show greater understanding, and that it would make it possible to put a stop to the bands sacking the city. I tried, for a long time, to make him understand that by now the war was lost and that what was happening was senseless and shameful . . . Vajna replied that he refused to talk about surrender. According to him the city must be defended to the last man . . . (From the diary of Giorgio Perlasca)

There is always someone in the bathroom. I have got used to looking away if someone is sat on the toilet, and it was worse in the brickworks where one had to squat next to others. Évie's mother carries her in whenever she needs to use the toilet or washbasin. It's not just her legs that are thin; she is generally very skinny. She must be very light, but I can also see how strong Aunt Klári is. She carries sacks and lifts children. When she is with Éva she talks quietly, but at other times she shouts. It's not that she wants to, as I gather from the way that she smiles while she is shouting.

The physicist says to her that if needs be he will carry Évie to the bathroom. Don't be silly, Laci, says Aunt Klári. You have enough to do lugging yourself around. He takes off his spectacles is the same way as when he makes notes, picks Éva up and really does carry her around with the greatest ease. He stands guard before the door in the hall while she is on the lavatory and tells me to stand in the door to our room to stop anyone else from entering.

In the main room the physicist and Aunt Klári draw up two of the chairs beside the big sideboard and sit down hand in hand; they must be very fond of each other. Meanwhile it is possible for me to grab a few minutes with Vera in Évie's room. Previously no one else had been allowed to do so.

Mother says that Uncle Laci had been trying for a position at the university; his wife was with her parents in the village of Érd, just beyond Buda. He was unable to get to her there, but he had thought that he could reach the university, which was perhaps safer, but Aunt Klári had kept him back. She had heard her shouting at him, Laci, that's enough of your nonsense. You're not going one step further. Quick march into the house.

Father is allocated to the guard at the gate, so I go down with him. It is a three-man guard; they wear ICRC armbands. They take over from the previous shift, and the warden instructs them that they can only allow in those who can show they have papers from the legation. If there is a pounding on the door they had best step aside because a shot might be aimed at the gate.

I set off to look for Baritone. I want to know his name, and I may ask him for one of his revolvers after all, but I can find him nowhere.

The warden and Uncle Laci are playing chess in the bathroom, with Uncle Laci sitting on the closed toilet and the warden on the rim of the bath, the pocket chess set being on Uncle Laci's knees.

I go downstairs again. I can hear a singing voice from the cellar.

Baritone is standing in the middle and singing, his arms spread out, his head thrown back. The flame of the lamps is quivering; the shadow of his outstretched arms can be seen on the wall. The man who was said to be amnesiac is standing next to him with one of Baritone's arms almost brushing his face, as if he had not even noticed him, and sitting under the other arm is a young girl.

He is singing Papageno's aria from *The Magic Flute* – that was another opera I saw performed by OMIKE, and very interesting it was, too. Fair-haired and with an oval face, the little girl is entranced as she listens to the singing. I can see many bearded faces. Father has not shaved for a long time now, but he is not sporting much of a beard. He said yesterday that even as a young man he did not have much growth at a time when other boys would be wearing a moustache at the very least. One joke that the other lads played on him in Kiskunhalas was to assure him that he needed to rub chickenshit on his upper lip to make it grow better.

Baritone clutches his hands to his heart and bows deeply. A few people applaud. The fair-haired girl is laughing.

We go out into the stairwell, and I tell him that we have not yet introduced ourselves. I am Gyuri, he says, so I, too, tell him only my given name.

You sang wonderfully.

His eyes are glowing. Now I don't see them as being dark so much as coal-black.

Papageno was a role Andor Lendvai sang. But there were only two performances. The very last two performances.

I was lucky to catch it, then; I had no idea it was one of the last two performances they gave.

I have lost any desire to talk about the revolver.

The warden and Uncle Laci are still playing chess in the bathroom.

Our roommate, the little girl's mother, has obtained a jug of drinking water and asks who would like a drink. Uncle Laci says put it away for the children.

The doctor whom I had got to know in the cellar comes out from seeing Évie and says something to Aunt Klári. He reports to Évie's father that things are fairly quiet in the cellar. There have been no more deaths; the amnesiac is an ex-first lieutenant. You know, he says, he has now withdrawn completely. All he says to anyone is *Who are you?* and has given his medals away to children.

That's perfectly in order, says Uncle Laci. At least he's honest and doesn't hide the fact that he recalls nothing. The whole country is suffering from amnesia; here no one ever remembers anything, but they put on this act of knowing everything. When he is feeling irascible his words become bitty; his teeth are bad, with some black and quite a few missing. His glasses have only one arm, and he flails them around in his hand.

The doctor returns to the cellar. He says he will give the morning's injections; he still has two days' worth of supplies.

Uncle Laci declares checkmate. He says it could be seen to be coming three steps before; it was bound to happen, having the castles in that position was impregnable even if two lesser pieces were brought into play. He picks up his notebook and lists for the warden's benefit the bad moves he had made, telling him that he himself had been looking at sequences three moves ahead. If you commit an error, then you should be working out the moves from there, he says. You assessed your position badly, so your sequence of moves was also bad.

The warden says that the game was still open up to the penultimate move.

Poppycock, says Uncle Laci. You didn't see what led to the penultimate move; you have to look for where the mistake began. If you don't locate that, then that means you're heading for the end from the very start.

This isn't physics, Laci, it's chess, says the warden.

Rubbish, my friend. Of course, it's chess. If it were physics you would long be dead. Rematch?

They set up the pieces again.

We have a hard time getting to sleep. The little girl on the other bed is crying. She is hungry.

I dream that I go up to the fourth floor in a trio with Gyuri and Vera. Gyuri steps over to the window, looks down and says, The city is miraculous, like a stage, and there seems to be artificial snow falling, see. He points down to a piece of scenery with a river painted in blue. I'm singing Papageno. Vera undresses and catches cold; she will be ill. I can't leave her and I clasp her to me. She loops an arm round my neck and presses her pubes against mine. More, that feels so good, she whispers in my ear.

I awaken to hear the girl crying again. Her mother gives her a biscuit. I am alone on the couch; Vera is lying beside Mother. I can't see Father anywhere. My underpants are wet. Everyone is looking at me. Mother, the little girl's mother, the little girl herself, only Vera is turning away. I go out into the bathroom and rinse my underpants.

Morning arrives.

The warden and Uncle Laci are again playing chess.

XIV

I tell Györgyi on the telephone that perhaps it's best if I leave a copy of the most recent section of my manuscript at the porter's lodge at the school as I am going that way anyway.

She is silent.

Does that suit you?

Do you want to go over the area yet again?

Now it is me who does not reply.

We're good at falling silent together.

Like being connected.

I am making progress alongside the block of memories. When I read through the draft for the first time I made notes on the text, but I don't know why I note things down again.

I decide to search out the first set of notes and place the current ones next to that. The gap between the two dates may reveal something about the difficulties of storytelling. While I think this, it seems to me that the interval between the two dates is more important than the actual date of 1944 that I again note down while transcribing the text.

Clearly, though, it does not exactly make my situation easier that the importance of telling this story forces itself out in front of the story itself.

I hand over the large envelope to the school porter.

The teacher had already mentioned it to him. He'll pass it on to her straight away.

I continue on my way towards the Praktiker DIY Store. Just before the sun was still glowing red, but now the valley is getting dark.

I board a tram and travel as far as the corner of Bem Quay and Halász Street where the cyclist had knocked me off my feet. I take a stroll upriver as far as the Erzsébet Bridge where I board a number 7 bus. I glance at my watch in front of 76 Amerikai Road then go on towards the old KISOK football ground, the underground tram depot.

I did the journey in eight minutes according to the clock at the next corner between Dorozsmai Street and Dorozsmai Lane, although my own watch says a different time.

The wristwatch used to belong to Father. Mother gave it to me after he died in 1953, and I have worn it ever since.

The route we took was Mexikói Road then Thököly Road.

I note down the time shown by the main clock at Keleti Railway Terminus.

Again there is a disparity of two minutes when compared with my watch.

Yet more clocks are to be seen in the shop windows, billboards and the hotel entrances in Baross Square in front of the station – each one points to a different time.

I can well remember that the big clock on the corner of the Outer Circle, in front of the National Theatre by the number 6 tram stop, was visible from the marching column.

The clock in that position now is smaller. According to the hands on the clock the time disparity is growing; by the time I get down to Lajos Kossuth Street on my way to the Pest end of the Erzsébet Bridge it has changed again, now decreasing.

The clocks' mechanisms cannot be reconciled with what the hands are showing.

I go into a watchmaker's, who checks the watch for two days. He says that over that time it has gained five minutes. He resets it.

I set off again.

I try to conjure up within me the bygone feelings of that bygone route. It does not work. It is not what was experienced in the past that preoccupies me but once again the disparity between the times on different clocks.

I am travelling around the city in a time that is not apprehensible in the act. Fő Street under Buda Castle. Bécsi Road. I take a number 1 tram upstream as far as Árpád Bridge and the corner of Váci Road, at the Pest end of the bridge in the XIIIth District. At the József Attila Theatre I take a taxi then from the Pest end of Margit Bridge. I go on foot to the Dohány Street Synagogue. I have a look to see which office has its signboard by the side entrance in the entrance doorway to the OMIKE hall of yesteryear, not far from the memorial to Carl Lutz.

I abandon any idea of finding any logical correlation between the various times. I have made notes on the disparities between clocks in the street and the shops, made notes of the discrepancies between what the hands of my own watch show in the John Bull Pub on Vadász Street, the Andrássy Hotel on Mihály Munkácsy Street, in Nagy-fuvaros Street, at the porter's lodge of the hospital on Szabolcs Street and at the corner of Pannónia and Csanády Streets.

Using fibre-tipped pens of different colours I map out the route that lives in my memory and the routes I have covered over the last three days. Each colour signifies a different time zone. The lines are layered upon one another, and that modifies the original colours.

In this way the different times form a *shared space*. That *shared space* is my city, able to accommodate the gazes of both cyclists, Mother's gaze as she waves from the column leaving the brickworks, Vera's long unseen face, even my old duffel coat, the face of the watch-maker as he says about Father's wristwatch, It's still a marvellous Tissot watch to this day, sir. As far as I can see it's a series made right after the war or more likely pre-war, I'd say. The *space of unsyn-chronizable times* also includes Györgyi's gaze as she reads what I have written and no doubt feels what I felt when I wrote her into the story. I note down that I am not going to go to the Ruszwurm café. I shall not order a coffee, so I can more easily conjure up Gizi's gaze as she brings the coffee in person and sits down for a few minutes next to Mother.

I shall have Bőzsi's name added to the memorial wall in the Jewish cemetery next to the New Public Cemetery on Kozma Street, out to the east of Pest or else on a plaque in the garden of the Dohány Street Synagogue or else among the many thousands of names in the Holocaust Museum and Memorial Centre on Páva Street – that's what is left for me.

My city is constricted to a labyrinth mapped with coloured fibre-tipped pens, even though in my sensations it is expanding. As the drawing is completed I see edifices that have become ruins behind their magnificent façades, empty streets in the cover of an Outer Circle crawling with people, drains stuffed full of corpses in the shadow of splendid underground stations, hordes of rats in place of cars. I find it interesting that my sense of being at home is not changed.

I note that there are facts, documents and sources that represent real resources: my preserved letters. After fifty-eight years it would be fitting to study what I had to say – those really are the words of a fourteen-year-old boy. The written form might also provide an opportunity for drawing conclusions, but I am well aware that the interpretations of sources in themselves raise matters of the interpreter's point of view, the methods of archiving and the drawing of conclusions.

Györgyi telephones. Her voice is unsure. I have a feeling she has found some pretext for calling off our meeting, but she does not consider it to be an appropriate pretext, and while she is holding the telephone receiver she is trying to dream up something else.

When I called her from Locarno I supposed that perhaps she was unable to separate herself from the written simulacrum of her or what she imagined about her mother's history from the way I had written it nor me even from the fourteen-year-old boy.

When and where can we meet?

Whatever suits you, I say. It could be the Andrássy Hotel, the one you couldn't make last time.

She gives me her own address as her preference.

Perhaps that was what had made her sound so hesitant, the thought of what I would have to say about that.

The gates to Miklós Radnóti Teachers' Training Gymnasium can be seen from a second-floor window of the house on the corner of Abonyi Street and András Cházár Street. I attended the school there for eight years, when it was called the Jewish Gymnasium, but after the First Jewish Law of 1928 tightening the *Numerus Clausus* of 1920, which restricted the university entry of Jewish students, many, myself included, chose to call it the Abonyi Street Gymnasium.

Even now I can smell the sweaty reek of the sawdust-strewn gym hall as meanwhile I watch a Volkswagen Beetle driving where, in December 1944, Vera and I, hand in hand, stealthily slipped from Francia Road towards Mihály Munkácsy Street.

While I was drawing my various routes with the coloured fibre-tipped pens I felt the same sense of being at home at most points of my city, but I am not satisfied with that way of designating it – it lacks a sense of how a feeling of being at home and not being at home can go together.

In Györgyi's hallway there is no man's hat or slippers. It would not be right for me to go through things in her bathroom to check whether there were two toothbrushes on the shelf.

Györgyi is wearing jeans, a white polo-neck and a denim waistcoat. There are a lot of photographs on a chest of drawers. An oval table and six chairs, large and small sideboards, glass cabinet on the wall between two windows. I don't ask if the furniture had been her mother's; that would be superfluous. Dining-room suites like that aren't produced any longer.

On one of the photographs are her mother and father standing in a garden with arms around one another's waists. Her father is taller than the snap taken on the terrace by the lake in City Park: he is in a freshly ironed shirt, white trousers and white shoes, as if he were getting ready to play tennis. It seems she obtained two copies of the photograph of her mother and grandmother standing in the gateway of a house in winter coats marked with yellow stars. I can now see that her mother at the age of sixteen looks older than in the other photograph, which must have been taken at least five years later.

She brings my manuscript in from the other room, carefully closing the door behind her as if she were safeguarding there something of herself that she keeps fenced off from others; there is no entry there, not so much as a crack left in the door. That is presumably where she read my manuscript.

She would like to ask me about several things but not now. She feels it is not yet time for that, she says.

I can relate to that as I feel the same. With some things one has to wait for the right moment, I say. I can see she surrounds herself with photographs.

It is a tactless challenge, my voice is even a touch aggressive, but she smiles. She does not find it hard to say, in a voice that mimics my own aggressive tone, Yes, with photographs, but you knew that already. You could have been ready for that, given what you wrote about me.

What she was thinking of, she says after a slight pause, is that she was coming out of school. It was hard to bear passing in front of a block of memories on a daily basis. Every day she went to the tram stop along the road on which her mother and grandmother had been made to line up.

I can't understand why she is laughing. It is not a hysterical laugh.

I ought to forget it, she says. The time has come for that, hasn't it? There are times when it does not come to mind even if I am beside the stone block, but then what comes to mind is precisely the fact that it is no longer coming to mind. She ought to be relocated to a school in, say, Zugló. Yes, that would be more practical from the point of view of travelling if she were to teach in a nearby school. Of course, it might be, she repeats, that getting transferred would not alter anything, but it might be a solution all the same. What did I think?

It would be wrong for me to leave her an escape route.

My stern voice sounds like a duty policeman who has brought a perpetrator to the station. It startles even me that my voice is like that; it startles her, too. It fills her with satisfaction, but then what sort of solution is she thinking of? Why does she presume that there is a solution to find?

The shape of her face also seems to have altered, acquiring angularity. The chin juts forward; the eyes are drawn together. I had never noticed she was that tall. She has a shrill voice as well. She thinks I don't know a solution is not possible – thinks I don't understand that it is not possible either for her or for that man about whom she is writing?

I ask her what makes her think that I and the person in the manuscript – whom I call the seeker – are different? She tells me to stop playing games; I know she is a specialist in literature and history.

She asks what I would like to drink, vodka or cognac? That's all there is, she says in a still-sharp tone.

Whatever you're having.

She pours out two cognacs. She downs her own drink with an unpractised action, a few drops are left on her lip and roll down to her chin, but she does not take out a handkerchief. Seeing that I have spotted the drops on her chin she wipes them off with her wrist.

She calls me over to the window and points down at the street. Opposite is the edifice of the old gymnasium that I attended, as did her mother – the boys using the entrance in what was St Domonkos Street,[12] the girls an entrance in Abonyi Street. She says this is the apartment my parents lived in. That is the first time she has used the expression *my parents*. When only she and her mother were left, when she was a girl, she would stand at the window waiting for her mother to get back home. Since then, whenever she looks down at the street it passes through her mind that her mother is crossing the road and carrying two shopping-bags. She had been out at the cemetery, she says, visiting her mother's grave. She had also had her grandmother's name engraved on the gravestone with the year of her birth, the fact that she had died a martyr's death in Ravensbrück with, as she puts it, the customary text: 'Her memory is preserved here'. She had also paid a visit to Luca's grave, which is badly neglected. She had bought another bunch of flowers at the cemetery gates and taken that back to place on it.

I tell her that I wanted to have Bőzsi's name added but had not decided on which memorial site to have it engraved at.

We talk about Bőzsi as if it were about a common acquaintance.

She is sipping a second glass of cognac. She takes off the waistcoat and laughs. Her chest heaves; her breasts are bigger than I had imagined.

She asks if I really did meet Vera later on, and did what I described really happen.

I thought that would engage her attention. The two cognacs had helped her to ask the question.

Let's be clear about one thing: it's a novel.

So, do I exist, or did you just invent me?

I say that when we alighted from the number 1 tram at the corner of Thököly Road she had been like a shadow following me, although had it not been for her I would never have got as far as I had got.

That's brilliant. I haven't been a shadow before.

I look at her the way she is looking at me. Through her expression I see the face of the girl who, tears in her eyes, reports to her at the gates of Ravensbrück that, in the view of a fellow pupil, it had all been put up at a later date.

In other words, you did go to bed with Vera?

What are we talking about now?

In an impassive voice she says that, among their various traumas, it can surely come as no surprise, can it, that she had been troubled. Luckily she herself had never had problems with achieving orgasm, but it was not to be discounted that her mother might have, although of course they had never talked about that.

I ask her why she is telling me.

Maybe you need information like that as well.

That may be, but you are talking about it like when an assistant impassively but audibly reads out the case histories to a sex therapist and counsellor in the waiting-room.

Tell me, by what right are you sticking your nose into my life?

I get the vague idea that it was you who asked me to.

Only you are making things public.

I'm sorry about that, but the sort of thing I do is attended with that risk.

All the same, on what basis?

Why, are you not sticking your nose into my life? Anyway I have brought the photographs that you posted to me.

Keep them in case you still have need of them.

But from what you just said I got the impression that you didn't want me to make certain things public.

So what if I did? I am more curious about why you kept very quiet about certain things that are very much my business.

That was a long time ago, and at the time Luca made me promise. I had forgotten all about my old notes, and I dug them out only when we met.

She goes to the bathroom. She has washed her face and applied lipstick when she comes back. In my gymnasium there was a physics master who was the spitting image (that's what she says) of your physicist in Pannónia Street. Even down to the way he would gesticulate during lessons and the way he held his spectacles by one of the arms. And, by the way, I thank you for everything, she says.

What are you getting at?

Everything, like I said. I have tried telling my students that it is necessary not only to concern ourselves with what we don't know but also with what we know, whether we really know it. Only now I think differently, and I am afraid.

Would *you* stick your nose in?

What I am afraid of is that someone who has an insight into ignorance and poor knowledge will be ostracized – whether they are Jewish or not. They don't know why, but they sense that person has an insight and they are afraid of that, and what I am afraid of is that they are afraid of me. Aren't you afraid?

Sure I am.

What do you do then?

I try to think that the worst thing is being afraid of myself.

I don't understand you.

Well, when I forget something I don't forget it, but I pretend I forgot it.

You don't forget anything.

I'm not sure about that, but I see you are well read up on me.

I see you are surprised that I'm familiar with Hungary's history.

What are you driving at?

That I know it is not just being a Jew that's hard.

Her eyes were never tearful when she spoke about her mother and grandmother. I can well imagine that she would sing the national anthem along with her students at ceremonies to mark the start and finish of the school year and high days and holidays.

You may think it is nonsense, I say, but I also thank you for everything.

What in the blue blazes for?

For the blue blazes of being so trusting with me.

Is that what you sense from what I just told you?

From that, too . . .

Fair enough, but I suggest that we drink no more cognac.

Do you have any vodka?

At last she laughs.

I never thought of myself as being as you describe, and maybe I'm not.

I would be grateful if you would go to number 36 Pannónia Street and look at the old cellar.

So you don't want to use me just as a shadow but as a tracker dog as well? Do we need to go together?

No, I would like you to go on your own. Everything vanishes. Even the cellar cannot be what it once was. Gradually everything vanishes: not just people but objects, memorials. I have faced up to that, and it would also do you good.

Her expression is mocking, like that of students who have heard her say the same thing umpteen times before.

If Luca had not said that it was you who told her mother in the brickworks that she could step out of the column before it set off, then I would not have dropped in on her when she arranged for you to visit.

I don't have any recollection to this day of having spoken to Luca's mother in the brickworks.

As an eighteen-year-old student I was hugely impressed by a writer, even fancied him a bit . . .

The age difference between us is twenty-eight years, even then . . .

I still fancied you.

You are too attractive to be saying things like that.

She places a hand on mine.

I felt sorry for that fourteen-year-old boy.

There's no need, I say. That would bother me, even trouble me.

We plant a kiss on one another's cheeks.

It's easy for you, she says. You can pick up your path wherever you want.

Wherever, I think to myself, but who picks up his trail and gets anywhere? I ought to tell her about that feeling, too. I ought to tell her that when the assistant found me in the car park of the Grand Hotel in Locarno and hauled me off to the floodlit terrace, where the cameras were already rolling – in other words a start had been made on the performance in which no one was who they were in reality – it turned out that the two harlequins, and to this day I don't know if they were a man and a woman or two men or even two women, that they too were part of the supporting cast. Their role was to marvel at us as spectators, in other words as posterity, so to speak, not as the *witnesses* that we were but as the *survivors* that we were called. I ought to tell her about the shame with which I was filled when, on stepping on to the terrace, I felt that I, too, was nothing more than the role that had been allocated to me. And I also ought to tell her that I was delighted just beforehand when she said that pain and suffering were universal, and that agrees with what we call history – true, she didn't quite say it like that, but that is how I would put it. Then I also ought to tell her – I suppose that both of us knew – that on reaching the end of our path we arrive at the beginning.

She may sense that if she were to ask I might say one thing or another, but I can see from her look that she knows where the boundary lies beyond which she must not step.

She puts an arm round my waist and leads me over to the window.

It was from here she watched her mother as she got back home, shopping-bags in hand. I might also be looking at my own self from here, walking along that same pavement with my school bag as a fourteen year-old. We can imagine the things – she, the shopping-bag; me, the school bag – without which we are unable to conceive that we are seeing what the other sees. She repeats that it is easier for me because, as she puts it, I can pick up my path wherever I want, and I don't declare that for me that means I shall later describe her room, list the objects in it and, above all, try to describe the photographs placed on the chest of drawers, but as for what knowledge I discern in her gaze . . . for that, most certainly, it would be hard for me to find the words; if, indeed, there were words that could be found.

XV

Once again they are burying people in the yard.

Once again family members are standing beside a freshly dug pit. Gyuri again sings the Kaddish, but this time they must have found it harder to assemble ten men, as I can also see two boys among them. Again I watch from the balcony as wives, husbands, children and parents throw a handful of soil into the pit.

They are also carrying out a burial in the yard of the house next door, the other side of the wall. They, too, lower a corpse wrapped in sacking into a freshly dug grave. There, too, there are people standing around, making signs of the cross and murmuring prayers – I assume the Lord's Prayer. I learned that; I could recite it, too. They look up and listen to what Gyuri is singing, and the sound of the Kaddish rises towards heaven.

There are others on the balcony. A member of the team keeping watch on the gate comes, and he says that the fighting is now in Dráva Street. German reinforcements have arrived at the Comedy Theatre; it is said that an artillery battery of the Hungarian Army has also moved in as well as an Arrow Cross stormtrooper unit. The biggest ruckus will be here in Pannónia Street, says a man who has escaped from a forced-labour brigade. It's a good time to go down into the cellar.

The warden is informed that only one day's drinking water is left.

There is shooting in the streets, and no one will volunteer to take buckets to Ernő Hollán Street, parallel with this but two streets nearer the river, where drinking water can be drawn from a tank.

The physicist, chewing a crust of bread, invites me to play a game of chess in the bathroom. I sit on the lavatory seat, he on the rim of the bath. If either of us has things to do we'll go out then come back and resume the chess.

There is now very little water left in the buckets even to flush the toilets.

I opt for a Spanish opening. I get entangled in the moves. We'll analyse it later, says the physicist. Let's just play this game out. Are you able to see that I'm going to lose? It's pretty obvious, he says. He turns to the warden, who has come in in the meantime. The end is already apparent at the start, Józsi. That's how it is and not just in chess.

If you can see the situation so far in advance why did you not say so in time? says the warden.

I did, only the idiots carried on blindly. Like I said, they are blind.

So that makes me an idiot and blind as well?

As far as being an idiot goes, yes, Józsi, but blind you aren't. It could never be said of you that you don't see what is before your eyes. Just don't forget what you see.

I move one of my knights. Not bad, says the physicist. We'll analyse that later. Given your position, that was the best move possible – not that it will help you, of course, but, given that you have closed the way for most of your pieces, it was a good move.

I won't forget, says the warden. I was only worried about Klári. She is taking on too much.

There's no need to be worried about Klári. I've known her longer than you. She's very tenacious, more so than you even.

I like their way of talking. I think I understand. I try to pay attention to them, although it's hard enough concentrating on the chess, but at least this takes the edge off my hunger. I'm thirsty as well, having had nothing to drink since this morning.

It's good if you can see positions that other people don't see let alone remember. All those many blind people who watch every last thing but see nothing and don't remember anything.

I can see from his expression that he excuses me my silence. It's good to hear the warden say, You know what, Laci, you've missed your calling. You should have chosen to be a priest. Nonsense, the physicist gesticulates. He moves his queen and announces, Check!

Bombs are now falling without any howling from the sirens.

Light bombs, says the warden. The most they will do is punch a hole in the roof, and the return fire now is mostly shooting submachine guns into the air. There's no need to go down to the cellar.

I slip a pawn in front of the attacking queen.

What I don't understand is how it could have happened, says the warden.

That's what I'm spelling out, says the physicist, slapping the warden on the back. You should always keep your eye on the previous error.

A woman comes in and announces that she saw from the window that Arrow Crossers were leading four men with yellow stars on their coats towards the Danube.

People shouldn't go outside for water with yellow stars on their coats, says the physicist. There are no volunteers so far, says the warden.

Units of the German 13th Panzer Division Feldherrnhalle withdraw from Újpest. The fighting continues at the railway embankment along Mexikói Road in Zugló. In City Park the 2nd Company of the Budapest Police Assault Battalion retook the building of the Industrial Hall. Fighting commenced in sewers under the districts of the city centre. German troops are retreating factory to factory from Lehel Street next to the railway lines out of the Western Station. Feldherrnhalle units are still holding the Dagály Street–Aréna Road line along the Outer Circle.

Vera comes into the bathroom and watches the chess match.

'Artillery ammunition has given out; ammunition for the infantry may only be issued on condition that it is only to be fired sparingly on orders. Fuel has given out, the situation of the wounded is catastrophic,' the Joint German–Hungarian Army Command HQ reports.

The Germans blow up Miklós Horthy Bridge and, at night, the Franz Josef Bridge over the Danube.[13]

Do you reckon the big mistake was on 19 March? the warden asks the physicist. The fact that the Germans were allowed to enter Hungary without a single shot being fired.

By that stage it was bound to happen.

Vera whispers in my ear that she has a raging thirst. The man from the guard on the gate who earlier said that fighting was going on by Dráva Street comes in again. Bursts of submachine-gun fire can now be heard from the bank of the Danube, he reports. You think we can't hear? the warden bawls at him without getting up from the rim of the bath. I had not heard him yell like that before. Vera runs out of the bathroom. The Russians can't yet be at Dráva Street, the warden says to the guard. The shooting would sound different. You've not been on the frontline, that's for sure. I know these things better than you.

By that stage it was bound to happen, the physicist reiterates.

So was the mistake entering the war then?

Of course it was, Józsi, of course, the physicist says, but that, too, was bound to happen.

Could we have stayed out?

Yes, of course, Józsi, says the physicist. But then before that the idiots had committed themselves to Hitler.

Hitler reannexed the territories Hungary lost after the First World War – Transylvania, the Felvidék in the north, Bačka, the Baranya Triangle and Medjumure in Serbia . . .

Yes, of course, the physicist is starting to gesticulate, but those idiots didn't have the faintest idea of the price that would have to be paid for that. Well, this is the price!

But once the Trianon Peace Treaty was signed there was no other choice . . .

Yes, of course, that's how the beginning and end meet, Józsi, that's what I've been saying. The first mistake leads to all the other irreversible mistakes.

I don't follow . . .

Look, Józsi, the Trianon Treaty was an appallingly unjust award. After that two paths lay open: either prove to the British, the Americans and French that we would try to be a peaceful, democratic country and over time show we deserved to have the faulty decisions alleviated and corrected – which is what István Bethlen wanted – or the second route was war. There was no third way. The idiots chose to lick Hitler's arse . . . Understood?

The physicist notices that the warden is no longer in the bathroom – he had scooted out with the man from the guard on the gate. He says it over again, just as with the chess . . .

Mate in two moves, isn't it, I say.

Two moves, he says. That's not bad at all. If you have patience you could make a useful player.

Friedrich Born, the authorized representative of the ICRC in Budapest, notes:

On 14 January an Arrow Cross stormtrooper unit broke into the Orthodox Hospital on Városmajor Street. Patients and staff were bundled out into the yard in groups of five or ten and shot to death, those who were lying in their beds being shot in bed. One hundred and fifty people were murdered, including 130 patients, the rest being doctors, nurses or other hospital employees.

I go down to the gate.

The warden is giving instructions to the men who are just about to take over the watch. I ask him if it is all right to go out in front of the gate. He says, Be careful.

Houses are smoking in József Katona Street, the next road. An Arrow Cross patrol is approaching from the right. A German panzer has parked at the junction with the Outer Circle, with German and Hungarian soldiers swarming around it. An officer is shouting out orders – even though his voice does not carry as far as our gate I can see from his hand gestures that he is giving orders. A machine gun is blazing away from one of the upper windows of the Comedy Theatre, but I cannot see who they might be shooting at from there. The two Arrow Crossers turn at the corner and hurry away in the direction of Pozsonyi Road, the parallel street two blocks nearer the river. Father is calling. I should get back inside. The tank starts moving but does not come back up Pannónia Street and instead turns off towards the Western Station. Now a second machine gun is chattering from another window of the Comedy Theatre. Father and the warden also step out on to the pavement. The gate of the house opposite opens. That is not a yellow-star house. Two women with pails come out. The warden shouts over to enquire whether they, too, have no drinking water. They reply that they haven't but it is still being distributed in Holló Street, and they're going to try to reach that.

In the stairwell, the warden makes a renewed attempt to seek out volunteers. There's no curfew, says Father, but you can't go out wearing a yellow star. Agreed, one can't go out with a yellow star, says the warden, but one can have a go without one. The patients and children have to have drinking water.

Gyuri is standing by the stairs; I have no idea where he came from. Right then, shall we go? he asks. Are you willing to take it on without a star? the warden asks. Why, do you see me wearing one? He is again wearing the rust-coloured pullover; it is pretty threadbare. It's risky, says the warden. You can be stopped at any time for a check. Gyuri grins and reaches for his back pocket to haul out a revolver. A few seconds go by and then he pulls out the other revolver from a side pocket. You were a soldier, says the warden. I hope you know how to use them. He checks the cartridge clip of one gun and puts the safety catch on. When we get back you'll have to let me have the other as well; you may put the others at risk if a raid is made on the house and they come across it.

We go upstairs. The warden still shouts out in a renewed effort to seek out volunteers. The doctor appears from one of the apartments. We need you here, says the warden.

The physicist is standing before the door to our apartment, two buckets in his hands. Father says farewell to Mother. He, too, is given two pails. He does not say farewell to me, so I ask him if I can go as well. It's not far, I say. Mother grabs me by the hand and pulls me beside her. I cannot see Vera anywhere. The warden also brings two buckets. He tells his wife, Five minutes there, five back, and even if one has to queue up for the water they'll be back in half an hour or an hour. In the meantime do whatever is necessary on his behalf; she can count on the doctor and the guards at the gate. Aunt Klári purses her lips. I don't know how she manages to speak like that or, rather, not speak so much as, say, Józsi! Now it is me who is clutching Mother's hand, not she mine. Father smiles, Hear that, he says. Five minutes there, five back, and even if we have to wait then half an hour or an hour at most. Once I get back we'll collect some chicken shit, and I'll daub that on my face to make my beard grow at last.

Four of them take eight buckets. As we accompany them down the stairs I work out that this will be between 250 and 300 millilitres per person. If it's distributed carefully that will be enough for two days.

We don't say goodbye at the gate.

The warden goes first.

Gyuri is carrying both buckets in his left hand, his right hand thrust in his pocket. The physicist seems to be explaining something to Father, gesticulating as is his habit, with the buckets dancing around in his hands. Father is nodding.

Aunt Klári gives Mother a kiss. Mother says we had better go up and not leave Vera on her own. Aunt Klári gives instructions to the guards in a voice that's steelier than the warden's. There are four guards on the gate, and their leader salutes her with a hand raised to his beret. Yessir! he says to Aunt Klári.

Vera is playing paper-scissors-stone and allowing the little girl to win occasionally and rap her on the knuckles. Clever girl! You win, she says. The little girl has a very serious face while she plays. She does not get angry if she fails to hit Vera's hand; she is very attentive. She's got good reflexes, says Vera, her voice like an adult's.

In the vague hope of being able to see Father and the other three from the window I go up to the fourth-floor apartment that we vacated. I cannot see them. They may well have already reached József Katona Street, perhaps just turned into it. The roof of the Comedy Theatre is smoking. In Tátra Street the upper storeys of the houses are alight. A platoon of soldiers is drawing back from the direction of Csanády Street by St István Park. As far as I can see, a Hungarian officer is yelling orders to a mix of Germans, Hungarian regulars and Arrow Crossers. Two German panzers arrive from the Outer Circle, behind them a few SS with submachine guns, about half a company of police and gendarmes blazing away from gateways. The tanks are firing rounds of shells.

I go over to the other window of this corner apartment from which I can get a view of both Pannónia and Főnix Streets. A thin strip of the riverside houses is also visible above the rooftops. Far away in the distance, on the Buda side of the Danube, is the castle. One of its wings is in flames. It seems the entire city is smouldering. A fighter-bomber swoops in so low that I can see the pilot for a few seconds. It is being fired at from Margit Bridge and crashes after being hit.

I can't tell if the underside of the sky is ruddy from fires behind Castle Hill or the sunset.

A dense cloud of smoke is floating above the Comedy Theatre and is spreading over the whole city.

The reddish light in the west is not caused by flames; it's different. Flames flicker, whereas this light illuminates everything, casting a ruddy glow on the smoking house roofs and being reflected from the walls in the twilight. Burning roofs could not be playing in such a purple colour. Where is the sun? Where can that all-illuminating light over the ruins still be spreading from? I can hear the scuttling of rats from over in the corner of the room; they have come up a fair old way to get here; they have not contented themselves with the sewers, cellars and stairway passages. Sounds can be picked out better in the all-illuminating twilight, otherwise I would most certainly be unable to hear the scuttling of the rats for the detonations and rattling of machine guns. It's as if everything were becoming brighter yet, meanwhile, the smoke is swirling more densely around everything and ruins are piling up on ruins, as if something I am seeing now that I had never understood was suddenly comprehensible; as if the piling up of ruins on ruins were the goal, which is incomprehensible and yet, if I nevertheless grasp that this is the point of it, I may perhaps make progress. This evening while we are playing chess, or even if there is no chess game, I am going to talk this over with the physicist. I would like to tell him that here, at the window, I have a feeling that I have seen a bit of what he said about the beginning and end of things meeting. He had been explaining something of the kind to the warden. In my mind I don't call him Uncle Laci but the physicist. One has to begin at the beginning: I think that is what he was explaining. Although who can know? No one can know where the beginning is. So it's not just me; others are also ignorant of where the beginning is. That does not set my mind at rest. There's no point in seeing the end if I can't find the beginning, only the fact that we are in it. If there were an opportunity I could say this nicely to the physicist; everything around me is so familiar, I am so much in it. The machine-gun barrel of the German panzer is rising, the turret revolving, the machine gunner cannot see up here. He fires a burst. A fragment from the wall bounces on to my hand, and my wrist starts to bleed, so I tie my handkerchief round it. It is not painful.

More than an hour has passed since they set off with the buckets.

I find no one in the apartment on the second floor; I dare not look in on Évie's room, but Vera and the little girl are snuggling up to each other on the landing. Vera has cracked lips. The little girl is sucking a small piece of iron. She says she was given it by her mummy. Vera asks her for it, carefully wipes it on her coat, then she, too, starts to suck it.

The apartment was not unoccupied after all. Both Mother and Aunt Klári were in Évie's room.

Two hours have passed since they set off with the buckets.

Mother gives me a hug;. I can't see her face in the dark.

Aunt Klári suggests we should move down to the cellar, as the firing is very intense; she will stay upstairs with Évie.

Vera says that she would not like to go down into the cellar.

A lot of people are seated on the stairs.

There are yells for Aunt Klári from downstairs. I can hear thumping on the front door and race up to the fourth floor. Many houses in the street are on fire. I lean out and can see there are two Arrow Crossers pounding on the gate, letting a burst fly and running away towards the Outer Circle. I dart down to the gate. Aunt Klári is making her way up. I tell her that two Arrow Crossers fired at the door but ran away. She says fortunately no one was injured. I go back to the fourth floor.

There has been no news from the water carriers for three hours now.

I do not want to be near Mother. I do not want her to say something. I do not want to try to say something to her. Vera is getting on well with the little girl and the piece of iron which they are taking turns to suck.

Three hours is easily enough time for them to have returned with the buckets.

Three hours is easily enough time for them to have got back.

Three hours is three hours.

I am not alarmed.

Anything can happen at any time – that knowledge is part of me. No one can deprive me of it. I cannot forget it; it is so much a part of me that if I did then I would forget myself.

I need to look for Mother. It could be that she is already down in the cellar.

The house is under fire.

One of the walls of the house at the corner is collapsing.

Vera and the little girl will surely be sucking the piece of iron in turns.

Later on I'll give the little girl the conch shell that is hidden in my haversack. It may appeal to her, and she will forget she is thirsty for a few minutes. Maybe she will sing into it. The little girl and her mother resemble each other. I noticed straight away when I first saw them that have similar countenances, but – how can I put it? – the mother's face seems like a child's and the little girl's like an adult's.

I can hear submachine-gun bursts coming from the Danube bank.

The blood has soaked through my handkerchief over the wound made by the splinter.

I lean out of the window.

Two people are running from József Katona Street, dangling buckets as they run. Only empty buckets swing as easily as that.

Two people are running towards our gate, not four.   .

I race downstairs and slip, knocking my knees. I limp. I kick an old woman who is sitting on the turn of the stairs. Beg pardon. There are yells at every hand, yelling on every floor, yelling at the cellar door.

Mother is on one side of the gate, Aunt Klári on the other. The four guards at the gate are right next to one another, one with a pistol. I had only seen a pistol on Gyuri, but the man with the beret has a pistol which he is aiming at the gate. I cry out, they're coming, although I don't call out that two are coming. Mother and Aunt Klári are about to open the gate, but I yank Mother back and the man with the pistol yanks Aunt Klári back. She very quietly orders the guards at the gate to open it up. The man with the pistol waits, looks at Aunt Klári, salutes and opens the door. The house on the corner is burning with a ruddy glow. There are burst of submachine-gun fire. Two men dive through the gate, the empty pails flying out of their hands. Aunt Klári hugs the warden to herself. That's the last time you leave me, she exclaims, embracing him. Why the shouting if her mouth is right by her husband's ear? Father retrieves one of the pails that had been flung aside, sits down on it, the bucket being hidden by his winter coat as if he were squatting. Mother and I got either side of him and haul him off the pail. The lad took away my pistol when all four of us were shoved into a group that was being harried towards the bank of the Danube. He was shot dead straight away. Uncle Laci started shouting at the Arrow Crossers and did not leave off, so he was shot at the next corner. I wanted to block my ears; the screaming was unbearable. Who was screaming? Bombers were flying over, the Arrow Crossers were dropping down flat on their bellies. The warden and I jumped under a gateway, says Father. The screaming was unbearable; it started from low down, by now a shrieking. I can't understand how Aunt Klári can still be hugging her husband so joyfully and yet meanwhile is capable of yelling as she is. The warden is muttering, as far as I can make out, the same thing as Father said. Aunt Klári is giving him kisses on the cheek and meanwhile shouting, and I suppose they must be able to hear her in the cellar and on the upper floors, because it is quiet there. Maybe everyone is disposed to give way to the shouting: it spreads out, penetrates the cracks, even permeates me as if it were breaking out of me. Vera looks on in terror, perhaps terrified by how she can hear me shouting when my mouth is closed. The leader of the guards on the gate is also looking at me, but why so long? Father resumes his seat on the bucket, stands up and embraces Mother. They step over to me and embrace me. The screaming is even louder; that cannot be taken away from me either; the screaming is also part of my knowledge. Aunt Klári's mouth is an O shape, the sound fills everything. Vera puts her fingers in her ears, the little girl races up from the cellar, takes the piece of iron from her mouth, hands it to Vera. The doctor pokes a syringe needle into Aunt Klári's arm, and the shrieking becomes fainter. The burning houses are throwing out light. The warden details four new guards for the gate.

NOTES

1 Now György Dózsa Avenue (XIVth District).

2 Katalin Karády (1910–90) was a leading actress in Hungarian movies made between 1939 and 1945, after the release of *Halálos tavasz* (*Deadly Spring*), her first screen role, made her an instant star. She is better known outside Hungary for being awarded the honorific Righteous Among the Nations for rescuing Hungarian Jews from the Nazis and their allies.

3 Number 60 Andrássy Avenue was a building used as a notorious prison by the Arrow Cross Party from 1937. After the end of the war it became head-quarters for the secret police (ÁVH/ÁVO) during the Communist era. It is now a museum called the House of Terror.

4 A greeting – which translates as 'persistence', 'endurance' or 'perseverance' – used by the the fascist Arrow Cross Party in Hungary.

5 Having been called Hitler tér (Hitler Place) from 1938, this was renamed Körönd (Circus) from 1945 and Kodály Körönd in 1971.

6 Now known as the Oktogon.

7 Now Köztársaság (Republic) Square (VIIIth District).

8 Called the Városi Színház (Municipal Theatre) from 1917 to 1940, in 1953 it was renamed the Erkel Színház (Erkel Theatre of the Hungarian State Opera House).

9 Now Miklós Radnóti Street (XIIIth District).

10 The Locarno Pact was part of a security conference that took place between 5 and 16 October 1925 under the auspices and jurisdiction of the League of Nations, the main part of which was the Treaty of Mutual Guarantee between Germany, France, Belgium, Great Britain and Italy – the Rhine-land Pact. While Germany was willing to recognize the borders of its western neighbours, it was not willing to recognize the borders of Poland and Czechoslovakia. To offset that refusal France (but not Great Britain) contracted mutual defence pacts with both countries.

11 Országos Magyar Izraelita Közművelődési Egyesület (Hungarian National Jewish Cultural Association).

12 Now called András Cházár Street (XIVth District).

13 Now the Sándor Petőfi and Szabadság (Liberty) Bridges.

THE BORDERLANDS OF HUNGARY, AUSTRIA
AND FORMER CZECHOSLOVAKIA

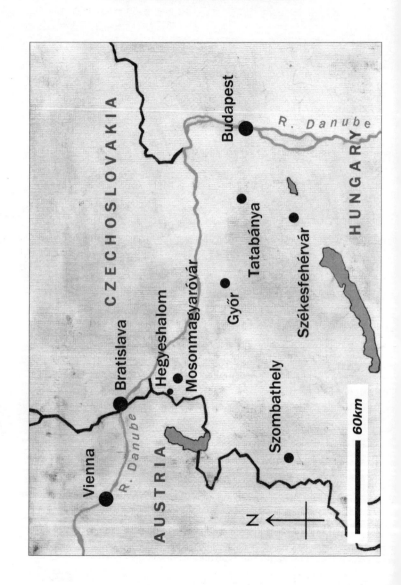

THE DISTRICTS OF BUDAPEST

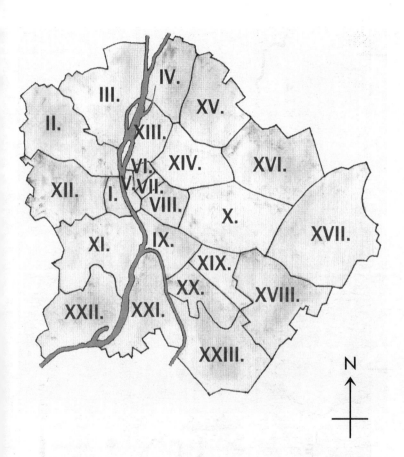

CENTRAL BUDAPEST
SHOWING THE POSITION OF THE WARTIME GHETTO

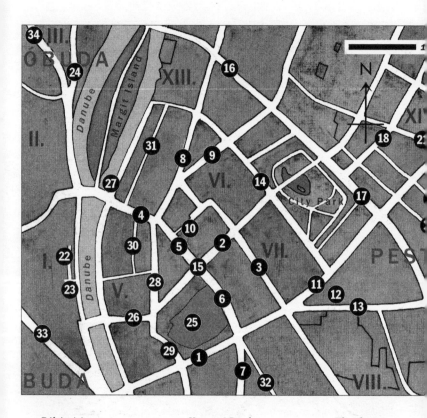

THE BUDAPEST GHETTO (1944–5)

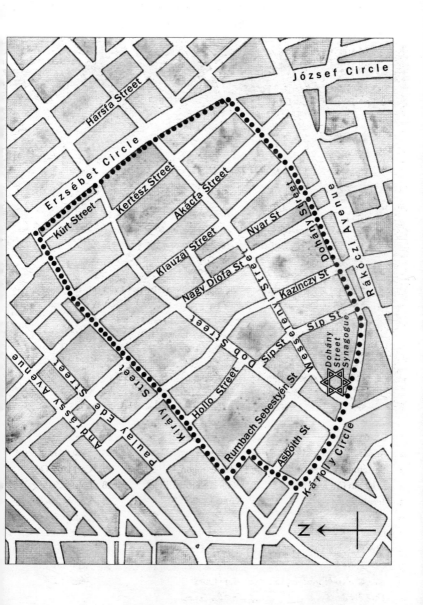

SOME AUTHORS WE HAVE PUBLISHED

James Agee • Bella Akhmadulina • Tariq Ali • Kenneth Allsop • Alfred Andersch
Guillaume Apollinaire • Machado de Assis • Miguel Angel Asturias • Duke of Bedford
Oliver Bernard • Thomas Blackburn • Jane Bowles • Paul Bowles • Richard Bradford
Ilse, Countess von Bredow • Lenny Bruce • Finn Carling • Blaise Cendrars • Marc Chagall
Giorgio de Chirico • Uno Chiyo • Hugo Claus • Jean Cocteau • Albert Cohen
Colette • Ithell Colquhoun • Richard Corson • Benedetto Croce • Margaret Crosland
e.e. cummings • Stig Dalager • Salvador Dalí • Osamu Dazai • Anita Desai
Charles Dickens • Bernard Diederich • Fabián Dobles • William Donaldson
Autran Dourado • Yuri Druzhnikov • Lawrence Durrell • Isabelle Eberhardt
Sergei Eisenstein • Shusaku Endo • Erté • Knut Faldbakken • Ida Fink
Wolfgang George Fischer • Nicholas Freeling • Philip Freund • Carlo Emilio Gadda
Rhea Galanaki • Salvador Garmendia • Michel Gauquelin • André Gide
Natalia Ginzburg • Jean Giono • Geoffrey Gorer • William Goyen • Julien Gracq
Sue Grafton • Robert Graves • Angela Green • Julien Green • George Grosz
Barbara Hardy • H.D. • Rayner Heppenstall • David Herbert • Gustaw Herling
Hermann Hesse • Shere Hite • Stewart Home • Abdullah Hussein • King Hussein of Jordan
Ruth Inglis • Grace Ingoldby • Yasushi Inoue • Hans Henny Jahnn • Karl Jaspers
Takeshi Kaiko • Jaan Kaplinski • Anna Kavan • Yasunuri Kawabata • Nikos Kazantzakis
Orhan Kemal • Christer Kihlman • James Kirkup • Paul Klee • James Laughlin
Patricia Laurent • Violette Leduc • Lee Seung-U • Vernon Lee • József Lengyel
Robert Liddell • Francisco García Lorca • Moura Lympany • Dacia Maraini
Marcel Marceau • André Maurois • Henri Michaux • Henry Miller • Miranda Miller
Marga Minco • Yukio Mishima • Quim Monzó • Margaret Morris • Angus Wolfe Murray
Atle Næss • Gérard de Nerval • Anaïs Nin • Yoko Ono • Uri Orlev • Wendy Owen
Arto Paasilinna • Marco Pallis • Oscar Parland • Boris Pasternak • Cesare Pavese
Milorad Pavic • Octavio Paz • Mervyn Peake • Carlos Pedretti • Dame Margery Perham
Graciliano Ramos • Jeremy Reed • Rodrigo Rey Rosa • Joseph Roth • Ken Russell
Marquis de Sade • Cora Sandel • Iván Sándor • George Santayana • May Sarton
Jean-Paul Sartre • Ferdinand de Saussure • Gerald Scarfe • Albert Schweitzer
George Bernard Shaw • Isaac Bashevis Singer • Patwant Singh • Edith Sitwell
Suzanne St Albans • Stevie Smith • C.P. Snow • Bengt Söderbergh
Vladimir Soloukhin • Natsume Soseki • Muriel Spark • Gertrude Stein • Bram Stoker
August Strindberg • Rabindranath Tagore • Tambimuttu • Elisabeth Russell Taylor
Emma Tennant • Anne Tibble • Roland Topor • Miloš Urban • Anne Valery
Peter Vansittart • José J. Veiga • Tarjei Vesaas • Noel Virtue • Max Weber
Edith Wharton • William Carlos Williams • Phyllis Willmott • G. Peter Winnington
Monique Wittig • A.B. Yehoshua • Marguerite Young
Fakhar Zaman • Alexander Zinoviev • Emile Zola

 Peter Owen Publishers, 81 Ridge Road, London N8 9NP, UK
T + 44 (0)20 8350 1775 / F + 44 (0)20 8340 9488 / E info@peterowen.com
www.peterowen.com / @PeterOwenPubs
Independent publishers since 1951